DEAD BEFORE DAWN

AN AMOS CARVER THRILLER

JOHN CORWIN

RAVEN HOUSE

BOOKS BY JOHN CORWIN

DEAD ON ARRIVAL

Ex-special forces operator, Amos Carver is being framed for murder.

Carver hasn't killed anyone. At least not for a few years, and certainly not in some backwoods Georgia town. He would never harm the person they're accusing him of murdering. But nobody believes him. And no one is willing to help prove otherwise.

The town might look almost dead. It might look like it's barely clinging to life. But it's very much alive. Rotten to the core. And the unknown forces running it want him dead.

They can come. They can try. But there's not a chance in hell Carver is going down without a fight.

CHAPTER 1

C arver saw the pistol lying on the road a hundred yards away.

It was hard to miss. Pink. Highlighted against the blacktop. And it was lying in the eastbound highway lane almost dead center.

At first, he dismissed it as a toy. But as he hiked closer, a feeling deep in his gut told him it was the real deal. There was only one person he knew who carried a pink gun. She was the reason he'd slogged five hard miles down the highway in the blistering heat of the Georgia summer sun.

Her pistol in the middle of the highway told him why she hadn't been waiting to pick him up when he got off the bus. It told him he should've come a day earlier. He could have. There was nothing stopping him from leaving yesterday or the day before. No job holding him down, and certainly not a woman. He just hadn't felt like leaving his comfortable beachside accommodations down in Florida.

Now he was here in Georgia, and it might be too late.

Exactly four cars had passed Carver during the hike. Three headed into town, and one headed away from it. The drivers and passengers had looked middle-aged. Touristy. Probably hikers. They would have had to be blind not to see the hot-pink Sig-Sauer P365 sitting on the road.

Carver was already slowing his pace. Already considering what he'd find when he reached the pistol. A body? A trail of blood? Nothing?

There was a small mountain on the right side of the highway. A long, paved driveway climbed the mountain to a big house perched on the side. There was forest on the right of the driveway and a big pasture to the left.

Forest stretched for miles on the left side of the highway. Carver angled toward the forest, eyes searching the road ahead. Something wasn't right and he intended to find out what it was.

He slipped into the trees. It was a little cooler in the shade, but not by much. A gentle breeze would have been appreciated, but Mother Nature wasn't obliging. The underbrush was thick. Making any kind of progress would be noisy and hard. Oh, he'd done it plenty of times. Too many times to count. Some of those times were seared into memory. Others were long forgotten. He wasn't sure where this time would fall on that list.

It might be nothing. Might be an overreaction on his part driven by his cautious nature. This was backwoods Georgia, not Serbia. Not Iraq. Not one of countless far more dangerous places he'd visited. But that wasn't going to change his approach.

It's the simple things that get you killed. Underestimating the opponent, the terrain, the situation. Rhodes loved to quote tidbits of wisdom before a mission. She was usually right.

He didn't know anything about this situation or why Rhodes asked him to come. She hadn't told him much. Just a slip of paper asking for help.

Just asking for help had been enough. She was family. Not by blood, but by service. Blood might be thicker than water, but real family was forged with blood, sweat, tears, and pain. Carver learned that early and never forgot it. That's why he was risking a heat stroke on a highway in the middle of nowhere.

That was why he was being cautious. Rhodes wasn't the kind to ask for small favors. She or someone she knew was in big trouble. Big enough trouble to call in Carver. There were at least four other people she would have called first if the trouble required an even hand. If the response needed to be measured. Well thought out.

Not to mention they hadn't been on the best of terms the last time he'd seen her.

Rhodes was a thinker. A strategist. By the time she made a decision, she'd already discarded multiple plans. So why was her gun in the road? What series of events had led to that?

Why hadn't any of the drivers stopped out of curiosity and looked at the gun? Picked it up and asked the same questions?

Carver hugged the tree line since cutting through the thick underbrush in the forest would take too long. He envisioned what he'd find. Rhodes lying dead or wounded at the edge of the forest. With her last gasp, she'd thrown the gun on the road. Figured it would be impossible to miss. Someone would stop and help her.

That seemed the most logical course. Carver might have done the same, but he'd never own a pink gun. Not because he didn't like pink. Guns were tools. He wouldn't buy a pink hammer or a pink knife. Black was a better choice, especially in tactical situations. Not that he'd been in such a situation in a while.

He continued walking. Eyes scanning. Ears alert. Senses sharp.

Looking for a body lying at the edge of the woods, just twenty feet from the road. But he saw nothing, not even a hand protruding from the underbrush. Maybe he had this all wrong. Maybe Rhodes had been in a car and tossed the gun from the window. Maybe someone had taken her, and she'd dropped it like a breadcrumb.

Too much speculation and only one fact—a pink pistol was lying in the road.

He hugged the edge of the forest like it was a wall. Sliding quietly along in the grass. A breeze rustled the leaves. Birds chirped. Insects buzzed. He was nearly there. Only ten feet away.

Time to find out what had happened.

CHAD DORSEY smashed the tablet against the granite countertop. The screen shattered. He hated remote management. Hated relying on others to do what needed to be done. A small problem had gone unnoticed. It had nearly grown out of control. A cancer on his plans.

"The problem is being taken care of, sir." Tony looked calm. Just another day for him. "That's what contingency plans are for."

"I'm well aware of that. The question is why you waited so long to fix it." He regarded the shattered screen. Slid it across the counter. "Have it erased and get me a new one."

"I can just have the screen repaired."

Dorsey bit back a retort. Went back to the matter at hand. "You told me this might be a problem a long time ago. Now it is. What are you doing to fix it?"

"Better not to say."

"But I want to know." Dorsey picked up his Remington M700 and aimed at pedestrians on the street below. They looked like ants from his penthouse. When he zoomed in, he could see their faces. See the boredom of their little lives. He could end that boredom at the pull of a finger.

"It's best to have plausible deniability." Tony stood next to him. "That's why I'm not taking care of matters myself."

"We're so close." Dorsey laid the rifle on his leather couch. "Just a few more days and it's a done deal. Unless this blows up in our face."

"It won't. This kind of stuff is my specialty."

"Good." Dorsey nodded to himself. "Good."

"My plan is going to tie up loose ends like a bow on a birthday present." Tony grinned. "I love this kind of stuff."

"Thank you, Tony." Dorsey stretched and wondered what he'd do for the rest of the day. His girlfriend was still in Europe, safely out of the way for the time being. This was a crucial phase. He didn't need her distracting him.

But he did need some sort of distraction.

He turned back to Tony. "You're dismissed."

A hint of a smirk touched Tony's lips. The order seemed to amuse him. These former military types looked down on those who'd never served. Dorsey didn't care. His money gave him all the power he needed.

He looked down at his casual attire. "I'm going to change. Tell the driver to be ready in ten minutes."

Tony nodded. "Business or pleasure?"

"Business today. I want to visit the office."

"I'll set it up." He took out his phone and tapped out a text.

Dorsey went to change clothes and returned moments later. Dressed in his black military fatigues, he felt more confident. Felt like he was in charge again. He was just as capable as anyone who served. He was a crack shot with multiple firearms. A master sniper.

And if Tony didn't fix things soon, Dorsey would take care of things himself.

CARVER STOOD TEN FEET from the gun. It definitely belonged to Rhodes. She loved hot pink. She preferred the Sig Sauer P365 for its compact form factor and stopping power. Carver didn't like it for half those reasons.

He preferred a Sig 226. It stood up to abuse better. It was a bigger gun and felt better in his bigger hands. Plus, the barrel was longer by almost two inches. It meant you could hit something with greater accuracy from farther away.

He walked over to the gun. Looked up and down the highway. The road vanished around a curve about a half mile away to the northwest. About a mile away in the other direction it was lost to sight over a rise. Not a car in sight. Not a human in sight. He turned in a circle and looked at the forest twenty feet away.

If Rhodes was injured or dying and threw the gun all this way, it meant she had enough strength to drag herself onto the road. It meant part of her would be visible from this vantage. He didn't see anything or anyone. But the underbrush was thick, so it was possible a body might not be visible from here.

He looked down at the gun, looked back at the forest. Tried to imagine the trajectory. Tried to imagine a circumstance that would warrant throwing a pistol out here instead of keeping it close to fight whatever wounded you.

It's all wrong. He looked up and down the road again. His reasoning was way off. It didn't make sense. It seemed best to leave things as they were. It was only another mile, maybe two into town. He'd tell the police what he found and let them investigate. They had the tools to do it and he didn't.

Picking up the gun would disturb the scene.

It was one of those rare times where he regretted not at least having a burner phone. "Rhodes?" Carver cupped his hands to his mouth. "Rhodes?"

He listened. No answer. He tried again.

"Rhodes!" He called her name several more times. If she was nearby, she was dead or unconscious. He didn't think she was nearby. Some other set of circumstances led to the gun being here. But it was better to check the immediate area. Comb the nearby forest in case she was here.

If she was nearby and alive, she needed help.

He looked to the north at the mansion on the mountain. At the pasture stretching down one side of the slope. Cows grazed on the grass. They were black and white. The kind of cows raised for milk, not for carving into steaks. A few large trees dotted the pasture here and there.

Sunlight glinted from something far up on the hill. He squinted and looked harder. It looked like someone was prone under a tree right at the crest. Or it might just be a cow. Maybe the sun had glinted off a cowbell. It was too far away to make out.

Maybe someone in the house had seen what happened here. Since no one had come down here to investigate, it seemed more likely that they hadn't. It was up to him to search the nearby forest before going to town. The gun was going to remain in place. If other drivers hadn't picked it up yet, there was no reason to think anyone else would.

He walked toward the tree line.

There was a faint hiss of static. Like a radio. His gaze fixated on the spot. The bushes rustled. There was shouting. Carver backed up a step as a man in a beige police uniform burst from the bushes. Behind him were two men in civilian attire. Jeans, t-shirts. Both were packing heat. Glock 19s in neat nylon holsters.

One of the civilians pointed at Carver. "That's him!"

The officer planted his feet and pointed his pistol. "Freeze, asshole!"

Carver was already standing still, hands up.

The same civilian kept pointing at Carver. "He's the one I saw running from the scene!"

"Same here." The other one spat on the ground and wiped tobacco-stained lips. "Hard to miss a guy that tall holding a pink pistol."

"Pick up the gun and toss it over here," the officer said.

Carver was four feet away from the gun. He made no move to pick it up. This was an ambush, and he was the target. The glint on the hill had been a lookout. They'd been waiting for him. They'd expected him to bend over, pick up the gun, and check it out. They needed him to touch it to put his fingerprints on it and transfer gunshot residue to his hand.

It was a neat little operation, carried out with the kind of precision he admired. It reminded him of jobs he'd done, but his hadn't failed as spectacularly as this. There was no way he'd touch that gun, not if a tank rolled up out of the forest along with a platoon of soldiers.

His mind considered the tactical situation.

Was the spotter on the hill also a sniper? Unless the guy was an award-winning crack shot, he wouldn't have a chance of hitting Carver. At first glance, the two civilians looked like military wannabes with their camouflage cargo pants and handguns in holsters. But they weren't the average rural Georgia civilian.

They were in good shape. Slim, muscular. Sharp eyes and honed reflexes. They weren't touching their guns, but their hands were ready, and the holsters were unsnapped. These boys were ready to go if Carver made the wrong move. The cop was nothing special. Plump around the midsection, pale, and sweaty. That run from the forest had tested his cardio to the limits.

"I said, pick up the gun and toss it over here." The cop pointed the gun at Carver's head. His plastic name badge said *Settler* on it.

Carver kept his hands up and swiveled to look back up the hill at the spotter. There was no movement. No glint of a scope. It had probably been binoculars.

One of the civilians grunted. "Fuck it. I'll just put the damned gun in his hand."

A car appeared over the hill heading into town. Not just a car, a black and white with a light bar across the top. A moment after it crested the rise, the lights came on and it sped toward them.

That brought up another question. Where had these men come from? Where was their car? Had they been watching and waiting from the woods all this time? This heat was no joke. They'd been marinating in their own juices for a while. Or maybe there was a trail, a clearing, somewhere to park a car and wait while the lookout did the sweating.

"Fuck!" Settler ground his teeth. "I told you we should have—"

"Shut it." The shorter, more muscular civilian made a zipping motion over his lips. "We can still make it stick."

Carver watched everything without a word.

Don't say anything until you understand the situation. Rhodes had told him that all the time. Told him he was too quick to judge. Too quick to act. This was one of those times where understanding was paramount.

Carver was starting to understand. He could see the puzzle pieces fitting together nicely already. He hadn't touched the gun, so this would make things a little easier.

Settler reached to his belt and lifted a pair of handcuffs. He handed them to one of the men. "Cuff him."

The shorter man took the cuffs and strode over to Carver. He looked confident. "Hands behind your back."

Carver obliged.

Settler recited Miranda. "Do you understand your rights?"

Carver said nothing. He didn't have to respond.

"Fuck it." Settler ground his teeth again. "You're under arrest."

Chapter 2

The oncoming police car screeched to a stop at the side of the road. It was a new Charger. Shiny black paint, *Morganville Police* written in white on the sides. The door opened. A woman slid out of the driver's seat and walked around the door. Eyes narrow, she assessed the situation.

"Settler, what in the hell is going on here?" Her accent was mildly southern, but not as redneck as Settler's. She looked at the civilians. "Who are these men and why are you holding this man at gunpoint?" Her eyes locked onto the pink gun. She frowned. "Is that Rhodes'?"

Settler worked his jaw back and forth, like he was figuring out what to say. Then he said it. "These men saw him shoot Rhodes. He shot the Chief."

Her gaze flicked from the gun to Carver. Back to the gun. Back to Carver. "What? Where?" She looked around frantically. "Where is Rhodes?"

"Up at the old Miller cabin." He managed to look sad. "I'm real sorry, Holly, but she's dead."

Holly went white as a sheet. "No. That can't be!" She looked at Carver, eyes filling with anger. "Why?"

Carver had nothing to say. Rhodes was a cop? The chief of police in this hillbilly town? That didn't make any sense. He hadn't seen her in over three years. Maybe that was enough time for someone to become a new person.

"I asked you a question!" Holly's fists tightened. "Why did you kill her?"

Carver said nothing. The woman was being fed a lie and nothing he said would turn that around. She trusted Settler, a fellow cop. She didn't know Carver from a hole in the wall. Besides, there was a severe lack of information. Rhodes wasn't the same woman he'd known years ago, and he didn't know anything about anything right now.

Silence was his best bet.

Shaking with anger and maybe shock, Holly looked around. "Where's your car, Settler?"

"Up at the cabin." He shrugged. "These two called it in when I was over on eighteen, so I went up the gravel road."

"Eighteen?" She looked confused. "I thought you were assigned to one thirty-six today."

He shrugged. "You know I like the coffee from Evan's better than the 7-11."

Eighteen and one thirty-six were the local highways. Carver remembered them from the map. This road they stood on was Highway Eighteen. It ran north by northwest from the highway junction where the bus had dropped him off. Kept going into Morganville. It went directly through downtown, made an S shape in the middle, and continued on past it.

"Put him in my car." Holly motioned for the short guy to move Carver.

The short guy looked uneasily at his buddy then shoved Carver. The force barely moved him. He gave the guy a look, then walked to the back door of the cruiser on his own. The civilian pushed down on the top of his head then used his hip to bump him inside. It was smooth and professional. This guy had done it before.

He wasn't a cop. He was something else. Both he and the other guy had a military look to them. They'd done some time, but they were too young to have done their twenty. They were in good shape and still wore their hair short but not buzzed.

Their clothes looked too fancy for hiking in the forest. They wore shiny leather boots. The jeans were form-fitting, not rugged outdoor wear. Then again, what did Carver know about fashion? He preferred cargo pants for utility. Style wasn't even a thought when he got dressed.

The short guy closed the car door and Carver enjoyed the cool air spilling through the metal screen between him and the front seat. Holly spoke to Settler and the civilians for a moment. Motioned toward town, then nodded and got in the car.

The Charger rocked on its shocks when she slammed the door. Still shaking, she looked at Carver in the rearview mirror. There were tears in her eyes. She wanted to say something, but her professional side took over. She put the car in drive and steered around the supposed crime scene.

She got on the radio. "I need an ambulance and CSI up at the Miller cabin immediately. Chief Rhodes has been shot."

Chief Rhodes. Carver couldn't believe how wrong that sounded. She was just Rhodes. No rank. No callsign. They'd all had ranks at one time, but not after they'd been given the boot. Then they'd been reduced to anonymous chess pieces in a different game.

"Shot?" a shocked male voice answered. "Dispatching now."

She hung the radio back on the receiver. Her eyes darted to the road, then back to him.

Carver now understood the situation well enough to talk. This woman had obviously been a close friend of Rhodes. Or maybe she just respected her. That was important. She would be the key to getting out of this mess.

He spoke. "Do you know how to test for GSR?"

She blinked, eyes darting back toward him in the mirror. "CSI does that."

"But can you?"

Her eyes narrowed. "Why?"

"Because I never touched that gun. I haven't touched a gun today and I certainly haven't fired one today."

"You think a simple GSR test will set you free?" She barked a humorless laugh. "You could have washed your hands in the stream on the way down the hill."

"My prints aren't on the gun either." He considered telling her Settler was dirty. That the civilians with him were helping frame him. But then he'd sound like a conspiracy nut. She might even be in on it. Sure, she was sad about Rhodes, but that didn't mean she wouldn't cover for her comrades.

"You could have wiped the prints." She shook her head. "You've got two witnesses placing you at the scene. That's all we need."

"Who were those men with Settler?"

She remained silent for a moment. "I don't know. You'll have to ask him."

"You've never seen them before?"

"I ask the questions around here, okay?" She glared at him in the rearview mirror. "You're the suspect."

"They're strangers then. Not locals." Carver nodded. "Small town like this you probably know everyone."

She wiped her eyes and stared forward at the road. Said nothing.

"You trust Settler?"

"With my life." The reply was almost automatic. "He's a good man. Helped me out after my daddy's accident."

"Your dad died?"

"Yes." Holly sounded exasperated. "Why am I answering your questions? Just shut up!"

Carver went silent again. Cops were cops. Either you were on their side, or you weren't. Settler was more than a cop to her. He was a personal hero. Someone who helped her out during a tough time. He looked old enough to be her father. Maybe that was the relationship. It certainly hadn't looked like more.

Even if they didn't have that bond, they were still cops. They'd have each other's backs no matter what. Same with military police, same with special forces, and so forth. A tribe by any other name was still a tribe. His prints weren't on the gun, and there was no GSR on his hands or clothes. The two witnesses would be the issue.

He had other proof on his side. Provided CSI calculated an accurate time of death and didn't doctor the results, he would be cleared. That, unfortunately, was no guarantee. He'd have to see how this played out before making any radical decisions.

What was obvious was that Rhodes had been investigating something. She'd been killed for it. They'd known Carver was coming to town and created the perfect frame. It was a damned shame. A waste of a brilliant mind.

Carver stared out the windshield as the town came into view. Heat shimmered off the blacktop in front of a large wooden sign.

Welcome to Morganville

Founded 1852

Population 3,557

The sign was faded, rotting. The highway was the only thing in this town that looked like it had been maintained, probably because it was a state highway. The strip of dark new asphalt crossed side streets with potholes and sealed-chip surfaces. The buildings were mostly red brick. Some were boarded up and closed.

The first building stood alone. The Olde Towne Pub was made of wood. The graying plywood was coming loose in places. A lone car was parked in the front. It didn't look as if it were fit to be open.

The highway became Main Street inside the city limits. Right at the curve ahead stood a tall, polished building with a grand dome crowning the top. City Hall looked like the only place that had seen maintenance.

A small mom and pop thrift store was open. A kid's clothing shop and a sandwich store were also open. The other dozen buildings on this side of City Hall were closed.

Holly followed the curve past City Hall.

There was a squat brown building, the public library, a rotting gazebo, and some more brick buildings. Two larger buildings stood separate from the others: Morganville Phone Company, and Morganville Power. The entrances and windows were boarded up. That was hardly surprising. Those companies had probably been bought out years ago by larger corporations.

Both buildings occupied a lot of real estate. They'd probably been big players back in the day. Now they looked like graveyards. Behind the electric company fence were rows of old coal-powered generators. Rusting iron boilers three stories tall. Stacks of rotting power poles.

Holly turned right onto a side street. The smooth silence of the new asphalt vanished. The tires on this road sounded like they were going over gravel. She swerved around a pothole and turned into a parking lot. A somewhat newer brick building was here, covering about a third of an acre.

The name of the place was about as uninspiring as the rest of the names: Morganville Police Department. It looked moderately maintained, but it was clear that most of the taxes in this deserted municipality went to City Hall. Probably right into the mayor's pockets.

There were two new Charger patrol cars parked out front. A pair of shiny new pickup trucks, an older pickup, and two compact cars. A drive on the right side continued to a gated chain link fence. There was no guard shack, and the gate was manual. The kind that grated open on metal tracks.

Tattered vinyl on the fence barely concealed what was on the other side. There was an ancient police van and an assortment of old cars. It was probably an impound and a motor pool. Carver had the feeling that this town had once been a lot more prosperous. It had the look of a place with a grand history but had since fallen on hard times.

Those hard times had hit a long time ago. It took decades for the neglect to show like this. He hadn't done any research on the town. He'd just looked at a map. Wondered why Rhodes wanted to meet him in such a place. Maybe to finally plant a knife in his guts like she'd wanted to do three years ago.

He'd come anyway. Rhodes wasn't the kind to send out a 911 unless she really meant it. He'd suspected a trap. She was the kind who could plan something elaborate. Lure the target over the bullseye so Carver could put a bullet between their eyes from a few hundred yards away. She knew he hated long-distance kills more than anyone. She still set them up just to mess with him.

They'd been friends. No, more than that. They'd been family, once upon a time. Then they'd just as quickly become, if not enemies, adversaries. Carver had destroyed everything.

DORSEY WAS UNHAPPY.

"You assured me this was handled, Tony."

Tony wasn't the least bit ruffled. He'd seen far worse and wasn't worried. "It didn't go as smoothly as hoped, but it's still handled, okay?" He took a water from the minifridge and twisted off the cap. "If we'd handled this like I suggested long ago, this wouldn't be an issue now. We'd have two dead instead of four."

"I make tactical business decisions every day. The risk at the time was too much. There was far too much heat."

"That's why I suggested waiting a couple of years and keeping an eye on the loose ends." Tony shrugged. "Let the heat die down."

"At that point we seemed to be in the clear." Dorsey sipped his whiskey and grimaced. The eighteen-year Macallan tasted more bitter than usual. Probably because of his sour mood. He looked up at the glass shelf. The minibar in his office rivaled that of what one might find in a restaurant. Several bottles of alcohol were worth more than the annual salary of most Americans. The Karuizawa 1981 alone was worth at least eighty thousand.

He'd been saving that for a special day. For the day when the final pieces of his plan fell into place. He was almost there. The Pentagon backed his plan. Most of Congress backed his plan. The President had recently come onboard, but his term was ending this year. Reelection wasn't guaranteed.

There were three major holdouts and they all had to be appeased. If the situation wasn't handled correctly, then everything would fall apart. Two people he should have killed long ago could cost him billions. He should have listened to Tony. The man could make people disappear in his sleep. Now it was too late. More people would have to die. He had to remain a safe distance away.

He opened a spreadsheet on his computer and looked over personnel. "These guys handling it, they don't look like anything special."

"They aren't, and that's the point." Tony took a sip of water. "They're off the book nobodies who can't be connected to Breakstone. I told you this is my thing, okay? The easy part is over. This is the hard part, and I knew it'd be hard. But it's still going to be over by tonight."

"You have a Plan B?"

"This is the same plan, contingency two."

"That's the same as a Plan B."

"No, a Plan B is if everything goes to hell. Everything is going to plan within the original parameters. The finale was adjusted to account for that. No plan survives first contact with the enemy." Tony stared at the whiskey decanter on the desk. His fingers tightened ever so slightly on the water bottle, then he took a long sip. "Sam is on standby. He's keeping a distance, but he can be on the ground quickly."

Dorsey looked relieved. "Why didn't you tell me?"

"Because I didn't think you needed to know. I tried to handle this without you knowing a thing."

"But I noticed." Dorsey tapped a finger on his temple. "I'm perceptive. I'm tactical. If I hadn't broken my arm, I was ready to volunteer for the war, you know. My dad's military friends said it was a shame they wouldn't let me in."

TONY TOOK A LONG drink and held back what he really wanted to say. "Yeah, you could've made general by now." If he had a dime for every guy who said he would've served, but offered an excuse like this, then he'd have a lot of dimes. Dorsey was nothing special except that he'd taken an idea and made a lot of money with it. Great timing had done all the work. The war had ended, and a lot of people were getting out of the service. A lot of people were looking for work and he'd provided plenty of it.

That was good on him. But it made him think he was one of them. He wasn't, but Tony didn't really care that much. It was just annoying to hear it over and over and over. He took another gulp of water and stared at the whiskey again while Dorsey went on about how he could've won the war in months instead of dragging out the occupation for years.

The man didn't understand the reality on the ground. He thought everything could be tied up into neat little packages. He was wrong, but that didn't mean he didn't have some good ideas. Tony had come to him with a proposal years ago. It had morphed into Breakstone's mission. It had captured the interest of important people in Washington.

It started with a premise: Massive regional wars don't do anyone any good. They destroy the environment, the economy, and millions of lives. They require massive armies, massive investments in old technologies, and massive logistics.

Tony's idea expanded on what the CIA had been doing for decades. Minor power shifts here and there to nudge events. A death here, a scandal there, and suddenly you control a company or a country without killing thousands. But the reason it wasn't working for the CIA was politics.

Instead of cooperating, government agencies were warring for budgetary dollars. Sabotaging each other's efforts just to win political favor. It had crippled the American machine. Privatizing certain aspects would fix the problem.

The current problem was similar in scope. Two deaths two years ago could have saved two more lives. Now the death toll would be at least doubled. Tony didn't normally have a personal stake in these kinds of things. He was normally sent in to fix a problem or die trying. Uncle Sam didn't pay him much or feed him well. Hell, he wasn't even treated like a hero.

But Dorsey's company was different. It paid well. People listened to him. He even owned private shares. Now he had to make sure everything fell into place. This was his operation.

He'd kill as many people as it took to win.

CHAPTER 3

H olly radioed into the station for backup. A man waddled out of the building. His stomach strained the fabric of his police uniform. Sweat dripped down his face before he even reached the patrol car.

He approached the driver's side window and stood there, uniform dark with sweat. The name badge said Maberly.

Holly got out of the car and closed the door. Spoke with him for a moment, then unsnapped her holster. Drew her weapon.

Maberly opened the back door. "Get out."

Carver complied. No reason to make a fuss right now. The nylon cuffs bit into his wrists as he awkwardly slipped out, hands still bound behind his back. Maberly gripped his arm and pulled. Humidity washed over him like a sauna.

Carver could've easily taken out Maberly. Holly had taken a stance about ten feet away, though. Too far for him to reach quickly. Far enough away that she could fire her service piece in time. Close enough that she could shoot him without missing.

It was smart. She was following her training. Keeping herself alive in a dangerous situation. Not that she understood just how dangerous it was. Not necessarily because of him, but because of Settler and those two military guys. They'd killed Rhodes for some reason. They'd kill Holly if they needed to.

Or he might have it all wrong. Maybe Settler was a good guy. The two guys with him might have called in the crime. Settler had gone to the murder site, they'd described Carver. Settler and the others had given chase through the forest.

But Settler had told Carver to pick up the gun. No officer would have asked the suspect to pick up the supposed murder weapon. Not unless he wanted their prints all over it. The only excuse for that would be if Settler thought Carver had wiped his prints and wanted to ensure fresh prints were on the weapon before the arrest.

That wouldn't make Settler part of this. It would just make him smart, ensuring that the perp didn't get away due to lack of prints. It made the murder charges iron clad.

Carver didn't buy it. Unless and until Settler proved otherwise, he was part of this. He was with the two military guys. Them plus the lookout made four total. So, who in the hell was calling the shots? This little Podunk town didn't look like it had anyone worth squat in it. Not that he hadn't seen plenty of little towns mired in squalor that were hiding people worth millions.

Holly stayed back ten feet while Maberly guided Carver toward the building. A faded US flag hung limp on a rusting flagpole. An old trash-can ashtray overflowing with cigarette butts sat ten feet from the building. A sign behind it warned people they had to smoke twenty feet from the building.

Still holding Carver's elbow, Maberly reached out and pulled open the glass front doors. They were heavily tinted with film so old it was yellowing. The lobby was carpeted. It stank of cigarettes. Vinyl chairs with ragged padding were lined up along the front. Old magazines were piled on a laminate table. Some were nearly ten years old.

Straight ahead was a wall with a window and a speaker grill. Behind it was a small dispatcher's office with a desk on the right side and a chair that looked as if the padding had gone flat from bearing so much weight. There was a radio and a charging rack of handheld radios on a table against the back wall.

Maberly took Carver through the door on the left. They passed the doorway to the dispatcher's office. Walked down a short hallway. Stepped into an area with six old metal desks arranged in rows. Four of the desks were bare aside from a coating of dust. Only one had a nameplate: Holly Robinson.

There were four offices to the left, windows partially obscured with yellowing venetian blinds. Carver read the names on the doors. Kevin Settler, Detective Andres Davis, Detective Abe Ritter. The last two had no names.

There was a workroom with copier and supplies to the right. It looked like the door had been removed from the hinges. In fact, it was still sitting in the room against the wall behind the copier. This place was old, unkempt. It didn't even have cameras.

At the very back was the largest office. The blinds were open, but the door was shut. The nameplate was something Carver had been expecting, but it still shocked him.

Chief Jaqueline Rhodes

He stopped walking and Maberly bumped into him.

Maberly didn't react. He just turned to Holly. "Where to?"

She hesitated. "Where's Davis?"

Maberly gave her a knowing look. "Where do you think?"

She sighed. "Ritter?"

"Still hasn't reported in today. I think he said something about vacation last week, didn't he?"

"How the hell should I know?" Holly bit her lower lip. "Let's process him and put him in holding. We need to wait for forensics anyway."

"Okay." Maberly nudged Carver toward the workroom. "Sit down."

Carver sat on a chair. The back was open, so his bound hands hung behind him. He felt the dampness of fingerprint ink on his digits. Holly pressed the fingers to the paper then wiped his fingers off.

"They have more modern techniques for that in this day and age," Carver said.

"Not here." She finished wiping his fingers then walked around and filed his fingerprints. She turned on an old computer and tapped on the keyboard.

Maberly lifted a hand. "Stand up."

Carver stood. Maberly frisked him. Removed a roll of cash, a driver's license, and a map of Georgia.

Maberly grunted and bent down to feel around Carver's ankles. "Where's your phone?"

Carver resisted the urge to put him down. Holly was busy on the computer. He could knee the clerk in the face, slip around behind Holly, and take her gun. But that would just make him look guilty. He'd be on the run. Turning this into a fugitive situation wasn't what he felt like doing with the rest of his week.

He let Maberly finish. Aside from the clothes on his back, Carver had nothing else. The driver's license, unfortunately, was a necessity in this day and age. Even the seediest motels asked for IDs.

"No phone?" Maberly looked flabbergasted. "Who the hell doesn't have a phone?"

Holly took the ID from Maberly and continued typing on the computer. "He probably tossed it. I'll bet there's evidence we could use. I'll track down his service provider."

Carver sat back down.

"Did I tell you to sit down?" Maberly said.

Carver remained sitting.

Holly looked through some drawers. "I can't find the extra film for the mug shot camera." She groaned. "Let's put him in holding for now."

"You got it." Maberly nudged Carver's shoulder. "Get up."

Carver stood. Maberly nudged him toward the hallway between the chief's office and the workroom. He stopped at a metal door and worked a key into the well-worn lock. The hinges squealed when he pulled the door open.

Carver went through into a wide space divided into six cells. The cells were cinder block on three sides and barred on the front. Like most police stations, this was a short-term facility, made for town drunks and troubled teens. Serious offenders might spend a night here until they were moved to a long-term facility.

As a suspected serious offender, Carver wouldn't be here more than a day at the most. They'd book him, charge him, and have him sent to the nearest detention facility. That was an inconvenience he didn't want. All kinds of things could happen to a person in those places. It was a convenient place to get rid of a murder suspect. That would tie up the investigation into Rhodes's death, and that would be that.

It was better to make sure he never got moved. He'd already made a list of alibis. First, he needed to know the time of the death. Once he knew that he could prove he was on a bus at the time of death. Unless the death had occurred shortly after the lookout had spotted him. But if that had been the case, he would've heard the gunshot.

Due to lack of cars and noise, a report from a gunshot would've reached him on the highway. Because of the rises in the road, the twists, and the trees, the lookout couldn't have spotted him until he crested that final rise. That meant they'd shot Rhodes when he was out of hearing range.

There had been a closed down gas station at the exit where the bus had stopped for him to get off. There hadn't been a single living soul out there except for him once that bus left. Even if they knew he was coming by bus. Even if they knew the schedule, they didn't know the exact time he'd be getting off that bus.

Carver envisioned the killer's plan from beginning to end. They would have timed it as tightly as possible with his arrival so the time of death would match up. That meant they would have had to lure Rhodes to the Miller cabin on a tight schedule. They would have told her it was important. Maybe tied it to whatever investigation got her killed.

Depending on the distance of the cabin from the road, they would have shot her, run through the forest, and reached the road. Planted the pink handgun on the asphalt. Retreated a short distance into the forest and waited while the lookout watched.

The more Carver thought about it, the more disgusted he became. What kind of moron would toss a pink gun on the highway? The way they were framing him made him look like the dumbest killer ever. It was downright insulting.

"How far is the Miller cabin from the highway?" Carver asked.

Holly was collecting a key from a metal box mounted on the wall while Maberly waited.

"Uh, a mile I think." Maberly frowned. "As the crow flies. The road going up there is longer because it winds around a lot."

Holly snatched a key from the lockbox. "You ask a lot of questions for a murder suspect."

"I need to know the timeline so I can prove it wasn't me."

She unlocked the first cell. Maberly nudged him inside. Carver went. He raised his hands behind him, waiting for them to remove the zip cuffs.

"Dream on." Holly slammed the door shut.

"It's just common decency," Carver said. "You're going to feel bad once you realize I'm not guilty."

"Settler's got two witnesses who say you are." Holly squeezed her eyes shut and blew out a breath. "You can rot for all I care."

Maberly scratched his balding head. "He's your prisoner, Holly."

Carver added another request to the list. "I'd like a map with the Miller cabin marked on it, and as soon as you have it, a time of death for Rhodes."

Holly pounded the flat of her fist against the bars. "Shut up!" She spun on her heel and marched out.

Maberly looked Carver up and down, then turned and left. He closed the metal door behind him. The lock clicked into place.

Carver looked down at the bunk. The folded-up mattress smelled moldy. It was first class accommodations compared to some places he'd been. He booted the mattress open. Turned and bent over like he was going to touch his toes. Slid his arms down his legs and stepped one foot at a time between them so his hands were in front.

These weren't even proper flex cuffs. Just a heavy-duty zip tie wrapped in a loop around his wrists. He gripped the excess nylon with his teeth and pulled until the cuffs were tight as possible. He twisted them so the locking mechanism was dead center between his wrists. He clenched his fists and pressed them against each other.

Then he raised his hands over his head. In one quick, fluid motion, he pulled his arms down and yanked his elbows outwards. The zip tie snapped. Carver tossed the pieces into the corner and looked at the room. There was a bed, a chair, a metal toilet, and a sink. It was normal for a jail cell.

It was about eight feet tall, ten feet deep, and maybe six feet across. Nothing overly generous, but not too cramped either. A light bulb on a cord hung from a metal hook embedded in the concrete ceiling. He went to the bars and looked at the outer room. There were no cameras in here either. This town was apparently too poor to care. He was probably the first murder suspect in ages.

There wasn't much else he could do at this point. He just had to wait until he had more information. With a time of death, he could prove he wasn't the killer. If that failed, he had other means. His number one goal was to get out of this cell before they sent him to a long-term facility.

Because that was where they'd try to kill him.

JASPER WHITTAKER'S mole delivered the news. Chief Rhodes was dead. A suspect was in jail. Paola Barros translated it to Portuguese and sent it via encrypted text to Brazil. The answer was almost immediate.

Who gave the order?

"Tell them it wasn't me," Jasper said. "But it's a blessing, right?"

Paola translated and sent another text. *Jasper didn't authorize.*

There was a pause that stretched into thirty minutes before corporate responded.

We're sending the Brothers to make sure this is tied up neatly. Have Jasper find out more.

She flinched. There was no explanation as to why they thought this required direct intervention on their part. As far as she knew, the police chief had only been here once and that was to introduce herself to Jasper.

Jasper took a puff of his cigar. "They respond yet, darling?"

"Yes." She told him what they said.

He poured himself some more cheap whiskey and tossed it back like a shot. "That's good. We got things running smooth as silk up here. Ain't no reason for them to get worried." Grunting, he lifted his heavy frame from the chair. "I'll tell my people to get more information as it comes, okay, darling?"

"I'll tell them." She sent another text.

He walked over to the couch and dropped into it. The old cushions tried to swallow him. He got himself comfortable. "Darling, bring me a blonde." He puffed his cigar. "No, wait, a brunette."

Paola rose and turned to leave.

He snapped his fingers. "Bring me both. I'm feeling lively today."

She nodded and left his office. Walked down a carpeted corridor with executive offices. Most of them were empty, unused. Only the accounting office and a handful of other positions were filled.

Whittaker Paint had once been a thriving business. They'd manufactured products for multiple name brands. At its height, the company had been worth nearly six hundred million. Then they'd invented a new paint base that was naturally thick and dense. It was like putting on two coats at once. It was revolutionary and premium. Nathan Whittaker called it Ultra Prime.

The other paint companies were eager to order from them. Even those that manufactured their own paint wanted to add it to their list of offerings. There had been plans for expansion. A larger manufacturing plant. More employees. If that had happened, the business would've been worth billions.

Instead, a whistleblower told the EPA about toxic leaks into local groundwater. They tied that into health issues in the community. Some people had died. Bodies had been exhumed. Toxins in tissues had been discovered. The federal government had sued.

Nathan Whittaker had been grooming Jasper to take over his business for years. He'd handed over day-to-day operations to his son, and his son had made changes to save money. He'd thought the cheaper disposal barrels would be fine. He'd thought an onsite disposal solution would be millions cheaper than hiring a third party.

Jasper had known about the leaking barrels. About the possibility of toxins leaking into the groundwater. He'd been too busy living the high life to care. The EPA had given him a reason to care again.

Whittaker Paints had to pay hundreds of millions in damages. They'd had to pay for cleanup, for testing, for everything. Nathan Whittaker died of a heart attack shortly after the verdicts. His life's work had been destroyed in a matter of two years by his idiot son.

Paola had seen it all before. When a successor is chosen because of nepotism and not because of skill, they were often destined for failure. Her brother had taken a once successful farm in Brazil and lost everything within five years of their father's death.

Jasper was even dumber than her brother.

She exited the offices and walked down a metal staircase into the paint plant. It was a vast jungle of metal, tanks, catwalks and stairways. The massive tanks had once all been utilized. Now only two were in operation, both for Ultra Prime, the premium paint base that should have carried this company to new heights.

She continued to the concrete floor at factory level. Passed an area with an unused employee cafeteria. At its height, it had serviced over a thousand employees. Those employees had earned good money. Morganville had been a thriving community until Jasper Whittaker killed it, both literally and figuratively.

She went through a door. Down a long staircase. Into the pit. At the bottom was a large underground room. A group of men were playing cards nearby. That was all they did for the most part. Smoke, drink, and play cards. This was easy work.

Paola interrupted their game. Told them in Portuguese what Jasper wanted. One of the men scowled at her. Folded his cards. Got up and walked into the darkness beyond. Paola had only been past this point a handful of times. She preferred to never go again.

The man returned a few minutes later with a pair of women in tow. Both looked like the picture of perfect health. They were well taken care of, but not like humans. More like show dogs. Primped and prepared. It showed in their eyes. They were the walking dead. Makeup covered the bruises.

Paola turned and walked back upstairs to the office. The man escorted the two women behind her. When the women moved too slowly, he gripped them by the necks and pushed them along. They whimpered, but that was all the noise they made. They'd been trained. They understood what happened to the undesirables.

They reached the offices. Paola knocked on Jasper's closed door. "They're here."

"Come on in, baby."

Paola opened the door. The man put his hand against the smalls of their back and guided them ahead. He went to the corner and stood there. Jasper had already removed his pants. His belly hung well over his privates. The girls went closer. Forcing themselves to the task at hand.

Holding back her rising gorge, Paola closed the door. Even on a good day, Jasper smelled of sweat trapped between folds of skin. He reeked of cigars and alcohol. He was a man of vices, and so, corporate gave him what he wanted to keep him happy.

She sat down at her desk and stared blankly at the computer screen. Then she took a deep breath and opened the logistics program. She started filling out the forms for the next shipments of Ultra Prime. It was, indeed, a lucrative product. But the millions it earned went to Brazil now. Brilhante Tintas had purchased the formula after agreeing to bail out Whittaker Paints and saving Jasper from destitution. Then they'd promised him more and he'd gladly accepted their conditions.

Paola finished the forms. Her thoughts went back to the Brothers. Corporate only sent them for serious business. The murder of the police chief could bring the feds to the city. More attention was the last thing corporate wanted. She had a feeling the suspected murderer would probably end up dead very soon.

That would tie up the investigation. The feds wouldn't come. The incident would be mourned and forgotten.

That was the way the world worked.

CHAPTER 4

A detective shambled into the holding facility about three hours after Carver's arrival. He went to the cell and stared at the occupant. Carver could smell the alcohol from his bunk.

"I'm Detective Davis." He was a short black man in an old brown suit. The tie hung loose around the collar, and the shoes were heavily scuffed. They were the shoes of a habitual drunk. Worn down by the shuffling gait of the inebriated.

Carver was sitting sideways on the bunk, staring at nothing. "Hello, Detective."

"You killed Chief Rhodes." The accusation held no emotion. It was as if he were simply reciting a line. "Sign a confession and I'll ask the prosecution to go easy on you."

"What a bargain." Carver leaned against the wall. "Did forensics finish their work? I need information to prepare my defense."

The detective laughed. "Boy, they have an ironclad case. Sign a confession and do your time."

"Get me a lawyer and we'll see how ironclad it is."

"You got a lawyer?"

"Nah, the public defender will do just fine." Carver remained sitting. Arms crossed. The detective made no comment about the lack of cuffs. Maybe he didn't know Carver had been cuffed.

Carver put on his best southern accent. "Get that public defender in here, boy. I'm done talking to you."

HOLLY WAS confused. There were no juvenile records for an Amos Carver. No adult records either. The man had never had so much as a speeding ticket. He'd joined the Navy at age eighteen and that was about the only noteworthy thing.

The background check came back empty. Third party records also empty. No records of a cell phone or even a credit card. Not even a birth certificate to verify his age. It was almost unheard of in this day and age. So, how had he gone from a blank page to a killer?

She thought back to what he'd said in the car. Not so much what he said but how he said it. He'd said Rhodes in a familiar way. Like he knew her. Rhodes had been in the military too. Maybe there was a connection. This might not be a random murder. There might be bad blood between him and the chief.

Holly wasn't a detective. It wasn't her job to look into things like this. The smart thing would be to mention it to Davis and let him handle it. The problem was, he wouldn't handle it. The man spent his free time drinking. How he'd kept his job so long was a mystery.

Holly pulled up Rhodes's records. She looked at the background search that had been run before the department had hired her. It was clean as a whistle. Rhodes also had a military record, but hers was for the Army. She'd been a military investigator for five years. She was a war veteran. She had more medals than most people in these parts had teeth.

She thought back to the first time she'd met Rhodes. She'd shown up in town one day. Gotten a room at the Morganville Hotel downtown. The hotel was still in business thanks to hikers. They'd stay in town before heading out to hike in the mountains. It was just enough business to keep the place running.

But Rhodes hadn't come to town for hiking. She'd hung around a few days. Gone to church, even. She'd introduced herself to the folks there. Said she was interested in moving to the town. Morganville wasn't even a nice place to visit, much less live. Holly didn't go to church, but her friends did. They thought it was wonderful having fresh blood move to town.

After about a week, Rhodes had come to the police department looking for work. Her military investigations background made her overqualified for most positions. The detective positions were full, but Chief Livingston had been wanting to retire for years even though he was young. He'd had a word with Mayor Morgan and Rhodes moved into the top spot at the police station just like that.

Maberly, Settler, and others had been pretty sore about the whole thing. Just about everyone wanted that job for the salary and perks. Just about everyone thought they were overqualified. What they hadn't considered was Chief Livingston had been in the Army, just like Rhodes.

Rhodes was also highly personable. The woman knew how to make you feel like best friends in ten minutes and that was without pandering. She was a straight talker. Trustworthy. Holly felt like she could tell the woman anything and that information was in a steel trap. Safe from the world. She had the qualities everyone wanted in a police chief or any officer of the law. The other sad sacks hadn't stood a chance.

Rhodes had helped Holly with her own personal issues. With an abusive ex-boyfriend. With depression. She'd pulled her out of a deep hole and made her feel worth something even though Holly had hardly strayed from this town since being born.

Tears clouded her eyes. Rhodes had been a good woman. Now she was gone. A rare, real jewel crushed by that man in holding. An enigmatic man named Amos Carver.

The military records might not jibe, but there was a connection. Carver knew Rhodes. But how? Maybe she'd investigated him for a crime. But why would someone from the Army investigate someone in the Navy?

Holly printed the skimpy report and put it in a manilla folder. Walked it back to the holding cells where Davis was interviewing Carver. There was shouting coming from behind the holding facility door. Holly opened it and saw Davis was the one making the ruckus. He was gripping the bars to Carver's cell door, red faced and shouting.

"You don't tell me what to do here, boy! I'm the law!"

Holly cleared her throat. "I got his records for you."

Davis released the bars. Stood taller and tried to straighten his tie. But his tie was undone and hanging around his neck. He shuffled to Holly and snatched the record. Lifted the folder like he was weighing it.

"What the hell is this?" He opened it and plucked the single sheet from inside. Skimmed it. "What the hell is this?"

"His record." Holly did her best not to wither under his glare. "No cell phone, no credit cards, nothing."

"You were in the Navy?" Davis stormed back to the cell door. "What did you do, mop the decks?"

"Among other things." Carver looked calm. Almost bored. "I demand a lawyer right now, or the judge will throw out your case on technicalities." He focused on Holly. "Has forensics filed a report? I want time of death, place of death, and a local map so I can plot the timeline and show you I'm innocent."

"You will do no such thing." Davis bared his teeth. "I am the detective in charge. I wouldn't be surprised if I'm made acting chief to get all this sorted out."

A laugh barked from Holly's throat before she could repress it. She turned it into a coughing fit. "Davis, we can't deny the man his rights. If we do, you know old Judge Porter will throw out the case. Or the feds might even step in."

Davis threw the manilla folder and the file on the floor. "Public defender, you said?"

Carver nodded. "That'll do fine. And I need all that evidence ASAP."

"I'm not under your command, boy." Davis stormed out of the room and slammed the door shut.

Holly picked up the file and the folder. "You know—knew Rhodes, didn't you?" She noticed he wasn't wearing the cuffs anymore. Davis must have freed his hands for some reason.

Carver stared at her with his cold eyes. "You looked up her record, didn't you? Looking for a connection?"

"Did you know her, Amos Carver?"

"Get me the information I need to prove my innocence and I'll answer your questions."

"I'm trying to help you."

He shook his head. "No, you're not. You liked Rhodes. You think I killed her."

Holly hated his cool demeanor. He made her feel like she was the one behind bars. Like he was the one in charge. Talking to him now was stupid. He'd lawyered up. It was best to let due process take its course.

"She was a good woman." Holly wiped tears away. "The best. And you took her away from us."

Carver looked unaffected. He sat down on his bed and went silent again. Eyes narrowed and calculating.

Holly's hands tightened into fists. She wanted to shout at him like Davis had done. Tell him to rot in hell. But Rhodes had taught her the value of keeping her cool. Of sitting back and letting others make the mistakes. She left the holding facility and went back to her desk.

"Cooler heads will prevail," Rhodes often said. "Proper planning can overcome a winning hand every time."

And she'd proven it time and time again. Maybe not with criminals, but certainly with Holly's personal life. This man deserved to die for killing her.

CARVER WAS FRUSTRATED.

Rhodes had won over the whole damned town. As usual. He mulled it over. Why had Rhodes come to this town? How in the hell had she gotten a job as a police chief? Her experience as a military investigator had probably weighed heavily in her favor. But that wasn't what she'd been doing for years.

It was getting late in the day. Carver didn't have a watch, but he knew about what time it was. Tracking time was subconscious. It had been vital at one time. Then civilian life made it useless. But now it was coming in handy again. Did the public defender's office close at five? Or did they come in at any time of the day?

The metal door creaked open, and Davis answered the question. "Your lawyer can't come until first thing in the morning. Sleep tight, boy."

"When is dinner served?"

The door slammed shut.

Carver stared at the wall. Then he stood and examined the lock on the cell door. It was nothing special, but he had nothing to pick it with. He'd need at least two slender pieces of metal. Picking it from this side would be almost impossible anyway. He could fit his hands and wrists through the bars, but the lock plate was wide. It would be hard to position the tools correctly even if he had them.

Jericho would've been able to do it easily. That skinny little tech could slip his arms through and reach all the way around. No muscle mass made it easy. Sometimes being the little guy was advantageous. Sometimes Carver wished he was smaller, shorter. Everyone underestimates the small guy.

Underestimating Jericho was usually the last thing someone did.

Carver went to the corner and put his hands on the wall and the bars, using the leverage to stretch his pectoral muscles. He held the stretch a while then knelt next to the bed like he was praying and stretched his lats. He continued through his daily routine. Keeping limber was important. He was at the disadvantage. He had to be ready for whatever came next.

He lay down in the bunk and considered scenarios. It was most likely he would be transferred to a prison tomorrow. It was there that the job would be finished. A prison gang would kill him for the price of a carton of cigarettes. Rhodes would be dead. He would be dead.

Case closed.

A heavy metal clunk signaled lights out. The florescent lights in the main room went off a fraction of an instant before the lights in the cell blinked out. Carver lay on the bed, feet nearest the bars, eyes open to let them adjust. His pupils dilated as wide as possible. But there was no light. No way to see.

He closed his eyes and drifted to sleep. Tomorrow would be a big day. Maybe the last day of his life.

THEY CAME for Carver at one in the morning.

The metal door creaked open. Carver's eyes blinked open. He remained motionless. A flashlight played on the floor outside the cell. Whispers echoed in the darkness. Hard soles tapped on concrete.

Carver closed his eyes. Light seeped through his eyelids. The lock on the cell door clicked. The door squealed open.

"Don't pretend you're asleep," Settler said.

Carver opened his eyes and shielded his eyes from the blinding light. It was a police flashlight. Extra bright. Used to confuse and blind.

"Don't move." The short guy spoke this time. Carver couldn't see him, but he recognized the voice. "We've got guns on you."

Carver kept still.

"Sit up slowly."

Carver kept still. "What's your name?"

"Won't matter to you in a few minutes."

"Okay, so what's your name?"

"You can call me Ruben."

"And your friend's name, Ruben?"

"Shut up, asshole." It was the other guy speaking this time.

"Stand up." Ruben said it patiently, but his patience was wearing thin.

Carver stood.

"Face the back wall."

He complied.

"Hands behind your back.

Carver complied again. Flex cuffs tightened around his wrists. The same kind they'd used on him before.

"Stay there," Ruben said.

Carver turned around and watched them. It was tight in the small space. The flashlight lit the place well enough to see three men wearing rubber gloves. Ruben, Settler, and the other guy.

Settler stripped the sheets from the bed. He stood on the edge, reached up and was barely able to touch the metal hook in the ceiling.

"Let Jimmy do it," Ruben said.

"Jimmy, Ruben, and Settler." Carver nodded. "I feel like we're becoming friends already."

Ruben waved his Glock at him. He stood behind the others, his back nearest the bars. "Shut it."

If he shot at Carver, he stood a good chance of mortally wounding Settler or Jimmy in the process. The bullets would ricochet in the tight space. This guy was playing it all wrong.

Jimmy twisted the sheets lengthwise. Fashioned the end into a noose. He managed to loop the middle over the ceiling hook. "You sure that thing is gonna hold?"

"It'll hold," Settler said. "Just make sure it's high enough."

"Don't matter if it's six inches or ten feet as long as his feet don't touch the ground."

"I like it," Carver said. "I'm blamed for killing Rhodes. I kill myself, case closed. Question is, what in the hell did she do to get herself killed?"

"You'll die never knowing," Ruben said.

"Tie this off, Settler." Jimmy gave him the slack.

Settler wrapped the end around the bars. "How high?"

Jimmy stood on the bed and put his head through the noose. "A little higher."

Settler pulled it tighter.

"Little more." The noose hugged Jimmy's neck.

Settler adjusted it.

Jimmy nodded. "Perfect."

Settler tied it off.

It was hanging time.

CHAPTER 5

Tony's phone dinged. He checked the text message. "It's done."

"Yes!" Dorsey poured them each a finger of whiskey. Held up his glass in a toast. "Damned good work."

Tony clinked his glass against Dorsey's. "Told you it'd be easy." He looked longingly at the whiskey then set down the glass. It was late, but Tony felt wide awake. He felt like celebrating. "I'm gonna head out. See you in the morning."

Dorsey took another sip. He glanced at the Karuizawa 1981. "Just a few more days and I'm cracking the seal on that bad boy."

Tony grinned. "We're in the clear now. Easy sailing from here on out." He left the building. Went into the parking deck and climbed into his truck. Breathed a sigh of relief. They'd delivered. He hadn't been sure those boys would be up to the task. Then again, there had been three of them. Three grown men were more than enough to handle one guy.

He sent another text. *It's time for the other bodies to be found.*

The reply came a moment later. *We'll take care of it.*

Tony put away his phone. He thought long and hard about where to go next. Couldn't go to the strip club. Couldn't go to the bar. Couldn't go anywhere with drugs or alcohol. He wasn't going to fall into that trap again. After sitting in the running truck for a good fifteen minutes, he gave up. Backed up and drove home.

It was going to be just another lonely night.

JIMMY TOUCHED the noose still around his neck. "This is high enough."

"Yeah, it's good." Settler tightened the knots. The sheet was firmly tied to the bars.

Carver nodded in approval. "Looks good to me." The time had finally arrived.

He reared back and kicked Jimmy on the side of his knee. There was a crack. Jimmy swung off the bed. His shout turned to a gurgle as the noose tightened around his neck. Carver kept moving. He slammed his shoulder into Settler. Settler slammed into Ruben. Ruben crashed into the bars.

Settler slumped. Carver brought his knee up into Settler's chin. There was a crunch as bones broke. He rammed his shoulder into Ruben again. He was a short man, so his head was about level with Carver's shoulder. The impact rammed his head into the metal bars. They rang with the impact. They rang again with the following blow.

The gun fell from limp fingers. Not a shot fired. Just a whimper as Ruben slumped.

Jimmy's legs flailed. He was trying to get his feet on the bed. Carver watched him swinging.

"Need some help, friend?"

Jimmy croaked and gasped, fingers prying desperately at the bedsheet. Carver gave him a solid kick in the side. Jimmy swung harder. Bounced off the bars. The noose went tighter. His neck snapped and his body went limp.

Carver worked his cuffs under his legs again. Broke them again. He pocketed the pieces. He felt Settler's pulse. There wasn't one. He checked Ruben. He was still alive. He untied the sheet from the bars. Jimmy flopped on the bed, slid off onto the floor. Carver checked his pulse. Nothing. Always best to be safe.

Jimmy was dead. Settler was dead. Ruben was on his way out.

Carver was in a cell with two corpses and a man whose fate he hadn't decided on. He could question him, but this wasn't the place for that. He dragged the bodies out of the cell and left them heaped up near the exit door. He examined the cell for blood. There was a little on the bars. He borrowed a strip of Jimmy's t-shirt and wiped them down. Wiped up the spot where Settler had bled on the floor. He found another pair of rubber gloves in Ruben's back pocket. He put them on.

Carver searched the bodies. All three had cell phones. All three had pistols. He left them in the holsters. Jimmy and Ruben didn't have wallets. Only thick wads of cash. Hundreds and twenties. No IDs, no credit cards. Nothing personally identifiable.

Settler had a worn leather wallet. Inside was a ten, a five, and two ones. More importantly, he had the keys to the cells. Carver pocketed them. He turned on the phones one at a time. They all required fingerprints or faces.

Carver opened Ruben's phone first. He seemed like the one in charge. Sure enough, there were some texts from an anonymous contact using an app that encrypted and deleted texts automatically. The last few texts were still there.

Going to finish the job now.

The reply: *Text me when you're done.*

Carver tapped out a text. *It's done.*

The message text turned gray. An instant later, it turned blue, and a checkmark appeared. It had been read. Carver looked over Settler's phone. There was next to nothing on it. Nothing in the encrypted texting app. Nothing in his normal texts except for messages about automatic payments for his cell phone and utilities.

Jimmy's phone was chock full of pictures and videos. Mostly sex videos. Carver played one and determined it was Jimmy having the sex. The women in the videos were attractive, but they looked dead in the eyes. Prostitutes maybe. He scrolled through the videos but found nothing of interest.

The encrypted text app was empty. Jimmy's regular text app was disabled. Carver tried to find out who the phone was registered to, but either the information wasn't on the phone, or he didn't know how to find it.

Another text arrived on Ruben's phone. *it's time for the other bodies to be found.*

Carver stared at the message. What other bodies? He typed back a reply. *We'll take care of it.* Rhodes wasn't the only one they'd killed. There were more.

It was ticking past two AM. Time to move.

Carver stepped through the metal door and back into the main station. It was dark and empty. No surprise a town like this didn't have a night watch. He went to the front. The only car out front was a black SUV. The streetlight either wasn't working, or it had been turned off. Unless someone drove into the parking lot, they wouldn't see the SUV from the road.

He returned to the holding area. Took a pair of flex cuffs from Settler's belt and fastened them around Ruben's wrists. Fastened another pair around his ankles. Fastened a third set around his elbows. That was about as close to properly restrained as it got with those things.

He took the car keys from Ruben's pocket. The logo matched the model of the big black SUV out front. Carver hefted Ruben over a shoulder. Took him outside and popped the rear hatch. The dome light didn't come on. That was a little detail people often overlooked. Interior lights flashing on in total darkness were a good way to throw a mission.

The vehicle smelled of chemicals. It looked like it had been washed recently. The carpet in the back was immaculate. It seemed Ruben liked to baby his car. Now it was his hearse.

With Ruben secured in the back, he made two more trips inside. Dumped Settler and Jimmy in the back. Closed the hatch. Went back inside one more time and looked around. The floor was clean. Nothing left in the cell. Nothing under the bed. It looked like nothing had happened.

Carver went outside, climbed in the SUV and cranked it. It was loud in the stillness of the wee hours of the morning. Almost three AM now. A bottle of blue cleaner was lying on the floorboard in the back. It was strong stuff. Just mist a surface and it would obliterate fingerprints. Handy to have in a situation like this even if it was just meant to keep a car clean.

Leaving the lights off, he drove out of the parking lot and toward town.

There were two ways to handle this. Disappear the bodies or make it look like an accident. Driving the SUV into a tree with the bodies properly placed might work. But the blood was already settling, coagulating. It might not be convincing enough for a seasoned medical examiner.

He drove to the old power company. Got out and opened the chain link gate. Drove inside and closed the gate behind him. There was a lot of refuse laying around, so he turned on the headlights. He steered around rusting generators, broken down utility cars, and other junk that had been stored there for ages from the looks of it. He reached the old coal boilers, all lined up in the far back. They were huge.

Back when they were operational, someone would shovel coal into the hopper. The burning coal heated up the water in the tank above. The steam turned the generator. Electricity was generated. The tanks were rusting, but they were still in one piece. Mainly because the steel was so thick.

The access port on the back of one of the boilers was open. Some poor sap back in the day had to climb inside and clean the tank occasionally. Scrape the scale left by the hard water. Make sure the steam pipes weren't blocked. Blocked steam pipes caused explosions, and nobody wanted that.

Carver leaned inside and shined the flashlight around the tank. Nothing inside except dust, rust, and a few leaves. The top of the pipes had been sealed off, so rainwater didn't get inside. The bottom was shaped like a cone, designed so water could be easily drained when necessary.

It was perfect. He sprayed the bodies with the cleaner first. Rolled them over and sprayed the other side. He considered removing their gloves. Did he want it to look like they'd been up to no good or keep it ambiguous? He decided to leave on their gloves. It would add mystery to the crime scene. Keep the locals confused.

He hefted Settler, dumped him in first. Dumped Jimmy next. Then he slapped Ruben gently to wake him up. Time to answer some questions.

But Ruben's skin was clammy. His pulse was gone. He'd died in transit.

"Great." Carver didn't blame himself. He'd done what he had to do to survive. He was mostly disappointed that Ruben couldn't provide answers. He checked Ruben's ankles and found an ankle holster on his right leg. It held a Glock 42, a slim, subcompact six-shooter. A thin knife was sheathed on his left shin. He cut off the flex cuffs and pocketed them. Sprayed Ruben down with cleaner.

The other two hadn't had any backup weapons. Ruben had come prepared in every way except the way that mattered most. He hadn't planned this out. Hadn't considered who he was dealing with. Backup weapons were useless if you were too dead to use them.

He dumped Ruben into the tank with the others. He considered the phones. He couldn't hold onto them for now, so he put them inside on a ledge, so they didn't slide down the conical slope to the bottom. They didn't seem to have any useful information on them anyway.

He removed a sock from Ruben's foot and dumped the money inside. The weapons also stayed with him. Except for Settler's service piece. That stayed behind. Taking weapons back to the jail cell was too risky. He doubted they'd frisk him again, but if they moved him to another facility, they'd almost certainly frisk him again there.

Carver drove the SUV back out and closed the gate. He drove to the only hotel he'd seen in town. It was the one place where the parking lot had a decent number of cars. The only place an unused vehicle might go unnoticed for a few days. He parked the SUV in the back, closed the doors, and locked it. He looked around, making sure no lights came on. He'd driven slowly so the engine noise wouldn't wake up any light sleepers.

He went back to the boiler. Put the keys on the ledge next to the cell phones. That arrangement would certainly make investigators wonder what had happened. Make them think a lunatic had committed the crime. He closed the boiler and went back to the street.

Carver walked around town. Looked at the boarded-up buildings. Loose boards on the back of the abandoned hardware store allowed him to slide inside. The place was dusty. No signs of vagrants or squatters. The empty shelving was still in place. He put the weapons, money, and everything else on the shelf except for the jail cell keys.

Should he keep at least one weapon? The only one he could conceal on his person was the Glock 42. The full-sized pistols would be too hard to conceal. If he was moved to another facility, maybe he could dump the pistol in the patrol car before being frisked again. Or he could just keep it and claim the police missed it on the first frisk.

He thought about it long and hard and finally made a decision.

The next stop was the police department. He used Settler's key to lock the front door behind him. He found the locker room off to the side of the workroom. They had bathrooms and showers. He cleaned off and put his clothes back on. They were stale with sweat, but he'd kept blood off them at least.

He went into the kitchen. There was some yogurt in the fridge. Some chips in the cupboard. He ate them. Wished there was something more, but that would have to do. He went back to the holding room, hung the keys in the lockbox. Walked through the main door and into the darkness. Closed the door behind him.

Carver carefully made his way to the cell. Felt around for the bars and the open door. He went inside and closed the door. It latched. Then he lay down on the bunk, took a deep breath, and went to sleep.

—— ◆ ——

CHAPTER 6

T he two men arrived in town shortly after dawn. They'd taken the redeye flight from Los Angeles to Atlanta. A car had been waiting for them in long term parking. They drove north up the interstate and stopped in a small town about thirty minutes from the destination. After a few hours of sleep, they'd cleaned up, eaten at a local diner, then driven the final miles.

They didn't know much about the target. He was tall, fit, and in jail. He had blue eyes, black hair buzzed short. His skin was light brown. Maybe tanned, maybe Latino. It was hard to say. The description was good enough. A town this small wouldn't have many folks in jail. A town this small wouldn't keep a suspected murderer in their own jail for more than one night.

The mole had said he was staying overnight. It was likely he'd be transported twenty miles west to the county jail today. Might be done with a prison bus, or just a single car. It was hard to say with small towns like this.

They had contacts in the county jail. The place wasn't a long-term penitentiary. It was a halfway house for people awaiting trial. A place where criminals with shorter sentences did their time. That said, there were some dangerous folks inside. A carton of cigarettes might buy an execution. But that would be too suspicious. It was better to pull off an execution while the prisoner was in transit.

Make it look like an accident.

It meant at a minimum two people would have to die. The driver and the target. It was too messy trying to take out just one guy. Much easier to just kill everyone. No witnesses. No fuss. The factory had moles in the local police department and at the county sheriff's office. That would make it easier to manipulate the chess pieces. To rig the game for the desired outcome.

The men drove through town, following the S-shaped highway. They noticed the parking lot behind the lone hotel was the only place with many cars. The diner next door was full of tourists getting breakfast before hiking. The men followed the highway past City Hall. Past the old phone company and power company. They turned onto the chip-sealed road leading to the police station.

One of the men spoke in Portuguese. "This town is a trash pit."

His brother nodded in agreement. "I would burn it to the ground."

His brother laughed. "Think of the men who have to work at the factory."

"I try not to." It was a dead-end place. Lucrative and necessary, but still a dead end. Los Angeles was the top of the pile. The Brothers took care of business there mostly. Sometimes they traveled east, sometimes north. Atlanta was a hot spot. New York, not so much. They removed roadblocks, greased the gears, kept things moving for corporate.

There were a few others in the company that did the same work, but the Brothers were the best at what they did. This was a case of a quick fix. They'd told corporate what would probably happen. One cop dead plus the suspect, worst case. Best case, just a dead suspect.

"Dead cops bring heat," corporate told them. "Minimize the heat."

Corporate depended on them to be the best. Times like this were when they proved it. It was still smart to give a worst-case scenario. Make it sound like there was no way around a huge mess. That way when they pulled it off with one death, it would look like a miracle.

Antonio plotted the route to the county jail. State route 79 offered the most direct route. It was a long stretch of road that went from two lanes in Morganville up to four lanes divided once it left the town. Highway 18 went the same way but was two lanes. It wound around the mountain, along a lake, and over a river.

It was the better route for them. It offered the perfect opportunity for an ambush.

Antonio texted the mole in Morganville and the one at county. Then his brother, Tiago, turned around the truck. He took Highway 18, and they marked off several suitable ambush locations. One spot was better than most. It was on a blind curve. A hundred-foot drop on the right. A cliff on the left.

There was a large white wooden cross with fake flowers. It was a memorial for some kid named Johnny. He'd lost his life years before when trying to take the curve too fast. There were two more smaller memorials for people who hadn't learned from Johnny's mistake.

The memorials were a good omen. This was a dangerous spot. A good place to make an accident happen.

Antonio texted the moles again. Told them what needed to happen.

The moles texted back. They'd make it happen.

"We're set."

Tiago tapped the steering wheel. "Let's make the contingency plan."

Antonio plotted the alternate route on 79. They drove from one end to the other. It was a logistical nightmare if this route was taken. There was only one place for the ambush. A small stretch of country road connected the town to the highway. There was a curve about halfway through, but it wasn't sharp enough to cause a natural slowdown. It was, at least, a blind curve.

It wasn't perfect, but it was doable.

Antonio dropped a pin on the map. Then they went to get the equipment they'd need. That would be easy enough in these parts. He searched the map for road construction. Found the nearest location.

Tiago wheeled around and they headed for the construction zone. One way or another, the target would be dead before he reached the county prison.

CARVER WAS tired and hungry.

He'd woken at six AM sharp. That was sleeping in for him. His stomach rumbled, but there wasn't much he could do about it. All he could do now was wait on the public defender.

Maberly brought in a bottled water and a bagel at seven. He slid them both through the bars.

"This is seriously all I get for breakfast?"

"Eat it or don't." Maberly shrugged. "Ain't none of my concern." He turned and waddled back to the door.

"Wait, where's the lawyer?"

Maberly checked the time on his wristwatch. "Should be here any minute." He left.

Carver downed the bagel and the water in short order. It didn't help much. He passed the time stretching and doing calisthenics to warm up. His knee was a little sore where it had broken Settler's skull. His shoulder ached from ramming Ruben repeatedly into the bars.

Otherwise, he felt pretty good. He'd avoided turning the situation into a fugitive hunt. He'd thwarted an unexpected attempt on his life. He did feel slightly ashamed for not considering the possibility that they'd come for him here.

The hanging attempt had to have been one of the dumbest things he'd ever seen. They should have brought ten guys with them if they really wanted Carver hanging from the ceiling. It was even dumber than their pink gun in the road gambit.

Carver would've risked getting shot. Would've gone down in a hail of gunfire if necessary. But he wouldn't have let them hang him without it costing them dearly. At least that way they would have had a harder time keeping the scene clean. They might have said he tried to escape, but that wouldn't explain why he'd been shot at two in the morning by a person who wasn't even a cop.

Carver wasn't even that upset about not getting answers from Ruben. Even if the man hadn't died, it was unlikely he would have offered up any information. At least not without time and torture. There hadn't been time. Carver would have had to kill him because he had nowhere to secure him.

The bodies were well hidden, but they'd soon start to stink something awful. Being sealed up inside the boiler might be enough to contain it but the odor might attract scavengers.

As long as it bought him a few days, he'd come out of this okay. The supposed witnesses were now deceased. There were no prints on the gun and no GSR on him.

The main door squealed open. Carver looked through the bars, expecting a man in a suit. Instead, a guy in a lab coat walked in, a kit in his hand.

"Put your hands through the bars, please." The man put on rubber gloves and unfolded a small TV tray to put his kit on.

Carver did. "Testing for GSR now after all this time?"

"Yes." The man opened the kit. Took out a plastic vial and pulled off the top like a cork. A rod with a black tip was attached to the inside of the lid. He pressed it to the skin up and down the left index finger and the web between the finger and the thumb. He closed it. Opened another. Repeated the process on the other hand.

He removed a clear box with a cotton swab inside. Removed it and ran it up and down the same areas. He put it back in the clear box. Took out a small ampule. Removed the tip and squeezed the liquid inside onto the cotton.

"Little late for a field test, don't you think?" Carver couldn't believe how sloppy the investigation had been so far. "You want to test for GSR as soon as possible."

"The results will still be valid. You haven't washed your hands."

Carver had no comment. "How long for results?"

"An hour." The man examined the cotton swab, but whatever was supposed to indicate a positive result didn't happen. He sealed the other vials in an envelope, collected the kit, the TV tray, and left.

Time kept on ticking. Carver's stomach growled louder and louder. He was starting to regret not turning this into a fugitive hunt. At least he'd be eating better. A squirrel, a possum, anything would do right now.

At long last, a man in a shabby navy-blue suit burst through the door and walked to the cell. "Mr. Carver?"

"That'd be me." Carver stood at the cell door.

The man looked at a form. "They didn't even take your mug shots?"

"These folks don't know their elbow from an asshole."

He grunted. "I am Oscar Bennet, your attorney. Sorry for being late, but I wasn't notified about you until late last night and didn't check messages until late this morning."

Carver didn't care about his excuses. "I need some information."

Bennet looked up from the form. "Yes, I suppose we need a lot of information."

"Time of death, witness statement from the bus driver, length of time for someone to walk from the exit to the place I was arrested." Carver watched the attorney write it down. "Get me that information and we'll prove I didn't do anything."

Bennet looked up and around. "Let me get us moved to an interview room." He walked to the metal door and pounded on it. Maberly appeared a moment later. Nodded. They disappeared behind the door.

Maberly returned alone with a pair of metal cuffs in hand. He opened the meal slot in the door. "Hands through the opening."

Carver complied. The metal tightened around his wrists. He backed up a step and Maberly opened the door. The clerk led him down the hall and into a room next to the offices. Inside was a large oak table that looked remarkably nice in the otherwise dingy station. The chairs were vinyl, thickly padded.

Carver sat at the corner near the attorney, facing the door. "Looks more like a conference room than an interview room."

"I asked for this one. The real interview rooms are small and uncomfortable."

"Surprised they complied."

Bennet shrugged. "My old man was a cop here. He retired a long time ago."

"Good to have connections."

Bennet opened the thin folder with the form in it. "Time of death is listed as twelve thirty yesterday. Place of death is right outside the Miller cabin."

Carver did the calculations in his head. "How far is the cabin from the road?"

"One point four miles."

"Are there trails or a direct path from the cabin to the road?"

"None that I'm aware of. It's dense forest and a slope."

"I got off the bus at twelve forty-one. I hiked five miles down the highway before I reached a pink gun in the road. There's no way I could have reached the cabin before twelve thirty unless I learned to time travel."

Bennet made notes. "I'll call the bus station. Ask the bus driver for a statement."

"His name is Albertson. Short, chubby, thick brown hair combed to the side."

Bennet raised an eyebrow. "You remember a lot."

"Being observant keeps you alive."

His other eyebrow went up. "That's an interesting way of putting it. I'll call them and ask for Albertson."

"His statement alone should give me an alibi. But my prints aren't on the gun, and I don't have GSR residue on my hands either."

"We should have confirmation within the hour." Bennet made another note. "You could have wiped the prints, of course and washed your hand in the stream that runs through the forest."

"So I've heard." Carver leaned back in his chair and enjoyed the softness. "Can I get something to eat? I'm starving."

Bennet looked over the edge of his reading glasses. "They didn't feed you?"

"A bagel and water."

Bennet sighed. He stepped out of the office and returned moments later. "I'm having breakfast sent over from Rose's Café."

"I could use some coffee too. Black."

Bennet left the room again and returned with a foam cup filled to the brim with coffee.

Carver sipped it greedily. It wasn't food, but it was a close second.

"There is the matter of the two witnesses." Bennet studied the report. "Ruben Brown and Jimmy Dasante."

A sip of coffee covered the smile threatening Carver's lips. "I mean, they can say they saw me all they want, but they can't beat physics."

"Physics?"

Carver nodded. "Like I said, I can't time travel. I got off the bus ten minutes after the time of death."

"Unless you weren't on that bus. Maybe you shot the sheriff—"

"But I didn't shoot the deputy."

Bennet didn't smile. "I meant to say the chief."

"I was on the bus. Albertson should remember me." Carver wished he'd kept the ticket and the receipt. Maybe the fact that he remembered what the driver looked like would be enough evidence.

"I'm just putting myself in the prosecution's shoes. If we can't prove you were on the bus, then there's nothing to say you weren't there." Bennet consulted a small map of the area. "You were spotted at two twenty-two. Arrested shortly after."

"That's about right. It took me almost two hours to walk from the bus stop to that point." Carver took another sip of coffee. "Physics."

"Why do you keep saying physics?"

"I'm saying I was on a bus, and it was physically impossible for me to be where they said I was at that time unless I broke the laws of physics." The more Carver said it, the less confident he was that he was using the word right. Rhodes had always been the smart one. She gave him a hard time whenever he tried to sound smart. It was hard to believe someone outsmarted her.

There was a knock on the door. Bennet answered, and a woman brought in a paper sack. He thanked her and opened it. Removed a foam container and set it in front of Carver. Opened it.

The smell of eggs, bacon, and potatoes wafted into the room. Carver took the plastic fork and started shoveling food in his mouth with the cuffs on.

Bennet continued studying the papers. "I'll make some phone calls. See if we can square your alibi."

"I'll be waiting." Carver demolished the food and started on the cup of orange juice next. He hoped they could contact the bus driver quickly. His life might depend on it.

Bennet returned after being gone for twenty minutes. "I called the bus depot. They're tracking down the driver."

"Good."

"Unfortunately, in the meantime, county is sending a transport to take you to county lockup. It's not too far, so I can meet you there after the bus driver gets back to me. If that matter can be cleared up today, we should have you out of there first thing in the morning."

ANTONIO READ the text from the mole.

A single marshal would come from the county lockup to retrieve the target. The mole would ensure they used Highway 18 both ways. They were due to pick up the target within the hour.

"We're on." Antonio checked the time. "Let's eat and go setup."

Tiago looked at the text. "This will be easy. Minimum casualties."

"Easy." Antonio agreed.

They went to the local diner and ordered some breakfast sandwiches to go. Then they parked on the county road connecting the town to Highway 18. The marshal's car would have to pass this spot on the way to pick up the prisoner. Antonio looked up images of the county marshal cars on the internet, so he'd know exactly what he was looking for.

The images showed a black Ford SUV with Sheriff or Marshal in gold lettering on along the side. It would be easy enough to spot.

They settled in for the wait.

"Wonder why they're so concerned about this guy." Tiago leaned his seat back. "Killing a small-town cop is no big deal."

"They think this guy is a local asset for a competitor." Antonio remained upright. He was the lookout. "Someone who maybe thought the cop was on our payroll. Or maybe they wanted to draw some heat. Cause a big investigation. The feds come in and start poking around, they might find out about the factory."

"Just like Arizona." Tiago shook his head. "That was a mess."

"Yeah. Just one little thing can bring down the whole house." Antonio took a bite of his sandwich. "This way we tie up the crime nice and neat. With the only suspect dead, there's no reason to bring the heat."

"As long as it looks like an accident." Tiago sipped his coffee. "Otherwise, we'll make it worse."

"Nah. This is gonna work."

Tiago grinned. "Yeah, I think so."

This had worked before, and it was going to work now.

CHAPTER 7

C arver shook his head. "I can't go to a penitentiary. I'd prefer to stay here."

Bennet chuckled. "I'm afraid you don't have much of a say in that."

"I'm afraid for my life."

The attorney blinked. "Explain."

Carver wasn't sure he could without sounding like a conspiracy nut. "I'm just a guy who won't do well in a penitentiary."

"It's not a penitentiary. It's a county lockup where they send people awaiting trial." Bennet shook his head. "The dangerous people are kept in a different section. You'll never see them."

"A lot can happen to a person in prison."

"This isn't the movies." Bennet gave him a long hard look. "Do you really think someone will try to kill you in there?"

"I think so, yes. Can you get a judge to keep me here?"

"Let's back way up, Mr. Carver. Remember, I'm your attorney. Anything you say to me will be held in the strictest confidentiality."

Carver nodded. "I understand."

"Did you kill Chief Rhodes?"

"No."

"Why are you concerned there is a threat against your life?" Bennet clicked his pen. "Is it because other police might think you're a cop killer?"

"Well, there is that possibility," Carver said. "Things happen to cop killers."

"It's not reason enough to convince a judge." Bennet shook his head. "Nothing is going to happen to you. Plus, you'll get three square meals a day."

"Sounds delightful." Carver lifted his coffee. "They don't have enough evidence to hold me as it is. I don't even know why I'm still here."

Bennet checked his watch. "They have twenty-four hours, which means you have a few hours left."

There was a knock on the door. Bennet opened it. "Yes, Officer?"

Holly stepped inside. "Hello, Oscar. How's Charlie?"

"Charlie mentions you often." Bennet cleared his throat. "But I'm afraid there's no place for niceties under these circumstances."

Holly stiffened. "Understood. We didn't get his mug shots yesterday." She looked around Bennet at Carver. "I need to take them now."

"Do you people even follow procedure here?" Bennet put his hands on his hips. "No field tests, no mug shots, and you waited hours before letting me know I had a client. This entire process has been a sham and I'm certain the judge will see it that way."

"I couldn't find the camera film yesterday." Holly looked flustered. "But I need to get his mug shots now. County is on the way to pick him up."

"Already?" Bennet checked the time. "Can't it wait until after lunch? I'm still talking to him."

"You'll have to do it at the lockup." Holly glared at Carver. "Mug shots, now."

Carver remained sitting. He thought about what Bennet had said. County lockup might be a safe place, but there were no guarantees. "I prefer to talk to my attorney here."

"You're a prisoner. You don't get a choice."

"I'm a suspect, not a prisoner."

"You've been charged with murder, Mr. Carver."

"Just Carver is fine. And have I actually been charged?"

"Yes, you have." Holly touched her holster. "We can do this the hard way if you want."

"Carver, just go with her, please." Bennet stacked his papers and put them in a folder. "We can continue this at county."

"Fine." Carver stood awkwardly since his hands were still cuffed. He stepped out of the room and looked around the station. Not a soul in sight except the three of them. Maberly was probably at his desk, but with Settler dead and the detectives absent, Holly was on her own.

Holly put her hand on his back and guided him toward the workroom. She put him in front of a white backdrop. Handed him a placard with his name and number on it. He held it up. Smiled. The camera flashed. He showed his profile. The camera flashed.

Holly motioned him out. "Thank you."

"You're welcome." Carver couldn't decide if this place was run by idiots, or intentionally understaffed and mismanaged. Maybe Rhodes had been brought in to bring the place up to snuff. They needed a lot of help.

Holly clicked on her radio. "Where in the hell is everyone today?"

"I ain't seen Settler," Maberly replied. "He's supposed to bring in the statements for the witnesses today."

Carver barked a laugh. "They still haven't submitted statements?" He knew they never would, and it made him smile.

"Settler was taking care of it." Holly motioned him back to the conference room. "Wait in there with your attorney. County will be here soon."

"I can hardly wait." Carver went back to the conference room. Sat down and sipped his coffee. "The witnesses never submitted statements."

Bennet was writing notes on a pad of legal paper. "I'm sure they'll be here soon enough."

"Somehow, I doubt it." Carver repressed a grin. "They were either mistaken or outright lying about seeing me at the crime scene." His humor faded as he thought about Rhodes lying lifeless in a morgue somewhere. "Are there crime scene photos? Anything I can look at?"

"They haven't submitted any evidence to your folder yet." Bennet stood. "I'm going to talk to forensics and see if they've filed a report. The way this place is being run I should be able to have you out by tomorrow."

The problem was, Carver would have to survive that long.

DORSEY FIRED THE STEYR AUG full auto.

The concussive shockwave thumped through Tony's chest even though he stood five feet to the side. Without protection his ears would be ringing. Dorsey loved firing full auto just like in action movies. But he also knew it was best to fire single shot for accuracy. And he was a surprisingly good shot for a spoiled civvy.

When the magazine was empty, Dorsey removed the magazine. Pulled back the release to ensure the chamber was clear. He put it on the table to the side and looked over the other guns. "What's the committee status?"

"Assets are in place. Timing is still on track."

Dorsey chose a UMP45. "Good. I think it's time to stage the scene."

"Agreed." Tony looked at the tattered target downrange. "What about the detective?"

"He won't play ball?"

"He says he will, but I don't trust him."

Dorsey picked up a magazine for the submachine gun. "He has no idea how the dots connect?"

"Doesn't look that way."

"He might be useful then. Might help set the scene."

Tony nodded. "I'm on it." He left the range. Left the building and went to the parking garage. He got into a nondescript gray sedan and drove it outside the city limits.

He passed through suburbia and its cookie-cutter homes and strip malls. Reached the rural areas beyond. Took a right down a country road and wheeled into a long driveway to a house set far off the road.

A pair of men stood as he entered. Nodded, but didn't salute as they'd been conditioned to do in the military. Tony opened the basement door and walked down the concrete staircase. There was a chair with a table at the bottom. Across from the table was a seven-by-seven room enclosed in thick, clear plexiglass. Black curtains covered the sides and concealed the occupant.

Inside the cube was a man. A detective. He was an older guy, probably ripe for retirement. Instead of retiring, he'd continued to play detective.

Instead of retiring, he might have to be retired.

Tony's people had taken him a few days ago. Bag over the head. A shot to keep him asleep. They'd brought him here for questioning. Tony had trained these guys himself. Proper interrogation techniques. Using voice changers to preserve anonymity. White noise generators to muffle ambient sounds.

Even a detective worth his salt wouldn't know up from down in this place.

Inside the room was a camera, a speaker and a microphone. Right now, the occupant was mumbling to himself. "Butter, flour, sugar, baking powder." He paused. "Salt, milk, cinnamon, and peaches."

"We looked that up," Blake said. "It's a recipe for peach cobbler."

"Then our techniques are working." Tony sat at the table in front of the cube and spoke into the microphone. "Good evening, Detective." It wasn't evening, of course. But it was important to distort time as much as possible. His altered voice echoed back over the mic inside the cube. He sounded like Arnold Schwarzenegger.

The detective flinched at the first sound to penetrate the white noise generators.

One of the men snickered.

Tony gave them a sideways look, then switched the program to a deep voice. "Have you thought about our last conversation?"

The detective looked up at the camera. "I'll do what you want. Just please don't kill me."

"As I said before, detective, we wouldn't kill you. Your wife would be the first to die followed shortly by your daughter and her husband." Tony let that sink in before continuing. "I know you don't want your grandkids to grow up orphans, so that's why I know you'll cooperate."

Tears trickled down the detective's face. "Please, just tell me what you want."

"I want to know everything about your investigation. The truth this time."

Detective Abe Ritter nodded. He looked like a man who hadn't slept in a week, though he hadn't been here longer than two days. The dark circles under his eyes stood out in stark relief to his pale, wrinkled skin. "Do you work for them?"

"Let me remind you that I ask the questions, not you." Tony pressed a button.

The shock collar locked around Ritter's neck activated. He yelped in pain.

"I ask the questions." Tony pressed the button again.

Ritter cried out in pain. "I'm sorry! I'm sorry."

"That's only level three, Detective. Don't make me turn it up more. Don't make me bring your daughter here. I'll strip her naked and put battery clamps on her nipples."

"Please no!" Ritter pounded on the plexiglass wall.

"Sit down, Detective."

Ritter sat on the small bed.

"Now, tell me everything about your investigation. Don't leave out a single detail."

"I noticed a lot of shipments to the paint factory. Truckloads of raw materials. I thought maybe they were ramping up production. I thought maybe there was a chance they might get this town back on its feet again."

Tony made notes. The factory was getting sloppy. "Continue."

"It's been like this for months. But nothing ever improved. So, I went there in person to talk to Jasper, and he gave me this long spiel about raw materials, and machinery, and maintenance. But he never explained what they were actually doing with whatever was coming on those trucks."

"Keep going."

"I hid in the woods on the backside near the loading docks. I watched with binoculars to see what they were taking off the trucks. There were pallets of five-gallon drums of paint base." Ritter rubbed his eyes. "Then the forklift removed these long wooden crates with numbers on the side. They're the same kind of boxes people ship guns in, I'm certain of it."

Tony made a few more notes. "Riveting story, Detective. Keep going."

"Then the trucks left without any cargo." Ritter stared blankly at the floor. "I knew something was strange about that, but Davis didn't agree with me. He said I didn't know squat about the industry and that I should mind my own business."

Tony remained silent and let him continue.

"But I just couldn't leave it alone. So, I went back. I tried to find a way into the factory, but the fence was too high and covered in razor wire. Everything about that place looks rundown but that fence is brand new and well maintained." He shook his head. "I never really thought about the place before. Whittaker Paint has just always been there. When I was young, they employed eighty percent of the town. Then the damned EPA almost put them out of business."

"What did your wife think about it?"

Ritter flinched. Blinked. "I didn't—"

"Don't lie, Detective."

The man shivered. "She thought it was none of my business. She said I should finally retire so we can buy an RV and travel."

"A wise woman, Detective. A very wise woman." Tony grinned.

"She's the only person I told besides Davis." Ritter clasped his hands in prayer. "Please don't hurt her."

"Continue your story."

Ritter looked at a loss for a moment. "I just kept hiding in the forest and recording the trucks coming in, how much paint they removed, how many pallets. Then I tried to find a guy who could help me get in there. Take a look around in secret. Then the next thing I knew, I was here."

"And where is here, Detective?"

"I have no idea. I don't even know what day it is or how long I've been here."

"One week and three hours," Tony said.

"No, it can't be that long. My wife must be worried sick."

"Your wife thinks you took a trip to your fishing cabin. As we speak, she's watching her daytime television."

Ritter shuddered. "That's everything I know. I swear it on my mother's grave."

"Detective, I think it's safe to say that we own you, don't you agree?"

His six-foot frame shrank in on itself until he looked a foot shorter. Like a sad, thin puppet with cut strings. "Yes."

"Good. You will return home today. You will say you felt a little sick and returned early. Then you will go to work as if nothing ever happened. You will not continue your investigation. In fact, you will become our inside man. For this, you will be rewarded. After you've served us for a short time, then you will be free to retire. Does that sound fair?"

Ritter nodded furiously. "It's very fair. I accept! I accept!"

Tony turned off the microphone and glanced at his students. "Very well done. I hardly had to do anything."

The men were grins all around.

"Did you hear me?" Ritter said. "I accept."

Tony let the man sweat it out for another five minutes to keep this experience vivid in his memory. "Relax Detective. Your incarceration is almost done."

TWENTY-TWO MILES away, Antonio crouched in the forest waiting on the mole to tell him the target had left. Everything was set. The ambush was ready.

He checked the scope on his rifle again. Checked the bullet in the chamber. He twisted the silencer off the end and looked through it one more time to ensure it was perfectly clean. Then he put it on the end and gave it a half twist to reconnect it.

The road was quiet. Maybe one car had passed through in the last fifteen minutes. From his vantage point he'd be able to see the Marshal coming from half a mile away. He likewise had a clear view of the road past the sharp curve below. He could see Tiago's position from here.

His phone vibrated. The target was on the way. This would be over twenty minutes from now. A message would be sent. Any rivals seeking to disrupt their territory would pay the price.

CHAPTER 8

A middle-aged man entered the conference room. He was thin. His thick beard tried vainly to give him a tough appearance, but a stiff breeze would probably knock him over. His beige shirt and black slacks identified him as a deputy.

Carver knew without a doubt he could disarm Holly and this man in under thirty seconds even while handcuffed. Unfortunately, that would turn this into a hostage situation. He might be innocent of the current crimes, but then he'd face jail for that. The only choice was to move forward with the farce.

Maybe he was wrong about the county lockup. Maybe he'd be safe enough there. Everything would be cleared up by morning. Then he could get on to the real business about who killed Rhodes and why she'd summoned him here.

The man spoke. "I'm Deputy Dixon here to transport the prisoner."

Holly held out a hand and shook his. "I'm Officer Robinson."

Dixon nodded at Carver. "This him?"

She nodded.

"He don't look like much."

Carver stood and towered over him. "Sorry, I didn't eat my Wheaties this morning."

Dixon backed up a couple of steps, hand on his holstered gun. "Boy, don't you do that again."

"Or you'll do what? Tickle me?" Carver went to the door. "Can we go? I'd like to get this over with."

"I tell you what, boy." Dixon ran a hand through his beard. "We don't take kindly to cop killers in these parts."

"Do people take kindly to cop killers in other parts?" Carver gave him a direct look. "Or is that unique to this fine town?"

"Shut your mouth, prisoner." Holly pushed Carver toward the door.

He didn't budge at first, then turned and slowly walked to the exit. All his instincts told him not to go with this deputy. To take them prisoner. Lock them up in their own jail. His gut told him that going to the county lockup was the wrong decision.

Taking hostages or becoming a fugitive might work in the short term. Long term it was a dealbreaker. He'd just have to hope whoever gave Settler and those men their orders hadn't realized the job wasn't done. Once they did, they'd send someone else after him. Maybe someone was waiting for him right now.

ANTONIO was waiting. Watching. He scoped a car that appeared in the distance. Zoomed in. Put the crosshairs on the driver's head. The driver turned down another road and disappeared. The last three cars that he'd seen had taken that route. Few of the locals continued along this road.

He checked the time on the text. Five minutes had passed. Fifteen more to go. He texted the mole. *When did they leave?*

The reply came a full minute later. *I thought they left but the prisoner is being difficult.*

Antonio clenched a fist. *Tell me exactly when they leave. Do not waste my time by telling me when you think they have left.*

I'm sorry. I'll keep a close eye on them.

DETECTIVE DAVIS emerged from the break room and looked Carver up and down. "What's he still doing here?"

Deputy Dixon signed a transfer form and handed it back to Holly. "We will notify you when we arrive."

His radio crackled with static. "Code twelve. Available units respond."

"Thank you, Deputy." Holly opened the front door.

More static. "Kilo One Two responding."

"Bronson Construction reporting stolen equipment. Please respond."

Dixon turned down the volume on his radio and opened the front door.

Holly smiled at him. "Busy day at county?"

"Always busy." Dixon looked around the lobby. It was clear he didn't think much of the place. "I gotta get going." He opened the front door and ushered Carver outside.

A running black SUV waited next to the sidewalk. Sheriff was written in bold gold letters along the side. Red lettering on the back said K-9.

Holly frowned. "You brought a dog with you?"

Dixon shook his head. "I was the only one available for prisoner transport, so I left Lulu at the station." He took Carver by the elbow and opened the back door. There was a single seat installed next to the metal wall of the dog cage.

Carver leaned over and squeezed into the space. There was metal behind him and metal in front. Small square holes cut in the metal gave him a limited view in the front and the back. A sheet of metal covered the inside of the window. It was like being shoved into a metal box.

He put on the seatbelt with his cuffed hands before Dixon did it.

Holly looked him over. "Looks like a sardine can."

Carver nodded. "What if I told you I suffer from claustrophobia?"

Dixon sneered. "I hope you do."

"You've both said some very mean things." Carver shook his head disapprovingly. "I hope you feel ashamed when you find out I'm not guilty."

"Shut your mouth, boy." Dixon slammed the door.

Carver watched the others through the slits in the window. Davis, Holly, and Maberly were outside talking to Dixon. Bennet walked past and into the parking lot. Dixon walked around the front of the SUV. Climbed into the driver seat. Clicked on the radio.

"This is Dixon. Leaving Morganville now with prisoner."

A voice crackled in reply. "Copy that."

He shifted into drive and pulled out of the parking lot. Drove down the rutted street to the highway. Turned right and headed north. He stopped at the Highway 18 junction. Looked both ways and crossed the highway.

Another voice crackled on the radio. "Highway seventy-nine is still backed up. Recommend you take eighteen."

Dixon replied. "Copy that." He made a U-turn and went back to Highway 18. Took a right and gunned the engine.

"Do you normally take Highway Seventy-Nine?" Carver asked.

Dixon didn't answer.

"Is it unusual for you to take this route?"

"Shut it, prisoner."

"It's a simple question."

"Seventy-Nine is faster." Dixon stared at him in the rearview mirror. "Now, shut it."

"Who was that on the radio?"

Dixon didn't answer.

"Seriously, who told you to change course?"

"Keep your mouth shut, boy."

Carver peered through the slits at the road ahead. "Someone might try to kill me, so just stay on your toes, okay?"

Dixon pulled over and screeched to a halt. He turned in his seat. "Shut your damned mouth, or I'll tape it shut."

"Don't say I didn't warn you." Carver turned the best he could and looked out the back window. The road behind them was empty. The road ahead was empty. This was a great place for an ambush.

Carver sat back and went over scenarios. How would he do it? How would he kill a prisoner in his situation without drawing more heat? Shooting him and the cop would send the wrong message. It would show that there was a third party who wanted him dead. Signal that Carver wasn't the one who killed Rhodes in the first place.

They could stop the car. Force the cop out of the car. Get Carver from the back. Kill the cop and make it look like Carver shot him. Then shoot Carver and make it look like they both died in the shootout. But it was unrealistic. There was no escaping this metal box. Not unless he found a blowtorch under the seat. There was no realistic way to set up that scenario.

Another option. Stop the car, kill Carver. Knock out the cop. Once again, that would send the wrong message. It would prove Carver was innocent. They'd want something that would leave questions in the minds of investigators. An accident would be the best route.

Dixon pulled back onto the road and gunned the engine. He glanced at Carver in the mirror and shook his head. "If I had a dime for every asshole that tried to pull conspiracy theory routine on me, I'd be rich."

Carver watched the road ahead. He swept his gaze from one side of the road to the other. Trees grew up the side of a mountain on the left. There were more trees to the right. A metal railing. A steep decline. It was beautiful country. It was why the tourists flocked out here for hiking.

The SUV climbed a hill. Crested the rise. The road curved sharply to the left a half mile ahead. The road banked, presumably to help cars that had too much speed coming down the mountain.

There was a wall of rock on the inside. On the outside, a metal railing and a steep drop. A large white cross with flowers and two smaller ones. Carver peered up the cliff. The trees were thinner there. Just a few bushes and some weeds. The bushes moved. Was someone hiding there? Or was it just the wind?

This is it. This is the perfect spot for an accident.

It wouldn't take much. Shooting out the right front tire might do it. Someone up on that ridge would have the perfect angle at the perfect moment. That was how Carver would do it. Was someone really up there? Or was he just being his normal paranoid self?

They closed to within a quarter mile. A hundred yards. Fifty. If someone was going to shoot out the tire, now was the time to do it. They hit the curve and the deputy slowed to take it.

A yellow dump truck barreled down the curve toward them. Bronson Construction was written in black letters along the side. It wasn't slowing. Wasn't turning. It was in their lane.

That was when Carver knew exactly how they were going to do it.

HOLLY WAS RESTLESS so she decided to go to the county morgue. She'd been putting it off for too long. Ever since Settler told her what had happened, she'd been in denial. Rhodes couldn't be dead. She was too smart, too fast to be killed by a savage like Carver. It just didn't make sense.

Forensics still hadn't released any information. Morganville was too small to have its own CSI team, so they relied on the county. Rhodes's body would be at the same facility. Maybe the medical examiner had some answers by now.

Either way, Holly needed to see the body. Needed to confirm with her own eyes that Rhodes was dead.

She got up from her desk. Walked down the hall and stopped at Maberly's door. "I'll be back in a few."

He rotated his chair. Put down a bag of donuts. Powdered sugar was on his chin and his shirt. "Have you heard from Settler today? He hasn't checked in."

"Nope. He still has to submit statements from his witnesses." She glanced at the empty desks. "Where's Ritter? He's normally in by now."

"I double-checked with his wife." Maberly smacked on a donut. "He's taking the week off. Fishing."

"Wonderful." She rapped her fingers on the door. "Davis is probably back at the bar by now."

"Probably." Maberly plucked another powdered donut from the bag. "Want one?"

"No, thanks. Just let me know when you hear from Settler. I want an ironclad case against this Carver guy."

"He's a bad dude." Maberly bit into a donut. "I can tell."

Maberly had all the instincts of roadkill, but Holly agreed with him this time. "Yeah, he is." She left the building. Climbed into her patrol car. Steered onto the old road and linked up with Main Street.

She took 18 like she normally did when she went to county. It was a little slower, but more scenic. She saw the black smoke rising before she climbed the hill leading to Johnny's Curve. It was a sharp curve. A bad place to be speeding. A kid named Johnny Nelson had learned that fatal mistake in the eighties and earned himself a place in local history. Another kid and a drunk adult had followed in the decades after.

Someone else might have learned that lesson today.

Heart in her throat, Holly sped up. Drove up and over the hill and down toward the curve. The smoke was coming from the sharp drop to the right of the curve. It was right where Johnny had gone over. The memorial sign that had been on the other side of the metal railing was gone along with the railing.

"Oh, sweet Jesus." She hurtled down the hill. Screeched to a stop at the shoulder near the bent ruins of the metal railing. Holly looked over the ledge and saw a vehicle burning far below. The smoke was too thick to see what it was.

She turned back to her patrol car to radio it in. Another vehicle was parked just around the curve, partially concealed behind a boulder that had fallen there years ago. A witness maybe? Holly climbed back in the car. Wheeled around and sped over to the boulder. She parked behind it. Got out and walked around it.

A man stepped out from the other side.

Holly gasped and jumped back. "Are you okay?"

Deputy Dixon looked pale as a ghost. His hands trembled. "It came out of nowhere. Smashed my front bumper off and went right over the edge."

"What did?"

"A dump truck." He wiped sweat from his forehead. "My God, that thing nearly took us out. If the prisoner hadn't screamed at me, I'd be dead right now."

"A dump truck?" Holly marched to the other side of the SUV and opened the back door. "What the hell happened?"

CARVER LOOKED up at her calmly.

He wasn't feeling so calm on the inside. He'd almost died thanks to assassins with creative imaginations. Sending a dump truck hurtling down a steep incline at the exact time the SUV was turning the curve was a brilliant way to cause a fatal accident. If he hadn't seen it coming, hadn't shouted at Dixon, they'd both be in a crater at the bottom of the mountain right now.

The assassins had used a spotter on one side. Someone on the other side of the curve had probably jammed the dump truck accelerator down. They'd aimed it like an unguided missile. Hoped it would look like an accident. Carver had seen it coming. Dixon hadn't even been paying attention.

Carver had screamed like a banshee to get the deputy's attention. Dixon had slammed on the brakes. Even then it was almost too late. The dump truck slammed into the front bumper. Spun the SUV ninety degrees and dragged it to the edge of the cliff.

Dixon had kept his foot on the brake, screaming at the top of his lungs. Carver had been screaming too. If the dump truck had dragged them another foot, the front wheels would have gone over, and nothing would have stopped the police cruiser from following. The metal box would've been his coffin.

A good ten seconds after the dump truck went over the side, Dixon was still screaming. He put the cruiser in reverse and got them away from the cliff. Then the cruiser limped up the road where he parked. The front wheels were wobbling like the axles were bent. This cruiser wasn't going anywhere.

Carver had seen something in the trees. A man running. Probably the spotter. He'd been ready for a shootout, but the killers hadn't come for them. They didn't want to turn this into another big news story. They needed it to be an accident. Killing Carver was supposed to quench the fire, not feed the flames.

He kept on a calm façade for Holly. "We almost got taken out by a dump truck without a driver."

"Without a driver?" She looked around the car at Dixon. "Was there a driver?"

"How the hell should I know?" He was still trembling. "Damned prisoner screamed, I looked up and slammed the brakes at the last second. All I saw was the grill of that damned truck."

Holly walked around to the front of the vehicle. "You're not getting anywhere in this thing. How about I drive you back to the city?"

"I have to file a report." Dixon leaned unsteadily against the hood. "I'm waiting on backup."

Carver stood next to Holly. Stared at the deputy. "Who told you to take Highway Eighteen?"

Dixon drew his gun. "Get back in the car, boy!"

"If I wanted to escape, I could've done it a dozen times before now." Carver locked eyes with him. "It's in my best interests to clear this up so I can get to the real business at hand."

Holly didn't seem concerned that he was standing so close. "Which is?"

"Finding out why they killed Rhodes."

"I said get in the car, boy." Dixon walked around the car, hands shaking.

Carver stood firm. "That dump truck didn't have a driver. Someone stole it from Bronson Construction and set it up here to take us out so it would look like an accident."

Dixon jammed his gun to Carver's chest. "You get in the cruiser, or I'll put you down."

CHAPTER 9

S irens echoed in the distance. Moments later, an ambulance and two county sheriff's cruisers crested the rise and hustled downhill toward the crippled SUV.

Antonio watched through the scope. "How did it miss?"

Tiago crouched next to him. "It hit the car. I saw them going over the edge. The timing was perfect."

"Somehow, the driver realized it would hit them." Antonio put the crosshairs on Carver's head. "He hit the brakes just in time."

"Don't shoot him." Tiago pushed down on the barrel of the sniper rifle. "We can kill him in the prison."

"Can we?" Antonio shook his head. "Who are our assets?"

"You'll have to ask corporate."

Antonio grimaced. "They won't be happy we missed our opportunity today."

Tiago gritted his teeth. "Who does this man work for?"

"I don't think corporate knows or they would have told us." Antonio watched Carver through the scope. "I'll see who we know at the prison. We'll have another chance to kill him soon enough."

CARVER WATCHED the emergency vehicles approach with apprehension. One of them would herd him over to the county lockup and he'd be a sitting duck for the killers. If they were connected enough in the town to kill the police chief, then they surely had someone on the inside at the jail. Someone at the sheriff's department had purposefully directed them along this route.

Humans were creative, especially when it came to finding ways to kill other humans. A bribed jail worker would be eager to earn his pay. Knowing the jail inside and out, he could probably list ten different ways to kill a prisoner without suspicion. Just because it was a county lockup didn't mean there weren't dangerous criminals there. Criminals who might be willing to take on more jail time if the price was right.

Nerves were tense. Holly and Dixon were staring at the smoke. Carver slipped out of sight behind the SUV. Knelt and removed the ankle holster. He wiped it down and tossed it in the bushes. He'd planned to ditch it in the cruiser, but this was better.

Four cops slid out of the police cruisers. The paramedics clambered from the ambulance and went to the edge of the cliff.

"How many people were in the dump truck?" A paramedic asked.

"Zero." Carver leaned against the SUV. "Don't waste your time."

The paramedic ignored him and looked at Dixon.

Dixon shook his head. "It all happened so fast I didn't see."

"Hot damn, Dixon." A burly man with a thick beard walked from his cruiser. "What happened?"

"What's the prisoner doing standing around?" A gruff old man with a mane of gray hair looked Carver up and down. "Secure him, for God's sake."

Dixon snapped out of his funk and seemed to realize Carver was still standing free. "Get in the car, boy!"

"I think it's best if I take Carver back to Morganville until you boys get this sorted." Holly took Carver by the elbow. "He can survive one more night in our little cell."

"He's on the schedule already." The gray-haired guy pushed past Dixon and took Carver's elbow.

"Well, if it ain't Sheriff Cox in the flesh." Holly held onto Carver's other elbow. "It'd be easy enough for you to change the schedule. You run the place."

He raised a gray eyebrow. "You look mighty keen to take the prisoner, young lady. Why remand him to us if you want to keep him?"

"I just think a lot has happened that you need to deal with right now." She nodded at the oily smoke drifting up from below. "Y'all need to get some people down there to investigate, don't you? Probably need to coordinate a major rescue."

Cox looked about ready to relent. "Yeah. It's no big matter to me if we get him today or tomorrow. But you'll have to submit new paperwork."

The big man with a thick beard and no neck came up behind Holly. "I'll take him right now, Sheriff. You ain't got no need for me out here anyway."

Cox nodded. "Sounds good, Hawkins." He looked at Holly. "Good with you?"

She nodded and stepped out of the way.

Carver just watched the whole thing unfold like a spectator. He looked at the eyes. The body language. The intent. Holly seemed to be having second thoughts about him. She might just about believe that someone tried to kill him. Once they found the stolen dump truck with no driver she'd know for sure.

Cox seemed all business. Hawkins looked eager to please his boss. Dixon looked ready to faint. Carver didn't detect anything suspicious from their body language. Reading people had been part and parcel of his work. Making the correct conclusions had been life or death in most instances. He just wasn't getting an overtly bad vibe from anyone. At least nothing enough to warrant suspicion. They were just folks doing their jobs.

So, Carver let Hawkins lead him to another cruiser. This one had a bench seat divided in half by a metal partition. Thick metal panels blocked access to the rear or the front just like Dixon's. He got inside. Buckled himself in like a big boy. Watched Hawkins talk with his partner a moment before coming back to the cruiser.

The SUV rocked when he climbed inside. He was a big boy. Not fat, not fit. Just somewhere on the line between being muscular and being a candidate for early onset diabetes. He spun the car in a one-eighty. Gunned it up the hill.

"You killed the police chief, eh?" Hawkins wasn't even looking in the rearview mirror at Carver.

Carver kept quiet. He'd be a free man sometime tomorrow. Best just to enjoy the ride and the free meals until then.

Hawkins kept talking. "It don't take a genius to see that you were in the military. I heard Chief Rhodes was in the military too. I'll bet you two crossed wires in the past and you wanted revenge." He nodded. "She was some kind of military investigator. Did she investigate you?"

There wasn't anything to say, so Carver stared out the window and enjoyed the scenery. This guy was treading all over Miranda right now, asking questions without a lawyer present. Unfortunately, it wasn't grounds for dismissal since there was no proof it was happening.

Hawkins went quiet. He aimed the car around the curves, over hills, and down country roads. They reached a large facility out in the middle of nowhere. Several cruisers were parked out front, all with the same black paint job and gold lettering on the sides.

The drive led to a gated area behind the facility. Big prisons were typically double gated. The driver would go through the first gate. That gate would close, and the next one would open. The driver would unload the prisoner in a secured yard with several guards.

This place didn't operate like that. Hawkins just parked out front. He got out, opened the back door, and motioned Carver out. Took him by the elbow and walked him into the front.

Unlike Morganville Police Department, this place looked clean and modern. New brown brick. New signage. The glass doors were clean, and the lobby didn't stink like cigarettes. A man at the front desk greeted Hawkins with paperwork.

Hawkins signed a form. Handed it back. He took Carver through a metal door and closed it. Took him to a lobby that was all cinder block and metal. A man behind another window had Hawkins sign another form. There was a buzz and a metal door popped open. A pair of guards stepped outside and took Carver by each elbow.

"Enjoy your stay." Hawkins turned and left.

TONY WAS HAPPY about the way things were going.

Ritter was a new asset. The police chief was done. The prime suspect was dead. Another day ticked down on the clock and the finish line was in view.

He wasn't too happy about one thing, though. His men hadn't reported in. They were done. Mission complete. There was no reason for them to hang around town or go radio silent. They'd dropped off the radar. This behavior was what got them kicked out of the military. During their time in the Marines, they'd gone drinking in town and failed to show up for duty. Not just once. Multiple times.

They'd course corrected in time to prevent dishonorable discharges. Then they'd gotten into a bar fight with a civilian and his friends. They hadn't won the fight. It would have ended there, but they'd been furious. They sneaked off base. Found the guy and killed him. Made it look like an accident. But the incident had been so soon after the fight, the civilian police demanded an investigation.

The military police got involved, but Ruben and Jimmy had covered their tracks well. There was a big fuss, a big investigation. Nothing was proven, but the brass took the opportunity to discharge the pair. Better to get rid of them then than wait for an international incident.

Tony's specialty was scooping up those kinds of folks. They were military trained and ready to do just about any kind of work for good pay. The military didn't pay squat, so anything north of an E-8 salary was a huge upgrade.

Sometimes you'd have trouble with folks like Ruben and Jimmy. Most times the money was enough to keep them on the straight and narrow. Or at least keep them from taking an unofficial vacation without notification.

So why hadn't they updated him on the other bodies? Why hadn't they finished their mission and returned to HQ?

If everything else wasn't going so well, he'd send a couple of men out to search nearby bars. They were certain to be in a drunken haze somewhere near Morganville. They weren't the brightest bulbs in the box, but at least they got the job done.

There was a knock on the open door to Tony's office.

Tony turned around and grinned. "Well, look what the cat dragged in."

Sam walked inside and looked at the empty alcohol cabinet. "Damn, you really did give up drinking, didn't you?"

"For now." Tony shrugged.

"I heard the queen bitch finally ate a bullet."

"That she did." Tony sat on the leather couch. "I miss the old days. You and me running lead. Causing chaos."

"You're too busy playing executive." Sam sat on the chair opposite the couch. "Our friend in Washington put me in touch with someone who can help us take down JSEC. That should be the straw that breaks the camel's back."

Tony pumped a fist. "That's exactly what we need right now for the final push. Dorsey has three stubborn holdouts. How soon can it happen?"

"Oh, it's already in the works. Their handler is our guy now. Two days, easy."

"Perfect timing." Tony was all smiles. This day couldn't get any better.

"Dorsey still playing dress-up?"

"All the time." Tony chuckled. "Puts on full military fatigues and parades around like he was in the Navy SEALS."

"Dumbass." Sam snorted. "If we keep him handled, then it's smooth sailing."

"Oh, he's handled."

"Good." Sam got up and stretched. "I've got to head out west later today. I'll be back in time for the finale, though."

"Good." Tony stood up. Gave his friend a firm handshake. "You take care, brother."

"You too, brother." Sam gave him a two-finger salute and left.

Tony wished he could drink. If JSEC was really going down this week, it was reason to celebrate.

CARVER LET the guards lead him inside the jail.

The clerk buzzed them in through another locked door, then talked to them at the window on the backside. "He's assigned to four oh one."

The guards hustled him off without a word. They got in a lift, and it went down.

Carver looked at the floor indicator. They'd been on level two. Now they were going down...to where?

The elevator groaned to a stop on S1. The doors slid open. Carver hesitated. The guards pushed him forward and out. He stepped into a concrete space with a row of showers and machines that looked like they belonged at an airport.

"Step inside, hands up." The guard drew his truncheon and poked him in the ribs. "Unless you want us to do a body cavity search."

"It's been a while." Carver winked. "Be gentle with me."

"Get into the machine, asshole." He poked him in the ribs again.

Carver stepped into the cylindrical container. Put his hands over his head. The machine whirred and rotated. The guard looked at a monitor. An outline of Carver's body appeared bit by bit. There was a white spot on his abdomen. Another on his shoulder. A third on his leg. He knew those white spots intimately. He remembered the bullets that had made them.

The guard motioned to the showers. "Clean up." Another poke with the truncheon. He pointed to an orange jumpsuit on a bench. "Then put that on."

Carver turned on the water. There was only one valve. No hot water. He removed his clothes and stepped under the water. Lathered with the strong-smelling soap.

The second guard said something to the first and snickered. The other grinned and nodded. Maybe they thought washing in cold water was some kind of punishment. Maybe it was amusing to them. Carver kept a close eye on them and his surroundings.

He finished. Dried and put on the orange jumpsuit. It was a little short, but it was clean. He put his clothes in a plastic bag and handed them to a guard. The guard herded him back to the elevator. This time they went to the fourth floor.

There was a rectangular open space with tables just outside the elevator, like a cafeteria. There were windowed metal doors lined up around the open area. Two sets of stairs led to a second level of identical doors, each one numbered in the 400s. Inmates in orange jumpsuits milled around the tables, eating and talking.

A few glanced at Carver but none seemed to care that another had just joined their ranks. The place was full. A beehive of activity. A pair of guards milled around the area. Cameras were everywhere. The security room was on the second level. The windows were laced with heavy metal mesh to keep people out even if they were broken.

A man sat in front of a bank of monitors. A woman stared out of the window at the inmates. Not a second slipped past when the inmates weren't being watched. Carver felt safe. There would be no midnight hangings here unless the killers controlled the entire jail.

His escorts took him to 401. The room looked unoccupied.

"Lucky you. Your former roommate just graduated." The guard nodded at a pile of sheets. "You've got this all to yourself."

"Can I eat?" Carver glanced at the meals on the tables.

The guard pointed to a male inmate with a cart loaded with trays of food. "Go visit the lunchroom lady."

The woman in the security room entered through a metal door near the elevator. Beyond her was a hallway that seemed to stretch on forever. Carver imagined this place was set up like most modern prisons. A maze of hallways. Each floor set up in subsections, each with its own security room and set of guards. A labyrinth of concrete and metal. Anyone who tried to escape would probably get lost before they got anywhere close to an exit.

The woman held a clipboard. She looked him up and down. "Carver, Amos. This your first time in jail?"

"I was in jail yesterday."

"I'm aware of that. Is this your first time in jail?"

"First time in this county."

She raised an eyebrow. "You've been arrested before?"

"I guess it depends on your definition of arrested."

She looked confused. "The definition is pretty straightforward."

"I'm sure Morganville PD ran a background on me. Maybe you could look at that."

The first guard jabbed him in the ribs. "Answer her, asshole."

He gave a sideways glance at him. This rib poking was getting old fast.

The woman looked at her clipboard. "Mr. Amos—"

"Carver."

"Mr. Carver—"

"Just Carver is fine." He looked at her nametag. "Johnson."

The guard bumped him in the ribs with his truncheon again.

"Belinda, please."

Carver nodded. "Okay, Belinda."

"Carver, how many times have you been in jail?"

He didn't know offhand. A lot of times as a juvenile. A few times domestically as an adult. A few times abroad, sometimes while on duty, other times while not. He tried to sum it all up in his head but couldn't come down to a single answer. "I don't know. Better consult my background record."

"Your background record shows nothing. Either you're lying or it was expunged."

"Okay, let's just say I've never been arrested then. I think that sounds a lot better, don't you?"

Belinda stared at him for a moment then wrote it on the clipboard. "What are you doing to ensure you won't be arrested again?"

"Not getting caught."

The same guard jabbed him in the ribs with his truncheon again. "Answer seriously, asshole."

"That is a serious answer."

"No, it isn't." The guard jabbed the truncheon toward his ribs again.

Carver caught the end in his hand before it touched him. He stared down the guard and spoke in a low voice. "I've been poked a whole lot harder by people a whole lot meaner than you, big boy. Maybe you enjoy poking people in the ribs with that thing. Maybe it makes you feel like a big man. You might feel safe in here. Think you can get away with it. So, keep it up and let's see if you keep getting away with it."

CHAPTER 10

The other two guards in the room ran over, batons out. "Release the weapon!"

Belinda backed up eyes wide. The other prisoners were watching and clapping. Probably the best entertainment they'd had in a while.

Carver let it go and smiled at the guard. Took note of his name badge. "Test me again, Wilson."

Wilson's partner, Mims, glared at him like he might step in and do something.

Belinda tucked her clipboard away. "I think the questionnaire can wait."

One of the room guards clicked on his radio. "Sir, we have a code violation here, prisoner four oh one alpha. Requesting an isolation lockup."

"Affirmative. Isolation approved."

"Roger." A guard with the name Michaels on his name badge pointed his baton at Carver. "You don't touch the personnel. You don't touch our weapons. Tonight, you're going to learn."

His radio crackled. "Belay that isolation order. Prisoner will remain to assigned room."

Michaels scowled. "What the hell?"

Carver shrugged. "Guess I learned my lesson already."

Wilson and Mims headed for the elevator. Wilson sneered and pointed his baton at Carver as the doors closed.

"Get in your room. No supper." Michaels pointed to the room.

Carver shook his head. "I'm having dinner. Either you bring it to me, or I'm walking over there and getting it myself."

Michaels got in his face. "Your time here can be real easy, or real hard."

"How hard you want to make it, Michaels?" Carver stared down at him. "I'm out of here tomorrow at the latest. Then I'm a civilian again. Then I'm free to find the people who tried to make it hard for me, Michaels. So, I'll ask you again, how hard do you want it to be?"

Michaels faltered. "Get your damned food and get in your room."

"Okay, daddy." Carver winked and went to the lunchroom lady man. "What's on the menu?"

PLANNING TO KILL someone is a lot easier when you know the right people.

The locals knew the right people. The right people liked money and they knew the best way to kill someone within their domain even if that domain was supposedly airtight and secure. Even a county jail had dangerous inmates. They were just kept on different floors away from the nonviolent offenders.

Sometimes a nonviolent offender made an enemy on the outside. That person on the outside might have the right people on their contact list. They might send a few bucks their way to make sure there's a mix-up and the wrong person ends up on the wrong level at the right time. Of course, that was just one way the right people could make an accident happen.

There were other ways too.

Antonio didn't care about the method. He just needed it to look like an accident.

The right person told him via text, *Consider it done.*

Antonio was satisfied. It would be done.

CARVER FINISHED his beef stew, or whatever it was. He took the tray back to the lunchroom lady man's cart and then went into his cell. He climbed on the top bunk. The mattress was thicker than the one in the Morganville jail. It was a little more comfortable than the floor, but not by much.

Inmates still milled around the common area. The talking was just a buzz in the background. Carver closed his eyes and relaxed. He had to kill a few hours and then he'd be out. A good night's sleep and then freedom.

Lights out came around nine. A klaxon buzzed and the prisoners went to their cells. Another buzz and the doors closed automatically.

A guard walked to the window and peered inside at Carver. He moved on to the next cell, making the rounds. Then the lights clicked off with a heavy clunk. Carver got out of bed and peered through the window. Dim light from the security room lit the common area.

Places like this had to cost a lot of money to run. Keeping a security guard to monitor the cameras twenty-four seven was expensive. Multiply that against the number of security rooms and they had to be spending a fortune.

He climbed back onto the bunk and closed his eyes. At least he could catch up on his sleep tonight.

TONY SENT TWO men to find Ruben and Jimmy.

He called them at eleven and they hit the road by eleven fifteen. They'd start the search at the local motels and move out to the bars. There was only one strip club in the county and only a couple between Atlanta and Morganville. Tony said to check them on the way just in case.

"Don't come back until you find them." He'd told them. Now he was at home staring out the back window at the swimming pool. He was annoyed, verging on angry. Once he found Jimmy and Ruben, they were going to get a friendly warning. By friendly, he meant they'd get tied down, punched, and waterboarded.

That was usually enough to convince their recruits to follow protocol. This wasn't the military, but it was run like the military, just without all the red tape and simpering officers. The rules and regulations were few, and the money was good.

Punishment might range from docked salary to suspension without pay for lesser offenses. But for people with special backgrounds like Ruben and Jimmy, the punishment had to be harsher. These people didn't learn lessons unless they were drilled into their subconscious.

Tony was good at it. Interrogation and punishment were his bread and butter. He'd cracked some of the toughest nuts in the world. Jimmy and Ruben were going to learn that the hard way.

The men texted him at different intervals. No sign of their quarry at any bars or strip clubs along the highway to town. No signs of them at establishments in town. Then they started checking motels. It was likely they'd holed up somewhere cheap with prostitutes and alcohol. That was how Tony had found them not long after they'd been discharged from the Marines.

Tony just hoped the morons had staged the other bodies and set up everything else. It was critical that all the puzzle pieces be in place so this whole mess could finally be closed.

The past had to be buried once and for all.

CARVER WOKE UP at five sharp. His cell was still dark, so he stared blindly toward the ceiling until the lights thunked on thirty minutes later. A klaxon buzzed and the doors slid open.

He'd never been to this jail before, but he already knew what the schedule was like.

The inmates funneled into a doorway at the back of the section. Carver followed them down the hallway. It bent around a couple of times and ended in a large common bathroom. There was a long pee trough along a wall and rows of showers all along the center place. Pipes ran across the ceiling and down columns to shower heads. It was wide open with no nooks and crannies to hide in.

Inmates showered quickly, grabbed towels from piles on nearby benches, then slipped back into their orange jumpsuits. Guards watched from all sides of the room. Carver counted ten and figured they were from every subdivision on this level.

He took a quick shower and dressed. Then headed back toward his section. He was following the long hallway back to his section when a side door opened. Wilson and Mims stepped out.

Wilson blocked the hallway and pointed his baton through the door they'd come out of. It was obvious that something was about to go down. Did Wilson think he was going to teach Carver a lesson? There was only one way to find out.

Carver went through the door and into the corridor. Pipes and wires ran along the ceiling. The walls were a little closer, like this was a back alley to the main thoroughfares in the building. He looked back at his escorts.

"Start walking," Mims said. "Sheriff wants to have a word with you."

Carver wasn't sure if that was true. Maybe Holly had said something to Sheriff Cox and now he had questions. Maybe Wilson wasn't looking for payback after all.

The hallway continued straight and stopped at a metal door. Mims buzzed it open with his badge and they entered a box with doors on all sides. Mims buzzed open the door opposite and the hallway continued on the other side.

This door ended at an elevator. Mims touched his badge to the panel next to the buttons and hit the down button. The elevator doors opened, and they piled inside. Rode it down to the first floor. This hallway had more pipes and cables running overhead. The pipes here were bigger. The water rushing through them was louder. Machinery clattered.

Carver knew right then they weren't going to see the Sheriff. Something else was about to happen. But he played stupid and kept walking. Mims buzzed open a door at the end. Wilson prodded him through with his baton.

Carver turned on him. Wilson grinned and the metal doors clapped shut.

THERE WAS NO DRIVER in the dump truck.

Holly stared into the blackened cube that had been the cab. The diesel tank under the passenger side had ruptured on the rocks. Sparks had set off the blaze. The only thing left was melted vinyl and the metal frame.

The truck had tumbled sideways during the fall and slammed to earth on the driver's side. If there'd been a human inside, they would have died on impact. Their broken bones would be the only thing remaining. But there were no human remains inside.

A long rod that looked like part of a tire jack was wedged in the remains of the driver's seat. It wasn't the kind of thing you'd find in a big industrial truck. An ordinary car jack wouldn't be remotely large enough to lift a truck this size. Truckers wouldn't even attempt to change a flat tire anyway.

There was also a scrap of nylon rope wrapped around the steering wheel. It had turned into a molten blob on the metal. The rest of it had pooled on the door like candle wax. Holly imagined someone using a car jack to wedge the accelerator down and using rope to hold the steering wheel steady.

They'd aimed the truck downslope, wedged the accelerator into place, and let the unguided missile take its course. Perfect timing would have required a spotter on the eastern side of the curve.

She followed the steep, winding trail back to the road. She went to the bent railing and looked down. Then she walked back to her cruiser. Climbed inside and drove up to the top of the hill. It was about a hundred yards from here to the curve. That was a lot of space for error if the truck didn't continue straight.

She looked down the opposite side of the hill. A county road crossed the highway here. A sliver of orange in the bushes caught her attention. Holly drove to the area and got out. She pushed into the trees and through the bushes. A roadblock lay on its back. There were two signs on it: Road Closed Ahead, and Detour with an arrow pointing to the side.

Anyone coming from this direction would have taken the county road instead of the highway. Cars coming from the same direction as Dixon's cruiser didn't matter. They would have seen the back of the sign and just gone around it.

Holly imagined sitting in the dump truck. Lining it up on the wrong side of the road so it slammed into Dixon's cruiser just as it turned the curve and came up the road. A full impact would've taken both of them over the side. Then the killers could have gone below, removed the car jack and the rope from the scene and left.

Maybe they thought the nylon rope would melt and leave no clues. Maybe they thought the police were too dumb to notice the car jack in the cab. Holly doubted it. Anyone smart enough to pull this off wouldn't leave clues lying around. But since the truck missed the cruiser, they couldn't go down and clean up the scene.

They couldn't shoot Carver or Dixon because then everyone would know that Carver wasn't guilty. He was just a convenient fall guy used to close the case.

She got back in her car and drove halfway down the hill. There was an incline leading into the forest. It looked like someone had slashed some branches out of the way with a machete. Holly pushed inside. A thorny vine was cut. Several bushes had been downed. It formed a passable trail, one that was made as someone walked through.

At the end there was a small clearing. The pine straw was disturbed. A pair of indentations in the soft soil looked like something left from a bipod. One of the killers had been prone here, watching the road with a scoped rifle. He'd gauged the speed of the cruiser and coordinated with the guy handling the truck.

Their timing had been perfect. Carver's shout had been the only thing between life and death. If the killers had failed here, it was doubtful they'd give up now.

It meant Carver might be in danger right this moment.

CHAPTER 11

Carver was in danger.

He was in a laundry. A pair of beefy men with swastikas tattooed on their necks were waiting on the other side. One of them tried to slap a pillowcase over Carver's head the instant he was through.

Carver twisted sideways. He braced against the first man and kicked the other in the knee. The man screamed and went down. Carver swung his knee up and tried for the groin of the other guy but hit his thigh instead.

The first guy shoved him away. Carver used the momentum and brought his foot down on the second guy's face. The man's head bounced on the concrete. He was down for the count. The first guy spread his arms like he wanted to grapple.

Laundry machines and pipes blocked a clear view across the room. He and this guy were the only people standing in this row. There were voices and the hiss of steam somewhere else in the area, but they were out of sight.

"I don't suppose they told you who wants me dead, did they?"

The thug lunged. Carver let him. He dropped to a knee and pummeled the guy once in his groin. He could have landed a blow on the guy's face or elbowed his throat, but he didn't want his hand all banged up. Not when he might have to fight a lot more people to survive this. The groin was nice and soft. It was also the weak spot for most men.

The big man howled. Bent over and grabbed his crotch. Carver took the pillowcase the man had tried to use on him. He wrapped it around the guy's neck. Braced his knee on the man's back. Pulled hard. The man struggled. Grasped at the pillowcase. He didn't have enough oxygen to work with. His brain gave out a few seconds later, and he went down hard on top of his buddy.

The men were wearing red jumpsuits. Carver didn't know much about civilian jails, but red usually meant danger. The jumpsuits were probably color coded. He frisked them. The jumpsuits didn't have pockets, but that didn't mean they couldn't conceal something. Necessity was the mother of invention. They might store packs of cigarettes up their assholes for all he knew. Carver didn't find anything. Then again, he also didn't feel like digging around in assholes.

Carver walked down the line of laundry machines. Around the corner. Down an aisle past ironing boards and piles of laundry on tables. The other rows were empty until he reached the front. A group of black guys were arguing with a group of white ones. Judging from the swastikas on their necks they were buddies with the two he'd encountered.

Carver pushed past them. One of the white guys shouted and tried to grab him. He slipped under the grasping hand. Gripped it and twisted sideways. The man screamed and went to his knee. "Try to touch me and we'll have a serious problem, okay?"

"Let me go!"

Carver turned to the other gang. "He's all yours." He kneed the guy in the chin. Just a love tap to knock him senseless, then walked past the other gang.

There was laughter. Shouting. Probably some fighting.

A group of guards ran past him. A young guy stopped abruptly. His eyes widened. "What the hell are you doing down here?"

"They sent me to pick up a clean jumpsuit from the laundry, but I got lost."

"Someone sent you down here?" He whistled. Mouth dropped open. "Okay, someone messed up real bad." He reached for Carver's elbow. Stopped and looked him up and down. "Uh, you follow me. Ok?"

"Lead the way, Spaulding." Carver had noticed the name badge had a red bar at the top. It probably indicated that the guard worked in the dangerous area of the jail.

The guard flinched. Looked down at his name badge. "Follow me." He led Carver to an elevator. They rode up to level four. Spaulding took him straight to the security room.

The man inside opened the door. Looked at the guard's badge. "What are you doing on my level? And what are you doing with him?"

"He was in the laundry. Someone sent him to get another jumpsuit."

"Who the hell asked you to do that?" The security guy looked scandalized. "And how did you get down there?"

Carver shrugged. "I think his name is Wilson. He and Mims took me down the elevator and then told me to get a new jumpsuit and meet them back at the elevator."

The security guy clenched a fist. "Get this guy back inside and don't breathe a word of it to anyone, got me?"

Spaulding nodded. He turned to Carver. "If you know what's good for you, you'll keep quiet."

Carver mimed zipping his lips. "It never happened. Can I get breakfast now?"

The security guy brought out a pack of cigarettes. "Want these?"

Carver shook his head. "Breakfast is good. I'm famished."

The door buzzed open. Carver went inside and grabbed breakfast from the lunchroom lady man. Scrambled eggs, sausage, and toast were on the menu today.

Spaulding spoke to the server. "He can take two trays today."

Carver gave him a thumbs up. "Thanks for having my back, Spaulding."

Spaulding looked a little pleased and a little confused. "Yeah, just remember what we talked about." He exited the metal door.

"Better take the extra tray now," the lunchroom lady guy told him. "If you don't, someone else will."

Carver took another. Found a table and sat down facing the security room. The food wasn't half bad. It wasn't as good as the restaurant food from the day before, but it was gourmet compared to most prison food he'd sampled.

He'd just taken the first bite from the second tray when Wilson and Mims appeared in the security room. They looked at him with a mix of anger and terror. Carver gave them a friendly smile.

It stood to reason this kind of stuff wasn't uncommon around here. Employees could be bribed. It was the same the world over. Most of the time they took money for small stuff. Cigarettes. Alcohol. Drugs. Anything to make prison time a little more bearable. Dropping off a guy to be summarily executed by other prisoners was something else altogether.

Wilson seemed relieved before he left the room. He figured he was in the clear since Carver hadn't mentioned the real details. What he didn't seem to realize was that it was by design.

A skinny guy sat down next to Carver. "You barely got here yesterday and you're already taking two trays? Better not let Davos find out.

"Who's Davos?"

"He's the long termer in these parts. He's got some pull."

"What's he in for?"

"Money laundering, I think."

Carver nodded. "Must be really dangerous then."

"He's got people outside with money. If he doesn't want you to get a meal, you won't get it. If he wants to ban you from borrowing library books, he can do that too."

"Very dangerous." Carver looked around. "Where is he?"

He pointed to a short guy entering from the hallway. His thick hair hung damp. He looked grumpy. "That's him. Better take a tray back so he doesn't know you've been double dipping."

"How does someone get jailed for money laundering in this rathole of a county?"

The skinny guy laughed nervously. "I don't know. I don't ask questions. I'm out of here in three months."

"For what?"

"My boss fired me, so I punched him a few times."

"That shouldn't be a jailable offense."

"I know, right?" He picked up Carver's empty tray. "I'm putting this up before Davos notices."

Davos was short, stumpy. He looked like he'd carried some weight around the midriff but lost it recently. He entered the room like a king, wet hair shining. A group of other guys followed him like puppies. A tall guy with a fair amount of muscle shadowed him like a bodyguard.

Carver kept watching. Davos sat down at a table. His bodyguard sat next to him. One guy fetched Davos a tray and set it in front of him. Another guy grabbed a tray for the bodyguard. It didn't matter if it was in the slums, the prisons, or a civilian office. Humans set up a hierarchy. Someone at the top, someone at the bottom.

Most people understood that power was the most important commodity in places like this. Money, power, and popularity were just currency. Some combination of the three would put someone at the top. A lack of all three would land someone at the bottom.

Carver didn't much care about the power this guy wielded. He was curious about something else though. Money laundering wasn't about small-time amounts. There was no need to launder a hundred grand or even a quarter of a million dollars. But once you got over a threshold you had to start making that money look legit or the taxman would notice.

Small time drug dealers went down mostly because they bought that fancy house and fancy car despite having no declared income. That was where people like Davos proved their worth. They usually did their work for a ridiculous percentage unless they were working for a big-time organization.

It was surprising this guy was still alive. They normally didn't survive to trial. Drug organizations didn't want someone with so much information being taken prisoner. The launderers were usually the people prosecutors were most keen to strike deals with. They'd do little to no jail time for reeling in the big boys.

If this guy was a long termer, it meant he hadn't snitched. Either he was too scared to talk, or too smart to talk. Either way, he was still alive and kicking.

Carver picked up his tray and walked to the table. He sat down before one of Davos' entourage could take his seat.

The bodyguard stood. "What do you think you're doing?"

"I need a moment alone with Davos."

"If you don't move, you'll get a moment alone with my fists."

Davos watched, amused.

Carver looked up at the big guy. "Look, I just put down two guys in red jumpsuits in the laundry. Don't waste my time."

The big guy blinked. "The laundry?"

Davos chuckled. "So, you're the guy who got sent downstairs?"

"You heard about it?"

"My contacts told me someone on this level was taking a trip downstairs. People who take that trip don't normally come back."

Carver nodded. "I took a trip downstairs. Now I'm back upstairs. And I'd like a word with you."

Davos waved a hand and the others melted away like snow in summer. "I'm very curious as to what makes you a target. Why don't we trade information?"

"I like information."

"Good." He steepled his fingers like a criminal mastermind watching the pieces fall into place. "Why were you sent downstairs?"

"I'll tell you if you tell me who you were laundering money for."

"I was working alone."

"Bullshit." Carver took a sip of coffee. "You want to protect your clients. I respect that. I'll give you some context."

"Context is always appreciated."

"Someone wants me dead."

"Obviously."

"That someone might be your former employers."

Davos drummed his fingers on the table. "Hypothetically, any large criminal organization has a need for vanishing people from time to time. But any such enterprise would be extremely judicious about it. Killing draws unwanted attention. This method would certainly fit the MO of such an organization."

"There have been three attempts on my life since I arrived in that little slice of Heaven known as Morganville." Carver studied the scrambled eggs. Were they powdered or real? They tasted funny. "I'm trying to find a connection."

"You don't know why someone would want you dead?"

"Oh, I know why, just not the who." He nibbled on the eggs. The texture seemed genuine.

Davos leaned closer. "Why?"

"I'll tell you but answer this first. Would such an organization kill the chief of police?"

"That would be a method of last resort. It would mean other methods had failed to secure this hypothetical chief's support." Davos' eyes gleamed. "They would make it look like an accident, not a hit, I think. Anything else would draw too much attention."

"That's where I'm finding a disconnect." Carver decided the eggs were the real thing and took another bite. "The chief was killed with her own gun. At least that's what I think happened. Some crooked cops and military types tried to pin the murder on me. Case closed."

"Except you survived."

"I survived. Then someone else tried to kill me in a staged car accident and again by sending me downstairs."

"You are a very popular man, Mr. Carver."

"Just Carver."

"Such a hypothetical organization might have highly trained killers who are proficient in making accidents happen." Davos leaned back. "But the attempt to pin a police chief's murder on you sounds very clumsy."

"It was clumsy as hell." Carver had been scanning the room. Looking for anyone who seemed overly interested in this conversation. He'd spotted a guy almost immediately. Young, brown hair, medium build. He'd sat at a table as close as he dared without drawing the ire of Davos' entourage. "Speaking of clumsy, I have some information for you."

"I'm listening."

"Do you think such a hypothetical crime organization would lay off me if a former employee asked them to?"

"Hypothetically, there would be no way to get a message to them. It's doubtful any such hypothetical organization would listen to someone who had a very limited field of expertise and has become useless to them due to incarceration."

"And yet, such a hypothetical person hasn't been sent downstairs."

"Not yet." He pressed his lips together. "What information do you have for me?"

Carver leaned across the table. Davos leaned closer.

"That young guy with the brown hair and glasses has been trying really hard to listen to us. I wouldn't be surprised if he's a plant."

Davos leaned back. "I wouldn't be surprised. The FBI is desperate to learn the identities of my connections. Thankfully, I was a very careful person. I know how to use the same connections wealthy people use to keep their money away from prying government eyes."

"I'm not saying I approve of it, but I don't like civilian law enforcement. Especially not the FBI."

"You're an interesting person, Carver. It's plain to see you were military, but you're still quite young. You look like you're searching for something."

"Maybe." Carver shrugged. "I think we're all looking for something."

"Amen." Davos took a sip of coffee. "Consider yourself my guest while you're here, Carver. If I think of a way to send a hypothetical communication to a hypothetical crime organization, I will let you know. Unfortunately, it's doubtful such a hypothetical communique from one such as me would be listened to."

"That's a lot of words for you'll try, no guarantees."

"I am a verbose man."

Carver nodded. "No verbose way to tell me who that organization might be?"

"I'm afraid not. I wouldn't. Any such hypothetical clients of mine would be held with the strictest confidentiality."

"You can just say no." Carver finished his breakfast and stood up. "Nice talk."

"Likewise." Davos nodded as a king might to a departing servant.

Carver dropped the tray off with the lunchroom lady man and went back to his cell. Davos almost certainly knew who was behind the attempts on his life. He also agreed that the crooked cop and military guys had been clumsy. It seemed that once they failed to finish off Carver, the organization had brought out the big guns.

They should've just brought out the big guns in the first place. They should've planned things out a lot better. It was like sending in the fourth string offense to win the game.

He sat on the edge of his bed and watched the other inmates. Watched the guy with the glasses. A guy like Davos wasn't going to say a word about who he worked for. Not even to people he trusted. He was smart and he wanted to live even if it was behind bars. The guy with the glasses was going to come up empty.

Carver whiled away the morning just watching and listening. And thinking. There was a lot to think about.

The intercom beeped. "Inmate Carver, report to the security desk."

CHAPTER 12

C arver went to the metal door. It buzzed and a guard opened it. Ushered him through. It wasn't Wilson or Mims, so that was good news.

"Come with me." The guard turned and headed down the main corridor to the main elevator.

More good news.

They went to the first level. The guard handed Carver a plastic bag with his clothes in it then showed him to a private room. "Get changed."

Carver took off the clean jumpsuit and put on his dirty clothes. They smelled like stale sweat. He left the plastic bag and the jumpsuit on the floor. Opened the door and rejoined his escort.

"Where's the jumpsuit and the bag?"

"On the floor."

"Get it."

"I'm not your servant." Carver gave him a dead-eyed stare. "I'm getting out."

"You will—"

"I will leave this place because the charges have been dropped."

The guard went into the room and jammed the jumpsuit into the bag. He walked it over to a window and a female guard behind the counter took it. She looked amused by the interaction.

The guard led him out of the secured area and into the front offices. He took Carver to the drive out front. A Morganville PD car idled there. Holly got out. She smiled.

Carver smiled back.

"Get in, Carver."

He climbed in the front seat. Leaned back until the faux leather creaked.

Holly sat down and closed the door. "We didn't have any evidence. The charges were dropped for now."

"Yeah, but you don't believe them, or you'd demand I sit in the back." Carver put on his seatbelt. "Can I finally get to work?"

"On what?"

"On finding Rhodes' real killer."

"We're not going anywhere until you tell me everything. You're hiding something."

"I want to see Rhodes."

Holly clenched the steering wheel. "I was going to see her yesterday. Then everything happened and I forgot."

"Drive us there. And tell me what they found at the dump truck crash."

"You're pretty demanding for someone who just got out of prison."

"It's a county lockup, not a prison." Carver shrugged. "You said so yourself. I was wrongfully detained, so I can be as demanding as I want."

"That's not how it works."

"That's how it works if you want more information."

She clenched the steering wheel a little tighter. Put the cruiser into drive and gassed it forward. They went back to the highway. Took a right. Drove about a hundred yards to a big nondescript building sitting alone on several acres of cleared land. The sign out front looked older than the one on the jail. It said *County Medical Examiner*.

There was no signage on the building except a street number. Holly parked in front. Took a deep breath.

"How close were you and Rhodes?"

"Not close. I just respected her a lot. Smartest woman I ever met."

"How'd she get hired?"

"I don't know. I guess she impressed the mayor."

"He's the one that makes those decisions?"

"Yep."

"Was there a former chief of police?"

"He retired when Rhodes came to town." Holly stared into the distance. "I know they met a few times. He just suddenly told the mayor he was retiring, and that Rhodes was the person to replace him."

Carver nodded. "How old is the former chief?"

"Mid-fifties. Kind of young to be retiring." She shrugged. "But he looked happy as a jaybird. Sold his house and moved to the Florida Keys."

"How hard is it to sell a house around here?"

"I don't remember the last time a house sold in Morganville. But his sold really quick and for asking price too."

"How much?"

"It was crazy. Five hundred grand I think." Holly chuckled. "Everyone knows everyone's business in Morganville. A lot of houses went on the market right after that, but none of them sold. Guess it was a fluke."

"Who lives there now?"

"Nobody ever moved in. It was bought by an investment firm that flips houses."

Carver filed the information away. "Rhodes make any enemies while she was chief?"

"No, she was really nice. Relaxed. Treated the locals like they were special, so everyone loved her. She went to church and was active in the community." Holly wiped a tear from her eye. "Chief Livingston didn't do much at all except go fishing. He just ran things on autopilot. Rhodes seemed like she really wanted to make a difference."

"You went to church?"

"I'm not religious, so no. But I did help her, Charlotte, and Renee organize things a few times."

"Who are they?"

"They were close with Rhodes. Not sure why, honestly, because they just didn't seem on par with her."

"On par?"

"They weren't the brightest bulbs in the box." Holly shrugged. "But what do I know?"

"Have you talked to them yet?"

She shook her head. "Not yet. Even if I did, it would just be informal. Detective Davis or Ritter will be the ones to handle the investigation."

"I wouldn't rely on Davis to investigate a baby's soiled diaper."

Holly laughed. "You got that right." Her face turned serious. "Okay, so spill the beans. What haven't you told me?"

"Let's go look at the body first."

"Carver, that's not right. I just told you everything I know."

"Which isn't much."

"Why were you smiling so much when I told you how Rhodes got the job?"

"I'll tell you. But first I have to trust you."

"Why wouldn't you trust me now?"

"Because you're a stranger. And you threw me in jail."

Holly glared at him. Opened her door, climbed out, and slammed it.

Carver got out and headed toward the front door. Holly caught up and used her badge to buzz the door open.

A clerk looked up from her computer. "Hey, Holly. I was wondering when you'd come by."

"It was supposed to be yesterday, but the wreck over at Johnny's Curve took up my entire day."

"I heard about that. So awful! Did the truck driver die?" She tightened her thick sweater around her and shivered.

"No, it looks like he bailed at the last minute."

The clerk's eyes widened. "Really? Brake failure?"

"I'll tell you all about it, Brenda. But I need to see Rhodes."

Brenda nodded sadly. "Okay, honey. Herbert's in the back today."

"Thanks." Holly went down a hallway.

Carver looked around at the white, sterile environment. It smelled like bleach, and strong chemical cleaners. The building was cold. Almost frigid. As they walked down the hallway to a pair of swinging double doors, the odor of death became stronger. It smelled different than normal. Clean and clinical. Not like it smelled in the field. There, it reeked of feces and rotting meat.

Herbert was a tall, unassuming man. Balding head covered by a bad combover. Glasses. Deep forehead wrinkles, probably from puzzling over corpses all day. He wore a lab coat and a thick butcher's apron.

A corpse with a partially disassembled skull lay on the table in front of him. The brain was out and on a scale. A life reduced to the weight of body organs. People were hunks of meats on sticks. Bones and flesh. All it took was a bullet to snuff the spark that gave them life.

It wasn't a pleasant thought, but it didn't bother Carver much either. He'd seen a lot of death. Caused a fair amount of it. Spared it in the right situations and let the walking, talking meat keep on doing its thing.

"Hold on a moment, Holly." Herbert wrote a note on a pad, then carefully removed the brain from the scale and set it aside. He looked up and seemed startled to find Carver there. "Oh, who is this?"

"Good question." Holly shrugged. "I think he knew Rhodes."

"Yes, very sad." Herbert's voice didn't echo sadness. He seemed clinical about it. Probably a good way to approach this business. He went to a wall of metal refrigerator doors and opened one. Slid out the stainless-steel tray.

Rhodes lay on it, one eye closed, the other eye missing. The hollow-point bullet had entered from the back, expanded inside like an umbrella, and taken her eye and part of her face with it. There was no doubt in Carver's mind how it happened. She was with someone she trusted. They betrayed her. Shot her with her own gun in the back of the head.

Her body was covered in bruises and bullet holes. Someone killed her with the first shot, then beat the corpse and shot it up.

Holly watched him carefully. "You don't seem bothered, Carver."

"Should I be?"

"You knew her, right?"

"Did I?"

"Damn it, Carver!" Holly clenched her fists. "Tell me something, anything!"

"Someone Rhodes trusted took her own gun and shot her in the back of the head. The hollow-point made a bigger hole exiting than it did entering. Then they kicked the body and shot it more post-mortem."

"Exactly." Herbert nodded approvingly. "No ligature marks. Livor mortis indicates body wasn't moved. Judging from the dirt on the uniform, the victim was standing and fell with a leftward spinning motion to land on their side. Then they were shot and kicked several times as if the shooter hated her."

Carver nodded. "Is there a report about the general scene? Footprints, other markings?"

He looked at Holly. "Is he an investigator?"

She looked at him numbly. "Yes."

"Interesting." Herbert gave him a file. "All the information is in there."

Carver went to an empty stainless-steel table. He opened the file and looked over the notes and pictures. There was an old cabin. A gravel driveway. Dried blood. A bullet casing. Pictures of Rhodes. Her remaining eye was open in the picture. Her mouth was open slightly. Had the killer given her a chance to say anything?

More importantly, who'd pulled the trigger?

There were no footprints. Some indentations in the gravel, but nothing that could determine a shoe size. The scene was clean and open for interpretation. Just how it was supposed to be. If Carver had picked up that gun, he'd still be in jail. It wasn't enough evidence to convict, but it was enough to hold him.

Why in the hell did you call me out here, Rhodes?

Now he was in deep. Sink or swim. Find the reason she was dead, and the reason others wanted him dead. He couldn't just walk away from this. He imagined Rhodes would be happy to know she'd snared him in one of her elaborate schemes again. She took perverse joy in watching him try to puzzle out her plans.

Carver liked to think he'd learned a thing or two from her. He just didn't have the patience for it most of the time. He was better at twisting things to his liking on short notice. People liked easy explanations. They liked a simple solution. The best way to resolve a situation was by avoiding anything elaborate and keeping it simple.

It didn't always work out, but it worked out enough times that Carver didn't feel the need to draw up an entire battleplan.

He read the rest of the file. No statements from Settler and his buddies. Nothing but what CSI had collected. A lot of blanks to be filled in and it was now Carver's duty to do the filling.

"You look like you just ate a shit sandwich," Holly said.

He closed the file and gave it back to Herbert. "Thanks."

"Did you see anything that stuck out?" Herbert asked.

"Rhodes trusted the person that shot her. They lured her out there. Put a gun to her head. Took her gun and shot her." Carver tapped a finger on the metal table. "They might've talked to her. Tried to buy her maybe. But if they knew anything about her, they didn't bother to do that and just shot her."

"You do know her." Holly gripped his arm.

"From what you told me, she was a decent sort. Honorable and all that. Church going. Probably hard to corrupt."

"Don't give me the runaround Carver!"

Carver tipped an imaginary cap at Herbert. "Thanks doc." He headed out. Walked down the hallway and outside.

Holly chased after him. She grabbed his arm again. "You'd better—"

"Let's go somewhere to talk."

Her body trembled. Maybe with anger, maybe with relief. Maybe with both. "Okay." A tear ran down her cheek. She wiped it away and got into the cruiser.

Carver dropped into the passenger seat. "Somewhere with food without a lot of nosy people."

Holly nodded. Gunned the car out of the parking lot and headed further north along the highway. She got the cruiser well above the speed limit on the straight road. The few cars out and about got out of the left lane when they saw her coming.

They slowed just outside the city limits of another little town. She pulled into a parking lot at an old brick building that had probably been a warehouse. Now it stood two levels tall and was full of trendy restaurants and souvenir stores. Tourists milled around a train. Others filled the restaurants.

The mountains formed a backdrop against the scenic town. It looked like an interesting place to visit. Carver might have made it around to these parts eventually. He might have even stuck around a while to explore. That was going to have to wait.

Holly took him to an upscale bar. A gastropub, they called them. They sat in a back corner away from the others. Most of these folks were locals anyway. They could probably talk about anything with them around.

A waitress hustled over. "What can I get you to drink?"

"A beer," Carver said.

"Sir, we have an extensive list." She pointed to a long list on the inside the menu.

"Pick me something as close to a normal beer as possible. The darker the better."

"A stout?" She nodded. "I've got you."

"And this burger." Carver pointed to a big bacon burger. "With fries."

Holly smiled at the waitress. "The grilled chicken Caesar salad with the dressing on the side. Water to drink."

The waitress left.

Holly turned to Carver. "Okay, talk."

"You buying lunch? I don't have any money. It's still at the station."

"Yes. Talk before I stab you with a butter knife."

He held up his hands in surrender. "Okay. Let's talk."

CHAPTER 13

Carver started talking. "I knew Rhodes. Knew her well. Military."

"But how? She was Army and you were Marines."

"I was Navy, not a jarhead." He leaned back. "Rhodes was the smartest woman I knew. Hell, she was the smartest person I knew. Made most of the upper brass look like chumps. Of course, most of them were and still are."

"You didn't answer my question."

"Let's just say we joined an interbranch organization."

"So, a cooperative task force between the Army and Navy?"

"Something like that."

"Care to be more specific?"

"Not really." He watched the waitress bringing his beer all the way from the bar. It was black as pitch. Just how he liked it.

She put water in front of them both and the beer in front of Carver.

He took a sip and nodded. "Good choice."

The waitress smiled. "I'll be back with your food soon, okay?"

She left and Carver started talking again. "Let's just say that our work was covert."

"No, let's just say what it was in specific terms." Holly picked up the butter knife and pointed it at him.

"I can't."

"Top secret then?"

"Even more than that."

"There's something higher than top secret?"

"Yeah. It's called nothing, nada. Things that don't exist."

She whistled. "A joint taskforce so covert that it doesn't exist."

Carver took another sip of beer. "It's nothing special, really. There are tons of nonexistent personnel and agencies in government, both civilian and military. Hell, even local police departments sometimes have them."

"They would be illegal."

"Yeah, of course they're illegal. That's why they don't officially exist."

Holly rotated her glass. "How long did you know Rhodes?"

"Long enough."

"Damn it, Carver. Straight answers, please."

Carver thought back to his first mission. Hard to believe it was so long ago. "We met ten, eleven years ago."

"You liked her?"

"Sometimes."

Holly stared at him. "You have an economic use of words."

"I try to use just enough to get the point across."

"It's not working. Did you hate Rhodes? Did you like her? Would you kill her?"

"No, yes, no." He took a sip of beer. "Okay, I hated her a couple of times. She punched me a few times. The first few times she was just angry. The last time she was furious."

"So, this brilliant woman from a nonexistent beyond top secret military organization just quit and decided to become a cop?" Holly shook her head. "Doesn't make sense."

"No, it doesn't." It was Carver's turn to spin his glass while he mulled it over. "She was meant for great things. Not taking a meaningless job in a nothing town. No offense."

"You're an asshole. I understand why Rhodes punched you."

Carver kept staring at the beer. Kept spinning the glass. What would bring a superstar like Rhodes here? He hadn't kept up with her after the task force was disbanded. Nobody wanted to talk to him anyway. He'd gone three years without a word from anyone until Rhodes' message reached him.

How she'd found him was a mystery. He'd kept off the grid for good reason. There might be some people who thought he'd be better off permanently silenced. If he was in their position, he would have done it years ago. Now it didn't matter. If he was going to talk, he would have done it by now.

Holly tried to interrupt. "What are you thinking?"

"Just asking the same question over and over in my head. Why did she come here?"

"How long has it been since you saw her?"

"A little over three years."

"Why were you in town? Did she ask you to come visit her?"

"You ask good questions, Holly. Maybe you ought to leave that town. Become a detective somewhere that matters."

"Answer my questions, damn it."

He took a drink. Set down the glass. "I was living in Clearwater. I gave scuba lessons."

"Well, if you were in the Navy, I guess you're good at it."

"Good enough, I guess." He rotated his glass again. "I was getting paid under the table. No name, no social security number, nothing. Somehow, Rhodes got a message to me. Begged me to come visit. Didn't say why, just said I needed to come see her right away. It was important."

"That's word for word?"

"Close enough." He recited it from memory. "Carver, come see me right away. I'll tell you why when you get here. Just trust that it's important and that it will clear things up between us. The answer is at the tip of my finger. I'm in Morganville, Georgia."

"Cryptic. Just like you."

"She knew how to pique my interest." He laughed. "Rhodes could manipulate the most bullheaded general into doing what she wanted. She knew all the right buttons to push for anyone if she had enough time to know them." He stared at his beer. "I was comfortable where I was. I didn't want to see her. But guess what? I came anyway."

"You sound like you're proud of her."

"Yeah, I was. Proud to serve with someone like that. A genius."

Holly teared up. "I know the feeling. I felt proud for the first time in a while having someone like her in charge of our department."

Carver tried not to feel bad, but he did anyway. Rhodes was the kind of person who left a lasting impression. That was why he felt so guilty for everything that happened even if he had nothing to do with it.

Holly noticed. "You look a little upset."

"I am." He looked around at the smiling faces. The hyper kids. The tired parents. The young twenty-somethings drinking their fancy beers. He wasn't made for something like this. He was made for other things. People aimed him like a missile and let him go. Rhodes did it. Maybe she'd done it knowing she might die. It was hard to say.

Carver wished he could've evolved into something better. Something smarter. Maybe not like Rhodes, but somewhere in between. Now he was just an unguided missile circling around an unknown target. The enemy was firing flak and decoys to take him down, but he would keep searching for a target or die trying.

His burger arrived and he downed it without another word. Then he went to the bathroom to wash his hands and returned to finish his beer. It felt good to be free again. To be loose in the world. He didn't feel adrift like he normally did. Like the ground would shift under his feet and he'd be in another country.

That was how it had been in the service. That was how his childhood had been. Always on the move. Never in one place for too long. Someone else always calling the shots. For a long time, he'd thought that was all there was to life. Then the worst had happened. He'd been discharged and discovered a new side to life.

He'd been like a kid in a free candy shop for a while. Then he'd had to find a job because that candy cost money. He'd gone from one side of the United States to the other and back in the space of the last three years.

Now he felt anchored again. Felt the tether of duty firmly around his neck. But this time he had a choice. Cut the tether and run or stay and find out who did this to Rhodes and why.

It was an easy decision.

He was staying. Someone somewhere was going to find out they'd made a terminal mistake. All Carver had to do was survive long enough to find out who it was.

"What was it you were smiling about earlier?" Holly asked.

Carver came back to the present. "The former police chief. I think Rhodes manipulated him. Knew what would make him move. What would make him recommend her for police chief."

"You think she bought his house?"

He nodded. "She set up a shell company. Made it look like an investor who wanted to flip the house."

"And she just had five-hundred grand laying around?"

"Oh, yeah. She was a trust fund baby. A rich kid." Carver grinned. "She told her old man to go to hell and joined the military. Something like that. She never did tell me the whole story."

"Wow." Holly's radio squawked. She turned up the volume and listened to Maberly's frantic voice. "...repeat a major situation here. I need someone back at the station to help me now!"

She squeezed down the button. "Copy that. On the way."

"Oh, thank god, Holly. What's your ETA?"

She motioned for the server. "Twenty minutes."

Carver raised an eyebrow. "Is Maberly normally like that over the official channel?"

"No." She thanked the waitress and paid with a credit card. Signed it when the waitress brought it back. Then they booked it out of there. Hopped in the car. Holly took it slow through town, then pushed the cruiser hard when they hit the highway.

Carver asked more questions. "How is it you're the only one who responded? Are your detectives deadbeats or something?"

"Settler should've answered, but I haven't heard from him at all today."

Settler won't be answering anything anymore. She was going to find out sooner or later. Probably sooner rather than later.

TONY WAS SHOUTING at the walls of his house. "What in the hell is going on?" He should have known better. He'd sent two somewhat capable guys on a mission that required absolute capability. They'd completed phase one of that mission but had vanished before reporting progress on phase two.

What in the hell were they doing?

His search team hadn't found a trace of Jimmy and Ruben anywhere. They'd circled Morganville and the places around it. Nothing. Then they'd closed in on the town itself. Drove around looking at houses to see if Ruben's SUV was parked anywhere. They'd found it at a hotel.

The clerk hadn't seen either of them. Didn't recognize them from the pictures. Nobody in town did. That was because they'd only been there for one day and for one purpose. That purpose had been achieved. Or so Tony had been led to believe.

But Ruben's SUV was sitting somewhere it wasn't supposed to be. It was sitting somewhere he wasn't. That man never went anywhere without his vehicle. Jimmy had a car, but he never drove it. He rode with Ruben. That was how it had always been with those two.

Now the backup team was spending valuable man hours searching for them. If they were holed up with drugs and hookers somewhere, it would not end well for them. Tony himself would make sure of that.

He'd kept all of this from Dorsey. No sense in upsetting him. He had enough on his plate with the bigwigs from Washington. These next few days would be filled with delicate negotiations and backroom dealings. This mess needed to be dealt with to ensure everything went smoothly.

HOLLY SLOWED as she rounded Johnny's Curve. Emergency vehicles were still trying to retrieve the burned-out husk of the dump truck. A yellow pickup truck with the words Bronson Construction in black on the side was parked on the shoulder. A couple of men with yellow ballcaps were standing near the edge of the cliff.

Carver tapped the dashboard. "Can you stop for a minute?"

"For what?" Holly saw the construction company men. "We can talk to them later."

"I just have a quick question."

She sighed and pulled over. "Hurry. Maberly sounded frantic."

Carver hopped out and ran across the road. One of the construction guys glanced at him. Did a doubletake. Seeing a man in civvies get out of a police car was causing dissonance in his head. Carver held out a hand. "I'm Carver."

The other guy shook it. "I already gave the police a statement."

"Are you the owner of the company?"

"Yep. I'm Charlie Bronson."

"Nobody saw anything, right?"

He nodded. "Everything was locked up behind our fence. They got in and out without security seeing anything."

"Do you have security camera footage?"

"We gave it to the sheriff's office." Bronson shook his head. "We skimmed the footage around that timeframe. There were a couple of guys in our uniforms who did it."

"Stolen uniforms?"

He nodded. "One of our construction sites was hit first. They took a roadblock sign, some cones, hardhats, and shirts. They took a key that got them into our main depot where they took the dump truck and keys."

"Can you send that footage to Morganville PD as well? We think this is connected to some other crimes."

"Yeah." Bronson nudged the other guy. "Have Gary email it to Maberly."

Everyone knowing everyone in these parts was coming in handy. Carver crossed the road and climbed back into Holly's cruiser. She gunned it and wheeled it back onto the road. They hurried back into town. She slowed down on Main Street.

Lights flashed in the storage lot behind the old power company building. She rolled down the street and angled into the open gates. A woman stood outside an ambulance. A man with a dog was talking with her. A small crowd had gathered, but they were being held at a distance by Maberly.

He was drenched with sweat. The afternoon heat was already shimmering off the asphalt. Shining off his sweaty, balding head.

"What in the hell is going on?" She jammed the car into park. Hopped out.

Carver enjoyed the air conditioning for a few more seconds. The bodies hadn't remained hidden as long as he'd hoped. He looked over the crowd. Most were in shorts. Most had backpacks and hiking gear. Curious tourists.

But a couple of guys hanging near the back of the crowd stood out. They wore black cargo pants. Both were open carrying M9 Berettas inside holsters. One had a survival knife sheathed on his thigh. Jimmy and Ruben's pals, no doubt. They could connect him back to the source of these problems.

Under normal circumstances he'd take one of them for questioning. But this wasn't a foreign country. This was domestic soil, and he was a civilian. That didn't make much difference to his way of thinking. But he didn't know where he'd take anyone for questioning. He was on his own. No tactical support. No extraction zone.

He'd have to play the long game. Follow them. See if they led him somewhere interesting.

Holly spoke to Maberly. He gestured wildly toward the boiler tanks. Carver knew what happened without asking. The guy walking the dog found the bodies. The dog probably got free from the leash or something. Followed the smell of rotting meat to the tanks. Started barking like crazy.

The guy smelled death when he got there. Opened the tank door and freaked. Called 911. Maberly called the ambulance and tried to manage the small circus as tourists tried to get closer for a look.

Another paramedic appeared from behind the tank. He motioned the other one over. She unfolded a gurney and pushed it behind the tank.

The military guys bypassed Maberly while he was talking to Holly. They went around the crowd, entered the fence. Jogged over to the paramedics. Maberly noticed them at the last minute and started shouting. He tried to run after them, but in his shape wasn't catching up to anyone. The men disappeared around the boiler tank.

The paramedics shooed them away. The men ignored them and emerged little while later. They looked grim. Upset. One of them was making a phone call. He spoke for a moment, then they hurried back. Hustled past Maberly and outside the fence. Veered toward the hotel parking lot.

Carver watched them from the comfort of the patrol car. When they vanished from sight, he grabbed Holly's Morganville PD ballcap from the seat and put it on. It wasn't a great disguise, but it was better than nothing.

He edged around the building and saw the men standing near Ruben's big black SUV. They were grim faced. Talking animatedly like men who were making contingency plans they hadn't expected to make. They'd thought a problem was handled. But it wasn't. In fact, it was far from handled.

The problem was watching them. Deciding how to handle them. Deciding whether they'd live or die.

One guy lifted his phone to his ear. Nodded a few times. Hung up. Then they climbed into a big black Jeep Gladiator with angry headlight mods and red halo rings. It had a hood-mounted exhaust, mud tires, and a winch on the front. All the trappings of someone who liked to offroad.

But the Jeep was spotless. Didn't look like it had ever seen an unpaved road. It rumbled to life and peeled out of the parking lot. Raced down the highway and out of town. The license plate was covered by tinted plastic. The sunlight glinted off it, making it impossible to read from Carver's position.

The Jeep vanished into the distance, and with it, Carver's only leads.

CHAPTER 14

P aola listened to Jasper shouting.

He was angry at one of the girls. A slap echoed. A girl cried out. Gurgling and gasping.

Paola's phone buzzed. An encrypted message from the Brothers. They needed more information on the target. They wanted to talk to Jasper. She banged on the door and walked inside.

Jasper was choking the life out of the Asian girl. She was limp in his big fat hands. He looked up in surprise. Dropped the girl like she was less than nothing. "What's the problem?" He shouted, spittle flecking from his lips.

"The Brothers want to meet with you. They want more information on a target."

"Darling, I can hardly understand you through all that accent." He motioned her closer. "Come here and whisper it to me."

Paola remained where she was. "The Brothers are coming. I suggest you get dressed." She went to the Asian girl. Checked her neck. There was still a pulse. The other girl was huddled in the corner of the room. Even the drugs weren't enough to calm her.

"Stupid bitch doesn't know how to please a man." Jasper fiddled with his crotch. He could barely reach it past his bulging belly. "Where the hell are my pants?"

The man who escorted the women back and forth from below was sitting in a chair across the room. Looking at his phone.

Paola clapped her hands and shouted at him in Portuguese. "Get the women below. The Brothers are coming."

He snapped from his distraction and went over to the unconscious woman. Nudged her with his cowboy boot.

Paola threw up her hands. "Just pick her up and get her out of here."

The man stared at her with dead eyes. He held her gaze. Didn't move. Then he slapped the woman so hard Paola jumped back in surprise and shrieked.

The Asian woman moaned. The man lifted his hand again.

Paola shielded her. "You're damaging the goods! Corporate will not be happy."

"Let the man have his fun, Paola." Jasper struggled to pull up his white briefs. "They don't let 'em screw em, so let him beat her."

"When was the last time we found an Asian woman you liked?"

He grunted and heaved back into his pants. "I don't remember."

"Exactly. You're very particular. And you want to just ruin this one?"

"She can't give a blowjob to save her life."

Paola resisted the anger. "Jasper, you're too large for her mouth. You need to train her patiently." Having seen his erect manhood many times, she rated it no more than four inches and narrow. Hardly too big for any mouth.

He chuckled. "Damned right I'm big. I make the ladies scream."

"So, you want to trash the only Asian you've liked in a long time?"

"All right." He nodded at the guy. "Ernesto, take care of that gal. Make sure she's nice and healthy for next time."

Ernesto slung the girl over his shoulder. Turned to the other one. "Come."

She crawled out of the corner, sobbing. "Help me, please."

"Come!" It was probably the only English word Ernesto knew.

Paola hadn't even known it was his name until then. Most of them were just anonymous. Dangerous and lurking.

"You can do what you want with the other one." Jasper laughed. "Those white bitches are a dime a dozen."

Ernesto yanked the woman to her feet and dragged her behind him. She was skinny, almost frail. She followed, whimpering.

Jasper liked them skinny. Small. Spinners, he called them. He was too fat to spin anything on his manhood.

Paola checked the time. "The Brothers will be here in thirty minutes."

"What information can I give them that they can't get themselves?"

"I don't know. The target is still a problem. He's out of jail and on the loose."

"Maybe it's time we got the mayor involved. His dumbass decision to hire a halfway competent police chief started this mess."

Paola didn't care. The Brothers scared her. She wanted them finished and gone as soon as possible. She was already dead inside. This place had killed her. But her body did what was necessary to survive.

She left the offices. Went down to the factory floor. Pushed out of an exit door and sat on the bench outside. It was supposed to be a smoking area. Hardly anyone used it. It was the only place she could have some peace and quiet. Solitude. A moment to try and forget the horrors of the day.

If only that worked.

TONY HURLED HIS phone across the room. It bounced off the sofa, unharmed. He snatched it and glared at the message. Now he knew why Ruben and Jimmy hadn't reported back. They were dead and rotting, Settler along with them.

"Dumbasses!" He paced to his phone. Snatched it off the floor. How could three men fail against one? It didn't matter how big and bad someone was, fighting off three armed men should be impossible.

It meant Ruben had miscalculated. He'd done something stupid. The target had taken advantage of it. Now the scapegoat was free and out of prison. This had gone down worse than imaginable.

He glanced at the television. Dorsey was giving an interview to a national news station. Talking about how private security was the way of the future. How it eliminated bureaucracy. How it removed the politics, the pundits, the lazy brass at the top. How it was nearly ten times cheaper in every aspect except for large-scale invasions.

But large-scale invasions were out. The future was in micro-conflicts. Using small-scale conflict resolution to effect systemic change. Prevent big wars like in Afghanistan, Iraq, and Ukraine. Prevent environmental destruction, loss of habitat and climate change.

Chad Dorsey cared about the environment. He cared about the rights of underprivileged groups. He hired minorities to senior positions and gave them real input into all important decisions.

"We are here to make life better not just for Americans, but for all countries." Dorsey grinned. "I'll bet you've never heard that."

"I haven't." The interviewer, Barbara Keegan, was a rising star on national news. "But it's amazing to hear it."

"This is a winning strategy, Barbara." Dorsey gave her his million-dollar smile. "It's time we used military power to improve life, not to take lives. It's time we let people of all identities fight for what they believe in."

Barbara grinned. "No more restrictions about who can sign up?"

"None. Just a willingness to fight for what they believe in."

"I love that so much." Barbara put a hand to her heart. "Do they get to wear black?"

He grinned. "Of course!"

"No more politicians calling the shots and I get to wear black?" Barbara mimicked a happy dance. "Where do I sign up?"

Dorsey smiled back. "We'll be taking applications on our website. We have operational training facilities in major cities around the nation."

"Even in those that have seen large scale conflicts?"

"Especially in those," Dorsey said.

Tony switched off the television. Dorsey was going to be pissed. One micro-conflict hadn't gone as planned. Somehow, he had to nip it in the bud before it turned into something far worse.

CARVER ALREADY WANTED another beer.

The heat in this town seemed worse than it had in Florida. There was no breeze from the beach. No cooling waters. Only stagnant humidity. Damp, red clay. Insects. It was a different kind of heat than Middle Eastern deserts. It should have been nothing to him but living like a bum had made him soft.

He ditched Holly's police cap in the car. Walked over to Holly and Maberly. Sauntered past them toward the ambulance.

"Carver, where are you going?" Holly caught up to him.

"What's all the fuss about?"

She got in front of him and put a hand on his shoulder. "You don't want to see it. Maberly said it's awful."

"What is?"

"Settler's dead. So are those two guys who were with him." She shook her head. "Whoever is trying to kill you must have killed them."

"Why would they do that? They tried to frame me. That would indicate they're working together."

She shook her head. "It's confusing. I don't know."

"Any big criminal organizations in this town? This county?"

Holly barked a laugh. "Are you kidding me? Maybe the Jehovah's Witnesses."

"Who are the rich folks in town?"

"There are no rich folks." She turned around and looked at the ambulance. "Jasper Whittaker was rich once. But he lost just about everything when the EPA swooped in on the paint factory. There are a couple of doctors with fancy homes. Mayor Morgan has some money, but I don't think he's rich."

"Odd." Carver started walking toward the ambulance again. "Every small town has at least one rich asshole. At least one guy who's a villain."

She frowned. "This isn't a town out of an eighties action movie, Carver. This isn't Roadhouse or Footloose. There are real people leading real lives here. No wealthy rich all-powerful guy is running the city or the county."

"They're damned good at hiding then." Davos was evidence that something was going on. Or he might be just a node of a bigger organization. Stuck out in the middle of nowhere. Laundering money so far away from the source that it could never be connected. That was the only reason he was alive. Maybe he had family he was protecting too.

As usual Carver suddenly thought of a lot of questions he should've asked Davos. Now it was too late. No way in hell he was going back to that prison. Visiting Davos would expose both of them. Besides, Davos had told him enough. There was something going on in this town. Something big.

He just wished he was smart enough to see what it was. Rhodes had stumbled onto it. Unfortunately, she hadn't left him a clue about what it was. She'd used her cryptic ways to lure him in. A fish chasing the bait. It had worked pretty damned well.

"Are you sure you want to see this?" Holly said. They were almost to the tanks.

Carver wrinkled his nose. "Damn, that stinks."

The paramedics stood near an empty gurney.

"What's going on?" Holly asked them.

The female paramedic shrugged. "We're waiting on the medical examiner and CSI to get here."

The old man with the dog looked proud. Like he'd just won the lottery. "Holly Robinson, you look mighty sharp in that uniform."

"Thank you, Roger." She gave him a southern smile. "What happened?"

"You wouldn't believe it." He patted his dog who was straining toward the boiler tanks. "Old Tater yanked the leash right out of my hand and ran over here. He started barking like you wouldn't believe at those big tanks. I thought it was racoons, but the stink coming from inside told me it was something else." His voice went low. "I swung that door open, and the smell hit me like a ton of bricks. Then I saw the bodies inside!"

"Wow, that's some good police work, Roger." Holly patted his shoulder. "Did you give a statement to Maberly yet?"

Roger rotated slowly like stiff old men do and looked at Maberly. "You know what? I sure haven't. I'll go do that right now while it's fresh." He chuckled. "It's been a long time since anything this exciting happened here. Not since the EPA came in and almost put Whittaker out of business."

"You lived here all your life?" Carver asked.

Roger nodded. "My family goes back three generations in this town. We used to have a plantation if you can believe it. Got burned down a long time ago, though."

"I'd love to hear some stories about the old days." Carver smiled friendly-like. "Little town history is fascinating."

"Oh, I'd love to." Roger looked even happier. "Come over to the Moose Lodge sometime. Me and the other old timers have a lot of stories."

"I'll sure do that." Carver tested a southern accent, but it didn't come out right. "Thanks."

Roger and Tater wandered over to Maberly.

"What was that about, Carver?" Holly looked suspicious.

"History is important. Stories about a town's past can lead to truths about its present."

"Sounds like something Rhodes would say."

"It's exactly what Rhodes told me once." He chuckled. "She was right, of course."

"Of course." Holly went to the other side of the boiler. She gasped. "Damn it, Settler, what did you get yourself into?"

"I thought you said he was a fine upstanding citizen." Carver looked inside and saw it was just how he'd left it. He saw Ruben's car keys where he'd left them too. He reached inside and took them.

"What the hell, Carver!" Holly grabbed his wrist. "You're disturbing a crime scene!"

"Not really." He showed her the keys. "Let's find out what these go to."

She sighed. "Fine. But don't touch anything if we find it."

Carver walked back toward the fence. He pressed the key fob a few times. When they came in range of the hotel parking lot, the SUV beeped. "There she is."

"I've never seen that vehicle before." Holly frowned. "Why were the car keys just left lying out like that?"

"The killer probably emptied their pockets. Searched them."

She shook her head. "This is so confusing. Why would they kill their own people and dump them? What in the hell was Settler doing working with them?"

"Everyone has a price." Carver sauntered up to the SUV. Used the fob to unlock the doors. Another button lowered the windows. He did that and looked inside. "Looks empty. Perfectly clean."

"Odd. Nobody has a perfectly clean car."

"They do if they don't want to leave evidence." Carver nodded. "I can smell the chemicals. This thing was wiped down and abandoned. I'll bet even the door handles are clean."

"Damn it." Holly clenched a fist. "What is happening in this town?"

"What did Rhodes find out that she shouldn't have?" Carver opened the car door.

"Damn it, Carver, I told you not to touch anything!"

"The SUV is wiped clean." He pointed to the chemical streaks on the inside door handles. He knew because he'd been the one to do it. "You won't find any fingerprints. The real evidence is on the bodies."

"What are you doing?"

"These people put me through a hell of an ordeal, Holly." He climbed inside and patted the steering wheel. "So, I'm going to use their car. Seems fair to me." He cranked the engine with the push starter and put the air conditioning on high. The dark red leather interior was hot as an oven.

"It's a vehicle that might have been used in a crime and now you're polluting the evidence."

"Probably a lot of crimes committed by the guy who owned this car. But the car is wiped clean." He patted the passenger side. "Get in."

"I can't believe I'm doing this." She went around and got inside. Sniffed. "That's a very strong chemical odor."

He nodded and pointed to the plastic bottle of cleaner on the floor in the back. "Looks like they carried it around with them. Probably used it to wipe down crime scenes."

She opened the glove box. Saw it was empty. Opened the armrest. Got out and started looking under the seats. Under the floormats.

Carver sat back and let the air conditioning cool him down while she worked. CSI wasn't going to find anything useful. That cleaner was good for removing prints from just about any surface and he'd coated the bodies with it. Plus, he'd been wearing Ruben's gloves and left the SUV as immaculate as he'd found it.

Holly finally gave up. Climbed into the passenger seat and closed the door. "Carver, you need to rein it in a notch. If we're going to find out what's happening here, then we need evidence."

"I agree." He tapped his fingers on the steering wheel. "I need some names."

"State the obvious, why don't you?"

"These are names you can find for me. Names of prison guards."

Her eyes widened. "Why do you want the names of prison guards? I can't give you that information!"

"Can't or won't."

"Can't!" She shook her head. "That's private information."

"And yet, I already know their last names just from being in prison."

Holly stared at him for a long moment. "Why?"

"I think they're linked to whoever is behind this. They sent me downstairs."

She stared blankly. "I don't understand."

"Downstairs is where the violent inmates are. They sent me there to die."

Holly closed her eyes and shook her head. Like her whole world was falling apart and she wanted to wake up. "That can't possibly be true. There are cameras everywhere. They're very strict about what goes on there."

"Will you do it or not?"

She shook her head. "I can't. I don't have access anyway."

Then Carver would have to do it the hard way.

CHAPTER 15

C arver didn't want to go back to the jail, but it looked like he'd have to. Maybe an internet search would reveal something. He didn't have a phone or an internet connection, so he'd have to borrow it from somewhere. That wouldn't be too hard.

He didn't have anything against smartphones or the internet except that it made a person easy to track. At one time that statement would have sounded nutty. Like something someone wearing a tinfoil hat would say. But now everyone was content to walk around with a tracking device. Posting their innermost thoughts online for the world to see.

The military used GPS location from smartphones to drop smart bombs. Special forces used social media data to track down targets. It made precision a little easier when the target carried a beacon with them all the time.

Since Carver knew how it worked, he chose to play it safe. Being off the radar was hard these days, but for him it was absolutely necessary. Which made it all the more impressive that Rhodes had tracked him down.

"You look like you're thinking hard, Carver." Holly was watching him.

"You know a guy named Wilson or a guy named Mims at the county jail?"

She shook her head. "No. But the folks who work there come from all over the county."

"I thought everyone knows everyone."

"In these parts, yes. Not all over the county."

He nodded. "Ok. See you later, Holly."

She remained in the passenger seat. "Where are you going?"

"Find a motel. Get some rest." That was mostly true.

"You don't have money."

"I need my things from the police station. I want my arrest record destroyed."

Holly squinted like she wasn't sure she heard right. "I can't do that."

"Sure, you can." He nodded in the direction of the police station. "Am I driving you over there, or are you taking your cruiser?"

"I'll get your things back." She slid out of the seat. "But I'm not destroying your arrest record." She closed the door and went to her car.

He backed the SUV out of the parking spot. Nosed around the other cars and pulled onto Main Street. Bounced down the rutted road and parked in front of the station. Holly arrived a moment later.

Carver followed her inside. One person was there, sitting in the office behind the placard that said *Abe Ritter.*

"Abe, where have you been?" Holly put her hands on her hips. "The world is going crazy, and you went fishing?"

Ritter was an older guy. Looked right around the age of retirement, maybe sixty or sixty-five. He looked tired. Like he was ready to go to sleep and never wake up.

"Sorry, Holly." He tried on a smile, but it didn't fit. "You know us old folks need our R and R." His gaze wandered to Carver.

Carver could tell by the look in the other man's eyes that wherever he'd been, he hadn't been resting or relaxing.

She looked confused. "Did you just get here?"

"Just pulled in a few minutes ago, yes."

"And you didn't notice the commotion over at the old power company?"

He shook his head. "No. What happened? Did a kid get stuck in a generator again?"

"No. Roger's dog found three corpses in a boiler." Holly teared up. "Settler was one of them."

Ritter flinched like someone struck him. "Settler is dead?"

"As a doornail," Carver said.

The detective swiveled toward him. "Who are you, young man?"

"Just a guy." Carver focused on the unsettled look in Ritter's eyes. This might be a small town but there was a lot going on. "You catch any fish?"

Ritter looked confused for an instant. "Sure. A few."

"What kind?"

"Trout mostly."

Carver nodded. "River fishing?"

"It depends on my mood." Ritter looked like a man trying to remember what he had for breakfast. "Sometimes I go to a lake."

"Can we talk about fishing later?" Holly shook her head. "This town has seen four murders in two days. I don't even know how to process that."

Ritter nodded sadly. "I'll get to the bottom of it. I promise."

"I hope so, Abe." She dropped onto a chair at one of the empty desks. "We just aren't equipped for this."

"I'll get right over there." Ritter picked up a leatherbound notebook and stood. He was dressed in a brown suit and wore a pair of heavily polished leather shoes. He looked like an old school gumshoe detective. Someone who belonged in a black and white film and called women dames and their legs gams.

Holly watched him. "You still spending time out at the paint factory?"

Ritter flinched. Shook his head. "No, that turned out to be nothing."

"Maybe there is something going on out there."

"No, there's not. I'm sure of it." Ritter gave Carver another look, then headed for the front door. Carver added him to the list of people he needed to talk to. It wasn't just the demeanor of the guy. It was the fact that he hadn't even blinked when Holly said four people had been murdered. He hadn't asked who the fourth person was. It was like he already knew even though he hadn't been here.

Word about Rhodes's death hadn't gotten around yet. Roger hadn't known about it, and that was a good sign that the rumor mill hadn't spun it out to the locals yet. Rhodes had been quietly carted off to the coroner's office. Three of the people involved were dead.

Carver leaned against the wall. "Did you tell anyone that Rhodes is dead?"

She flinched from her thoughts. "Besides your lawyer, Maberly, and Davis?"

He nodded.

"No. I've hardly had a chance to process it myself. Why?"

"Where is Davis? You think he's at a bar somewhere running his mouth about it?"

"He's probably in bed." She checked the time. "He found out when he was already drunk. He questioned you, then he probably went home and drank until he passed out."

"What's his story?"

"It's really none of my business telling you."

Carver shook his head. "Everyone's business is everyone's business in this town. How about you give me a brief history of this fine police department?"

She idly wiped some dust off the empty desk. "When I was a kid, this place was full. Just bustling with life. The whole town was vibrant."

"Your dad worked here."

Holly frowned. "How'd you know that?"

"Most kids aren't gonna hang around a police station. They couldn't tell you how it was in here two days ago, much less ten or twenty years ago."

"My dad was a detective. My mom worked out at the paint factory. Ritter worked with my dad." She traced a line in the dust. Like making a timeline so she could remember the important bits. "Davis was a little older than me. Both his parents worked at the factory. Heck, most of the town worked there. All the little mom and pop businesses were alive back then. Just so full of life." Holly trailed off and stared at the line in the dust.

Carver gave her a moment. Growing up in a place you love only to see it die before your eyes was probably tough. Not that Carver would know. He'd been in so many towns in so many places that he couldn't relate to small-town childhood.

Holly marked an X on the dust line. "A lot of people were getting sick with mystery ailments. Some people got cancer. I think most people knew it had something to do with the paint factory. Most people knew it was recent because the factory had an excellent safety record. Nathan Whittaker did everything by the books. He loved this town. Loved the people."

She pounded a fist on the desk. "That spoiled brat Jasper ruined it all. The EPA swooped in and bankrupted the factory. Poor Nathan died of a heart attack. Almost everyone lost their jobs. It was like someone stabbed the town in the heart. Killed it so fast it made heads spin."

Holly swept the dust off the desk and watched the cloud settle to the floor. "Davis's dad was one of those who got cancer. He died. His mom was pregnant but lost the baby because she'd been drinking too much of the city water. When the factory went bankrupt, the government used most of the money to repair the environment. The scraps went to helping the people."

Carver nodded. "Typical government agency."

"The people were supposed to get millions to help pay doctor bills. The government said they'd make a fund to cover all that. But that fund ran out within a year. Everyone left the town. The businesses dried up. Left nothing but a husk. My parents made it out okay. They moved down to Florida."

"But you couldn't say goodbye. You stuck around."

Holly shook her head. "I couldn't say goodbye. This town is part of me. I can't just leave her to rot."

"So, Davis started drinking. Why'd he become a detective?"

"He went to police academy. He wanted to become a cop and nobody else in this town wanted to work here since the pay is so bad." Holly bit her lower lip. "The mayor took over for a while. Elevated Davis to detective. He tried to talk Ritter into retiring, but the old man said he had nothing better to do." She stared blankly at the floor. "Davis said he'd find a way to bring down Jasper Whittaker, but as you can see, he's been too busy staring at the bottom of liquor bottles to work on that."

"Where's his mother?"

"I think she moved to Alabama where she's originally from." Holly looked up at him. "So, yeah. That's how this town died. It's how Davis died inside. How most of us townsfolk died."

"You seem more alive than most," Carver said. "Like you care."

"There's still plenty to care about." She wiped her eyes. "Every time I see downtown, I see what this place used to be like. Others just see the bones. Like they're staring at a dinosaur in a museum exhibit."

Carver wandered into the workroom. Found his file just sitting out on the counter. He opened it and looked at his mug shot. The fingerprints. The arrest record. "How was the paint factory polluting the town?"

"Jasper cut corners. He fired the company that was moving toxic waste and paid to have a big hole dug under the paint factory. It was supposed to be lined with concrete and used to store barrels of waste. It cost just under a million dollars a year to use the waste management company. It cost them just over a million to dig that giant room under the paint factory. The problem was it would've cost another two million to cover the place in concrete."

Holly laughed like a person trying not to cry. "This town sits on a foundation of granite. If you go to the quarry, you can see what it looks like. Jasper thought that was enough to contain any leaks. But it wasn't. All those chemicals ran down the rock and into the underground water supply."

"Must have leaked a lot." Carver looked at the paper shredder in the corner of the workroom. He decided he'd rather burn the file. That was more thorough. He emptied the file. Folded up the contents and jammed them into his pockets.

"Jasper also cut corners with the storage barrels. He got cheaper ones without the proper lining. They corroded and started leaking. Apparently, he was also charging people to store other waste down there. Stuff that didn't even come from the paint company."

"So, how is this place still in business?"

"A paint company from Brazil bought it. They wanted to own the rights to Whittaker Ultra. Buck told everyone it was revolutionary. The thickest paint base ever. So thick just one coat was like three coats. Waterproof, weather resistant, non-toxic."

Carver walked out of the workroom. "Sounds like it was pretty toxic to me."

"There were toxic byproducts to making it." She shrugged. "I don't understand how it worked, but the paint itself was non-toxic."

"It's not important." He sat down. "Tell me more about this Brazilian company."

"You took your record, didn't you?"

He nodded. "Are there copies of my information anywhere?"

"No." She stared at him. "Your background check came back almost blank. Is that part of your former job?"

"A lot was wiped, yes. I prefer to keep it that way." Carver tapped the desk. "Tell me about this Brazilian company."

Holly stayed quiet a moment. Like she was making sure he understood she wasn't following his orders. "Brilhante Tintas bought the company for pennies on the dollar. They kept Jasper on to run the place for some reason. He keeps promising there's a big recovery coming, but it never comes."

"Is Jasper rich?"

"The family home was taken by the government along with all the Whittaker possessions. Everything was liquidated. Whatever was left wasn't much. The Brazilian company bought back the family mansion, but it's in their name, not Jasper's. So, no, I don't think Jasper is rich. He's just a fat old bastard who came out of this better off than everyone else. He doesn't even leave the factory these days. From what I hear, he lives out there."

It wasn't the first one industry town he'd been to. Sometimes it was a paper mill, or a steel mill, or maybe even a military base. The company would fail, or the government would move the base. The town would dry up to nothing. Become a husk occupied by the few people too stubborn to move on.

It wasn't just an American thing. It happened all the time in other countries too. But this was the first time he'd cared to understand it. To know every factor that brought a town to its knees. Because this time it was personal. This dead town had claimed Rhodes and it had tried to claim him. Something was very much alive and lurking. Something that was very protective of its secret.

And he had to kill it before it killed him.

CHAPTER 16

C arver had a list.

It was a small list, but it was still a list. It was enough to get started with. Rhodes probably would have already figured out what to do next just from glancing at it. She'd probably have looked at it and seen a bunch of connected dots. A map leading her to the rotten heart of this town.

She'd probably already figured out everything. That was why she was dead. Carver had to figure out what Rhodes had already known. He'd avoided the dying part so far, but it was still early in the game. Plenty of time to make a fatal mistake. Plenty of time to catch a bullet before the timer ran out.

Maybe Rhodes had made a map. Best to start with the low-hanging fruit first. "Holly, what's Rhodes's address?"

"I'll take you." She got up. Straightened her uniform. Went into the break room and cleaned the dust off her hands. Then she went into the workroom. Unlocked a door at the back and returned with Carver's money and paper map he'd been carrying with him.

"You got gloves?" Carver took the money and counted it. It was all there.

She picked up a box of latex gloves. "Playing it safe?"

"Trying to."

They went outside and dropped into her patrol car. She turned left out of the station. Navigated the rutted road and stopped at a modest little pink house.

Carver snorted. "Damn it, Rhodes."

"Hot pink. Her favorite color."

Carver thought about her pink gun in the road. "Yeah." He got out. The yard wasn't quite overgrown with weeds, but it was getting there. The sidewalk was cracked and blackened. The driveway was in similar shape. The house looked newly painted. It practically glowed.

"That's Whittaker Ultra on the house, of course." Holly looked a little proud when she said it. Like she took some credit for living in the same town as the manufacturer. "It was painted six years ago."

"That paint is six years old?" Carver looked at the general state of everything else. The gutters had weeds in them. The downspouts were missing. "This house was already pink when she moved here?"

Holly nodded. "The mayor bought up a lot of the land. He rented the house to Rhodes. I think she wanted to buy it."

Carver put on latex gloves. He slid out of the car. Strode up the steps to the stoop. Tested the front door. It was as bright pink as the rest of the house. It was also locked. He checked under the door mat. Checked the planters and a rock at the base of the stoop. No spare key. He hadn't expected to find one. Rhodes wasn't dumb enough to leave one out.

He went around back. The door was undamaged but unlocked. "You trust your CSI department?"

Holly didn't answer immediately. "They're from county. I don't know them that well, but I think they're trustworthy."

"Good enough. If I see what I expect on the other side, call it in. Maybe someone got careless." He nudged open the door with his gloved hands. The kitchen was on the other side. It was small, not very tidy. The sink was full of dishes. The cupboards were open, all their contents piled on the counters. The cabinets were open. A bottle of soap and a sponge were on the floor. There hadn't been much inside of them.

Carver peered through the kitchen door into the den. He wiped his boots off as good as he could on the outdoor mat.

"Hold on." Holly gave him a pair of plastic bags. "Put these on your shoes."

They both covered their shoes and went inside.

Holly clicked on her radio. "This is Holly Robinson at Morganville PD requesting a crime scene investigation at one zero two Westbrook Road."

The radio crackled a moment later. "CSI is already enroute to Morganville Electric Company." The voice sounded frazzled. Like there was too much going on to keep up with.

"Acknowledged." Holly shook her head. "I don't think they'll be here for a while."

"It's unlikely they'll find prints. But it's worth a shot." Carver ventured inside. Rhodes hadn't brought much with her. No furniture. Hardly any dishes or decorations. It had just enough to make it look like someone lived there. Just enough to convince people that she'd found her new home.

The mattress was off the bed. Torn open and propped up against the wall. The pink sheets lay on the floor next to it. The dresser was opened and empty. The bed and floor were covered with athletic underwear, cargo pants, thick socks. The kind of clothing that was all business and no pleasure. The pillow stuffing and mattress stuffing covered some of it.

The walls were mostly bare. There was nothing unnecessary here. It was a personal void. There were pictures of Rhodes with kids on one wall. Another picture of her with two older people. They might be relatives. Carver didn't know. All he knew was that this looked fake.

The pictures in this room were like a coat of paint. A façade. Rhodes wanted it to look like she'd personalized this place. Made it her own. Most ordinary folks would believe it. Welcome her to the community. But she hadn't been here to stay. She'd put minimum effort into this place. Her room on the base had been ten times more decorated.

She'd had a bookshelf with history books and tactical tomes. She had historical maps framed on the walls. Pictures from old wars. The medals her grandfather had earned in World War II, and pictures of her dad in Vietnam.

Her dad and grandfather weren't in any of the pictures in this house. Rhodes didn't have any siblings that he knew of. No kids either. So, who were the people in these pictures?

Carver laughed and shook his head. "Screwing with my mind from the grave, aren't you?"

"What do you mean?" Holly looked at the clothing. "Someone tossed this place."

"They didn't find anything. Rhodes was too smart to hide anything here." Carver pushed his weight down on the linoleum floor. The plywood underneath creaked. He scuffed his boots around. Tested the flooring at the corners. None of it was loose.

Holly watched him curiously. "How is she screwing with your mind?"

"This whole place is a setup." He walked into the bathroom. The old medicine cabinet had been torn out of the wall and was lying in the bathtub. The wall cavity where it had been was empty. Judging from the nails and the torn-up drywall, it hadn't been hinged or used to hide anything.

The green subway tile on the walls and floor were old and moldy. Some were cracked. Carver tested them with the flat of his fist. Nothing seemed loose. The bathtub was a standard steel type. He booted the side. It didn't budge. He kept walking. Kept looking.

There was no garage and no crawlspace or basement. It took just a few minutes to check the house. The pulldown attic stairs were already lowered. He went up into the sweltering dry heat. The insulation was old and flattened out. The paper was blackened and dirty.

Whoever had tossed the house had looked around and torn up some of the insulation. It was bright pink under the paper. Carver looked up in the rafters. There wasn't room to stand up in the attic so the rafters were short. There was nothing up here but heat and humidity.

He dropped back down. "She didn't leave anything here."

"If she did, someone found it already."

Carver shook his head. "She didn't leave anything here. I just thought it might be worth checking."

"How can you be so sure?"

"I just know Rhodes. She's always a step ahead."

"Was a step ahead."

Carver nodded. "Yeah." He went outside. "You said she was best friends with a couple of women?"

"Charlotte and Renee." Holly pulled the backdoor closed behind her. "They live just down the street."

"Together?"

She nodded.

"They're a couple?"

"I don't think so. They never acted like it." Holly climbed back into the cruiser. "It's not like they have to hide it in this day and age."

"How long have they lived here?"

"Three years. Maybe a little less." She cranked the cruiser. Steered off the curb and guided it down a quarter of a mile to a brick house.

It was well tended. Bright green grass, manicured flower beds. A white picket fence with a little gate. A rusty old wheelbarrow and some garden gnomes sat among the flowers. This place was loved. Rhodes's had been abused through neglect.

Holly threw the car into park and got out. "Let me talk to them first. They don't like men very much."

"You sure they're not lovers?"

"I just know that men, especially big ones make them nervous." Holly unlatched the gate. Stepped through and went up the bright white walkway. Knocked on the front door. It swung open. Holly glanced back at the car, surprised. She drew her gun.

Carver got out and hustled up the walkway. "Wait." He checked the door frame. It was broken. Kicked in. There was a dirty imprint on the otherwise clean front door. He should have seen it already, but he'd been too busy admiring the yard.

"Give me the gun."

Holly shook her head. "Carver, I'm not giving you my service weapon."

He sighed. Wished he'd picked up the weapons he'd taken from Ruben and Jimmy. The serial numbers were filed off, so they would've been untraceable. He put up a hand and glanced around the doorframe. Judging from the odor, whoever had been here was long gone.

He still had on the gloves and the bags over his shoes, so he went inside. Two bodies were on the floor in the den on a blood-soaked area rug. Two women. Bruised and cut up. Naked except for modest underwear. Like they'd been tortured then stabbed multiple times with the bloody kitchen knife on the floor.

There was something metallic under the nearest body. He knelt on the dry carpet and looked closer.

"Oh, Jesus!" Holly gasped. "This can't be happening."

Carver tugged on the object. It was nickel-copper alloy. Designed to withstand fire and the elements. Designed to outlast the person who carried it with them from the day they entered the military. Dog tags.

He turned them over and shook his head. The name on them was his along with his former serial number.

"Is that a clue?" Holly leaned over.

"It's planted evidence." He tossed them to her. "I was supposed to be framed for these women and Rhodes."

"But, why you?" Holly stared at the dog tags. "It's such an elaborate plan."

"It's a clue." Carver took the dog tags back. They were covered in dried blood. "These women were tortured and executed. They wanted it to look like I was angry. Like I hated them for some reason. Rhodes' body was full of bullet holes. The ribs were broken and bruised. Like I kicked her. Like I hated her."

"They wanted it to look like revenge."

He nodded. "Exactly."

"Revenge for what?"

Carver knelt and examined the women's faces. They were too bruised and cut up to make out features. Both had been about five feet and two or three inches tall. Both were a little round at the hips. One had long blond hair, the other was brunette. Their skin was pale white. He'd seen countless women like this. He remembered a few faces. A few names. A few places. But there wasn't enough here to place these women.

He looked around the room. The coffee table had cute little coasters. Decorative porcelain figurines. The lamps, the drapes, the couch, everything was color coordinated. Shades of gray and white.

Pictures of beaches. Mountains. Rivers, lakes, and streams. Wild animals. A gray cat. A gray pit bull mix with sweet eyes. Not a single photo of a person. Just places and animals. These women didn't want to be seen. Didn't want to put themselves on display. Even their underwear was the kind that went up past the navel.

Holly was shaking. Crying. "I can't believe this is happening. Who could do this?"

"Get a picture of that footprint on the front door." Carver figured it would give her something to do. "See if it matches up with the footwear on one of the corpses in the boiler."

"Y-you think Settler did it?"

"I think one of the guys with him did."

She straightened. Nodded. "I'll start looking for clues and call this in."

Carver went back to examining the women. He stood and walked a circle around the open den area. The floor beneath the area rug was fake hardwoods. It looked like vinyl. The kitchen was the same. He looked around. The kitchen table was knocked over. Broken dishes on the floor around it. Like someone wasn't satisfied with killing the women. Like they needed to smash up the place a little first.

There was something different about this scene. It hadn't been tossed. Hadn't been searched. It had been carefully staged. He'd staged enough scenes to know what it looked like. He was good at it. Rhodes' house hadn't been staged. They'd searched it.

The staging here would fool most local cops. Even the FBI would call it open and shut. The dog tags would prove it. Ruben and Jimmy probably planned to take some fibers from Carver's clothing, strands of hair, and sprinkle it around the bodies right after they'd hung him. Nice and tidy.

Rhodes and these two women dead by Carver's hands, as far as anyone else was concerned. A lone wolf with a dark history would be the perfect fall guy. But Carver had been chosen because of his connection to Rhodes, that much was obvious.

That meant these women might be connected to her somehow. There would have to be a reason why Carver would brutally kill Rhodes and these women. Would take out his revenge fantasy by mutilating corpses.

The den, kitchen, and eating area were one open space. He found a hallway and followed it to two bedrooms. This place had been recently renovated. It looked like the bedrooms had been enlarged. Each given a master bath with shower and tub and a large walk-in closet.

The rooms were as heavily decorated as the rest of the house. The aesthetic reminded him of something. Something Slavic, maybe? Russian? There were no Russian nesting dolls, but the designs reminded him of Eastern Europe.

What stuck out was the absence of personal photos. The cat, the dog, scenic vistas. No pictures of the women. No pictures of family. The bloody cat carcass was in the bathtub of the room on the right. The dog was in the one on the left.

Ruben wanted investigators to think Carver killed the animals and made the women watch, then spoiled their private place with the corpses. Ruben and Jimmy probably had made them watch.

The animals had been slaughtered like cows. Slit throats. Carver wondered if the killers made them watch or did it later as an afterthought. He noticed something blue caught in the dog's mouth. He looked closers. It was a piece of rubber glove. The dog must've bitten the killer. Nipped him on the finger. It might not have left a mark, but maybe it had.

He inspected the closets. The clothing was modest. Baggy pants and shirts. Long dresses. No athletic gear. Nothing remotely revealing or sexy. Everything about that was a clue. If these women didn't like men, wore this clothing, and weren't a couple, it meant just one thing.

They'd been abused. Maybe beaten. Maybe raped. The mental scars turned them into these people. But that hadn't necessarily turned them into close friends. It seemed likely they had shared trauma. Maybe they'd been abused by the same person or people.

That was why they didn't have pictures of themselves. They considered themselves damaged. Scarred. Broken. The last thing they wanted to see was a reminder. The mirror on the bathroom wall was a small decorative circle. Hardly enough for seeing the face, much less the body.

Most women loved the big mirrors. Lots of light for putting on makeup. Full-body mirrors to admire themselves in. This place didn't have any mirrors except the small ones in the bathrooms. The clues added up to a story. The story told Carver that the women wanted to live in a small, dead town. Far away from the crowds. Far away from men.

He found their purses. Simple bags. The drivers' licenses were a little over three years old. Charlotte Cunningham and Renee Smith. The pictures were blurry. It was strange because government issued IDs required clear images of faces. Yet both were virtually unrecognizable from their pictures.

He dug through the purses and wallets. No credit cards. No rewards cards. Nothing except a few hundred dollars and bank debit cards. These women paid for everything in cash. They took what they needed from the same bank.

This story was getting more and more interesting.

CHAPTER 17

Tony had a meeting with Dorsey.

He told him the problem persisted. The problem had survived. It was alive and walking around Morganville and they hadn't stopped it.

Dorsey looked too calm for someone who'd just heard the news. "He killed your men?"

"And the cop."

He worked his jaw back and forth. "Let's go. You and me. We can fix this and be home in time for dinner."

"I hope you're kidding. You can't go anywhere near this mess. It'll blow up in your face." Tony jabbed a thumb against his own chest. "I can't go near it either. Neither of us can be connected to this or it all falls apart."

"We can take a car from the impound like we did that other time. It's nice and anonymous. We find him and I can drop him from a hundred yards."

"Sir, we can't do that. It's too risky." Tony hated it when Dorsey considered himself one of the boys. He thought he knew what he was doing, but he really didn't. The only people he'd killed had been helpless or drugged. Dorsey loved the sport. Loved watching someone try to run.

"You know I can do it," Dorsey said. "No-scope three-sixty."

The man had never hit anyone with such a stupid maneuver except in his video games. "Do you want to keep your company? Your freedom? Let my men handle it."

"Your men haven't done shit!" Dorsey slammed his hand on his desk. "How in the hell do three men fail to kill one?"

Tony didn't have an answer. "I've already got another crew rolling. They'll take him out by any means necessary. It's already messy, so making it a little messier won't matter at this point."

"How will a daylight execution not bring them back to our doorstep?"

"I'm using people who aren't on the books. They're contractors. Specialists." Tony smiled. "And they'll make it look like someone took revenge for Rhodes. It won't lead back to us."

Dorsey ground his teeth. "I don't like being cooped up. You know how I am. You know how much I miss being in the field. God, I miss Afghanistan and Iraq."

"I know you do. But this life isn't all about action. Sometimes it takes a lot of patience. A lot of waiting."

"You think I don't know that? How long did we wait in Afghanistan? Something like eighteen hours. And I still no-scoped those insurgents."

"Yeah, it was awesome." Tony held out his fist for a bump. "No-scope three-sixty, baby."

"Exactly." Dorsey looked mollified. "Let me know when it's done. I'm so ready for this week to be over with."

"You and me both, boss." Tony left the room. Walked down the hallway and into the bathroom. Then he let the disgust show on his face. If this moron didn't give him so much money and a share in the company, he would've no-scoped his ass a long time ago. He'd had a dozen chances to kill Dorsey in Afghanistan and God knew he'd wanted to.

Dorsey went over there just before they'd pulled out American troops. He'd insisted on taking out some insurgents himself. All he'd done was kill four innocent sheepherders. But it had been enough to satisfy him.

Then they'd made a trip to Iraq. Gone into Baghdad in disguise. He'd killed a handful of civilians he labeled insurgents to prove that he had what it took to be like Tony. It was like a kid shouting, "Watch me!" as he does a wheelie on his bike or flips his skateboard.

Except in Dorsey's case, it was a grown man committing murder for show. Dorsey was a psychopath, or maybe a sociopath. Tony didn't know which one it was. He just knew that Dorsey had great business sense. He could convince people of just about anything. Make them think he was sincere and caring.

They didn't know he could just as easily stab them in the back and not feel a drop of remorse. Dorsey was gifted. A genius. But he was also sick in the head and dangerous.

That was why Tony had a plan for independence. A plan that would hand the reins of this company over to people who knew what they were doing. But everything had to go right this week. Problems needed fixing.

The consultants he'd hired were specialists. Carver would be in a body bag by the day's end.

CARVER WAS DEAD tired.

It was mid-afternoon and he was ready for a nap. He wasn't used to thinking about things so hard. Trying to be a detective was draining. Trying to frame the big picture was exhausting. Rhodes hadn't left him a clue and that was a big mistake. Missiles were aimed and fired. They were sent to blow up things. Kill people. They weren't designed to follow clues until they found who they were supposed to kill.

He'd taken the cash from the deceased women's wallets and added it to his own. They were for business expenses because this was becoming a job. He considered it fair exchange for justice. Ruben and Jimmy had probably killed these women. Carver had exacted justice. It was enough justification to keep him from feeling guilty. Plus, they had no need for it anymore.

Carver checked their phones. Both required fingerprints to open. Renee's index finger opened hers. He went through her texts. There were almost none, and those were mostly from Rhodes. He skimmed them. There was nothing useful. Rhodes hadn't texted her very much and Renee hadn't texted anyone else except the guy who mowed the lawn.

He checked her banking app. Used her fingerprint to unlock it. He skimmed the deposits. They weren't much, but it was plenty to get by in this town. What caught his attention was the company: *American Mutual Bank Trust Account.*

The money was coming from a trust fund, or at least that was what it looked like. Renee hadn't had a job.

He unlocked Charlotte's phone with her thumbprint.

Holly watched with sick fascination. "This doesn't bother you at all?"

Carver considered lying. Telling her it bothered him a lot. Mainly because she would think he was a sociopath. "It bothers me some. I don't like when people are murdered for no reason."

"That's a strange answer."

"It's an honest one." He checked Charlotte's banking app. She was receiving money from the same trust. He used her phone to google American Mutual Bank Trust Account. It was a bank. They managed the trust. It was exactly what it said it was. Why were two unrelated women receiving money from the same trust account?

Carver examined the banking app. There were times he'd stolen a target's phone. Manipulated balances and transfers through their banking app to make the activity look innocent or nefarious, depending on mission parameters.

This time he set up a scheduled transfer to send the money from Charlotte's trust to a bank account in the Caymans. He set the transfers to the max amount of the deposits which were three thousand each month.

It would take some time for the bank to find out the women were dead. For them to cancel the trust and do whatever else they were supposed to do with the money. By then, he'd have a few thousand dollars that would have gone to waste otherwise.

He went back through the texts and found one from Rhodes wishing Renee a happy birthday. He went to biometrics and clicked to add a fingerprint. The device prompted him for a four-digit PIN. He entered the birthday. It let him in. He added his fingerprints and his face. Changed the PIN.

He tried the same with Charlotte's phone, but the PIN wasn't her birthday or year of birth. He tried a few random numbers, but the phone locked him out for thirty minutes.

Holly watched him. "What are you doing?"

"Trying to find out why they were getting money from the same trust fund."

She frowned. "Renee and Charlotte were getting money from the same trust fund?"

"That's what I said."

"But they're not related. Not married. That's strange."

"I thought so too. But I don't know how to find out why."

"Call the bank?"

"Wouldn't do any good. They'd stonewall me. Tell me it's confidential."

"Maybe I can find out why." Holly took out her phone.

"They won't give it to you just because you're a cop."

"I know." She dialed a number. "Judge O'Brien, please. Tell him it's Holly Robinson." She walked outside.

Carver stared at the bodies. "I think I killed the guy who did this to you, but I promise I'll end the guy who ordered him to do it. I hope it's okay I'm taking your money. If I find out you have relatives, I'll give it to them instead, okay?"

He took their silence as agreement.

Money was one of those stupid things you never had enough of. Needed too much of for simple things. Carver had learned a few things working special operations. He'd learned that the government didn't care about him. That he was a tool, nothing more. Same thing went for everyone he worked with.

Most importantly, he'd learned how to plan for his future. How to skim a little here and there so he'd have a comfortable landing pad when he decided to retire. That pad had come in handy when the shit hit the fan. Now it was a mattress. A comfortable place to lay. It helped him do what he enjoyed the most. Sitting on a warm beach. Listening to the water crash against the shore.

He'd even had pictures of his favorite beaches. He took them everywhere as a reminder. Knowing that one day he'd be sitting on one of them. Drinking a cold drink. Forgetting the terrible things he'd done.

Then it hit him. The answer to that nagging question. Carver laughed out loud. "I'm an idiot." That was why he wasn't paid to think. It was why Rhodes could think circles around him. Sure, she wasn't great at chess, but her mental chess was out of this world.

Holly came back inside. "Why are you laughing like a madman? Have some respect for the dead, you psychopath."

Carver reined in his laughter. "Sorry."

"You're fucked up, you know that?"

He nodded. "Sorry."

"Don't apologize to me. Apologize to the dead women lying on the floor in front of you, asshole!"

"I'm sorry, Renee. I'm sorry, Charlotte." Carver stood and faced her. "You'll have to excuse me, Holly. I'm not normal."

Holly's anger softened. "Carver, you're just...unexpected. I don't even know how to explain it."

"You don't need to try. Just know that whoever did this to Rhodes and these ladies will pay for it."

She showed him a picture of a boot. The boot was on a foot. The foot belonged to a dead man named Ruben. "This is the boot that kicked open the door." Tears pooled in her eyes. "This bastard is the one who did this." Her shoulders shook. "And Settler was working with them!"

"I don't think Settler had anything to do with this. They probably coerced him into it." It was a lie sure as Carver was breathing, but it might soften the blow. "Settler was probably under threat of death."

She wiped her cheeks. "I didn't think of that. You think he was innocent?"

"I think so. He was probably afraid for his life." Carver didn't know how else to spin it, so he let the lie hover there. Let her take it or leave it.

Holly worked her jaw back and forth. "I think you might be wrong. But I'll give Settler the benefit of the doubt. He did enough for me that he deserves that much."

"Yeah, he deserves that much." Carver put a hand on her shoulder. "You don't bear the blame for the actions of others. People just do things. Sometimes bad, sometimes good. You're only responsible for you."

"I know that." She touched his hand. Pressed it harder to her shoulder. "But I can still mourn them. It's like the person I thought I knew died and something terrible took their place."

"Nobody is just good or bad. One of my COs was the nicest guy you'd ever meet. Everyone loved him. Thought he was the funniest guy in the world." Carver chuckled. "He could go anywhere and turn strangers into his best friends. But then I saw this same guy blow off a man's head from three hundred yards with a fifty cal. I saw him gut a guy for trying to kill a squad mate. He was good. He was bad. He was a lot in between."

"He did what was right," Holly said. "There's nothing wrong with killing someone who tried to kill your squad mate."

"Yeah, but his home life was miserable." Carver grinned. "That man cheated on his wife so many times. He just had a way with women, I guess."

Holly didn't seem to know how to respond. "On a brighter note, Judge O'Brien agreed to sign a warrant to find out who funded the trust."

Carver hadn't used a warrant once. Anytime his team needed something, they took it. By force, by trickery, by hacking. Whatever it took. There was no legal barrier they wouldn't breach.

It was nice having someone who knew how to navigate civilian legalities. "Okay. What do we need to do?"

"He'll sign it and his clerk will email it to the bank. Once that's done, they'll text me and I'll call the bank."

"That sounds too simple."

"That's how it's done sometimes." Holly checked her phone then tucked it into a pocket. "It'll take about thirty minutes."

Carver looked at the women again. "Goodbye, ladies."

"Respect, Carver."

"I promised them results, Holly. I'm showing them respect."

"In the weirdest way possible." She shook her head. "You are something else." She looked him up and down. "And you also look like a bum. Do you have any other clothes?"

"Not on me."

"You traveled here without packing anything?"

"I travel light."

"I'll say." Holly sighed. "There's a thrift store south of town. We can get you some fresh clothes there."

"I like that idea." He followed her outside. Closed the door behind them so the crime scene looked undisturbed. Then he got in her car and stripped off the gloves and shoe bags.

"We need a dozen CSI units to go over everything." Holly shook her head. "Maybe we need outside help, like the FBI."

"Don't make the call." Carver leaned back in the seat. "Keep your head down. This is going to get worse before it gets better."

Holly nosed away from the curb and followed the street. She turned down a road and whipped the cruiser up to sixty miles per hour. "You think I'll be in danger?"

"I know you will be. All of this was designed to be tied up in a neat little package." Carver dropped the gloves on the floorboard. "Since that didn't work out, they'll be calling in a cleanup crew."

"You know way too much about this stuff." Holly glanced at him then back to the road. "It's almost like you've done it before."

"Uncle Sam asks for a lot of things. Nothing is off the menu."

"You make it sound so sterile."

"The people in charge like it that way." He shrugged. "Whether it's a drone strike or sending someone to slash the throats of an entire family, they don't want to think about it. They want to go home. Smile at their spouse and pretend they're a good person."

"If it's for the good of the country, aren't they a good person?"

"That's open to interpretation. But if it helps them sleep at night, that's on them."

"Why were you laughing earlier, anyway?"

Carver had almost forgotten about that. "I figured out how Rhodes found me."

CHAPTER 18

Holly slowed the car around a curve. "Okay, so how did Rhodes find you?"

He tapped his temple. "Superior intellect."

"You don't have a phone, but you have a name and address, right? She probably used the phone book."

"No, I didn't have a physical address." He chuckled. "Rhodes remembered my favorite beaches. She probably went to the ones I talked about most. I'll bet she stood nearby and watched me, and I never even knew it."

"I'm surprised she didn't shoot you."

"Me too."

Holly slowed down. The car ahead was going the speed limit. "You sound serious."

"Because I am." Carver adjusted the air conditioning vent so the air hit his face. "Thinking what she thought of me, I wouldn't have blamed her."

"You're being cryptic again. Care to elaborate?"

Carver thought it over. The context might help. Also, it wasn't exactly top secret since it had nothing to do with a mission. "Let me think about it."

"You do that." She veered around the slow car. The cruiser roared past it. She let up and the car settled back into a steady hum around eighty miles per hour. They stayed silent for the next ten minutes. Holly steered into a small strip mall at an intersection with some restaurants. She holstered the car in a space between two trucks. Flung the lever into park. "Let's get you all gussied up, okay?"

"Just don't make me too pretty." Carver got out and stretched. "I don't want to stick out."

Holly laughed. "You have an easy way about you, you know that? Problem is, I don't know if you're being serious or funny."

"I'm not that smart and I don't have much of a sense of humor." Carver shrugged. "But I think I was trying to make you laugh that time."

"It worked." She hooked her arm in his. "Let's go get you pretty, flyboy."

"Flyboy?" Carver was amused and a little insulted. "You need to work on your military lingo."

They went inside. Bumped back through the front doors an hour later. Carver wore fresh black cargos, a black t-shirt, and new socks. The bag in his hand had three similar sets of clothing in it. He wasn't sure where he'd keep it. Maybe in Ruben's SUV.

"Why not jeans or shorts?" Holly hopped in the cruiser and started it. "Black is going to be hot as hell in this weather."

He had his reasons. Shorts and flipflops were fine for the beach. They were expected for tropical vacations. This place might feel like the tropics, but this was no vacation. This was serious business. Life or death. He was dressed for success. Maybe not so much for daytime under the blistering sun, but certainly for night.

The AC kicked on and blasted the hot air in the cabin. Swirled it around and managed to get it bearable. Holly backed up and went to the road. Steered back toward town. "What next?"

He took out Renee's cell phone and opened the maps app. "Finding a place to stay."

"How fancy?"

"Not the downtown hotel, that's for sure." He looked along the stretches of highway near the town. Found a motel that looked promising. He scrolled the other direction and found another motel. Either was good. The first one was located in a better spot for what he needed to do next.

Holly's phone rang. She answered. "Thanks, Rita." She frowned. "What? But how?" Shook her head a few times and ended the call. "You're not going to believe this."

"Warrant didn't work?"

"Exactly. And you're not going to believe who rejected it."

"The DoD."

She stared at him blankly. "I thought you weren't smart."

"I'm not. I'm experienced. Only a couple of entities that can do that to a warrant. The DoJ and the DoD. But Rhodes was military. She was here for a reason, and it wasn't a civilian reason." Carver pictured the two dead women. Were they former military? Did they have something to do with a previous mission?

"You had a fifty-fifty chance of being right. But you were going to say Department of Defense anyway since that's how you lean." Holly squealed around a curve. "Department of Justice is probably a curse word to you."

"Not really." Carver shrugged. "I was out of country most of my life. I never had to deal with them or think about them." He stared out the window at a field of cows. Mountains in the distance. Dark storm clouds on the horizon. "I never understood how it felt to be American until I lived here for three years straight."

"That's..." Holly shook her head. "I don't know how to respond to that. You sound so American, but you grew up abroad?"

"Yeah, on military bases mostly. But my mom hated staying on the base, so she took me into town almost every day. Made me play with foreign kids." He stared at the phone screen. "I didn't know any better. Never gave it much thought until I was older. Kids would make fun of me because I was American, and I didn't even know what it was."

"Kids would make fun of you for that?"

"Some people don't like Americans that much." He decided which motel he'd go to and tucked the phone into a thigh pocket on the cargo pants. "They blame the people for the politicians."

"I guess you'd know. If you were in a covert operations group, you probably did a lot of shady things for politicians."

"Shady is putting it nicely." Carver looked at more cows out the window. "We nudged events however they wanted them. A nudge normally meant killing someone important, or maybe a lot of important people. Not all of those nudges seemed to be in favor of American policy."

"You're awfully chatty now. I thought that was classified."

"It's vague enough so you don't know anything. Besides, I think it might be useful for you to have more background if we're going to be working together."

Holly whistled. "I'm in the big time now?"

Carver nodded. "You're in the big time. But remember I'm a target. If you're with me, you might be a target too."

"You're not going to try to stop me?" She glanced sideways at him. "You're not going to try to play the hero and save the damsel in distress from her bad life decisions?"

"I'm no hero and you don't need saving." He turned to her. "The people that needed saving are dead. Now we're just going to find out the who and why. Then we're going to kill the who."

"I'm a cop. I can't just go killing people."

"Cops do it all the time."

"Yeah, but not by choice."

Carver didn't debate the issue. He knew better. He'd seen it happen in every country. It was just part of life. "I'm going to the motel to rest."

Holly checked her watch. "But it's so early."

"I need some rest." The activities of the past two days had taken a toll.

Morganville city limits came into view. They breezed past the worn old sign and bumped down the rutted road to the police station. It looked like a circus down the street around the old power company. Blue and red lights flashing. Police cruisers and ambulances everywhere.

Holly parked. "Just hang out for a while. Let's see what they found out about the bodies."

"You do that. I need some rest."

She smacked the steering wheel. "You plan on walking somewhere? Nearest motel is a few miles out."

"I have wheels."

"You have an SUV owned by a dead man, Carver." She shook her head. "You can't just go driving that around."

"Sure, I can. He won't miss it."

She scowled. "Fine. I'll find out what's going on and we can touch base later. What's the number to that phone?"

"You're not upset I took a dead woman's phone?"

"At this point you've got me so turned around emotionally that I don't know what's up or down anymore." She groaned. "I've been to a murder scene, and I can't report it because it'll make me a target. I feel like I've got the weight of two bodies on my shoulders."

"Those women didn't have any nosy neighbors? No one to miss them?"

"The nearest houses are vacant. I think the closest person is a mile down the road."

Carver gave it some thought. "They were friends with Rhodes. Maybe mention that someone should tell them Rhodes is dead."

"Rhodes's death isn't common knowledge yet. I don't know if that would fly." Holly shook her head. "I'll just keep quiet for now even though it's killing me."

"Do you feel bad?"

Holly frowned. "Of course I do."

"No, I mean about everything you said to me yesterday when you thought I was guilty."

She huffed. "Get out of my car, Carver."

Carver slid out of the car. The SUV was parked down at the police station, so he'd have to make his way there. Holly wedged through the crowd outside the fence and went inside. Maberly was still guarding the gate. Gawking onlookers had spread out along the fence for a better look. Carver followed the fence and looked at the inside. They'd set up a barrier to keep people from seeing the bodies.

He turned around and crossed Main Street. Went around the closed-up hardware store. Everyone was focused on the crime scene, so he squeezed inside past the loose boards. The sock with the money and the weapons were still on the shelf. He took everything and slipped outside again.

Carver walked down the street to the station and went inside. The lobby was empty. The door leading to the back was locked. He looked through the window of Maberly's office. Checked out the computer screen. It was locked with a password.

Carver had wanted to dig through the records for Wilson and Mims, but it looked like he'd have to find their locations another way. He went outside to the SUV and cranked it. The fuel tank was only a quarter full. He turned up the AC and took out the phone. Searched the internet for Wilson and Mims in Morganville and the county.

Social media provided some results, but none of the pictures looked like the guards. The guards hadn't worn nametags and he didn't know their first names. Unless they had landline phones, it was unlikely they'd show up in a phone book search. He tried it anyway. Wilson came back with several results and none of them in Morganville or nearby.

Mims returned a rural address about thirty minutes from the county jail. Adam and Sherry Mims. It seemed worth checking out. He backed out of the parking lot. Set the GPS on the phone and followed the little blue line on the screen. The phone battery was low. He opened the armrest and pulled out the charger cord he'd found earlier when searching. It fit into the bottom of the phone and started charging it.

Carver passed by a gas station on the way out of town. It was a tiny joint with two pumps, but it was open for business which was more than he could say for most places in this town. He veered into the drive and parked in front of a gas pump. Got out of the SUV.

An old man with coveralls humped outside. "We're full service, sir. You want premium for that beast? It'll get better gas mileage."

"Regular is fine." He watched the old guy pump the gas. "How safe is this town?"

The man scratched his scraggly beard. "Used to be real safe. Guess that's changed."

"Before today you'd say this town was about as safe as it can be?"

"Maybe." He shrugged. "There were rumors that Jasper Whittaker was up to something, but ain't nothing ever come from it." He finished pumping the gas. "That'll be eighty-two dollars and thirty-nine cents."

Carver picked out a hundred bucks in twenties and took the change. "Thanks." He climbed back into the SUV and started following the blue line on the map again. He banked around Johnny's Curve. The bent railing and some skid marks were the only signs of the accident. Everything had been efficiently removed and cleaned up.

He stopped at the boulder. Walked around and found the gun and the ankle holster where he'd stashed it. He dropped it into the passenger side floorboard then got back in the car.

Once again, he followed the blue line. It took him past the prison, past the medical examiner's office and north up a county highway. Led him curling up a mountain past old houses perched on narrow plots just off the road.

The address belonged to a rusty blue single-wide trailer. There was a barn surrounded by old pickups and cars. None except a compact pickup looked functional. Carver pulled into the driveway. He slipped on Holly's Morganville PD cap and got out.

Went up the rickety wooden stairs to the screen door and knocked. There was movement inside. Some thumping about. The inside door swung open. An old man stood there. Definitely not Mims.

The old man looked at the ball cap. "Can I help you officer?"

"I'm looking for Adam Mims."

"Me? Or my boy?"

"Sorry, sir, I was just told he's a guard at the county jail. They don't tell me much."

The old man chuckled. "You're the low boy on the totem pole, eh? Got you running errands?"

"Yeah. Some scumbag prisoner we arrested the other day got into a fight and might have injured two guards. Mims is one of them. I wanted to get a statement from them, but I can't do it while they're at work."

"Yeah, they're real strict over there." He looked Carver up and down. "Tell me what this is really about."

"I'm sorry, sir—"

"Don't bullshit me, boy. You ain't with the Morganville PD, I know that much. "You're FBI or something, judging from that fancy SUV and your half-assed attempt to look like a normal civilian."

The old man was sharp as a tack, so Carver switched tactics. "Those boys might be in bed with the wrong people. I'm trying to find out if that's true."

"Well, shit." The old man cackled. "His problems finally came home to roost like I knew they would."

"You don't seem too concerned about your son."

"He ain't my boy, he's Sheryl's. He was a boy when I married his mom and adopted him. That boy never listened to me. Always in trouble." The old man shook his head. "Him and that Wilson kid were always looking for shortcuts in life. When that didn't work out for them, they became guards. But I knew it wasn't for no legit reason."

"So, you think he's involved with the wrong people?"

"Think it? Ha!" The old man scuffed the threshold with his slipper. "I know it. He tried to buy his momma a new car on a guard's salary. I told him to keep that dirty money away from us. Sheryl and I fought like cats and dogs over that boy and I'm just sick of it."

"Did he get his mom a new car?"

"No. I think he was just bragging. Trying to make it look like he was a success." He spat to the side. "He and Wilson showed up in a brand-new three-quarter ton pickup a week later. Truck like that costs a hundred grand easy. Sticks out like a sore thumb to anyone with a brain. Ain't nobody affording that pickup on twenty dollars an hour."

Carver nodded. "I think you're right. So, if we arrest him, it won't matter to you?"

The old man laughed. "Put him away for ten to twenty. I'll finally be able to say I told you so to his momma."

"We've been trying to do this covertly, so I haven't called the prison or asked for his address. Can you give it to me?"

"Yeah. Him and Jerry Wilson bought the old Kleiner farm off Route Two." He rattled off an address. "Stupid boys. They deserve what's coming to them."

"This is part of a larger ongoing investigation, Mr. Mims. Do you have any knowledge as to where he's getting this extra money from?"

Mr. Mims shook his head. "I don't know, and I don't want to know. I'm sure he's on some crime lord's payroll."

Carver nodded. "Thank you for your help, Mr. Mims. Please don't mention this to anyone. We're hoping to catch some big fish in this net. Maybe Adam and Jerry will turn state's witness and avoid too much jail time but learn a valuable lesson in the process."

"Doubt it." Mr. Mims backed up a step. "I don't suppose there's a reward for my help, is there?"

"There isn't, but you've been very helpful." Carver made a show of looking around, then peeled a hundred from the roll of money he'd taken from Charlotte's and Renee's purses. He gave it to him. "The Bureau thanks you."

"Ha!" The old man snatched it and looked it over. "God damned feds." He shut the door in Carver's face and a chain rattled into place on the other side.

The ruse had almost worked. Carver felt a little stupid for even trying it. Rhodes would have developed a five-step strategy with bullet points before ever stepping out of the car. She would've wrapped that old man around her finger in no time.

But at least now he had an address. Two possible links to whoever wanted him dead. All he had to do was ask them the right questions.

Maybe they would get him one dot closer to the truth.

CHAPTER 19

A gray Nissan Pathfinder hummed down the highway leading into Morganville. Five men were cramped inside. The air conditioning couldn't keep up with the body heat. The close quarters made it even more miserable.

Nobody complained.

It was nothing compared to what most of them had been through. These conditions were easy. Almost pleasant. The driver rolled down the window and started smoking. The others put their windows down. The breeze was more pleasant than the stifling warmth of five big men in close quarters.

A larger SUV would've been far more practical. But it would have stuck out. Most hikers drove cars like this. It would allow them a certain degree of anonymity. It would also keep the target from noticing them right away.

They were dressed in hiking gear. Athletic shorts and t-shirts. Hiking boots. Some of them wore cargo shorts. They'd mixed it up to make their appearance more authentic. Once they arrived, they'd set up shop somewhere near downtown. Watch the town. Locate the target and eliminate him as quietly as possible.

Then they'd plant evidence linking him to other murders.

The quick, clean operation management had hoped for had turned into a mess. This was the cleanup crew. Their specialty was turning situations around. Turning a loss into a win. They were batting a thousand so far. Over fifty missions, no failures. They were good at what they did and didn't hesitate to do it.

The driver flicked cigarette ash out of the window. "They should've waited for us. Damned target is going to be alert now."

"Nah." The guy squeezed in the back between the other two men shook his head. "He thinks it's over. Thinks he's in the clear."

The man to his left yawned. "I'm still on Ukraine time, boys. I can't sleep on those corporate jets."

"Yeah, too soft. Too cramped." The driver laughed. "Give me a C seventeen any day."

"Amen, brother."

The car went silent again as their thoughts turned toward the town ahead and the target they were tasked to eliminate. They knew by tomorrow morning they'd be heading back to Atlanta with another successful mission under their belts.

CARVER DROVE TO the address Mr. Mims had given him.

There was a long gravel drive through overgrown pastures. At the end, a big white single-story farmhouse. A metal garage on the right, turned so the doors faced the house. The gravel turned to a concrete pad at the end.

A midsized sedan was parked there. A jacked-up red pickup sat on the other side. Like a giant next to a normal sized person. The blinds on the windows were shut. No one would see Carver coming.

He guided the SUV up the gravel driveway. Nosed around the giant pickup and parked on the other side. No one would see the SUV from the road. He gauged the terrain. The gravel road continued into the pasture behind the house. It turned to a rutted dirt trail about a hundred yards distant and went around the bend of a small mountain.

There was a big silver propane tank in the back. The kind used to supply an entire house for heat and utilities since there was no city service here. A gas company truck would make the rounds in this rural area and fill up the tanks every so often. There was also a big green lid in the back yard. Probably a septic tank.

Rural living at its finest.

He got out and walked to the passenger side of the SUV. Opened the door and laid the Glocks on the seat. He quickly field stripped them. Checked the barrels and springs, then reassembled them. They looked clean enough. They might even work perfectly. You never knew until you pulled the trigger.

Carver popped out the magazines. They were full. He popped them back in. Put on Ruben's belt holster for open carry and slid a Glock inside. He strapped on the ankle holster. Checked the pistol for ammo, and slid it back in. He held the other Glock in his hand.

It was doubtful Wilson and Mims would try anything. It was still better to be safe than sorry. He went around the backside of the house. Slid along the back wall to the nearest window. He peeked inside. The blinds were shut. He edged to the next window. The blinds were shut on it too. Carver poked his head out and looked down the back of the house. All the blinds looked shut. Just like on the front.

He gave his next move some thought. Knocking on the door wouldn't cut it. He'd have to either smash inside or sneak inside. Dealer's choice. Before committing, he needed to know his options. Carver crept onto the concrete patio. Tested the back door. It was unlocked. Probably not much of a reason to lock the doors this far out in the country. Or maybe they left it unlocked while home.

Carver knelt on the hinged side of the door. Gently twisted the handle. The latch clicked. He eased open the door. It moved silently on oiled hinges. He held the Glock ready. The room on the other side was tiled. A kitchen cabinet was right next to the door. He rose slightly and peered over the counter.

The kitchen was dark and empty on the left.

He pushed the door open and peered around the other side. There was an open pantry and a small utility room. Also, empty. He closed the door quietly. The kitchen was a long narrow rectangle. Had an old gas stove. a stainless-steel sink. A white refrigerator with food stains on the door.

Beer cans were piled into a big industrial-sized trash can. Small red roaches climbed along the sides. The place smelled of sour beer. It was definitely a bachelor pad. A woman probably hadn't seen the inside of this place in a while.

The television droned nearby. Sounded like a sports announcer. Maybe an action movie. It was hard to say. Carver didn't watch much television. He peered outside the kitchen door. There was a tiled dining space with an old wooden table. The table was piled with mail. A cheap chandelier hung over the table. It was turned off.

Beyond the table was the den. There was a gray cloth couch against one wall. A couple of end tables against the sides of the couch. A huge television mounted on the opposite wall. There were several gaming consoles connected to the television. They looked new. Carver didn't know much about them, but he'd seen plenty in soldier's barracks. It was easier to play soldier in a video game than in real life.

A football video game seemed to be playing itself on the television. It looked and sounded like the real thing. The crowd roared. Football players shouted and grunted. It was loud enough to drown out Carver's footsteps.

To the right of the kitchen door was a hallway. It led past two doors in the middle and ended at two doors in the end. Probably a bathroom and three bedrooms. Ranch-style houses were usually built like that. He'd broken into enough of them to know.

The hallway was dark except for a trickle of light from the doors at the end. The door on the left moved like someone bumped it. He heard muffled talking. It was hard to understand over the sound of the television.

Carver slipped down the hallway. Peered through the crack in the door on the left. Shadows moved inside. Someone was talking. He rotated and looked through the door of the other room. A ceiling fan was spinning. The bed sheets were messy. Clothes were piled on the floor. No one was inside.

He checked the middle doors. One was a small bedroom. Dark and empty. The other was a small bathroom. A closed door on the other side presumably led to the bedroom on the left.

If Wilson and Mims were joined at the hip like Mr. Mims suggested, they were both in the same bedroom. Maybe the reason a woman hadn't been here was because they didn't like women. Maybe Carver didn't want to poke his nose inside that room just yet. Or maybe it was the perfect time to catch them.

The door wasn't cracked open enough to see the bed. Carver listened hard. He heard bumping around. Someone talking. Whatever was happening, this was a good time to surprise the pair. But first, he needed to be sure he'd covered all his bases.

Carver slid back down the hallway. Looked over the den. The foyer. The kitchen. Ensured no one else was in those areas. He cracked a blind and made sure no one was in the front yard. Without someone watching his back, he had to do it himself. Had to be certain he was in the clear.

He went back down the hallway. Held a Glock at the ready. Put the side of his foot against the bottom of the door and nudged it open. The door swung inside. The first thing Carver saw was Wilson naked on top of Mims. The second thing he saw were all the pills scattered on the bed. Used needles on the floor.

The third thing he saw was the most important. The other two men in the room. The men who were staging the scene—death by overdose. The men were about five feet six inches tall. Dark tanned skinned. Not muscular, but in good shape.

One had a long, ragged scar on his cheek. His hair was cropped short, military style. The other guy wore his hair longer. Shaved around the sides, but long on top like a model. He was a pretty boy, but his eyes told a different story. That look and the way he was moving the naked bodies told Carver that this was something he'd done a lot.

The other one had a gun in his hand so fast, it was a blur. The gun pointed at Carver. Carver had his gun trained on him already. Neither fired. The other guy stared at him from across the room. He spoke a few words in another language. It sounded almost Spanish, but it wasn't. Probably Portuguese.

There was an open closet door in the back of the room. The closed door was the one that led into the bathroom.

Wilson struggled weakly. Wild eyes darted back and forth. He looked up at Carver with something like relief. Mims groaned. Carver was surprised they were still alive. Judging from the empty needles and pills, they wouldn't be for much longer.

"Are these the guys who paid you to kill me?" Carver said.

Wilson nodded weakly. Tried to speak, but only mumbled. The drugs were kicking in.

"I think this is the first time I've walked in while the players were still setting the stage." Carver kept close to the door frame. The walls wouldn't stop nine-millimeter slugs, but it would give him a chance to slip away if things went south. "Why do you want me dead?"

The men stared at him. The second one still hadn't drawn a gun. They were obviously content to let Wilson and Mims die while he watched. They didn't want to shoot a gun and spoil their carefully arranged scene.

Carver likewise didn't want to shoot. He wanted answers, not corpses. But the language these guys spoke already gave him a strong clue. These guys were clearly from South America. They spoke Portuguese. That meant they were almost certainly Brazilian. The only Brazilian link to this town was the paint factory.

"Rhodes figured it out, didn't she? She knew something was happening at the paint factory. You killed her and sent mercs to kill me." It all made sense. "Let me guess. Human trafficking? Drugs?"

They didn't say a word. Just watched him and the men on the bed with dead eyes.

"That was quite a trick you pulled with the dump truck. Smart way to tie up a loose end. But trying to hang me in the jailcell was dumb. You could have sent six men in there and I would have fought them to the death. No way to make it look like I hung myself."

The unarmed guy glanced at the first one. He looked puzzled.

"Do you speak English?"

No answer.

Carver sighed. "Look, I don't have to kill you now, but I can shoot up the place. Make this pretty little scene look like a warzone. Give me some answers or I'll start shooting."

Wilson groaned. His eyes rolled up into the back of his head and he slumped forward. His naked body plopped wetly onto Mims. It looked like the prison guards had reached the end of the road.

"You're pissed because they failed to get me killed, right?"

The one without a gun spoke. "You die." He slid his finger across his throat. "You die."

"Okay, you don't speak English." Carver considered his next options. He decided it was better to be rid of the assassins right now. Didn't matter how dirty the crime scene got.

The other guy seemed to read his intentions. His eyes narrowed. He fired the first shot. Carver was already moving when he saw the man's eyes narrow. He fell sideways to the floor. The center of the door behind him exploded into splinters. Two more shots blew holes through the drywall. Dust rained down on him.

Carver squirmed down the hall on his back. Kept the gun trained on the door. More bullets exploded through the wood. Feet pounded on the floor. A door slammed open. Sounded like the bathroom door. They were trying to gain position. He rolled over and pushed to his feet. Dove out of the hallway and rolled to the side.

Bullets smashed into the dining room table. Splintered wood and mail flew into the air. This murder scene was going to puzzle the hell out of someone. Carver could think of a couple of ways to salvage it, but he wasn't going to give these two any recommendations.

Bullets kept coming until they didn't. Probably reloading.

Carver considered the situation. He could just camp out but there wasn't a lot of cover in the house. Plus, it was two armed men versus one. Unless they were stupid enough to venture out to the open part of the house, he didn't have a clear shot.

But he couldn't simply leave two assassins alive. He was in their crosshairs. They would continue to seek and destroy. They were a danger at his back that he couldn't permit. Somehow, he had to put them down.

He checked the front door. It was unlocked. The deadbolt lock was the kind with keyholes on both sides. No twist lock. There was a key in the lock. He slid the bolt shut. Locked the bottom door. Took the key from the deadbolt lock. He didn't want anyone coming in or going out that way.

He returned to the edge of the hallway. Carver fired down it and ran across to the kitchen. Return gunfire blasted more splinters from the kitchen table. He poked the gun around the corner and fired again.

"I can do this all day. I've got plenty of ammo."

"You die!" One of them responded. More gunfire.

"We'll see about that." It looked like Carver wasn't going to get any answers from them.

He couldn't run. Couldn't leave these assassins alive to make another try for him. He also couldn't fight. They had a safe position and superior firepower. If he didn't do something soon, they'd coordinate and come for him.

And then he would die.

CHAPTER 20

Carver had been in plenty of impossible situations.

This was different. He didn't have a team backing him up. He didn't have superior firepower he could call on to help him. He'd have to use all available resources to salvage the situation. And the biggest resource was sitting in the back yard.

Carver went to the small utility room. He yanked the dryer away from the wall. A flexible gas line was attached to the back. The dryer moved easily, so he yanked harder until the flexible gas line went taut. He kicked the hose hard. Kicked it again. It snapped loose. Propane flooded into the room.

He went to the kitchen. The gas range was at the end near the doorway. He pushed it away from the wall until the hose went tight. Then he kicked it free. Bullets whined past. Smashed into the door jamb. One crashed through the microwave hanging over the gas range. The digital display winked out.

That put a damper on his plan. But it was okay. There was a toaster in the corner. He tore up a paper towel and dropped the pieces into either side. Turned the level to extra crispy. Depressed the lever. It snapped into place. The toaster began to heat up. The air was so thick with gas, Carver was choking on it.

The back door used the same kind of deadbolt lock as the front door. Carver took the key from the inside. Quietly opened the door and closed it. He locked the deadbolt from the outside. Then he ran to the SUV, started it, and backed it away from the house and closer to the garage. From here he could see both the front and back of the house.

Seconds ticked past. Something crashed through the kitchen window. The Brazilian boys had figured out what was up. They'd charged into the front of the house. Discovered their predicament. Now they were trying to get out.

The toaster might not do the job quick enough.

A head poked out of the window. Carver fired a round. The head jerked back inside the window. Now he imagined them running to the back of the house. There were probably windows at the other end.

Windows shattered. Flames burst through the openings. A low boom echoed. The gas had ignited. The explosion wasn't enough to blow the house to pieces, but it was good enough to superheat the inside.

If the Brazilian boys were any good, they'd survived the blast. But the flames and smoke would get to them soon enough. Carver gunned the SUV. Drove through the front yard and spun around the side.

Sure enough, something was smashing out the back windows. Scarface's head poked out. Carver put a bullet into it. The head vanished inside. The other guy dove through the broken window. Guns blazing in each hand. Clothes on fire. Hair smoking. Screaming like a maniac.

It was a hell of a sight.

The passenger side of the SUV was facing the house. It ate the bullets. Carver slid out of the driver side and ducked behind the front tire. When the bullets stopped flying, he ducked around the front. Found the pretty boy gasping in the dirt. His magazines were empty, but he wasn't done.

He rolled onto his back. Drew a knife.

Carver aimed the gun. "I wish you spoke English." Fired. The back of the Brazilian boy's head popped like a can of shaken soda.

The house was a blazing inferno. Not long until someone saw the smoke even from miles away. He frisked the dead guy. Came up with a locked cell phone. He turned on the screen.

It asked for a five-digit PIN. No fingerprint or faceprint accepted. He kept the phone anyway. Might be a chance someone could crack it.

He tossed it in the center console. Then he hefted the body by the shirt and jeans. Swung it a couple of times and tossed it back through the window. Into the inferno.

The next stop was the driveway. Carver checked the sedan first. It was almost certainly the assassins' vehicle. It wasn't a rental, but it was clean as a whistle. Just some extra nine-millimeter ammo inside. He'd probably need it, so he took it. Dumped it into the center console of the SUV.

The pickup truck was close to the house, but it wasn't on fire yet. It was locked. Carver climbed onto the nerf bar and smashed the window. Unlocked the truck. The floorboard was covered with fast food bags and empty drink containers, but it still had that new car smell. The center console had a phone charger and shotgun shells.

A shotgun was mounted on the back. A Mossberg pump-action. It was good all around, so Carver took it and the shells. He made sure the shotgun chamber was empty. Put it on the back floorboard. Tossed the shells into the center console with the other ammo.

Then he gunned the SUV down the gravel drive. Veered onto the road headed back to town. He got a mile down the road and slowed. Looked back and saw the smoke rising into the hot blue sky. This far out in the sticks there wouldn't be a rapid response.

The house would be burned down to the bones. They'd find two skeletons with bullet holes through their skulls just inside the window. Two skeletons in a lover's embrace. Drug paraphernalia around them. Bullet casings scattered everywhere. If enough of the wood survived, maybe they'd see the bullet holes.

Carver imagined forensic experts trying to decipher the mess. It would take them a while to identify the bodies. Enough time maybe to give Carver a head start on the next stage of this operation. The paint factory was at the center of this. Someone there had something to do with Rhodes's death. He wanted to find out what it was and burn the entire place to the ground along with the people inside.

Brazilian assassins. A Brazilian paint company. Whittaker Paint Company. All three had to be connected. A town like this wouldn't have many foreign connections. Certainly not someone who would choose Brazilian assassins over Russians, or just plain old American thugs. Brilhante Tintas had a hand in this.

They'd started by using Ruben and Jimmy. Former military guys. A couple of guns for hire. They bribed Settler. Probably had others on the payroll. Hell, they probably owned the whole town already. Only a few people didn't know. People like Holly, maybe. Maberly, Davis, and Ritter were probably on the take.

Carver thought back to Holly's conversation with Ritter. "You still spending a lot of time at the paint factory?" It was an innocent question. But Ritter's response looked guilty. Like he was hiding something.

When you're solving a puzzle, look for the edge pieces first. Frame the puzzle with them. Follow the edges all the way to the center.

Rhodes liked giving advice like that. Carver had even solved a jigsaw puzzle using that advice. But it was never as easy as she claimed.

Morganville was a puzzle. A lot of little pieces. The town center. The police station. The paint factory. The people who killed Rhodes. The people who tried to kill him. Maybe the paint factory was at the dead center of the finished puzzle, but it was just a place. Who would be the person at the middle?

Jasper Whittaker? A Brazilian cartel leader? Someone he never could have imagined? Maybe the paint factory wasn't in the middle. Maybe it was just somewhere close to center.

So far, the edge pieces were Rhodes, the two dead women, Ruben, Jimmy, Settler, and the Brazilian boys. Part of a frame was in place. Or maybe it was the entire frame. What other edge pieces was he missing? It seemed like Abe Ritter might be one of them. It was better to piece together the edges before storming into the paint factory.

The hardest part was finding an edge piece that was still breathing. Through some small fault of his own, they were dropping like flies. He needed someone who could answer questions, not another corpse.

Carver pulled off the side of the road. Checked the shotgun. Checked the ammo. Loaded the Glock magazine. It'd be nice to have extra magazines instead of loose bullets, but it was better than nothing.

He sat back and thought about how to approach Ritter. Questioning a cop wasn't just something you did. They didn't like having the tables turned on them. They also had the threat of force on their side. Carver had dealt with military police more than he'd wanted to. This would probably be just as pleasant.

His thoughts wandered to other things. Nothing useful for the matter at hand. He tossed the lever back into drive and continued toward town. It took about thirty minutes to get back. He parked just before the curve in Main Street took him past the electric company. Got out and walked between the abandoned storefronts until he was on the side of the electric company fence.

It was still a circus. The ambulance was gone. The bodies were probably gone. Taken to the medical examiner's office. The crowd was still pressing around the fence, a little smaller than before.

There were a few new faces. Probably tourists who'd just rolled into town and stopped outside the hotel to see what the fuss was about. A small knot of men caught Carver's attention. They stood apart from the rest of the crowd. Talking and scanning the area. Looking for something or someone.

They were dressed like tourists. Fancy hiking boots, shorts, backpacks. A couple wore their hair long on top and shaved around the sides. One had a man bun. Another was shaved bald. On the surface, they looked no different than the other tourists around them. But their demeanor and vibe hit Carver a little differently. It was just a gut feeling. Nothing substantial.

They weren't the only ones who seemed out of place. There was another group of tourists who seemed way too interested in everything except for the scene playing out at the electric company. They stood on a hotel room balcony. Two of them were aiming their phones at the crowd, not the murder scene.

There was only one reason to take pictures of the crowd. They were looking for someone. A person of interest. They might be feds. They might be working for the Brazilians. They might just be men looking for attractive women. They could be journalists. They could just be making videos for social media. It was hard to tell these days.

Carver watched them. Watched the other group. Until he knew more, it was best to stay out of sight and keep working on the puzzle.

Don't get distracted. Stick to the matter at hand and get it done.

Rhodes's never-ending advice rattled in his brain. Ritter was the matter at hand. Finding him and questioning him was at the top of the list. The barrier around the crime scene was still in place. Carver couldn't tell if Ritter was inside. He didn't have anywhere else to go, so he walked down Main Street and kept going straight where it curved. He circled around City Hall and approached the police station from the rear.

Ritter might not be there now, but he'd eventually have to come back. Carver went inside. Maberly was back at his desk. He looked up. Blinked in surprise.

"What are you doing here? You were released."

"I need to talk to Holly."

He frowned. "She's at the old electric company. You'll have to wait until she's done."

"Is the whole station over there?"

Maberly's fingers rustled in a bag of chips. "Just about. Craziest thing I ever saw in my life."

"I'll bet. Detective Ritter taking the lead?"

The other man barked a laugh and almost choked on a potato chip. "Davis took it from him. I thought they were gonna duke it out in the parking lot."

"My bet would be on Ritter."

"Yeah. Davis can't stand up without a shot of whiskey in him." Maberly flinched as if realizing he was talking to a civilian, not another cop. "Well, uh, best go wait on Holly somewhere else. I can have her call you when she's back."

Carver thought hard about how Rhodes would handle this. "Maybe Ritter can help me. I saw a guy who looked really suspicious. He was watching everything with a big smile on his face. Like he's the one who did it."

Maberly frowned. "Leave the detective work to the police, Mr. Carver."

"Just Carver."

"Ritter's in a sour mood anyway. He probably went somewhere else to cool off after Davis pissed him off."

"Probably went home then."

Maberly laughed. "Doubt it. He's still working because he can't stand to be home with the old lady."

"Can't blame him." Carver nodded at the other man. "Tell Holly I came by."

He turned and left. Followed the fence along the back of the police station. Cut down an alley at the top of the curve of Main Street. Kept behind the buildings until he reached the SUV. The vehicle would probably be a liability. The people Ruben worked with would probably recognize it. But it was better than walking everywhere.

He circled around town. Took the residential streets to avoid Main Street. Emerged at the other side of town where the rundown pub was. There were a couple of cars out front. Carver parked on the dirt in the back. He went in through the service door and into the kitchen.

A guy smoking a cigarette looked up from his phone. "What are you doing back here?"

"Bathroom?"

"Other side of that door, buddy." He jabbed a hand at a swinging door. "On the right."

"Got it." Carver went through. A short hallway was on the other side. To the right were a couple of bathroom doors and a door at the end that said *Staff Only*. He went to the bathroom and took a leak. Checked himself out in the mirror.

There were a couple of specks of dirt on his face. His hair looked oily. Sweat beaded on his forehead. He was going to need a shower before he started stinking. He turned on the water. Rinsed his face. Combed his fingers through his hair. It was about as long as he'd ever worn it in recent memory. He preferred it buzzed, but then he looked too much like a former grunt.

Three years later and he still hadn't adjusted to civilian life that well. He still didn't blend in like he wanted. Or it might all be in his head, and he blended in just fine. It was hard to say. But he probably fit in about as well as those two groups of people back at the hotel area.

He left the bathroom. Walked out to the bar. Ritter was at a table in the corner staring at a glass of amber liquid. Carver dropped into the seat opposite him.

Ritter about jumped out of his skin. His face went white as a sheet.

It only took one look at the man to make Carver realized he'd been wrong. This man wasn't on the take. Something else was going on here.

CHAPTER 21

Ritter finally found his voice. "What's the big idea, mister? Can't a man enjoy a drink without a stranger interrupting him?"

"You tell me." Carver nodded at the drink. "Looks like three fingers and you haven't had a sip."

"You need to leave right now." Ritter looked around nervously. "Please."

"Can't be seen talking to anyone?"

"If you won't go, I will." Ritter reached for his drink.

"You're as jumpy as a house cat." Carver gripped his wrist. "Looks like we have something to talk about after all."

"I don't know what you're talking about."

"The paint factory."

Ritter shrank back. Jerked his wrist free. "I haven't told anyone anything. I swear to God."

"I believe you." Carver leaned back in his seat. "At first I thought you were on the take. Now I realize it's the opposite. Someone told you to keep quiet or they'd do something nasty to you, right?"

The other man looked confused. "Who are you?"

"You thought I was with the paint factory." Carver reached over and took Ritter's drink. Tried a sip. "This isn't half bad. It's not the cheap stuff." He took another sip. "Not the real expensive stuff either."

Ritter watched him. He tried to scowl but looked more afraid than anything. "Who are you?"

"You like the good stuff, but your guts are all twisted up inside. You want to drink to make it go away, but you're concerned you might have too much. Might run your mouth." Carver nodded. "It's a catch twenty-two. I've been there myself."

"Please tell me who you are. Who you're with."

"I'm alone. Solo."

"I don't understand."

"Ritter, someone scared the shit out of you. I need to know who they are and what they wanted."

Ritter trembled. "I'm too old for this shit. I should've retired a long time ago."

"And what? Sat at home and listened to the missus rattle off to you all day? Escape to the fishing cabin until she came looking for you?" Carver took another sip of the whiskey. It had a nice burn. "Tell me what happened and maybe I can make it go away."

The other man's face went slack. Like the emotion just overcame him. "This is Morganville, for God's sake. I never expected to deal with something like this."

"There's something going on in this town. I need you to tell me what it is."

Ritter took the glass away from Carver. Tossed back the rest of the whiskey. He raised two fingers at the bartender. The other guy nodded. Grabbed whiskey from the top shelf and started pouring it. Carver looked at the label and realized it wasn't whiskey. It was dark tequila. He never had been good at identifying alcohol just from drinking it.

"Ritter, I want to get rid of the problem. The people behind it are the reason I went to prison."

"They threatened my wife. My daughter." He shivered. "She's got two little boys and a girl. A husband. If it was just me, I'd be okay with dying, you know?"

"I know."

The bartender dropped off two glasses. Glanced at Carver uncertainly, then walked away.

Ritter watched him. "I don't even know who's in on it." He turned back to Carver. "I don't know anything! I had a good quiet spot I'd park my car at. I'd sit there, drink coffee and read books. But the tourists started showing up one day and ruining my peace."

"Tourists are thick as fleas up here."

"Yes, they are." Ritter shook his head. "The mayor hates it. That's why he's never rebuilt downtown. He says he doesn't want to survive on tourism. He wants real industry again. Like the paint factory."

"Let's get back to the matter at hand, Ritter."

The other man nodded. "I started looking for a new quiet spot to enjoy. One day I drove out to Factory Road and found a hill with a good view. It turned out to be a nice, quiet spot. Wasn't anything else to do but read, you know? Town's half dead and there's zero crime."

"The town's mostly dead, Ritter."

Ritter nodded. "Yeah. It's just a husk."

"Tell me everything."

The other man took a sip of his tequila. Winced. "I just started noticing how many trucks go into that place. Big rigs that can haul a lot of paint and supplies. So, I started wondering what they could be bringing in, you know? Because the paint factory hardly makes any paint. Just enough to qualify for tax breaks, I think."

"How many trucks?" Carver asked.

"Two big trucks a day. Minimum." Ritter shook his head. "I could tell they were going in full and coming out empty. I used to help my uncle with his over the road rig. You can hear the load in the shocks and see it in the tires. When they go out empty, the trailer rattles more and the tires aren't sagging a bit."

"Suspicious." Carver had no idea what supplies were needed to make paint. But if a factory was making a lot of paint, they'd presumably use the supply trucks to deliver the finished product. Or maybe they didn't. He didn't know anything about it. But logistics for civilian truckers had to be at least as good as military logistics.

"Of course, it's suspicious." Ritter tapped his glass. "These trucks aren't owned by Whittaker Paint or by the mother company, Brilhante Tintas. They're contracted long-haulers. These people want to go in full and leave full. They want to get paid both ways. Unless they're getting paid double coming in, they wouldn't take a job like this."

"Were they getting paid double?"

Ritter shook his head. "I never asked one of them. This was just idle curiosity for me at first, you know? Then I got binoculars. Found better vantage points. Started watching the loading docks to see what was coming off the trucks."

"What was it?"

"Pallets of five-gallon paint buckets and these long wooden crates that looked like something you'd store weapons in."

"Got pictures?"

Ritter shook his head. "Not anymore. My phone was wiped clean."

"How long are these crates?"

"Seven, eight feet." He shrugged. "Hard to say, but it's close to that."

"I don't know if they ship weapons in crates that large, but I honestly never paid much attention to that side of things."

"I don't know either. Maybe they're parts for the paint factory. Could be any number of reasonable explanations for them."

"Agreed." Carver enjoyed a sip of tequila. "But then they threatened you. Obviously, something is going on there."

"It happened a few days ago. A bag over my head, and then I was in a dark room. Someone talked to me with a voice changer."

"Describe the room."

"Plexiglass walls. A camera and a speaker on the wall. A slot for food."

"The walls were clear?"

Ritter nodded. "Covered on the outside by curtains."

"What did the voice sound like?"

"Sometimes it sounded like movie celebrities. But the last guy just used a deep voice. He told me to keep quiet or my family would suffer. They'd let me live, if I did what they said."

"Tell me everything about your time there. What techniques did they use?"

Ritter rolled his neck back and forth like he was trying to work out a kink. "Nothing at all for hours. Just silence. There were these white noise generators that blanked out everything from the outside. I think they were lying to me about time of day and the duration of my incarceration." He finished off his tequila. "Someone punched my ribs when I was first there. Then I was tossed into the room."

"Then someone was real friendly to you after that? Offered you some water and food?"

"Yes, exactly." Ritter shivered. "I've seen enough movies to know it was a routine. But it works. And they made me crazy not telling me what time it was or how long I'd been there."

"Tell me exactly what they told you."

"They told me I'd be their inside man. If I did that, they'd reward me and then I could retire in peace. So, of course, I accepted."

"That's it?"

Ritter nodded. "Oh, and he said not to continue my investigation."

"Naturally." Carver spun his glass. "Have they asked you to do anything for them yet?"

He shook his head. "Not yet."

Carver took out Renee's phone. Downloaded a voice over IP app that gave him a burner number to use. "Contact me at this number when you find out."

Ritter frowned at the pink case. "That phone looks kind of girly for you."

"It's not my phone." Carver leaned back in his seat. He tried to imagine what Rhodes would do. Would she tell Ritter about the dead women? Would she give him some puzzle pieces to work out? Or would she realize the man was too scared for his family to do much of anything?

Carver settled on the last answer. Ritter was a man on the edge. He'd been taken by people who were proficient with interrogation and prisoner manipulation. They were the same techniques he'd used many a time. The same approach CIA operatives and military operatives took to breaking down a prisoner, so they'd cooperate.

Ritter hadn't taken much effort to break. He was just a small-town detective. Maybe he'd seen some wartime action, but that didn't make him capable of resisting interrogation. Hell, most ordinary grunts were no better than civilians at that. It was best just to let him be and hope he kept cooperating.

He was an edge piece to the puzzle. Definitely closer to the paint factory. Perched on a hill in his car, a book in one hand, binoculars in the other. Carver needed to visit that hill. It could potentially answer a lot of questions.

"How long were you casing the factory?"

"About a month."

"You watched it all day and all night?"

"No." He shook his head. "Just during the day."

Carver thought that was sloppy but kept it to himself. "You got bagged there or at another spot?"

Ritter drew an invisible line on the table with his finger. "The first hill was here." He traced the finger in a curve. "There's another dirt road that leads to a hill back here. I could see the loading docks from there. I was only there maybe for a week before they got me."

"Have you been back?"

"Hell no!" Ritter motioned to the bartender for another round.

"Tell me how to get there. Tell me as much as you know about the place."

Ritter told him. It wasn't much, but it was enough.

Carver polished off the tequila. "Keep your head down, Ritter." Then he left out the back of the bar. Climbed into the SUV and made his way to Factory Road. He took a roundabout way through the residential streets. Followed a pitted avenue to the highway that intersected Main Street in town.

Main Street was smooth and soundless beneath the SUV. About half a mile out, he turned onto another newly paved surface. Factory Road wended around the bottom of a small mountain. Or maybe it was a large hill. Carver found the dirt road Ritter mentioned. It was partially hidden by overgrowth on the outside of a curve. Most people would be looking toward the inside and miss it.

Carver pushed the SUV through the branches. They lightly scraped the sides. The road was rutted and partially washed out. He herded the car around the edge. More branches scraped the sides. He figured Ruben wouldn't mind.

The other side still had some gravel. The tires bit into it. He followed it around the hill and up to a flat spot about a hundred feet beneath the crest. Trees and bushes blocked the view. A small section had been cleared out by Ritter. He'd parked his sedan at that spot so he could see the mountains, fields, and valleys stretching into the distance.

Carver got out and enjoyed the view. A lush, green canopy covered the sides of the mountains. Houses were perched on the sides in some places, large structures. Easily visible from miles away. Most houses were small. Tucked beneath the trees, hidden from view. It seemed rich people liked to put their homes on full display.

If he had a house, he'd prefer to keep it hidden. Not standing naked on a cliff. Fully vulnerable to anyone who had a mind to target him. The right amount of structural stress could turn that home into a landslide.

Keep to the matter at hand. Rhodes's voice echoed in his head. Like a teacher chiding a student. She did that to him a lot.

Carver wished he had binoculars. He settled for his eyeballs. There was no railing. Just some logs arranged around the edge of the lookout. The tops of the trees below formed a natural barrier to keep the logs from rolling.

He went to the edge and had a clear view of Factory Road. It was about as straight as possible in this terrain. Parts of the hills had been blown up and carved out to make room. It ended at a guard shack. Tall fencing with razor wire stretched around the perimeter. The road continued on the other side for a short distance. Then it forked. One part curved left to a circular driveway in front of the factory business office.

The main road continued past the factory. It curved around the back. That was where the loading docks were. The factory was just a big rectangle. Nothing special about it. The exterior was gray. It looked clean. Almost new. Carver assumed they'd used that fancy paint on the building to keep it looking fresh.

A figure emerged from a side door. A woman with long dark hair. She sat on a chair and crouched over. Hands over her face. She stayed like that for almost fifteen minutes. Then she stood. Straightened her shoulders. Went back inside.

That was a person who looked stressed. Like they'd been dealing with a lot more than shades of paint. It was the body language of someone who was tied to a place they hated. Or they might just be having a bad day. Rhodes would be able to tell him in a heartbeat.

She'd also note that there was a garbage can and an ashtray near the chairs. This was a smoker's hangout. She might even mention that it looked unusually clean for a place where people came to smoke. Hardly anything in the trashcan. It was hard to tell if the ashtray was full or not.

Either it was cleaned regularly, or hardly anyone used the space. It seemed like it would be well used by factory workers. Smoking inside the paint factory couldn't be safe. Or maybe there was nothing flammable used in the paints. Carver didn't know enough about it to guess one way or the other.

"Overthinking as usual." Carver chided himself since Rhodes wasn't here to do it. He was trying too hard to build a scenario based on limited visual information. He didn't even have binoculars. This was probably the worse stakeout he'd ever conducted. There was too much riding on this to get it wrong.

He used the cell phone to find an outdoor gear shop. There were two of them to the south and a third to the north of town closer to the mountains the tourists preferred to hike. He hopped back in the car, navigated back to Factory Road, and headed out. A semitruck turned onto the road when he was a hundred yards from the stop sign.

The guy driving it was Caucasian. Stubbly beard, chubby in the face. Carver rolled down his window and waved him down. The truck ground to a stop. Carver looked up at him. "Hey, I'm lost. What's the best way back to town?"

The trucker barely thought about it. "Take a left at the stop sign and just follow it, buddy." He grinned. "You ain't got a cell phone with GPS?"

"It's broken." Carver shrugged. "I hardly know where I am right now."

"Yeah, I hardly know it half the time myself." The trucker laughed. "They tell me where to go and I just drive there."

"I'll bet." Carver made a show of looking at the truck. "How long of a haul has it been for you?"

"All the way from Florida, brother. Not too far, but far enough to make a dollar."

Carver whistled. "They must get all kinds of cargo from there."

"Yep. Europe, South America. This haul is from Brazil."

"First time to these parts?"

"First time to this place." The trucker nodded down the road. "The pay was too good to refuse even though it's one-way."

"One-way?"

"Yeah, full coming in, empty going out. I don't usually take those, but they offer full pay both ways and an on-time bonus, so ain't no way I'm passing that one up."

"Saves you gas on the return I'll bet."

"You bet it does, brother." The truck shifted. "Well, I gotta get on. Good luck finding town." He winked, grinned, and the truck labored forward.

"Thanks, brother." Carver hated the word even in this meaningless context. But he put on a grin and faked it.

Because now he knew for certain this place was generating a lot of money for a place that didn't distribute any paint.

CHAPTER 22

S omething shady was going on at the factory.

There was no question about that. The question was what? It didn't take much thought to connect South America and drugs. But you couldn't just send drugs on commercial ships and trucks. Could you? Maybe it was easier than Carver thought. The ships were massive, and the volume was so high that maybe it was impossible to stop smugglers.

Even so, it seemed terribly bold. The odds were high that a shipment would get intercepted, especially if they were sending enough to weigh down ten to twelve semitrucks a week. And what was in the crates? Weapons?

Carver pulled onto the road and headed to the northern gear store. It was a thirty-minute drive because nothing was close out here. It was all cow pastures, mountains, and clusters of small houses with rundown pickups parked on the grass.

He parked in front of the store and went inside. Grabbed some binoculars and a few other supplies. He stopped at the diner next door and had a quick meal. Paid for both places with cash. Then he went back toward town and stopped at a motel he'd passed on the way to the gear shop.

The clerk in the front wanted an ID. Carver gave him a fake name and fifty bucks to not worry about the ID. At first it didn't look like it was going to work. But then the guy pocketed the cash and gave him an actual key. Most motels didn't use the new keycard systems. That was why they were still reasonably priced.

Carver parked around the back of the building on the grass. He didn't want the SUV visible from the road. He walked around front. It was a single-story place with no breezeway.

It probably hadn't changed much from when it was built in the sixties or seventies. The furniture inside confirmed that. It was old, but clean enough.

He closed the curtains. Turned up the AC. Stripped down and took a shower. With the sweat and grime washed off, he put on a change of clothing. It looked about the same as the last, black cargos, black shirt. He checked the bag of goodies from the gear shop to make sure he had everything, then locked up the room and left.

On the drive back he kept a close eye on passing cars. Ruben's SUV was going to be a beacon for anyone who'd worked with him. Most people wouldn't give the car a second glance. He was looking for someone who did. Then he'd see if they followed him. Or came at him guns blazing.

They were probably desperate to kill him by now. No pretext of an accident. Just put as many holes in him as possible. Their careful phase was over. That didn't mean they'd be reckless, but out here in the middle of nowhere, they could kill someone and have no witnesses.

Carver passed a few cars going the other way. None of the drivers so much as glanced at the SUV. He took a turn on a county road about a mile before Factory Road. A couple hundred yards down, he turned on a gravel road. It was decently maintained for a distance. It turned rougher as it twisted through the hills.

It made a loop around a larger hill. Ritter's stakeout spot was about halfway up. The detective had parked his car in the grass. Hiked through a short section of forest. Camped out on a ledge overlooking the back side of the factory. Carver wondered if the people who snatched him just happened to find him here or if they regularly patrolled this road.

If they didn't want people snooping, they'd patrol the area. He kept driving. Another quarter mile down was a bare spot in the undergrowth. He steered offroad and pushed over some smaller bushes until the SUV was concealed behind foliage. It wasn't perfect, but someone would have to follow the same path to see it. He hoofed it back to Ritter's lookout. Opened his bag of goodies and got to work.

He set up fishing line in a hundred-foot perimeter. Hung bells on it. Anyone who tripped on the lines would ring the bells. Then he set up a camouflage blind right behind some bushes. It would conceal him from anyone approaching from the road. Between it and the bells, he'd have enough of a head start to avoid getting bagged.

Carver sat on the ledge and peered at the factory. The truck he'd passed on his way out was just pulling away from the loading dock. The door was down so he couldn't see inside. It was late in the afternoon so that was probably the last truck of the day. He settled in for the long haul. Set the binoculars on the tripod and angled it toward the target.

It would have been nice having a monocular with night vision. Maybe even a laser rangefinder, a windmeter, and his old Dragunov SVD. He'd claimed one as a trophy long ago. It wasn't the best sniping rifle he'd ever used, but it worked every time he pulled the trigger. Like many older Russian weapons, it was reliable.

He hadn't planned on shooting anyone from a distance today, but considering how his morning had gone, anything was possible.

The woman from earlier came outside again. Slumped on the chair, face in her hands. He zoomed the binoculars on her for a better look. She had olive skin. Dark hair. Almost certainly Brazilian. Her face appeared. Dark eyes stared desperately at the world outside the fence.

She was trapped in a cage. But it wasn't the fence keeping her in. It was fear. That was how cartels worked. You could leave anytime. But you wouldn't live long after you did. Once you joined their payroll they owned you.

The woman remained outside for fifteen minutes. Then she returned through the same door. Over the course of the next three hours, six workers went outside and smoked. All Caucasian. All probably locals. At five, a bell rang. The workers left. Piled into their cars in the rear parking lot and streamed out through the gate. Carver counted about fifty of them. Not a lot of people for a factory.

He stood and stretched. There were better ways of doing this. He just hadn't had the cash on hand to do it. High resolution cameras could watch the place all night and he could fast forward through the footage.

But he didn't have credit cards. He would have had to go to a bank. Used an ATM. That would have left a trail for someone to follow. Now was not the time to leave a trail.

He ate the field rations he'd purchased. Chased them down with lukewarm black coffee from a thermos. Hiked back out to the road, crossed it, and took a leak on the other side. Then he went back to his spot and sat down.

The sun didn't set until almost nine. A little after dark settled in, a door at the far end of the loading dock opened. It was the only rollup door that was level with the ground. The others were set up a few feet to match the height of the semitruck trailers.

A high-roof van pulled out. It was black, windowless, and unmarked. Carver zoomed in with the binoculars. They didn't have night vision, but the back of the factory was lit. It was too dark inside the van's cabin to see the driver. The van drove down Factory Road. The taillights were the only thing visible after a few seconds. They turned right.

A few minutes later, another van pulled out. Carver tried again to view the driver, but it was too dark. Another van followed moments later. Then another. The cabin light was on in the sixth van. Carver saw an olive-skinned man at the wheel. He had a scar on his cheek. The same dead look in his eyes that the Brazilian boys had.

They were the distribution team. But what were they distributing?

By the time the rollup door closed, eleven vans had left for parts unknown. Certainly not enough to distribute the amount of paint that had arrived on two semitrucks. Or maybe eleven trucks were just enough to distribute the paint. But why had they waited until this late to ship out?

Carver didn't know much about logistics. Other people usually took care of that. He certainly couldn't estimate shipping capacity for paint. There was only one way to find out more. He wasn't set up to do that tonight, though. This was just for collecting information.

The woman came outside one last time at midnight. She took a little longer than earlier before going inside. No one else came out. No more vans either. No one drove down the road he'd used to reach his lookout. If it was patrolled, it wasn't a regular thing.

Dawn eventually kissed the mountains on the horizon, and it was time to go. Carver packed up and went back to the SUV. He went back to the motel. Parked in back. Went inside and slept for four hours. At nine in the morning, he returned to the diner near the gear shop for breakfast. Then he purchased more rations from the gear shop.

He felt pretty good. Four hours was plenty of sleep for him. Six hours was optimal. Anything more was just lazy. He had a lot to do today. No time to sleep in.

Carver hopped in the SUV and navigated it toward the factory. He returned to the lookout spot and hid the car. Settled in behind the camouflage blind. Watched and waited. He took out Renee's cell phone. Scrolled through all the apps. There was a locked app called Vault. It required a fingerprint to unlock. His didn't work. Apparently, the app used its own stored biometrics. Not the ones used to unlock the phone.

It piqued his interest. The name implied it was like a safe. What was hiding in the safe? Certainly not money. The banking app relied on the phone's biometric credentials. What kind of secrets did Renee have?

He'd seen similar apps before. Some people used them to store passwords. Some to store extortion material. Top secret information. Account numbers for anonymous banks. Everyone from CEOs, to sheiks, to middle managers used similar apps. Most of them used complex passwords to guard them, not fingerprints. It was too easy to kidnap someone and use them to bypass biometrics.

If the wrong password was used too many times, the app would destroy the information inside. No one could recover it then, not even the best techs. More often than not, the information wasn't recovered without intense interrogation. Most people would give up the password eventually. Those who didn't usually died from the questioning.

Renee had used her fingerprint. The information she'd hidden couldn't be all that valuable. But it was certainly worth a look.

A black high-top van turned onto Factory Road. Slowed at the front gate. The guard opened it without checking a badge. The van continued around the back. The driver looked Latino. Probably Brazilian. A solid panel behind the driver blocked the view of the cargo space. There were no windows on the side. The back windows were too darkly tinted to see through.

Carver noted the time. Another van arrived an hour later. The next van was half an hour behind. The vans trickled in all morning. The last one arrived just after lunch. The drivers all looked Brazilian. Almost certainly not locals. Almost certainly not factory workers.

He took out a paper map of Atlanta and surrounding areas. Flattened it on the ground and started plotting points. The trucks had been gone all night. Had they been driving that entire time, or had they stopped to rest? The first van had been gone eleven hours. The second one twelve hours. He calculated the travel time to their destinations by dividing the total time in half.

Without a plotter, a protractor, and a straight edge, he relied on the phone's map app to calculate destinations. He checked driving time to various places. There were plenty of big cities within the travel radius. That was assuming the vans arrived somewhere and dropped all their cargo in one place. They might have multiple stops. But it gave Carver a rough idea of where they'd been.

Nashville, Charlotte, Chattanooga were all possible destinations. They were prime cities for drug distribution. It was interesting information but hardly the main thing Carver was interested in.

The factory side door opened, and the woman emerged for the third time of the day. She was crying this time. Her face looked fine. No bruising. No signs of physical abuse. Either this woman hated her job, or she didn't like what was going on inside.

Carver studied the layout of the building. There were large vents along the roof, all closed. They were probably for emergency venting in case of chemical fumes. They were possible points of ingress.

He'd searched the internet for the inner workings of a paint factory and found very little useful information. That meant gathering what he could from a detailed visual inspection. He hiked the forest perimeter. Examined the building from all angles. Looked for weaknesses in security.

There were four emergency exits along the rear of the building. Ten loading dock doors. Two emergency exits along the side of the building. Cameras above each of the loading dock doors.

The south side with the break area had five cameras. Enough to ensure there were no blind spots. The front and north side had enough cameras to ensure total coverage as well. The cameras near the corners of the building were angled just enough to cover any diagonal approach. All except for the northeastern corner. That was because the camera over the tenth rollup door the vans used was looking straight down. It wasn't angled to cover the corner. The camera on the northern side wasn't angled enough to see a diagonal approach.

It was the only weakness in the camera coverage he could find. Maybe it would be enough. Maybe it wouldn't. Finding out the hard way might be the only option.

Carver waited out the day. Watched the same pattern unfold. The woman sat outside for ten to fifteen minutes every two hours. The bell rang at five. The workers got in their cars and left. Just before nightfall, Carver drove the SUV to the highway and parked on the side, lights off. Headlights appeared on Factory Road.

The first van turned onto the county road. Its taillights vanished over a hill. Carver pulled onto the road, headlights off. He gunned the SUV and reached the hill. Saw the taillights in the distance. He followed it for miles. It eventually reached a more populated area. He turned on his headlights after the van went around a curve. He kept following it. The van turned onto a highway, then the interstate. Turned north.

It pulled into a mechanic shop in a small town about two hours later. Carver parked across the road at a strip mall and watched through binoculars.

The driver parked next to a gray sedan. He opened the back doors. Pulled out a medium-sized box. Loaded it into the sedan's trunk. He followed that with four more boxes. Closed the van and got into the sedan. Steered back onto the highway, the interstate, and continued northeast.

Four boxes didn't seem like much cargo. It certainly wasn't paint. Probably bricks of cocaine. Carver tried to calculate how many kilos it weighed, but that wasn't his specialty. It was probably a lot. He didn't even know how much a kilo sold for. Probably ten to twenty grand each if he had to guess.

The driver left the interstate just outside Charlotte. Pulled into a rundown area. Stopped at a bar. He went inside. Carver parked right next to him. Got out and stretched his legs. He went to the window and looked inside. The driver was at the bar, drink in hand.

This was going to work out just fine.

CHAPTER 23

Carver went to his goody bag. Pulled out a slim piece of metal. He went to the driver's car and slid the metal between the passenger window and door frame. Angled it up and felt it catch a rod inside. He lifted it. The lock popped up. He opened the glove box and popped the trunk.

The four boxes inside the trunk weren't sealed with tape. The flaps were folded in against each other. He lifted a flap and checked inside. There they were. Four clear-wrapped bricks of white. So typical. He was probably looking at close to half a million in street value.

There was a rock on the ground. It was about as thick as a brick of cocaine. The packages were stacked four deep. Carver pulled out one row. Put the rock on the bottom. Put three packages back inside. They were about even with the other packages. He folded the flaps back, closed the trunk. Closed the car doors.

Carver climbed into the SUV and backed it into a parking place on the side of the building. Then he went inside the bar. The driver was at a table talking to four people. They were all drinking. Empty shot glasses were on the table in front of them. It looked like a party.

There were three men, one woman. Various ages. The oldest looked forty, and the woman looked the youngest, probably in her twenties. They had tattoos, piercings. Nice clothes. The woman was Latina. Two men were white, one was black.

Carver sat at the bar. Ordered a beer. He leaned back and watched the driver's table. The group ordered more shots. Downed them. Then the driver paid the bill. Chairs scraped the floor. They stood. Walked toward the door.

The driver and friends went outside. Carver tucked a twenty under his beer then went out after them. He turned right outside and went to the side parking. Hopped in his car. The Brazilian and his friends were huddled together around his car. The driver handed out boxes, one to each person. The others took the boxes and put them in the trunks of nondescript cars. They were probably burner cars. Picked up from a cash lot. Fake registration. These people were dressed too nicely to have cars like this.

The other drivers slid into their cars and left. The Brazilian guy leaned against his car. Lit a cigarette and smoked it. He made a phone call. Spoke a moment and ended the call. Finished his smoke and climbed into the car.

There was no real reason to follow him, but Carver did anyway. The guy went to a motel. Knocked on a door. A scantily clad woman answered. He handed her cash and went inside. Apparently, he was done with his job. The other drivers would distribute the rest of the cocaine.

There was nothing special about this drug operation. Nothing he could see, anyway. They apparently had an effective way to get the drugs into the United States. Delivered them to the factory. The factory distributed them from there. Nice and simple.

Rhodes had probably discovered the operation. Gotten into their business. They'd found out and killed her. Tried to frame Carver and everything had blown up.

Carver had no obligation to Rhodes. No duty to keep up the investigation. Punish those responsible. That was for the cops to handle. But these people tried to use him as a scapegoat. They'd tried to kill him on multiple occasions.

It was just business. Smart business. Don't leave loose ends unattended. Carver understood that all too well. Killing and survival was his bread and butter. A trade he was well-versed in. The cartel was trying to handle a problem. This time, the problem was going to handle them.

Plain and simple, the cartel had messed with someone capable. They'd tried to frame Carver for the death of a former friend. A brother in arms. It just rubbed him the wrong way. Made his hackles stand on end.

If he'd come to town and found out Rhodes was dead, he'd have gone to her funeral, said a few words, and gone back to minding his own business. But now he aimed to stick around and make a point about messing with the wrong person.

He just had to figure out the best way to go about it. And he didn't have the tactical genius of Rhodes to plan it out. Carver wasn't the kind to sit down and make big plans. He just winged it most of the time. This was not a time to be winging it.

He started the SUV and headed back to Morganville, a kilo of cocaine on the passenger seat. He wondered who would get the blame for the missing brick. The Brazilian guy, or the delivery boy who'd taken it. One of them wasn't going to survive. Cartels didn't survive by being forgiving when product went missing.

Carver mulled over the situation while he drove. He mapped out the organization in his head. Top of the chain was Brilhante Tintas in Brazil. They bought out Whittaker Paint, saved them from oblivion, and turned them into a distribution point. Jasper Whittaker was probably living high on the hog thanks to them.

Whittaker Paint had a skeleton crew of locals. Just enough to make it look like they were doing some business. Clearly, they weren't doing much. The Brazilian delivery boys were the hidden muscle. The pair who'd tried to kill him were probably part of that crew. Or they might've been contracted out.

The military guys were contracted locals. No way they were involved in the drugs. It was just easier to use Americans as witnesses to frame Carver. Ruben probably pulled the trigger on Rhodes. He probably came up with the idea to use Carver as the scapegoat.

Somehow, they'd known Rhodes asked Carver to come see her. She'd probably talked to someone she trusted. Probably Settler. Holly thought he was a good guy. Maybe Rhodes had too. But then Settler had told the paint company. They'd seen the opportunity to clean up the mess before it went too far.

As far as Carver was concerned, the local facility would be the one to pay the price. There was no way he was skipping down to Brazil looking for blood. He just wasn't the guy to do that. But his honor would be satisfied by killing the top brass at the local facility. That would send a message to Brilhante Tintas. *Don't mess with me.*

Carver nodded to himself. It was good enough. He'd fade back into anonymity at another beach. If the Brazilians decided to come looking for him, then, and only then, would he take a trip south.

The reality on the ground was that he couldn't go away now. They were actively hunting him. If he just ran, that would only encourage them. It was like showing fear to a pack of wild dogs. They could smell it. They'd track your scent. Corner you. Attack. You had to put down the lead dog to stand a chance. Then the others would back off. Then you'd be safe.

By the time he reached his motel, he had a decent plan cooked up. It couldn't compare to anything designed by Rhodes, but it might be good enough to keep him alive and earn her and him some payback.

DORSEY FIRED THE Barrett fifty cal.

The watermelon downrange exploded. "That'll be his head." Dorsey was on his stomach. Eye to the scope. The bipod held up the barrel. "No one will ask questions. They'll still pin her death on the drifter."

Tony ran a hand down his face. "Look, I know you want to do this, but this isn't a game. It's already risky using our own assets for this."

Dorsey pushed up to his knees. Rose to his feet. "He must have run. That's why they can't find him."

"I don't think he ran. He's nearby, trying to figure out what's going on."

"If he runs, what then? We manufacture another perp?"

"He won't run. We can find another perp to use. It might fly. But I promise that this guy will be the best one to take the blame. His profile, everything fits."

Dorsey ran a hand along the fifty cal. "You think the new SUVs could handle a bullet from this? I kind of want to test it."

Tony shrugged. "Probably. But do you really want to shoot up a million-dollar armored SUV?"

"I'd like to know the armor works." Dorsey's phone buzzed. He glanced at the screen. "The Senate is voting tonight. Almost there."

Tony nodded. "We should have the votes now."

Dorsey grinned. "Just barely. But barely is still enough. Sam came through with that final holdout."

"I told you he would." Tony hated politicians. Their weaknesses were usually money and power. Promise them more of one or the other and they usually played along. But sometimes you had a self-righteous ass who didn't play by those rules. Senator Mancini was one of those.

Thankfully, Tony and Sam knew how and where to apply pressure. The same kind of pressure used to control people like Ritter. That pressure was in the form of Mancini's pregnant daughter. Sam had had fun with her and sent video proof to her father. Mancini had finally caved.

The huge spending bill had a lot of components in it. A lot of big interests. Sam was pretending he was with the oil companies. It was good camouflage. That way Dorsey's firm couldn't be fingered for the kidnapping.

Dorsey was a good talker. He could sway people with words. But he was a lot better at swaying them with money. The House votes were already in line thanks to him and Tony. But Dorsey was an absolute disaster when it came to strategy. He kept pushing out idea after idea about how to handle the Morganville situation. All he was pushing out were turds.

On the other hand, Tony was getting irritated by the silence from his men on the ground. These were seasoned vets. Meticulous professionals. They'd taken out plenty of hard targets. Targets much harder than the one they had now. And yet, they'd been there almost two days without results.

Was Tony going to have to get involved again? Would he have to risk a visit to the town? He was Dorsey's right-hand man. Highly visible. If something went wrong, it would all fly back in their faces. Hell, his last visit had been dumb enough. But it had been worth it. It still brought a grin to his face.

The local cops were going nuts. One of their own had been killed. Two other bodies had been found with the dead cop. Supposed witnesses to the murder of Chief Rhodes. They didn't have the resources to handle this. And when they found the dead women, it was going to grow even bigger. The feds would probably get involved. The tiny town would light up like a beacon. Things would be discovered, and all of Tony's planning would be ruined.

Carver was the perfect fall guy. His death would tie up all the loose ends. The feds wouldn't get involved. Law enforcement would settle back down. There would be some funerals, a small town in mourning, and then silence. If the voting went as planned, then the end of this week would pave the way to the future for the company Tony envisioned.

Dorsey watched as a young intern put watermelons on the pedestals at the end of the range. He mimicked aiming. Firing. "Boom. Pink mist."

Tony had seen him do it for real. But that was on foreign soil and in secret. If he flew off the handle and tried to down Carver himself, it was going to be a mess. He had to figure out how to keep this idiot under control before everything went south.

CARVER FIGURED OUT how he was going to do it.

The cameras were a problem. Not knowing what was waiting inside the loading docks was a bigger problem. He could get inside, but he'd be taking a big risk. Still, it was the best he could come up with.

First, he had some time sensitive errands to run. He went back to Renee's house. The bodies were still there undiscovered. The smell was stronger than ever. He wore a pair of latex gloves so he wouldn't leave prints. He also wore bags over his shoes.

He tapped on the vault app and put Renee's finger on it. It didn't open. He tried all her fingers. None worked. He tried all her toes. Same result. He boiled a pot of water on the stove. Let it cool a little, then dipped the fingers inside to give them some ambient heat. To ensure that the cold flesh was warm enough to activate the sensor. He'd had to use that tactic before. It always worked.

This time it didn't work. None of her fingerprints or toeprints unlocked the app. Carver warmed up Charlotte's prints and tried with her. No success. He already knew it wouldn't unlock with his prints. And now he knew it wouldn't self-destruct after a certain number of tries. But whose fingerprint unlocked it?

He got Charlotte's phone. Unlocked it with her fingerprint. She had the same app on her phone. He went through the process. Tried her prints and Renee's prints. None worked. It was damned peculiar. Why would someone have an app on their phone they couldn't open or use? Maybe it had something to do with the payments they were getting from the DoD.

He knew of women who'd gotten settlements from the DoD for sexual harassment. Maybe these two had served. Maybe something had happened to them. Now they were being paid hush money. That still didn't explain the vault app.

He couldn't change Charlotte's biometrics, but he needed to keep her phone. He went into the kitchen. Emptied the pot of water and put the pot back in place. Then he found a small thermos container. He opened the freezer. Found some artificial blue ice cubes inside. He fit a few inside the container.

There was a knife block on the counter. He took the cleaver. Went to Charlotte's body and removed the index finger. It was like cutting wood. No blood. He put the finger in the container with the artificial ice. Closed it. Rinsed off the cleaver. Put it back. Aside from the missing finger, nothing had changed. The crime scene was mostly preserved.

This had been a failed side mission. No new answers, just more questions. So, now what? Push ahead with the primary objective or waste more time? Because that's what it felt like he was doing. He was trying to be thorough. To pretend he'd planned everything out to the last detail. He was trying to be someone he wasn't—Rhodes.

Carver had to admit he felt lost. Like an ancient ship at sea on a cloudy night. No way to navigate by the stars. Only a vague notion of speed, direction, and course to guide him. All he had to go by were a scant few facts, a few observations, and a gut feeling.

Sailors called it dead reckoning.

The dead reckoning of a man like him was only useful for so much. But now everything was riding on it.

CHAPTER 24

Carver returned to town. He parked the SUV out of sight and walked to the police station. The lobby was empty, but there was a loud murmur echoing through Maberly's office from the back room.

Maberly looked harried. He was typing on his computer, a frantic look in his eyes. He glanced up at Carver. "What—what are you doing here? Why are you still in town?"

"Holly here?"

He blinked a few times while his brain registered the question. "Yes. But she's busy."

"I need to talk to her."

Maberly grunted. Rotated in his chair and shouted out of his door. "Holly, that Carver guy is here."

The door opened a moment later. Holly gave Carver a look and walked past him, outside. He followed her. She walked around the corner of the building and stopped. "Where have you been?"

"Here and there." Carver shrugged. "How's the investigation going?"

"The medical examiner said the men died violently. Two had broken knees. One looked like he almost choked to death but his neck was snapped. Two had blunt force trauma to the head."

Carver nodded. "Yeah, that'll kill a man, all right."

"But who would do that? Was it punishment for not killing you?"

"Probably." Carver leaned against a patrol car. "I did some digging into the paint factory. Looks like they're distributing cocaine out of there."

Her mouth dropped open. "What? Why didn't you lead with that?"

"It adds context to the situation." He looked around. "I figure Rhodes was investigating it. They got wind of it and had her killed. They knew she'd asked me to come to town, so they figured I was the perfect fall guy."

"How are they doing it? How did you find out?" Holly paced back and forth. "I have so many questions."

Carver gave her the gist of it. Told her about following the driver.

"You took a brick of cocaine?"

He nodded. "I don't know why. Just seemed like the thing to do."

She pursed her lips. "It's almost like you want to sow chaos."

"Maybe."

"Well, in either case, it's evidence."

"It's nothing." Carver booted a pinecone. "Anyway, I came to talk to you so you could get me inside."

Holly went still. "You want me to take you inside the paint factory? How am I supposed to do that?"

"You're a cop, right?"

"Last time I checked."

"I had a few ideas about getting inside, but this way seemed best."

She looked at him hard. "Me taking you inside seems best? What other cocked up schemes did you have for getting inside?"

"Riding on the top of a semitruck, but the cameras would see me. Other way was to sneak into one of the delivery vans, but there's nowhere to hide inside." Carver went to the next on his list. "Steal a van, but the guard would realize I'm not Brazilian."

"Explain how I get you inside."

"In the trunk of your cruiser. Needs to be at night."

Holly kept staring at him. "On what pretext?"

Carver shrugged. "Just say Rhodes had a note to meet with someone out there but you don't know what it was about. So, you wanted to ask them."

"Well, that's not a bad reason. I could use it to break the news that Rhodes is dead."

"They already know she is. They're the ones who ordered the hit."

"Yes, but they don't know we know." Her fists clenched. "Carver, what do you plan to do when you're inside?"

"Find some answers. Maybe let them know I didn't appreciate them trying to kill me."

"That worries me. Aren't there enough dead people in this town already? I think Morganville's population dropped by half in two days."

"It's time for a reckoning, Holly." Carver tried to look sympathetic, but he didn't really know how to. "There are millions of dollars in drugs funneling through that paint factory. That's why it's never going to produce more paint or fully recover. Because they don't want it to. They want a minimum number of locals working there. Everyone else is working for a cartel, including Jasper Whittaker."

Holly showed her teeth. "That fat bastard ruined this town. God knows he's done even worse since then, but he's untouchable. The mayor won't let us near him."

"I keep hearing about this mayor, but I haven't seen the guy." Carver glanced toward City Hall. "Where does he live?"

"About a mile outside of town. You passed by his property when you were walking into town."

Carver thought about the hill with the lookout. The big mansion on the hill. "That big house on the mountain?"

"Yes. He owns a thousand acres. He used to live in town in a small house. But when the town died and everyone started leaving, he suddenly started buying up property. He owns most of downtown now too."

"That smells funny."

"I always wondered where he got the money from. Maybe now we know."

Carver thought about it. "The Brazilians probably paid him to look the other way. That's why the police force here is so small. Probably a lot of people on the take. Hell, I'm surprised they didn't offer you something."

"Why would they?" Holly laughed. "Not like I can do anything. Plus, the fewer the people who know, the better."

The paint factory was the source, but who was the town boss? Carver's compass was swinging back and forth between Jasper and the mayor.

Maberly walked into the front parking lot. He looked at Holly's cruiser. Looked toward town, then glanced back. He spotted Holly and Carver on the side of the building. "Oh, I thought you'd left."

Holly shook her head. "You need something, Maberly?"

"Mayor's coming to town. He wants an all-hands meeting. I wanted to make sure you hadn't left."

"Goodness. Old Buck Morgan is blessing us with his presence?"

"That he is." Maberly chuckled. "I ain't seen the old coot in a while. Not sure I want to see him again."

Holly dismissed him with a wave. "Okay, I'll stick around."

"Good enough." Maberly went back inside.

Holly walked to a big oak tree with a concrete bench underneath it. She sat down. "Carver, I can't drive you into the paint factory. I won't be a party to whatever scheme you've cooked up. I'm going to call the FBI."

Carver sat next to her. "I know you think that's the right thing to do, but do you really think an operation this big could survive so long just because the local PD are looking the other way? There are other players in this game. Might even be some FBI agents on the payroll. If you make that phone call, you'll just be putting yourself in the crosshairs."

She shook her head. "I don't believe it."

"You don't, or you just don't want to believe it?"

"I don't know." She stared at the ground. "Why am I still in this town? Everything here is rotten to the core. And it's all because of Jasper."

"Okay, so let me clean it up."

"You just want revenge."

"Not revenge. Safety. They tried to kill me, Holly. They'll keep on trying unless I put a stop to it."

"What is wrong with you, Carver?" She peered into his eyes as if she might find a soul. She flinched. "It's like you're dead inside."

"I assure you, I'm alive."

"Do you feel happiness? Sadness? You're like a stone."

He smiled. "Are you a therapist or a cop?"

"Just explain to me how you can be so matter of fact about exacting vigilante justice. Because that's what you're doing."

"I've been doing stuff like that all my life, Holly. I did it as a kid and I did it for the US government." Carver chuckled. "Funny thing is, I found happiness after the worst day of my life. I realized there was no need to do it for me or for anyone else."

"I really want to know about the worst day of your life. Did someone shoot your dog?"

"Happened once when I was a kid. It wasn't really my dog, though. Just a stray."

"And that was your worst day?"

"No. My worst day was getting the boot from the military. From my unit. All of us got the boot. The unit was completely disbanded."

"What happened?" She huffed. "Let me guess. It's classified."

"We had to sign NDAs to keep our benefits." Carver shrugged. "Well, the others did. I was denied benefits."

Holly put a hand to her forehead. "You did something, didn't you? Killed someone you weren't supposed to? Maybe assassinated the leader of another country?"

"No, nothing like that. You're kind of right, though. They thought I did something." Carver laughed. "Funny thing is, what I was blamed for doing looked like schoolyard play compared to the things they tasked me with doing."

"Then why won't you tell me what happened?"

"Maybe I will sometime when this is over." Carver stood. "Are you going to help me get into the paint factory?"

"I can't, okay?" Holly stared at the ground. "I just can't."

"Fair enough. Just don't call the feds, okay? I took a risk by telling you because I thought you'd help me. But I don't want to be responsible for something happening to you."

"I'll think about it."

Rhodes once got his team inside a facility using a bribed cop. Carver had thought it would work for this situation even without a bribe. Holly was supposedly on his side now. But it hadn't worked. If anything, it had backfired. Now she might call the FBI and that would put a stop to his plans real quick.

Relying on people he didn't know or trust was usually a no-fly zone for him. Letting his guard down and trying to talk Holly into this just proved he couldn't persuade people with words. He was only good at persuading people with hard tactics. Now he just had to hope she didn't do something stupid.

"Don't look so worried, Carver. I won't do anything stupid, okay? Let's find more facts before you go blowing up half the town."

"Yeah, you're right." Carver decided it was tonight or nothing. Holly would sleep on it tonight and wake up feeling like she had to call the FBI. She seemed like the sort who tried to do the right thing. She'd had a good upbringing. He liked her for that. But good people needed bad people to protect them. That was just the way of life.

She smiled. Touched his arm. "Thanks."

A sleek black Tesla rolled into the parking lot. It stopped in front of the police station and the back doors swung up like the wings of a bird. A man in a teal suit swung his legs out of the back seat and stood. He looked like he was in his mid to late fifties, but in good shape. He had short gray hair. A ruggedly handsome face. He was grinning and had a twinkle in his eye.

The driver stayed in the car, but Carver got a good look at him. Black suit. Short hair. He had the look of a bodyguard about him. Probably former military, but it was hard to say without seeing the way he handled himself..

Holly whistled. "New ride for the old man."

"His name is Buck Morgan?"

She nodded.

"I'm guessing the town is named after his family."

"His great-great grandfather had something to do with that. There's a plaque with the history at City Hall if you're interested."

"I'm not." Carver watched the mayor stride down the sidewalk like royalty.

The mayor saw Holly and waved. "Hey there, young lady." He had a friendly voice. Like someone you could trust. "Who's your friend?"

Carver didn't believe for a moment that the mayor didn't know who he was.

"Well, it's a long story, Buck." She smiled and walked over to him. "Love the new car. And this suit goes great with your eyes."

"Aw, this old thing?" He hooked his arm in hers. "I thought I'd try something different."

Carver backed away, but the mayor beckoned him.

"Mr. Carver, why don't you come inside? I feel like you're as much a part of this thing as anyone else."

Carver kept backing away. "I've got a hair appointment."

"Oh, but I insist." Buck's voice went from friendly to threatening in a heartbeat.

Holly kept on a forced grin. "I think we've put him through enough, Buck."

"He's material to this, so I'd like him inside."

Carver didn't feel like making a scene. Plus, the mayor was obviously part of the problem in this town, so now was as good a time as any to get to know him. "I'd be happy to help any way I can, Mr. Buck."

Buck's right eye twitched. "After you, Mr. Carver."

"Just Carver." Carver went inside. The door to the back room was open, so he passed by Maberly's empty office and found the place about as full as he'd ever seen it. Davis, Ritter, Maberly, and a skinny white guy with a mullet were there.

Davis frowned. "What the hell are you doing waltzing in here?"

"Mr. Buck wanted me here." Carver sat on the edge of an empty desk. "Guess we'll find out why together."

The mayor entered and Maberly closed the door behind him. Everyone stood in a loose circle facing the front of the room.

Buck stood at the front in his teal suit, a friendly smile on his face. It looked real enough, but his eyes told another story. "My friends and colleagues, we have suffered a great tragedy.

My heart goes out to you on the loss of two members of our law enforcement family. Chief Rhodes and Officer Settler will be greatly missed."

Davis glared at Carver. Holly glanced his way. Ritter refused to even look his way.

The mullet guy nodded and wiped tears from his eyes. "I can't hardly believe it, Mayor. Who did it?"

"That's a good question, Jesse."

"The prime suspect is right there." Davis jabbed a finger at Carver. "Two witnesses placed him at the scene."

"Thing is, I checked his alibi," Holly said. "There's no way he could've been at the old Miller cabin during the chief's time of death. Medical examiner backed that up. The bus driver corroborated Carver's story."

"That and this man was in jail when the witnesses and Settler were killed," Ritter said. "It's obvious someone has a vendetta against this police department."

"My God!" Jesse trembled. "You think we're next, Ritter?"

"I'm hoping it's over." Ritter shook his head. "But I don't know. We just have to be vigilant."

Buck held out his hands. "Okay, simmer down, y'all." He turned to Holly. "I want to see the reports so we can verify Mr. Carver has an ironclad alibi."

"I think being in jail when the others were killed is about as ironclad as it gets, Mayor." Holly made a face. "Seems obvious whoever killed Rhodes also killed the others."

Davis rubbed his hands on his pants like he was drying the sweat off. "I guess being in jail does make it hard to commit murder."

"Fine, so Mr. Carver is out as a suspect." Buck looked agitated. Like he'd hoped to find some reason to lock up Carver again. "I just want you all to know that I have absolute faith you can find the culprits and bring them to justice."

Holly looked like she was trying not to laugh.

Jesse was crying again and nodding. "Amen, Mayor. We'll get whoever did this, God Almighty willing."

Davis sat on the edge of his desk. He was sulking or maybe wishing he could take a drink. Sweat beaded on his forehead. It was probably ninety proof perspiration.

Ritter glanced uneasily at Carver, then at the mayor, and then at the floor. Maberly stood near the door. He stared vacantly at his closed office. Like he wished he could just sit down. Or maybe he wanted the bag of potato chips next to the keyboard.

Buck nodded toward the interview room. "Mr. Carver, I'd like a word in private."

Carver pushed off the desk and went into the room. He sat at the far end of the table facing the door. Buck followed him in a moment later and closed the door behind him. He walked almost to the end and sat down one chair away from Carver.

His friendly demeanor evaporated. "Why are you in my town, boy?"

CHAPTER 25

The mayor looked like he wanted to gut Carver.

Carver wasn't worried. "You can just call me Carver."

The mayor stared at him darkly. "Answer the question."

"I heard it was a great tourist destination for hiking."

"Is that why you're here?"

"Yep. Lots of hiking." Carver maintained eye contact. "You get plenty of tourists through here. Why am I any different than the others?"

"I think you know why."

"I don't. Why don't you tell me?"

"I'd like you to be a guest at my home, Mr. Carver. You can tell me all about your hiking plans."

"I prefer staying in town. It's closer to the mountains."

Buck pressed his lips together. "You're staying at the hotel?"

"Yes, but I think this will be my last night." If things went as planned tonight, the last part of his statement would be true.

"That might be for the best." Buck stood. "Enjoy your hike, Mr. Carver." He left the room.

Carver went back out to the office area. Holly was talking to Jesse. Seemed like she was trying to comfort him. She saw Carver and patted Jesse on the shoulder. Left him and gave Carver a look like she wanted him to follow her. Then she went out the door to the lobby.

Carver went to Jesse. "What do you do around here?"

Jesse looked him up and down, uncertainty plain in his eyes. "I manage the motor pool. I keep the cars maintained and if they need a mechanic, I coordinate with them for repairs."

"That's an important job."

The other man looked pleased. "Yes, and so many people don't realize it!"

"Keep up the good work." Carver nodded at him then went out to the lobby. Holly wasn't there. He went outside and found her on the sidewalk. Buck's Tesla was pulling onto Main Street already.

"What did Buck want with you?"

Carver told her what he'd said. "The man's crooked as they come, Holly."

"Obviously. Him and his son are rotten to the core." She watched the Tesla vanish into town. "Why would he invite you to stay with him?"

"Probably so he can stage my death. Make it look like a hunting accident or something."

Holly frowned. "You say that so calmly."

"It's the truth. I go out there, suffer some kind of accident." Carver had a feeling there were more military types out at the mayor's. He was probably the guy who'd hired Ruben and pals to take care of the Rhodes situation.

Figuring out that connection made Carver feel almost competent. Buck Morgan and Jasper Whittaker had conspired to get rid of Rhodes so they could protect the goose laying golden eggs. They'd failed and the Brazilians had gotten involved. That made things a little more complicated, but Carver figured he could fit it onto his busy schedule.

"I think the FBI is the best next step." Holly grabbed his wrist. "You're in the clear, Carver. Let's keep it that way, okay? It's time to bump this up the food chain."

"If you call the FBI, all this will get swept under the rug. The paint factory will get advanced warning. They'll shut down drug distribution. The feds will show up, look around, and get pissed that you wasted their time. It's like the kid who cried wolf. Then they'll find out you called them, threaten your life or outright kill you, and go right back to business."

"My dad knew a guy there. I can call him."

"You trust him with your life?"

"Damn it, Carver, before you started running your mouth, I thought I could trust the FBI with my life. Now I'm feeling as paranoid as you are."

"Good. You've got good intentions, but you're going to get yourself killed." Carver walked to the oak tree and the concrete bench. "Just lay low and let me check things out, okay? Maybe there's a better way to bring them down."

"I'll get you inside the paint factory. You can take pictures and find more proof."

"I changed my mind about that." Carver had been giving his plan a lot more thought. If he used Holly to get inside, they'd know she helped him. If something went wrong, she'd die along with him. "I'm not going inside just yet."

"Okay." She frowned. "What are you planning to do then?"

"I don't know yet." He leaned on the oak tree. "I'll let you know, okay? In the meantime, keep your head down and your eyes open."

"Thanks for making me paranoid, Carver."

"You're welcome." He noticed a guy standing at the corner of the abandoned hardware store on Main Street. The guy was looking at him with a monocular. Carver pretended not to notice. He couldn't make out the guy's face, but his shirt was light blue and said *Blue Ridge Mountains* on it. He knew that because he'd seen the guy wearing it yesterday.

That guy had been with one of the groups of tourists who caught his attention. It only confirmed the connection between the mayor and the military freelancers. The mayor had sent them to town looking for him. If he'd accepted the invitation to the mayor's house, a whole squad of freelancers would've taken him down.

Holly sighed and looked at the police department. "Well, I'd better get inside and pretend that I'm looking for the killer."

"Good idea. Play the dutiful police officer." Carver turned and walked down the road away from town. He'd parked the SUV around the fence. He could feel the guy with the monocular watching him all the way.

A small dirt road connected with the next street over. Carver turned the car around and headed that way. He made his way north on the backroads until he was at a motel a few miles northeast of the paint factory. The clerk inside didn't give him any guff about an ID. He just typed the fake name Carver gave him into the computer and handed him a key to the end unit.

Carver parked behind the motel and went into his room. It smelled like a badly cleaned ashtray, but that was the norm for places like this. He lay down on the bed and let his mind unwind for a few minutes. Tried not to think about anything. Just kept his mind nice and empty. He was pretty good at that. Not thinking about anything for hours at a time was something he'd learned in the field.

Then he got up and accessed Renee's cell phone. Opened the map app and zoomed in on the paint factory. He switched to satellite mode. All sides were watched by cameras. The cameras had night vision, but that didn't matter. The area around the building was well lit. Lights on the side of the building illuminated up to fifty feet. The streetlamps extended that to about a hundred feet.

The chain link fence wasn't electrified but the razor wire on top discouraged scaling it. One option was to cut a slit and sneak inside. But the cameras would still be an issue. His other plans involved hitching a ride. If he could get right up to the side of the building he'd be in the camera's blind spot. Then he could slip inside.

But it was unlikely he could catch a ride. No matter which way he sliced it, the cameras on the northeastern corner might be the only weakness in their armor. Provided he wasn't wrong about their field of vision. If they were wide FOV cameras, then they'd spot him in a heartbeat.

And that was just the outside.

There were probably cameras inside as well, at least on the main factory floor. They'd want to keep an eye on the regular workers. Make sure they didn't wander anywhere they weren't supposed to. They might have cameras wherever they stored the cocaine. They wanted to keep anyone from stealing product.

He couldn't do much about any of their security precautions except avoid them. He'd done that more times than he could remember. This would be no different. Carver laughed to himself. It would be a lot different. He didn't have any equipment except a few stolen guns and some supplies from a gear shop.

"Dead reckoning, right, Rhodes?" Carver chuckled. He ate from a ration pack then went to sleep. It was going to be a long night.

MAYOR BUCK MORGAN texted his contact.

Why is this man still breathing?

The response came moments later. *We've got people on it. Did you do as we asked?*

Of course. Thank God those idiots haven't tried to call the feds.

Stay the course. We're almost there.

Buck stared out the window of his mountainside estate. The valley and Morganville spread out below. The mountains rose behind the town, framing it perfectly. It almost looked like it used to back before the big EPA scandal. One day he'd make it look like that again. If everything worked out as promised, he'd have enough money to rebuild the town and the factory. Then he could finally purge scum like Jasper Whittaker from the history books.

This place had been perfect when he was a kid. The gateway to the mountains. Happy families. Good paying jobs at the paint factory. Booming retail business. Nathan Whittaker had run a tight ship and so had Buck's father, Lance. It was amazing how one moron like Jasper could wreck everything.

"What's wrong, dad?" Jensen stood near the foyer, car keys in hand. "You thinking about Jasper again?"

"Can't stop thinking about that jackass."

Jensen stepped beside him. "They get that drifter yet? Tie up the loose ends?"

"Of course not. They're trying to give me a heart attack."

"I had him in my sights that day. I could've taken him out."

"Son, I wish they would have let you." He patted his shoulder. "Maybe you'll get your chance yet."

Jensen grinned. "I hope so." He went toward the door. "Mom's still in LA?"

Buck nodded. "It's best having her and your sister out of the way until this is done."

"Okay, so the only question is, blonde or brunette?"

"The only answer is, why not both?"

Jensen laughed. "Jasper said he has some new girls in inventory, so that won't be a problem."

"Tell him not to sedate them so heavily this time." Buck sighed. "I don't want another one dying on me."

"You and me both." Jensen twirled his keys in his hand. "Be back soon." He left the house and climbed in his truck.

Buck returned to contemplating the future. It was a shame that there would be no more girls when Jasper was gone, but that price was worth paying to rebuild the town he loved.

CARVER WOKE UP at one AM.

He showered. Threw on black cargo pants and a black long-sleeved shirt. He smoothed dark camo paint on his face and put a black ballcap over his dark hair. He put the nine-millimeter ammo in one belt pouch. Put the shotgun shells in the next two pouches.

He attached holsters to both sides of the belt for the Glocks. The ankle holster also went into place.

Carver drove down the gravel road that led to his lookout but parked it in bushes just off the side of the main road. He went to the corner of the fence where two sides met the post. The area was overgrown. A cut in the fence would go unnoticed unless someone waded into the bushes for a look.

The small metal cutters he'd bought snipped through the fence. He slid through the slit then took out his binoculars and zoomed in on the northeastern corner of the building. The side with a possible blind spot. Or so he hoped.

He had about two hundred feet of darkness until he reached the lit area. Then he'd have to carefully walk straight to the corner and hope he was right. Otherwise, he'd have unwanted company.

Carver tightened the belt with the ammo and guns and hustled through the darkness toward the paint factory. He reached the edge of the lit area. Focused on the place he was going. Sprinted across the open space. He felt exposed. Like all eyes were watching him. He reached the building. Pressed his back to the wall. Looked up.

The cameras were angled out toward the approach. They couldn't see what was right beneath them. He crouched and waited for two entire minutes. If he'd been seen, someone would come looking. No one did. He stood. Pressed his back to the wall and slid along it. A fire ladder was attached to the side just overhead.

He took the climbing rope from his backpack. One end had a weighted hook on it. He tossed it at the ladder. It bounced off the rung. It took three tries to loop the hook over the bottom rung. The weight dragged the rope back down to him. He hooked the rope to itself and pulled the loop tight.

Carver muscled his way up, hand over hand. He didn't want to walk up the wall because the cameras might spot him. He reached the bottom rung. Pulled himself up the ladder. Unhooked the rope and pulled it up to him. Then he climbed to the roof.

He went right, walked all the way to the corner to an access hatch. There was a lever on top. Rust around the edges. The roof flashing was peeling. Carver twisted the handle. It moved a quarter of the way before hitting something.

The locks on these were usually simple spring-releases on the inside. A tongue of metal on the inside handle pressed against a metal edge. He pulled up on the corner of the hatch. It moved slightly. He kept lifting, using his legs. The metal tongue began to give. The handle had to turn ninety degrees to free the tongue. Since it had moved forty-five of those ninety degrees, there was less tongue making contact with the ledge.

It bent just enough to slide loose. The hatch popped open on a hydraulic spring, nice and quiet. There was a ladder inside. Carver went down it. At the bottom was a metal catwalk, a thick grid of metal. It was ten feet below the ceiling and ran between vent pipes. The factory floor was visible below.

Carver followed the catwalk. It hooked left and connected to metal stairs. They went down to a landing that connected to more stairs. There were several flights going all the way down to floor level.

The factory was dimly lit. Only a few of the giant bell lights were on. There was a background hum echoing through the stillness. It was enough sound to cover his movements. His position gave him a good view of the floor. There were large stainless-steel tanks. Lots of pipes. Electric motors. Cables and wires.

If there were cameras, he didn't see them. It was hard to find anything in the tangle of pipes and metal. After a few minutes, he spotted one near a mixing tank. It was aimed to watch the operator. He located others watching the other mixing tanks. It was safe to assume there might be more but spotting them from up here wasn't easy.

There was a wall about halfway through the factory. Carver didn't want to risk walking down on the floor. There were closed doors that might be locked. He tested the stainless-steel pipes above him. They felt sturdy. He hooked his hands around the one just overhead and walked hand-over-hand until it intersected with a larger pipe. This pipe ran to the wall. He continued down it. Lifted his legs and scuttled through the hole in the wall to the other side.

There were conveyer belts loaded with empty one-gallon paint cans. The pipe Carver dangled from and several more just like it connected to more tanks. The conveyer belts ran beneath the tanks where they filled up the paint cans. At least he would come out of this knowing how a paint factory operated.

There was plenty of open space. Wooden pallets were piled high against the far wall. The loading dock doors were to his right. To the left, a stairway leading up into management offices. The windows were dark. He slid down the pipe to the top of a tank. Sat down to rest his arms and legs.

There was a hum and the sound of metal clinking. Elevator doors opened. Someone was coming.

CHAPTER 26

A man emerged from the elevator, pulling a pallet jack behind him. The pallet was loaded with five-gallon paint buckets. He pulled it to the doors leading into the paint factory. Used a keycard to unlock the doors. Pulled it inside.

The man wasn't one of the typical factory workers. He was one of the Brazilians. Why was he doing grunt work? Carver shimmied back up the pipe. Inched along it back to the hole in the wall. He hung by his arms and legs. Watched the guy pop open the paint buckets. He poured thick white paint through a metal grate on the floor. Then he reached inside the bucket. Twisted his arm back and forth. Pulled out a package covered in paint.

He set the package on the grate and went to the next paint can. Carver shimmied along the pipe and slid down to the top of a tank so he could rest. From his top-down view he could see inside the bucket. There was a plastic net attached to hooks in the middle of the bucket. It had been holding the package dead center.

The metal grate was over a stainless-steel overflow tank. The Brazilian guy continued emptying buckets and removing the packages until the last bucket was done.

He took a hose and rinsed off the packages. Then he flipped a switch. The tank slurped down the paint. Carver could hear it traveling up a pipe and flowing into one of the stainless-steel mixing tanks. The guy rinsed down the area and unwrapped the packages. Beneath wax paper was a white brick of cocaine wrapped in plastic.

That was why the guy was doing grunt work. The cocaine was smuggled inside the buckets. How it got through the x-ray scanners and port security was a mystery. It seemed risky as hell shipping it straight from the Brazilian paint company in their paint buckets.

They were one intercepted load away from getting shut down permanently. The paint buckets didn't have a name on them, so maybe they were shipping them from other places in Brazil.

Carver thought back to what Holly said about the Whittaker Ultra paint base. How it was so thick and dense that it remained new looking even years later. Maybe that was why they were shipping it in the middle of the buckets. Because the paint was so dense it blocked out scanners and x-rays. But wouldn't something blocking an x-ray also raise an alarm?

He'd dealt with port security before but had only taken a crash course to find out what he needed to know to breach it. Old-fashioned smuggling worked just fine but it was still a gamble. These people were shipping cocaine like it was no gamble at all.

Jasper would probably know. Carver just had to find him. From what Holly said, the guy practically lived at the factory. Probably in the management offices.

Carver climbed the pipe to the main trunk. Shimmied all the way back through the wall and to the management offices. They were on the second level up a staircase. Built up against the ceiling on metal I-beams. There was empty factory floor beneath them. It looked like it might have once held inventory.

The only way in looked like the front door. The emergency exits were on the exterior of the main building. The door the smokers and the woman used was just beneath the offices. Going up the stairs to the door looked like the only way to get inside.

He followed the pipes to the nearest tank and slid down to the top. The guy with the buckets would be back this way at some point. Maybe now, maybe later. It was hard to say.

Carver looked for cameras and didn't see any. He climbed down the metal rungs on the side of the tank and reached the floor. He skirted the light. Crept up the stairs. The office door was glass and metal. Just like the swinging glass doors on most business places.

He pulled. It swung outward. He stepped inside the darkness. Eased the door shut. The office space was large. A receptionist area with a desk and phone. A hallway with office doors and windows. At the far end were double doors. That would almost certainly be where Jasper was.

Carver crept down the hallway. A florescent bulb at the end offered some ambient light. He glanced into the open office doors. He couldn't see inside, but they felt empty. He paused outside the last door on the right. He could hear someone breathing. Tossing and turning. He turned on the cell phone screen to provide a little illumination.

There was a figure on the bed. It was the woman. Her eyes were rolling beneath closed eyelids. She was twitching. Probably having a nightmare. That was no surprise. Working for a cartel wasn't exactly a stress-free job.

He let her be and went to the end of the hallway. The hallway branched to the left and the right. At the end of the right hallway was a stairwell. It went down to the emergency exit that the woman used.

Carver returned to the double doors. They were locked. That wasn't a problem since they opened outward and not inward. There was nothing protecting the latch. Carver jimmied the latch with a pair of flat screwdrivers. He tugged and the door opened quietly. He slipped inside and closed the door.

Raspy snoring came from somewhere to the right. It was hard to hear anything else over the noise. Carver used the phone screen for illumination. He had a flashlight, but it was too bright. He walked forward, scanning with the phone screen.

There was an old couch. It was filthy. Sagging. A small form lay on the floor in front of it. Carver went closer. It was an Asian woman, huddled in the fetal position. She was bruised on the arms, legs, and face. But she was breathing.

Carver's hackles rose. Were these people into human trafficking as well? Or was this a prostitute?

He walked around the area. It looked like a large office that had been converted into an apartment. There was a bathroom with a tiled shower and a large tub. A kitchen. Two guest rooms. A hallway leading to the master bedroom where the snoring came from. The Asian woman looked like the only other being in the place.

Carver went down the hallway and found the source of the snoring. A big mound in the middle of a big bed. The room smelled like stale sweat and unwashed skin. Jasper was on his back. Eyes closed, mouth open. Rattling off snores like a rusty chainsaw. The man was obese. Carver couldn't shove him off the bed without risking a back strain.

He closed the bedroom door. There were no windows. No other way out that he saw. He found the light switch and flicked it on. Dim, yellow light filled the room. Jasper continued snoring. There was a cell phone connected to a charging cable on the side table. Carver picked it up. It felt greasy. Like it hadn't been wiped down once in its entire existence.

The screen required a seven-digit PIN. He put the phone down. The end tables were simple. No drawers, just tops. Carver felt under the only pillow on the bed. Nothing there. Unless Jasper was hiding a gun in a fat fold, he wasn't armed.

Carver drew a Glock. Put the cold metal tip to Jasper's temple. The man kept snoring. He prodded his head. Jasper grunted. Swatted at his face like shooing away a bug. Felt the gun barrel with his fingers. His eyes cracked open. He frowned. Rubbed his eyes and looked up.

His mouth opened. Carver slapped a hand over it. "Not a word, Jasper. Nod if you understand."

Jasper nodded.

Carver removed his hand. "No one can hear you scream anyway."

"You killed Paola?"

Carver nodded. "And the Asian woman. It's just you and me and the truth."

Jasper shivered violently. "Who are you? What do you want?"

"Who am I?" Carver leaned closer to Jasper. "You don't recognize me?"

Confusion spread on Jasper's face. "You're the man from the pictures. The man they brought in the Brothers to kill."

"Yes. Except I killed the Brothers."

He trembled. "Who in the hell are you?"

"I'll ask the questions." Carver prodded his temple with the Glock. "Tell me why your people killed Chief Rhodes."

Jasper's forehead bunched up. "We didn't kill her. You did!"

"I can assure you that she's the one person I didn't kill. But I did kill your dirty cop and Ruben and Jimmy. Enough with the lies, tell me the truth."

"Who are Ruben and Jimmy?"

"Stop lying."

"It's the truth!" Jasper moaned and quivered. "I swear it. Don't kill me, please. I have a lot of money. Take as much as you want."

"Who's at the top of the food chain here?"

"Pietro. He's the company liaison. He's the only guy I deal with from corporate."

"He's the one who wanted Rhodes killed?"

"No! We didn't kill her! Killing the chief of police is the option of last resort. It draws too much attention to the town. Risks the operation. When they found out you killed her, they thought you were with another cartel trying to stir up trouble. They didn't want any attention on the town. They decided to kill you. To make it look like an accident so the heat would die down."

Carver watched Jasper's face. His body language. The man was an absolute coward. This was the truth as well as he knew it. But it didn't make any sense. "Who hired the military guys, Ruben and Jimmy?"

"I never heard of them I swear."

"Rhodes never came sniffing around here? Never found out about the coke operation you've got going on?"

Sweat trickled down Jasper's forehead. "She never seemed interested in this place. She visited once after she got the job. Just dropped by and said hello and to let her know if we needed anything. That was the last time she came out here."

"Did you kidnap a detective?"

"Kidnap a detective? No, of course not!"

"Who's on your payroll? Settler? Davis?"

"Maberly and Davis. Neither of them knows exactly what's going on out here, though. I just pay them to keep me informed."

Carver nodded. "I believe you, Jasper. Which raises more questions than it answers. Because I didn't kill Rhodes. Someone else did and they tried to frame me for it."

"What?" Jasper wiped the sweat from his eyes. "Why would they kill her?"

"Explain to me why Brilhante Tintas is so bold as to ship the cocaine in paint. How are they not worried about random searches, x-rays, and scans?"

Jasper gulped. "Whittaker Ultra makes it impossible. It refracts light waves. Scatters them. That's why it stays so vibrant even after years of the sun beating down on it. It doesn't block x-rays, but it makes them bounce around. So, the x-rays pick up on the paint inside the container, but not the packages in the middle of the paint."

"That explains why Brilhante Tintas bought you out. They wanted the patent and the formula."

"We'd been shipping Ultra to them for years. They must have discovered what it did. They tried to buy us out even before the EPA destroyed us."

"Before you made stupid decisions and destroyed the company."

Jasper licked his lips. "You have your answers. I'll tell Pietro we have an understanding. Then we can all forget this ever happened, okay? No harm, no foul."

"What's in the long wooden crates you're shipping in? Women?"

"Women?" He laughed nervously. "No, those are spare parts for the machines. They don't need them, but they keep buying them. It helps it look like we're spending money. Makes it easier to launder the funds from the cocaine."

"Where did the Asian woman come from?"

"They bring me women. It keeps me happy." He licked his lips again. "You know how it is."

"Looks like you had fun with her." Carver grinned. "My kind of fun."

Jasper smiled back. "Yeah, exactly. I have plenty more women. Have whichever one you want. Do whatever you want to them. We can be friends and I can make you rich."

"You don't care if I snuff a few?" Carver bit his lower lip. "I love watching the light die in their eyes."

"Same here, friend." Jasper was excited now. He was making a new friend. "I can get you any kind of woman you want. Pietro's friends can get rid of the bodies. No muss, no fuss. I've been through plenty of them."

"Good to know." Carver swiped Ruben's razor-sharp survival knife across Jasper's throat. The big man's eyes widened in horror. He grasped at his neck. Convulsed. Carver stepped back and watched him bleed out. "Good to know."

He waited for the death rattle. Turned toward the door. The Brazilian woman was watching him, eyes wide. She backed away slowly. He pointed the gun at her. Motioned her over. "Paola?"

Tears welled in her eyes. She nodded. Shoulders slumped. Walked closer.

"You speak English?"

"Yes." Her accent was heavy, but clear.

"Tell me where they keep the cocaine and the women. Tell me how many men are guarding this place. Do all of that, and I will help you get away from here, okay?"

Tears rolled down her face. "There are normally twenty men. Eleven of them are gone on delivery runs. The others are in the pit. The big place below the factory. The women are held in a cargo container. The cocaine is in another container."

"Is the elevator the only way down there?"

She shook her head. "There are stairs."

"Tell me more about this pit."

Paola wiped her face. "Jasper had a big cave blasted in the bedrock to store toxic waste in. When corporate bought the factory, they had it enlarged. There are rooms for the men to sleep in."

"Is human trafficking a large part of their business?"

She shook her head. "They only do it for Jasper. Sometimes he shares the women with other men. The mayor's son took two women with him tonight."

Carver stepped closer to her. "Paola, thank you for your help. Can you stay here and be quiet while I go tend to a few things?"

"Why don't you kill me? I work for them."

"Have you killed anyone?"

"No, never."

"Do you like working for the company?"

"No, I hate it. But I'm trapped here."

"I don't see a reason to kill you, then." Carver walked out of the door.

"Wait." Paola touched his arm. "When you go down the stairs, you'll have to open a door. It's very squeaky. Most of the men are asleep by now, but they might hear it. They all sleep with weapons nearby."

"They have their own rooms?"

"Yes."

"Thank you. Can you tell me how to get to the stairs?"

Paola straightened a little. "Yes. Go out the office doors, down the stairs. Go under the offices and to the back wall. You'll see a closed metal door next to a blue water tank. The stairs are there."

"Where do the security cameras feed to? Is there a room?"

"There are monitors downstairs. Someone keeps watch on them all night. The cameras detect motion so the screen will blink to alert them that something is moving. But there are no cameras in the area beneath the offices or in the stairwell."

Carver left the offices and went downstairs. He'd come here for answers and only found more questions. But that was no reason to stop. These people tried to kill him, and it was best not to leave an enemy at your back.

Even if it wasn't the enemy you thought it was.

CHAPTER 27

Carver followed Paola's instructions.

He found the stairwell door. Went downstairs. Eased open the door at the bottom. It squeaked loudly in the stillness below. There was no background hum in the pit. Nothing to hide the noise. He slipped out of the light and into the darkness. Slow strides prevented scuffing and kept his footsteps nearly silent.

There was a light above the door. A few lights scattered throughout the space. Not enough to provide a visual of everything. The door was in a corner. Probably the back corner. The pit stretched out before him. Empty and unseen.

Someone grunted. There was a squeak, and someone wearing hard soles walked in his direction. Carver pressed his back to the wall. A man appeared in the gloom of a light about fifty feet away. He vanished into darkness. Reappeared beneath the door. He opened the door and looked up the stairs. Closed the door and looked around.

Carver stepped up behind him. Grabbed his head and in one smooth motion, smashed it against the concrete wall. Slashing throats was safer, but Carver didn't want to spill blood right here. Someone else might come this way. A massive pool of blood would draw attention. He hefted the man. Walked further into the darkness. Dumped him in a dark corner.

The man was still breathing so he twisted his head sideways. Felt the neck snap. The breathing stopped. Carver frisked him. Found a sidearm, a house key with a number on it, and a small wad of cash. No license or car keys. It made sense. These guys were probably smuggled here. Probably rarely left the premises. Or maybe they just didn't carry their wallets around with them while they were here.

The walls had grooves in them. Carved by a grinding machine. There were bits of gravel all over the floor. He'd have to be careful not to let it crunch under his boots.

He did the math. Twenty men. Eleven absent. One dead. Eight more on premises. He walked softly. There was a lot of open space. He could feel emptiness stretching into the darkness around him. Then he came to a wall. A pair of lights revealed plywood and doors. Living quarters had been built up against the rock wall. They were windowless and the doors were closed.

Each unit was about ten by ten. About the size of a bedroom. Another row of them had been built opposite of these. Twenty-five doors on each side. Fifty total. He crossed to the other side away from the lights and kept walking. He found the security room. It was slightly larger than the other rooms and had a metal door.

The door was propped open. He peered inside. No one was there. The guy who'd come to check the door must have been the one watching the cameras. There was no camera watching the door. He must have heard it and gone to investigate.

There was a huge television mounted on a wall. The camera feeds were tiny squares dividing up the screen. At the bottom were four larger images where some of the camera feeds were enlarged. Carver checked out his corner approach and confirmed it was a blind spot. Good to know he could still do some things right.

One of the screens blinked. He used the mouse to click it. The screen appeared in one of the enlarged sections. The guy who'd been emptying the paint buckets was coming back. Carver considered disabling the cameras, but with the watcher down, it seemed okay to leave them be for the time being.

He scanned the camera feeds and found the room with the cocaine, a room with women huddled on the floor, and a room with pallets of paint buckets. It seemed they brought them downstairs immediately. Probably to keep the regular workers from making a fatal discovery. He also found the elevator. Seeing places on the screen didn't tell him where to go. But the area was just one big square like the factory directly above it.

How difficult could it be?

Carver went to the nearest living quarter door. He tested the doorknob. It was locked. He went down the row, testing them all. Every other room was unlocked. The doorknobs had keyholes, so the occupants could lock the rooms when they left. It looked like the Brazilians had spaced themselves out since there were plenty of units available.

He checked inside the unlocked rooms. Used the dimmest setting on his LED flashlight to confirm they were empty. Then he went to the other side and repeated the process. In the distance, he heard the elevator clanking open. Twelve rooms on one side were locked. Eight on this side were locked. The others were unlocked and empty.

That narrowed down the rooms a little, but not by much. Some of the locked rooms belonged to the van drivers. Some were occupied. He heard someone talking. Laughter. Someone besides the paint bucket guy was up and about.

Carver went around the living quarters and entered another section of the pit. A distant light illuminated what looked like cargo containers. It was probably where they kept the women, the cocaine, and the cash. He looked in the opposite direction toward the elevator. He saw the man from earlier talking to two other men.

The other men sat at a table in a plywood break room. They were playing cards and drinking beer. The paint guy pulled the pallet cart to the side then opened a refrigerator. Took a beer and popped it open. He sat down and one of the men started dealing cards.

Carver calculated the odds of taking them all down quietly. It wasn't going to happen. There were AK-47s leaning against the wall. They were old and battered. The wood was scratched, and the magazines looked like they'd seen better days. But there was no doubt they worked and worked well. The men also had Glock 19s in shoulder holsters. One wrong calculation and this would turn into a firefight he couldn't win.

He had to assume that the other five Brazilians were similarly armed. Had to assume that seconds after hearing gunfire, they'd all rush to the scene. It would turn into a mess and unless the Brazilians were idiots, Carver would end up riddled with bullets. Taking that into consideration, he crept through darkness to the rock wall and slid toward the break room's exterior wall.

Like the living quarters, it was built of plywood and two by four studs. It sat on the rock floor. Cinder blocks and wood shimmed it level. It didn't have a door or even a wall on the front. It was just open. There was a microwave, a fridge, and an electric range inside.

Carver quietly scooped up a handful of gravel from the floor. It wasn't a lot. Just small bits and pieces. He slid along the plywood wall. Positioned himself right at the edge to the opening. He imagined the positions of the men around the table. Went through the order in his head. Counted down from three and swung around the corner.

He saw his mistake the instant he stepped inside.

There was a gun on the table in front of the man opposite him. It had been concealed by a bag of potato chips. That didn't change the plan. The nearest man was sitting down, facing away from him. Carver reached around from the side. His knife flashed. Three quick stabs in the throat.

He kicked the table forward with the bottom of his boot. It slammed into the midsection of the man opposite the first target. The man was reaching for the gun. The air burst out of him. The gun slid off the table. The third man was rising. Hand going for the holstered weapon. Carver threw a handful of gravel at the man's face. The man instinctively threw his hands up to protect his face. Carver thrust the knife three quick times into the man's stomach.

The man's hands clutched at his gut. He shouted in pain. The knife dove in and out of his throat three times. He went down. The third man was scrabbling for the gun on the floor, not the one in his holster. Carver kicked the table one more time. It slammed the man's head. Carver swung around the dying second man, unrelenting.

The third man was dizzy from the blow. Struggling to rise to his feet. Opening his mouth to shout. The knife plunged in and out of his throat two times. His shout turned to a gurgle. Carver shoved him back to the ground.

He picked up the handgun from the floor. Took the one from the man's holster. Same for the handguns from the other men. Ejected the magazines, cleared the chambers, and put them on the table. Then a Kalashnikov. Ejected the magazine. Cleared it and dumped the rifle on the table. Ejected the magazine from the second Kalashnikov. Cleared it.

Carver grabbed the third rifle and checked the chamber. It was loaded. He left it that way and leaned it against the wall. He added the magazines from the Glocks and rifles to his ammo pouches. Picked up the loaded rifle. Total time elapsed, maybe thirty seconds. Lack of practice had made him slow.

He hustled back into the darkness, AK-47 at the ready. Slowed his pace and crept to the living quarters. No one was stirring. Apparently, no one had heard the ruckus. They'd slept through it.

Carver remained in darkness and went prone in case someone had.

There were five men left and he didn't know which rooms they were in. He couldn't just start kicking open doors. Everyone would wake up and start shooting. He didn't have grenades or anything useful for taking out a group of guys.

The Kalashnikov might do the trick, but he didn't want this to turn into a shooting match. It didn't matter how good of a shot you were, all it took was one stray bullet to end your day real fast.

Carver maintained his prone position. He ticked down two minutes. No one emerged from the rooms. He pushed to his feet and went into the security room. He found a lockbox with keys hanging inside. The keys were numbered just like the rooms, one to fifty. Twenty were missing. Presumably the occupied rooms. They didn't keep backup copies, not here at least.

He had the numbered key from the first guy. He went back to the break room and took the keys from the three bodies. Went back to the lockbox and hung the keys on their respective hooks.

The empty hooks represented locked rooms. Some were occupied. Some were in use by the guys driving the vans. The visual was helpful. It helped him narrow down the possibilities by four more.

Keys one through three were in the lockbox. The first taken key was room four. Apparently, no one wanted to be next door to the security station. Every other hook was skipped except for rooms eight, twelve, sixteen, and twenty. Carver had taken those keys from the dead men and put them on their hooks. Sixteen hooks had no keys. Eleven belonged to the drivers.

Which five were currently occupied?

He puzzled it over for a while. There just wasn't an easy way to do this. The doors swung inward, and the door jambs were simple. Just like the doors inside a house. Kicking them open would be easy enough. But there might be a much easier approach.

Carver slid off his backpack and took the slim-jim from inside. He went to the living quarters on the opposite side of the security office and chose an unlocked, unoccupied one as a test subject. He slid the thin, flexible metal into the space between the door jamb and where the latch was. He worked it downward. Wiggled it. Put pressure on the door.

The latch gave and the door swung inward. On a scale of one to ten the noise level was about a five. It was enough to wake up a light sleeper. The metal scraped. Wiggling the knob made an unavoidable amount of noise. It was the quietest way into the rooms, but it would be inefficient.

Jimmying open every room until he located the remaining five men would take a while. Maybe all five were close to each other, or maybe they were scattered among the units. The only other option would be to knock on the doors and see if someone answered.

They wouldn't expect an enemy to come knocking. They'd be vulnerable. But that only worked if they came one at a time. The knocking might wake up others. Someone else might step out behind Carver and put an end to him.

The stairwell door creaked open in the distance. He hustled past the living units and slid into darkness. A figure moved through the shadows. A dim light lit a face. It was the woman. Had she changed her mind? Was she coming for Carver?

She looked frightened. Like she wanted to be anywhere except down here. Carver watched her. She looked around but didn't use the flashlight on her phone. She wasn't armed. He went up behind her. Touched her arm. She gasped. Put her hand over her mouth to stop a scream.

She blew out a ragged breath. Calmed herself.

"Why are you here?" Carver whispered.

She whispered back. "I was afraid you would have trouble."

"I am. Four men are down. I don't know which units the remaining five are sleeping in."

Paola shivered. "Show me the dead men."

He led her to the security room guy. She looked at his face. Nodded. Carver took her to the break room. She put a hand over her mouth and convulsed.

Carver put a hand on her back. "Deep breaths."

Paola nodded. Took a deep, shuddering breath. Looked at the faces.

"Do you know which ones are still here?"

"Yes." She grimaced. "I have to cook for them. Bring the meals to their rooms every night."

"Do the same men always drive the delivery vans?"

"Yes." She turned away from the corpses in the breakroom. "I know all the rooms."

"That's good." Carver put his hand on her back again. "You're going to be okay."

She shuddered. "Please don't touch me."

He pulled back his hand. "I'm sorry."

"Me too." Paola wiped away a tear. "Thank you for killing them."

"It was necessary."

She looked at his face. At his bloody leather gloves. She motioned him to follow. Led Carver to the security room. She got on her knees and looked under the security desk. Came back out with a small black magnetic case. Paola slid it open and removed a red key.

Carver reached for it, but she shook her head. "I'll open the rooms. You do what is necessary."

Carver nodded. "Are you sure you want to be this close?"

Paola nodded. "Yes. I hate them."

He blew out a breath. "Okay."

Paola took him to room sixteen. The key opened it quietly. Carver slipped inside and found a man slumbering on mattress. A Kalashnikov lay on the floor next to him. Carver tested the edge of Ruben's knife. It was starting to dull. A quick slash to the throat wouldn't work as well anymore. He pressed his hand over the man's mouth and jabbed him in the carotid artery at the same time.

The man's cries were muffled. He bucked and squirmed. His arms thrashed and hit the wooden wall. Carver removed his hand and backed off. The man was too weak to scream. Blood loss sent him into that eternal goodnight seconds later.

Paola watched, almost stricken. Tears welled in her eyes. She trembled violently and backed away from the door. Carver followed her back out.

He leaned to her ear and whispered. "Are you sure you still want to do this?"

She nodded. "I want to watch them die."

A doorknob rattled. It turned. A door on the opposite side opened, and a man with a rifle emerged.

CHAPTER 28

The man's eyes widened. He shouted in Portuguese. Aimed his Kalashnikov.

Carver whipped a Glock out of the holster. Fired. The bullet took the man in the forehead. He went down, the rifle booming. Bullets pinging off rock.

Paola dropped to the ground. She was quiet. Not a scream or a shout.

Carver almost admired that. But he didn't want her dropping to the floor. "Which rooms?"

She rattled them off in Portuguese. Blinked and shook her head. "Twenty-two, twenty-four, thirty-six."

"Run to the break room and hide." Carver gripped the back of her shirt and yanked her to her feet. "Go." He said it calmly. Quietly.

Rooms twenty-four and twenty-two opened. Automatic gunfire erupted. Muzzle flashes lit the apartments. The occupants were firing at the apartments on the opposite side. Toward the room their comrade had come out of. They hadn't bothered to assess the situation before firing. Bullets punched through plywood. Splinters flew. Within seconds, their thirty-round magazines were empty.

Carver was on their side. He pressed his back to the wall. They stepped from their apartments. Looked at each other. At the body sprawled across the way. One of them depressed the magazine release and rocked out the mag. Carver stepped out just enough to get an angle on them both. He aimed the Glock. Squeezed the trigger twice.

The furthest man dropped like a rag doll. The other man spun. Carver gave him a third eye and a hole in the chest. He dropped. That left one guy. The man in room thirty-six. A room that was riddled with bullet holes.

Carver sprinted across the aisle to the other side. Put his back to the units and slid down toward the last apartment. The door hung ajar. Blood trickled just inside the threshold. He shined his flashlight inside. The occupant lay face down, Kalashnikov sprawled in front of him.

Just some guys with guns. Little to no training. Certainly, no situational awareness. Not that Carver would complain. It made his job simpler.

He used the red key to unlock all the locked units. Checked inside just in case. They were all empty. No guns, no money, nothing inside. He frisked the bodies and disarmed them. Took their ammunition, their cash and went to the break room. Paola wasn't inside. She was huddled in a dark corner just outside.

She stood. "All dead?"

Carver nodded. "Aside from the sex slaves, we should be the only ones alive."

"But the drivers—"

"I'll take care of them too." He held out his hand. Remembered she didn't like that and dropped it. "Take me to the sex slaves."

She nodded. Walked away from the break room. Took him far down to six cargo containers lined against the walls. Most were closed and padlocked. Some only had metal rods latching them on the outside.

Carver rapped on the sides of a locked container. "What's in here?"

"The first is cocaine, the second is cash, and the third is weapons." She went to the first unlocked one. "Women." Pointed to the fifth and sixth one. "Alcohol and food supplies."

He lifted the latch and swung open the door. The smell of body odor washed over him. Urine. Feces. There were mattresses lined along the floor of the container. Women sprawled on some of them. Most of the women were huddled in the back. Awake with wide eyes. They'd probably heard the gunfire.

Carver shined the flashlight on himself so they could see him. He almost gave the standard speech. Almost said, "We're with the US military. We're here to save you." It was an old reflex. Now he didn't know what to say.

Paola said something for him. "This man has killed your oppressors. You're free to go."

No one moved. A few whimpered or cried. Finally, someone spoke from the dark back corner.

"Really?"

Paola nodded. "Yes, really."

A slim girl in dirty sweatpants and a t-shirt stumbled out of the darkness and toward Carver. She looked like a teenager. Maybe younger. "Who is this man?"

"Carver," Carver said. He imagined what Rhodes would do right now. Just opening the gates and freeing the women into the wild wasn't the right move. There were other things to consider. A lot of other things.

Jasper thought Carver had killed Rhodes. He didn't know anything about Ruben or Jimmy. The Brazilians had also thought Carver had killed Rhodes and was about to bring the heat down on their operation. They'd tried to kill him out of reflex. But they weren't the ones who'd started this. That trail led somewhere else. To a different part of the puzzle.

If these women went free and talked to the police, the DEA and other feds would swarm here like flies. Whoever had started this would sink back into the darkness. They'd wait patiently and come for Carver again when he wasn't ready for it.

It was best to stay on the offense. To be the one with the element of surprise. But how was he supposed to do that once these women spread the word? It was a problem. A problem he didn't know how to solve. He couldn't just lock them back up.

Carver had to put the genie back in the bottle somehow. Or keep the genie from talking. He turned to Paola. "Do you know these women? Their names?"

She shook her head. "Jasper gave them nicknames. They didn't let me look inside the container. I only saw the ones they brought out."

"Are there better lights in this place?"

Paola nodded. "The lights are controlled in the security room."

"Can you turn them on? I want it bright as day in here."

"Yes, of course." She hurried away.

The teenage girl was watching him. "I'm Tina Compton, from Los Angeles."

"How old are you?"

"Fifteen." Her lips trembled. "I went to a college party with my friend. I think something was in a drink because I blacked out and woke up in a basement with some other girls. I don't even know how long we were down there. One day, some Latino guy came in and took me. They drugged me and I woke up here."

"He was Brazilian," Carver said. "How long have you been here?"

"I have no idea. A couple of weeks, I think." She started crying. "They'd take girls out. Sometimes they'd bring them back all bruised. Sometimes they didn't bring them back at all."

"Did they ever choose you?"

"They did, but the fat man upstairs said I was too chubby. That I needed to lean out before I deserved him."

"He's dead now."

She nodded. Hugged Carver. "Thank you."

Carver patted her head. "You're welcome."

The other women were coming forward. Some spoke Spanish. The power clunked on. Big gym lights hanging from metal conduits on the ceiling lit up the place like the sun. The women looked haggard. Bruised and broken. Some had feces and other bodily fluids smeared on them. They all wore sweatpants and t-shirts.

Lights inside the container came on. There was no bathroom inside. Just a few large buckets. Two women remained on the mattresses inside. The sole Asian woman approached Carver and started speaking loudly in Mandarin. He knew enough to recognize the language, but he didn't speak it.

"Those women are dead." A short woman with long but dirty blond hair dropped to her knees. "I think they sedated them too much. They never woke up."

Carver freed himself from Tina and went inside. He checked the vitals of the two bodies. They were cold. Dead. "Yeah, they're dead."

Paola ran back into view.

Some of the women hissed when they saw her.

"You bitch!" The blond woman tried to lunge but fell to her knees.

The Chinese woman shouted in Mandarin. Tears streaked dark makeup down her face.

"Please, I didn't want this." Paola shielded herself behind Carver. "They killed my family. Made me work for them."

The pit filled with echoes of despair. Crying, cursing, screaming. Carver had heard worse. He finally thought of a plan. Raised his hands. "Everyone, please be quiet."

The noise died down. Women huddled together or alone. Watched him with uncertainty, despair, maybe a little hope.

"This is part of a larger operation." Carver made eye contact. It was important to make them feel human in his eyes. "This place represents only a small part of the organization behind this. There are eleven more men who will be returning in the morning. I have to neutralize them next. Then we move to phase two of the operation."

"What operation sends a single guy to take out sex traffickers?" Tina looked around. "Why isn't there a whole squad with you?"

Carver didn't have a good answer. "What I'm saying is, you have to go to a safe house until the operation is over. Then it can be made public."

"Some of us have families that need to know we're okay!" Another woman spoke up. "And someone needs to find the families of those dead women and tell them."

"I don't care." A painfully thin woman pushed her way through the others. "Please, just get me somewhere safe. Get me food, a bathroom." She began to sob. "I can't take this anymore. I thought I was going to die in here."

"Here's the dead honest truth." Carver sighed. "I'm all alone. Someone killed a friend of mine. I followed the clues to here. I found out these people were dealing drugs and sex trafficking. So, I killed them. But then I found out that they're not the ones who killed my friend. And if you make this public now, then the people responsible will find out and I'll lose my chance to find them."

"And kill them?" Someone said.

Carver nodded. "Yes."

Tina smiled. Touched his hand. "How long do you need, Carver?"

"I don't know. It might be days or weeks."

"How about one week? We owe you our lives but hiding out for weeks isn't possible. How would we even do it without money?"

"Can you give me one week?" Carver addressed the nine women. "One week?"

The English speakers nodded. Some of the women spoke in their native tongues. Paola spoke Spanish and three of the women nodded. The Chinese woman looked confused.

Carver took out Renee's cell phone and opened a translator app. He typed in English, and it spat out simplified Chinese. The woman listened to it and nodded. She took the phone and typed. Handed it back.

My family is in China. I have no one here. Please help me.

He typed back. *I will.*

The few women who didn't want to cooperate were finally persuaded by the others.

One woman pointed at Paola. "I want that bitch to pay for helping them."

"I wasn't helping them." Paola held up her hands. "I told you, they killed my family."

"She's the reason you're free," Carver said. "She didn't do this to you. She was as much a prisoner as anyone else."

Tina put a hand on the other woman's shoulder. "I believe you, Carver."

He finally had their cooperation, but now he had to figure out how to house them. How to keep them safe for one week.

"Two of us are missing," the blonde woman said. "They took them a few hours ago."

Paola nodded. "The mayor's son took two women. There's another woman in Jasper's apartment upstairs."

"Get her and bring her down here," Carver said. "Make her understand what needs doing."

"Are you going to get them back, Carver?" Tina took his hand. "You need to do something because they might kill them."

The mayor was the next link in the chain. The next puzzle piece. Only because of his possible connection to the military people. "Paola, does the son bring them back?"

She looked down. "Yes. Sometimes they're dead."

He nodded. Checked the time. "Who does he normally talk to?"

"Me. He doesn't like Jasper."

"Just you?"

Paola nodded. "But he usually keeps them for a few days. He won't return them today."

Carver thought it over. "The van drivers will be returning soon. I need to take them out next. Then I can recon the mayor's house. Find out what kind of security he has. I can't just rush in."

"Do what you need to do, Carver." Tina rubbed the top of his hand.

Carver wanted his hand back, but he didn't want to look insensitive. Rhodes told him it was one of his flaws. He was like a robot sometimes. All duty. No emotions. Carver had emotions. He had plenty of them. But they got in the way. It was better to ignore them and do the job at hand. By then he was usually too tired to deal with emotions.

He mustered up some feeling. Smiled at Tina. "Thank you. I need to find a place for you to live for the week."

"Jasper's mansion," Paola said. "The company was going to sell it, but they kept it in case cartel leaders visited and needed a place to stay."

"Where is it?"

"About fifteen minutes away. Sometimes one of the men would take me there to help a maid service clean it."

"You're beautiful," Tina said. "Did they sexually abuse you too?"

Paola shivered and looked down. "I'm sorry. I don't want to talk about it."

"Oh, no." The woman who'd shouted at her stepped forward. Hugged her. "Why didn't you say something?"

Paola shivered more. "Please don't." She pulled away. "I don't like being touched."

"Oh, you poor girl." The woman wiped tears from her face. "I understand."

Carver checked the time. The first van would arrive in two hours. "Paola, is there somewhere they can clean up and eat? I don't have transportation for them yet."

She nodded. "Yes. There are showers and food down here."

"Okay. Do the vans return on the same schedule every day?"

She nodded again. "Around the same time, yes. Vitor tracks the schedules and counts the money. If anyone is late or short, they answer to him. He uses an encrypted app to send the information to corporate. They had a man who cleaned the money, but he's been in prison a while and they haven't found anyone else to clean it."

Tina looked confused. "You mean launder the money?"

Paola nodded. "Yes, sorry. My English is not the best."

Carver nodded. "Get everyone cleaned up and fed, okay? Have them ready to go in two hours. We're going to use the first van as transport."

"Okay."

Tina clapped her hands. "Okay, ladies. Let's get rid of our stink."

Paola herded the women toward another building across the huge underground chamber. With the lights on, he could see that the pit had been blasted from the bedrock. Parts had been carved and smoothed a little. Others were raw and rough.

Some areas were covered in concrete. Most of it was just rock. It looked like a rush job. Then they'd built plywood structures like the security room, living structures, the break room. Dropped some empty cargo containers into this side. Run some plumbing to a plywood room near the living quarters. Probably toilet and showers.

This was the place Jasper had stored the toxic waste in. Poisoned the water supply. Destroyed the company and allowed it to be turned into a drug and sex-trafficking operation. It was a malignant tumor in a once-thriving town. A disease. But it wasn't the disease that had killed Rhodes. This place was strictly Brazilian. Didn't have any of the military types like Ruben and Jimmy.

The paint factory wasn't what set things in motion against Carver. It was only tangentially related.

Maybe the mayor was the person who'd started it. Maybe he'd thought Rhodes was a danger to the drug operation. A danger to his supply of sex slaves. He'd used his people to take her out. Tried to pin the blame on Carver. Tried to tie it up in a neat present for the Brazilians.

It didn't feel right. Someone like the mayor would want to stay out of dangerous situations. Protect his interests and his position. He would have told Jasper about the problem and let the Brazilians handle it. No need to dirty his hands with the affair.

Carver had barked up the wrong tree, then chopped it down. Now he had to clean up the mess and find the missing connection. It was there somewhere, a needle in a pile of bodies.

CHAPTER 29

C arver searched the other unlocked cargo containers. Tools were in one. Nothing as useful as bolt cutters, but there was a sledgehammer. He used it to smash open the locks on the other containers.

One had weapons and a workbench for cleaning them. There were some crates of 7.62 ammo for the Kalashnikovs. A couple of extra rifles and handguns. Nothing spectacular. He took several duffel bags and loaded them with empty magazines and ammunition. He filled another with handguns and rifles.

He retrieved the weapons from the bodies and put them in the bags too. Then he took it all up the elevator and stuck the bags behind an electric motor near the loading docks.

Carver went back to the other containers. One had bricks of cocaine and bricks of cash. It was more cash in one place than he'd seen in a long time. There was no doubt in his mind that Davos' imprisonment was the reason this cash had accumulated. They hadn't found anyone to replace their money launderer.

Avoiding the police wasn't the biggest problem drug operations faced. It was laundering all the cash. Carver had seen homes where the walls were stuffed with dollar bills. He'd seen mountains of green in warehouses. Unusable all thanks to the tax man.

Many criminals were caught because they were living a lavish lifestyle and not reporting any income to the IRS. They bought expensive cars and big houses, but their income didn't reflect their lifestyle. Because it was all cash under the table. The tax man was better at detecting criminals than the cops.

Finding a good money launderer was hard. Otherwise, the Brazilians would have funneled this cash out a long time ago. Keeping this much sitting around was bad for business. It was less money available to pay for people and supplies. Wasted capital.

Carver found more duffel bags and stuffed them full of cash. There was too much for him to take everything, but it would be enough to keep him liquid for a long time. He put the money with the weapons.

Then he found a nice spot in the loading bay and camped out near the rollup door the vans would use to enter.

Once the vans entered, they'd park in a row near the cargo elevator. Someone would unload bags of money. Take them down in the elevator. Store them in the cargo container with the drugs.

Except that wouldn't happen this time.

At nine fifteen in the morning, the first van rolled in. The driver was Vitor, the same one Carver had followed. He looked a little worried. The missing brick of cocaine had probably come to his attention. He was the one in charge of the money and the drugs. The one responsible for making things line up for corporate. But things weren't going to line up so well with a missing kilo.

Vitor was going to be off the hook for this one. Corporate wasn't going to torture him or cut off an arm. They wouldn't get the chance.

Vitor went to the back of the van and opened the doors. Carver stepped out from behind a storage tank. Approached from the side. Vitor was reaching inside the van for the bags. Carver rammed the butt of the gun into the back of his head. Vitor went down hard.

Carver dragged him onto the elevator. Took him into the pit. Laid him out next to a body in one of the plywood bedrooms. Put a bullet in his head. The gunshot echoed in the pit. He took the cell phone from Vitor's pocket. The other men hadn't had phones. Drivers needed phones since they left the premises. The phone was locked with a PIN. Useless. He tossed it on top of the body.

Paola watched him from a distance. Her dark eyes were free of emotion. She'd probably reached the point of overload. Stopped processing. It was normal. When it happened, it usually caught up a day or two later. Or maybe she didn't know what to think about him shooting an unconscious man in the head.

"I'm sorry." Carver holstered the Glock. "I didn't want to get blood in the van."

Paola nodded. "You're very considerate."

"I need you to get the women settled into the mansion. There are bags of money in the van. You can use the cash to buy supplies if necessary. Once I finish cleaning up here, then I'll come out there."

She nodded again. "What about the factory workers?"

Carver folded his hands over his chest. "Good question. Who do they report to?"

"There are managers who bring problems to Jasper. But it's a skeleton operation. They don't like to talk to Jasper. But it will look strange if I'm not in the office and they come by."

"Plus, Jasper's body is on the bed. And I don't know how to move it."

She smiled. "Yes. The big fat prick is dead."

Carver checked the time. "The next van will be here in thirty minutes. You need to get going." He thought of something else. "Can you get past the gate guard?"

"Yes. He knows I run errands for Jasper. I have to go to the grocery store for supplies as well."

"Driving a van won't be a problem?"

"I usually drive a van when I go to town."

"Good."

"After I take them, I'll come back and sit at my desk in case a manager needs me."

"You'll be okay here?"

She nodded. "I will do whatever it takes to finish this."

"Thanks."

Paola frowned. "You're very strange. So much killing doesn't affect you at all?"

"Of course, it does." Carver put a hand to his stomach. "I push it deep down. Then I'll deal with it later over some beers."

"You're human, after all?"

"Yes, I promise." He motioned toward the elevator. "Can you get the women into the van? It'll be a tight fit."

"They will fit." She walked away.

Carver went back up the elevator. He counted four sacks of money. Unzipped a bag and pulled out a brick of twenties. They were all the same denomination. About a hundred grand per bag. He lined up the bags on the floor. They could serve as seats.

The elevator clanked open a moment later. Eight women piled into the back. Most carried a duffel bag with them. Probably food and clothing. Paola had good attention for detail. It would be useful having her help him with the factory while he tried to solve the rest of the puzzle.

Paola hit a button on a remote inside the van. The rollup door clanked open. She steered toward the door. Another van rolled in just then. Screeched to a halt to avoid a collision. The driver stared in confusion at Paola. Pulled a gun.

Carver fired two shots. The windshield puckered inward. The driver slumped. Women in the van screamed.

"It's okay!" Paola shouted. "It's okay, he's dead."

Carver opened the other van's door. Shoved the dead driver to the side and climbed inside. He drove around Paola's van and parked at the end. It had been a close call. Had the regular workers heard the gunshots? The door leading into the other part of the factory was locked with a keypad. Maybe the managers had access.

He checked the driver's phone. It was also locked with a PIN. He left it for the police. Maybe they could unlock its secrets.

Carver got out of the van. He went to Paola's window. "Who has access to the keypad?"

"Only me and the men. The managers usually call me when they have a problem." She gripped the steering wheel. "They wouldn't have heard the shots. It's too noisy on the other side."

Carver nodded. "Okay. I thought the drivers followed the same schedule. This guy wasn't due for another twenty minutes."

"Sometimes they're early, sometimes late. I'm sorry."

"It's okay." He motioned her to leave. "Drive safe and slow." He would have given her the number to Renee's phone, but Paola didn't have a phone.

Paola nodded. "I will." She eased the van forward and out of the bay. The door closed behind her.

Carver hid again and waited. The next van appeared on time, according to what he'd put in his notes. The driver hopped out. He didn't notice the broken windshield on the other van. He walked around to the back. Opened the back door and looked around as if expecting someone. Probably waiting for Vitor.

A bullet through his temple ended the fruitless wait. Carver dumped the body in the back of the other van. He took the money bags from both vans and piled them with the weapons behind machinery. He checked the driver's phone. It was also locked with a PIN.

Carver figured that Vitor required them to lock the phones with a specific number. He wanted to keep tabs on their texts and other communications. It was a common thing in organizations like this. Nobody trusted anyone completely. Unfortunately, Carver didn't have a way to find that number. Plus, he knew the information would be useless to him.

He went back to his hiding place. More vans arrived. More drivers died. By lunchtime he'd put down the final guy. Tossed the body in the first van. The back end was sagging from the weight. Blood was leaking from the back doors. Carver opened the cargo elevator. Backed the van inside of it. Got out and took it into the pit. He parked it next to the living quarters and left it.

Then he went back upstairs and loaded the van closest to the door with all the money and weapons. It was far more than he'd ever be able to use, but there was no telling where this trail would lead him.

Paola returned when he was finishing up. She parked next to his van and climbed out.

He walked around and met her. "Did things go smoothly?"

"Yes." She looked at the other vans. "And here?"

"There's a van in the pit with bodies in the back."

"Good." She watched him with dark eyes. "I stopped at a store and purchased a cell phone with no contract. I will tell the managers that Jasper went on vacation. I will tell them to call me if they need something."

"Does he go on vacation? He looked too big to get around much."

"Yes, regularly. He went to Thailand a few times each year. I think it will be impossible to move his body, so it's best if no one from the front comes back here."

"Thank you for thinking of these things. It's not my strong suit."

"No one is perfect." She folded her arms. "I don't want to stay here, and I don't want to stay with the women. Where are you going next?"

Carver flexed his blood-encrusted gloves. "I'm going to my motel to rest, then I'm going to stake out the mayor's house. Can you drive the van out of here? The guard will probably have questions if he sees me."

"Of course." Paola motioned toward the front area. "Let me talk with the floor manager. I'll be back in a moment."

"I'll be here." He leaned against the van and watched her walk away. The long hours and physical activity had worn him down. He was aching for a bed. His mind wasn't as sharp anymore either. It was good Paola was helping him through the minutia that might otherwise sabotage his efforts.

Paola returned after a while.

Carver opened the cargo doors. "Any problems?"

"None." Paola opened the driver side door. "The floor manager hates Jasper, so he was happy. Our secret is safe for a few days. I hope it's enough for you."

Carver hopped into the back and closed the rear doors. "I hope so too." He sat down on the bags of money.

Paola drove them outside. Past the guard shack. Onto the highway. She pulled over after a short distance.

Carver got out and walked around to the passenger seat. Got in. "I have an SUV hidden nearby. Let's swing by and grab it, then we can go to the motel."

They did that. He drove it to the motel and parked behind it. Paola parked the van next to the SUV. He got out. "You can use the cash to get another room."

"Does your room have two beds?"

"Yep."

"I'll take one."

"You're comfortable with that?"

"Yes." She watched him carefully. "You stopped touching me when I asked you to. Plus, you don't look at me like you're interested."

"If I saw you on the beach, I'd be interested. I'd probably even talk to you. But this isn't the beach. This is life and death."

"You have boundaries, and you respect boundaries."

"People aren't too happy otherwise." He walked around the building and unlocked the end unit. Let Paola inside first, then followed. He went straight for the bathroom. Closed and locked the door. Showered and dried off. He went out with a towel wrapped around him since he hadn't brought a change of clothes.

Paola was waiting outside with clothes and a towel. She looked at the scars on his chest but didn't say anything. She went into the bathroom and locked the door. Carver put on a pair of underwear. He normally slept in the nude but figured this wasn't a good time for that. He climbed under the covers and fell asleep fast.

Tomorrow was going to be a busy day.

—— ◆ ——

CHAPTER 30

Paola poured herself a bath.

She was exhausted mentally and physically. She could hardly believe what had happened during the night. Couldn't believe she was free at last. When she'd seen Carver cut Jasper's throat, she thought she was next. That he was an assassin, hired by a competitor.

It was hard to believe he was a lone man trying to find out who killed his friend. Paola wasn't sure she believed it. But his actions hadn't shown otherwise. He was tall and muscular. He could do anything he wanted to her, and she couldn't resist. But he'd backed off the instant she asked him.

There was also something about him that scared her. The lack of emotion in his eyes. He didn't look dead inside, but he certainly didn't show much on the outside. It was frightening and reassuring all at the same time.

Paola slipped into the hot water and breathed in relief. She hadn't had such luxuries at the factory. She'd been as much a slave as the other women. She just hadn't been used like them. At least not here. It had been another matter in Brazil.

She blocked those thoughts from her mind and tried to relax. Tried to feel nothing. Her heart had stopped racing at least, but her stomach felt twisted and knotted.

I'm free, she thought. *I can go where they'll never find me.* The thought comforted her somewhat, and her nerves relaxed. Maybe she was worthless enough that the cartel wouldn't care that she was gone. Or maybe they would think she had been killed along with everyone else. If anyone could make it happen, it would be her new guardian angel.

She said a quiet prayer and gave thanks to God. He had finally delivered her from evil.

MAYOR BUCK MORGAN woke up on the couch.

Jensen lay naked on the floor next to the blonde. It had been quite a night and his head ached something fierce. He went to the bathroom for ibuprofen and water.

Buck picked up his cell phone and checked his texts.

The wife had sent some pictures of the sunset out west. *Wish you were here, my love.*

He texted back. *Miss you too, babe. All work and no play.* He finished off the glass of water and poured himself another. Then he went to the den to get the brunette and take her to the shower. He had a full bladder, and he didn't want it to go to waste.

The brunette wasn't there. He walked around the surrounding rooms. She wasn't there either. There was a knock on the door. A solid thump, thump, thump. He looked through the peephole and saw his bodyguard, Reggie, outside. The brunette was struggling in his arms.

Buck opened the door. Reggie shoved the girl inside. "She was making a run for it."

"Thanks, Reggie."

"Taylor caught her coming out of the back. He brought her to me."

Buck closed the door and looked down at the girl. He grabbed her hair and yanked her closer. "I told you not to run, didn't I?"

"Y-yes." She trembled with sobs. "Please, just let me go home. I want to go home."

"You made your decisions, little lady. You ran away from home. Listened to the wrong people. Now this is your life." He released her hair and knelt next to her. Smoothed her hair back from her face. "Some people's lives are meant to be a warning to others. This is you."

"I want to go home." She kept sobbing. "I'll be better, I promise."

"No more parties? No more drugs? You'll listen to your parents and go back to college?"

"Yes, I promise!" She shivered. "I'll do anything."

Buck sighed. "That's what I like. Someone who can admit their mistakes and promise to do better."

She looked at him, eyes hopeful. "You'll let me go?"

He slapped her so hard she slumped. "Of course not. You had what, nineteen years to do better? You made this bed, now lie in it." He grabbed her hair and pulled her after him kicking and screaming. He shivered in pleasure. This was real power. And if things went to plan, he would turn Jasper's penny ante operation into something even bigger.

He dragged the girl into his big tile shower. Her struggling weakened. She was tired. He released her hair and let her drop to the floor. He stood over her. Aimed and released his bladder on her.

His phone rang. Buck kept peeing and checked the caller ID. It was Atlanta. Finally. Just a couple more days and things were going to get better.

CARVER ROLLED OUT of bed.

Stretched. Cracked the curtains and looked at the parking lot. It was just as empty as yesterday. Actually, that had been earlier today. These all-nighters were messing with his sense of time.

Paola was curled under the covers on the other bed, breathing gently. She was an attractive woman. It was surprising that Jasper hadn't used her like the other women. The cartel must have told him not to for some reason. Whatever it was, it was her business.

He gently nudged her. Backed up and sat on his bed.

She gasped and jerked awake. Rolled over and looked at him. The fear turned to relief. "Yes, Carver?"

"I'm going to get breakfast. Want to come?"

She rubbed her eyes. Stretched like a cat. Nodded. "Yes. I'm hungry."

"Okay. Get dressed."

"What time is it?"

"About four PM."

Paola laughed. "And you still call it breakfast?"

"We're breaking a fast. And it's the first meal of our day."

"I suppose you're right." She pulled on shorts, black boots, and a t-shirt.

Carver watched her curiously. "Where did you get those clothes?"

"From my closet at the paint factory."

"Ah." He slid into another pair of black cargo pants. His clean clothes supply was rapidly dwindling.

Paola looked at the bloody clothes he'd been wearing the day before. "Maybe you should burn those."

Carver dumped out his last set of clean clothes and shoved the bloody shirt, pants, and gloves into the paper bag. "Yeah, I got sloppy. I should've done it earlier."

"You're tired. I can see it in your face." She reached up and touched his cheek. Ran her thumb under his eye. "You've been sleeping, but your body is still tired."

"Yeah." He grabbed some money and the bag of bloody clothes. "Let's go eat."

They went around back. Hopped in the SUV. Carver drove twenty minutes to a diner that was far outside of town. He got black coffee, pancakes, bacon, and eggs. Paola ordered the same thing, but with orange juice.

She regarded him curiously. "Tell me more about yourself, Carver."

"Not much to tell."

"That's not true."

Carver reversed it. "Tell me about yourself."

"There's not much you don't already know."

Carver grinned. "That's not true either."

"I suppose not." She watched him with her dark eyes. "You were military. I think you've killed a lot of people. You seem like the kind of person who is very calm until provoked."

"That sums me up, I guess." He sipped his coffee. "You were just a normal person in Brazil, but something happened. Probably got someone in your family killed. I'm guessing you had a brother who worked for the cartel, but he messed up. Now he's dead and they forced you to work for them."

"I do have a brother, but he immigrated to Europe years ago. My father worked for the cartel, laundering money. He decided to skim money and they found out. They killed him and my mother, then kidnapped me. They told me my father's secrets and said my service would pay back all the money he stole."

"You didn't know what he was doing?"

She shook her head. "My family wasn't wealthy by American standards, but we were very well off for Brazil. I thought my father was an ordinary financial manager. My father thought he was smarter than the cartel. We were both wrong."

"I can see how that would be bad."

She laughed. "You have a calm way with words, Carver."

The food arrived and they ate in silence. Carver considered telling her a little more about himself, but it didn't seem necessary. He'd been one thing, then another, then accused of being something else, and now he was just a civilian. The best he could say about himself was that he'd done his duty, saved lives, taken lives, and learned some hard lessons. Now he was just trying to take out whoever had set events into motion so he could secure his flank.

He didn't want to live life constantly looking over his shoulder. He wanted to go back to a peaceful existence somewhere nobody knew him. He wanted to be left alone.

"You look troubled." Paola gazed at him while she sipped orange juice. "Don't feel bad about what you've done, Carver. You saved lives. You're a hero."

Carver shook his head. "I'm not on a mission, Paola. I'm not here to do good, okay? Someone tried to kill me. I'm trying to find out who so I can put an end to it. Another nail in the coffin. Until I do, I'm a dead man walking. "

"You saved me. You saved those women and many women who won't end up in Jasper's harem in the future." Paola stabbed her scrambled eggs with a fork. "You're a gift from God."

He laughed. "You're so weird. Why would you believe in a God that took your parents from you and forced you to work with a drug cartel?"

"The sins of the father, I think." She ate her eggs. Shrugged. "I prayed for help, and you came. I kept my faith and God answered. What don't you understand about that?"

Carver finished his pancakes and stacked his plates. "It's sweet, but strange."

"Call it what you want, Carver." She wiped her mouth with a napkin. "I'm here to help my avenging angel with whatever he needs."

"Thank you. You thought of things I never would have considered." He leaned back. "I have a particular set of skills and one of them isn't making tactical plans."

"Tell me what I need to know, Carver." Paola smiled. "Isn't that what you Americans say in the military? Need to know basis?"

"It is." He waved the server over for a coffee refill. When she left, he started the story from the beginning. Told her about Rhodes, about Ruben, Jimmy, and Settler. About the Brothers. Told her everything all the way up to the last driver he killed.

Paola smiled. "Holly doesn't know you killed those men at the police station?"

"No, and I'd like to keep it that way." He sipped his coffee. "We'll need to talk to her. Let her know what happened at the factory."

"You think we can trust her?"

"Yes. She's got a good sense of justice combined with a load of common sense." He shrugged. "If the mayor is involved, then I'm going to need her help now more than ever."

Paola nodded. "You don't know how the two murdered women, Renee and Charlotte, are involved in this?"

"They're connected to Rhodes." Carver stared at his coffee. "Why she took such an interest in them, I don't know."

Paola took a pen and napkin. She made a circle with an RH in the middle. Two circles below it with RE in one and CH in the other. Rhodes, Renee, Charlotte. Another circle for the paint factory. Another for the Mayor. Another with a question mark in it. She connected the factory to the mayor. Connected the mayor to the question mark. Drew a dotted line from Rhodes to the mayor. Another dotted line from Rhodes to the question mark.

Carver looked at the circles. "That about sums it up. Maybe the mayor is connected to Rhodes. Maybe he's not. But he's definitely got connections with the paint factory."

"I think he's linked to everything. This is his town." Paola folded her arms across her chest. "You will need to know how many men are protecting the mayor. Where he sleeps. How to approach his house. It's on the side of a mountain, yes?"

"It is. On a plateau." Carver had looked at it on the map app, but he hadn't seen it in person since his first day here. "I think he has a view of the whole town from there. Some sides are covered in trees, so a covert approach is possible." He showed Paola the satellite view on the map app.

She rotated the phone and scrolled around. "One paved road leading up. It looks like there are dirt roads too."

"Yeah, leading to pastures."

"You should ask Holly to drive out there. She can pretend she's on business." Paola pushed the phone back to him. "She can tell you how many men are up there, and their positions."

Carver nodded. "That's a good idea. I'll ask her."

"Surely you already thought of that."

He shook his head. "No. I thought of using her to get into the paint factory. It was a bad idea. It would've gotten her killed."

"So, you went in yourself."

"Yes."

"Let's go meet with Holly now." Paola checked the clock on the wall. "She can go today. Then you can go in tonight. We still have a few hours of daylight left."

"I like that idea."

"You told me you don't have much time. I think the women you rescued will be okay for a few days, but I don't trust them to keep quiet for very long. They're desperate to get home, and I don't blame them."

"I understand that. It was a big ask, but if I don't find out who wanted Rhodes dead, then they might still be in danger. It might all be connected."

"Possibly." Paola folded her napkin. "The mayor and his son borrowed women often. No one else did because the women were mainly for Jasper. Human trafficking is not a major part of the cartel business as far as I know."

"It's the military connection I'm interested in. The mayor uses people who walk and talk a lot like Ruben and Jimmy. Former military turned freelancers. That's why I think the mayor might be the one who ordered Rhodes's death."

"I can see that." Paola wadded up the napkin and dropped it on a plate. "Let's go see Holly now."

Carver paid the bill and they left. He took a county road to avoid passing by the prison and the medical examiner. Ended up on the back side of town near the police station half an hour later. He parked behind the fence.

"You're very careful."

"Have to be." He slid out of the seat. "I think the mayor has people watching for me in town."

"Surely he has people in the police department already watching you when you come to town."

"True. But something feels different about the freelancers." He went into the lobby. Saw Maberly at his desk behind the window. "Is Holly here?"

Maberly frowned. "Why are you still here, boy? I'd be long gone by now if I were you."

"The mayor wants me to stick around." Carver went to the window. "Can you get Holly for me?"

He sighed. "She's on the west side helping animal control with a rabid racoon."

"Where, exactly?"

Maberly looked from Paola to him. "Who is that?"

"A friend. Just give me Holly's number and I'll call her."

"She's over on Westminster Drive. Third house on the right."

"Thanks." Carver left. Checked the location on the map. It was ten minutes away.

They arrived at a street with single-story shoebox homes. Nylon siding. Cars parked on cinder blocks in the driveway. A mess of children's toys in the front yard.

Holly's cruiser was parked on the side of the road. She was leaning against it. Watching a pair of animal control agents trying to lasso a furious raccoon. It wasn't going well. She did a doubletake when Carver parked the SUV behind her cruiser. She looked from him to Paola.

He dropped out of the car. "Got a moment?"

She walked around to his side. "Where have you been?"

"Doing some things."

Paola walked around to join them. "Hello, I'm Paola."

Holly frowned. "What's going on here?"

"Do you have a moment to talk?" Carver asked again.

She blew out a long breath. "Yes. Now tell me where you've been."

"Looking for clues."

"Okay, Scooby Doo." Holly laughed like she didn't believe him. "Tell me what you've really been doing."

"I will, but you might not like it," Carver said. He told her what he'd done at the paint factory.

Her eyes grew wider and wider as he talked, but she didn't say anything until he finished. Holly's eyes grew accusing. "You committed mass murder."

CHAPTER 31

M ass murder sounded heavy.

Carver didn't think of it like that. It was a war. A small war with a limited number of casualties.

"He executed people who needed to be executed," Paola said. "You know I'm right."

Holly went pale. Leaned against the car. "The mayor has been raping trafficked women he got from Jasper?"

Paola nodded. "His son picks them up most of the time."

Holly's face paled. "Jensen."

Paola nodded. "Yes, Jensen. The mayor rarely came there. I don't think the mayor and Jasper like each other very much."

"They don't." Holly leaned against the SUV for support. "Buck blames Jasper for destroying Morganville. He hates him."

"Makes sense," Carver said. "I think the mayor had something to do with Rhodes's death. I need you to take a drive up there and tell me how many men he has guarding his place. Get a good look at the layout."

"So you can roll through there and kill everyone?" Holly shook her head. "I can't do that. I'm an officer of the law!"

"I just need answers." Carver glanced at the animal control guys. They'd finally gotten the noose around the animal's neck. "Your police department is corrupt, Holly. And if you try to bring in the feds, nothing will happen. Do you want justice for Rhodes?"

"You're not looking for justice, Carver."

"You're right. I need to eliminate a threat so I can continue to live in peace." He wasn't sure what else to say. "You can help, or you can sit it out. Either way, I'm going to talk to the mayor on my terms. I need to find out who planned Rhodes's murder. Who decided to use me as the fall guy. It was a good plan, but the execution wasn't so great."

"I still don't understand why they'd kill Settler and those two men." Holly stared at the thrashing raccoon. "That part just doesn't add up." She turned to Paola. "I'm so sorry what you and those women were put through. I know it must seem like Carver is doing the right thing, but this is vigilante execution, not justice."

Paola's dark eyes lit with anger. "It is God's justice. These powerful men have been dealing drugs. Brutalizing and killing women. They make a mockery of your laws. Maybe you can't see that, but Carver can. Maybe his heart isn't in the right place, but his head is. He is doing what needs to be done. Can you help him, or will he go in alone with no idea of what to expect?"

Holly gently pounded her fist on the side of the SUV. "I went to school with Jensen. He always seemed so nice. I can't believe he's part of this."

Paola grimaced. "I watched him test women to see which ones he would take home with him. He made them orally pleasure him. Forced them to take objects into their bumbums." Paola shivered. "It made me sick. He enjoyed making me watch."

Holly looked confused. "Bumbums?"

"Their butts," Paola said. "In Brazil we call them bumbums."

Holly's gaze went distant. "This one girl in high school accused Jensen of rape. No one believed her. Everyone thought Jensen was a good guy." Holly stared into the distance. "He went to church. He traveled to Atlanta to participate in volunteer service. I guess it was all a lie."

"Bad people compensate," Carver said. "If someone is rabidly religious, it usually means they're atoning for some bad stuff."

Paola raised an eyebrow. "You think I'm rabidly religious, Carver."

He nodded. "Yeah, and you like me executing people. You'd probably do it yourself if you could."

She nodded. "I think I would enjoy taking vengeance on evildoers."

"Okay, I'll help." Holly watched the animal control men put down the raccoon with a .22 pistol. "I'll drive out there and see what I can see."

"The mayor might have had Renee and Charlotte killed," Carver said. "Maybe Rhodes found out about the women being trafficked. Maybe he thought Rhodes had told them."

"It's almost funny." Holly didn't look amused. "You thought the paint factory was behind everything. Jasper told you they weren't. You believed him and you still killed everyone."

"Because they were trying to kill me." Carver put a hand on her shoulder. "It's hard to live in peace when a cartel is after you."

"Either he kills them or he's a dead man walking," Paola said.

Holly gave her a look. "You're starting to sound like him."

"My accent isn't that heavy," Carver said. "But she's right. Unless I kill these people, I'll never be able to stop looking over my shoulder. They're above the law and have small armies protecting them. There's no other way to do this but vigilante style."

"Damn it, Carver." Holly pounded her fist on the SUV again. "I hate it, but you're right. Let me give you my number."

Carver punched her number into Renee's phone and texted her, *Hi.*

The message popped up on her phone. Holly slid into her cruiser and wheeled it around. She punched the accelerator and hit the road running.

Paola hopped back into the SUV.

Carver got in and drummed his fingers on the steering wheel. "Now, we wait."

"Where?"

"I need to get close to the mayor's house. I want to get a closer look through my binoculars."

"Okay."

Carver checked the map. Found the routes that would take him near the mayor's own personal mountain. He made a U-turn and got back on the county road. Headed east. A rough paved road took him south. It led him up a mountain to the east of the mayor's place. He found a spot that let him see most of the side. It was covered in trees. If there were any dirt roads, they were hidden by the foliage.

The house wasn't visible from this side. It was perched on a plateau on the west side. Carver didn't see any men. Any vehicles. Just a big cell tower straddling the peak. It probably served half the county from that vantage point.

He walked to the edge of the dirt road. Tried to get a better viewing angle down through the trees. They were too thick. If he wanted a better idea of the terrain, he'd have to go on foot. That wasn't part of the plan just yet. He climbed back in the pickup and continued along the dirt road.

It followed the curve of the mountain and dipped into a valley. It ended at a cow pasture on the eastern side of the mayor's mountain. Carver surveyed the route up the mountain from here. It was steep. A little rocky. He would be tired by the time he scaled to the top. Or he could climb to the same height as the house and walk laterally until he reached it.

But if he reached the top and there were a dozen armed guards there then things wouldn't go well. The Brazilians hadn't been well trained. These guys might react faster. They would be better shots. More coordinated. He needed to know what he'd be up against.

He turned the SUV around. Followed the dirt road back to the paved road. Followed it back to another road that intersected the state highway he'd walked in on that fateful day. He passed a lot of pasturelands. A lot of open space. A lot of cows. On the north side of the mountain, he took another long look. He could see the profile of the house from here.

It was jutting out just above the tree line below it. The lookout had been somewhere up there the day he'd come to town.

Carver drove to the highway. Steered south. Kept going past the spot where he'd found Rhodes's gun. He went past the pasture where the lookout had been. He kept going until there was forest on both sides of the road. Then he made a U-turn and parked at the edge of the trees. From here he could see the switchback driveway winding up between the northern pasture and the forest. He had a clear view of the house, too.

He looked through the binoculars again. Saw Holly's cruiser parked in the front. Saw her talking to a young guy outside the front door. Carver zoomed the binoculars as far as they would go. The guy was grinning. Laughing like he didn't have two abused women inside his house. Like he hadn't done an evil thing in his life.

Even from this distance he looked charismatic. Charming. Like he didn't have a care in the world. Holly was smiling too. Like she enjoyed the conversation.

"Can I look?" Paola asked.

Carver handed her the binoculars.

She watched for several minutes. "He shows all the classic signs of a psychopath."

"Agreed." Carver leaned back in his seat. "Menendez and Rocker used to call me a psychopath."

Paola lowered the binoculars. "Who are they?"

"Some people from my squad."

"What were their roles?"

"Recon, sabotage, recovery, snatch and grabs." He rested a hand on the steering wheel. "A lot of things."

"Did you like them?"

Carver shrugged. "About as well as I liked anyone in the squad. We were all family in the field. Looking out for each other."

"What about when you were in the States? When you were home?"

"We'd usually get a month of leave after a long mission. Everyone went their separate ways. Some of them had family."

Paola nodded. "And you?"

"Rhodes and I would hang out some. Go drinking. She wasn't married, but she had a brother in Louisiana. I went down there with her once. It was nice."

"You and Rhodes were close."

Carver gave it some thought. "Sometimes I feel like she watched out for me like a big sister to a little brother. Like she figured if she didn't invite me out that I'd just be alone."

"But you're happy like that, aren't you?"

"Yeah. Maybe not happy, but content. Just give me a good beach and sunshine, you know?" Carver smiled. "That's what I want when this is over. It's nice being on my own."

"Did you miss Rhodes at all?"

"Yeah. She was family." His throat went dry. "But I lost my family when they disbanded us."

"What happened, Carver?" Paola touched his hand. "I can hear the pain in your voice."

"It's classified."

"That's bullshit. Tell me. It's important."

Carver picked up the binoculars and watched Holly. She was talking to the mayor. Buck was smiling but there was suspicion in his eyes. He knew something was up. The man looked on edge and this visit from Holly was making it worse.

"Damn it." Carver sent her a text. *Leave now.*

Paola looked at his phone. "What's wrong?"

"The mayor isn't buying what she's selling."

"Is that an American saying? Because I don't understand."

"He's wondering why she's visiting him. I don't know what she told him, but he thinks she's up to something." Carver put the binoculars to his eyes. Holly looked at her phone. She waved and backed away. Smiling nodding. Saying her goodbyes.

Buck's driver came up behind her. Put a gun to her back. Holly froze. The driver took her gun and her belt. He put a hand on the back of her neck and shoved her inside the house. The mayor got out of the way.

Two more men walked into view. Both brandishing rifles. Both had sidearms holstered on their belts. Both wore black uniforms and headsets. They had the same former military look as the driver. Freelancers.

Buck spoke with them. They nodded and disappeared on opposite sides of the house.

"Shit." Carver put down the binoculars. "They took her inside at gunpoint."

Paola tightened her grip on his hand. "What do we do?"

It was almost seven. Another couple of hours before sundown. "I can't go in until it's dark."

"And then what? You don't even know how many men are there or where they're keeping her."

"There are at least three guards, the mayor, and Jensen. Holly and the two women Jensen took are inside the house. No guard dogs which is good."

"How do you know there aren't any dogs?"

"Because they would have started barking when Holly drove up. A sound like that would carry from way up there."

"You learned this from just watching for a few minutes?"

"Holly drew out the guards." He stared at the mountain. "If there are only three guards, it means the mayor isn't the person I'm looking for. He's just another steppingstone to the top."

"Why do you say that?"

"Because whoever put the plan in motion sent Ruben and Jimmy and at least four to five more guys into town after me. A person like that would have a small army around their mansion." Carver shook his head. "The mayor might be hiring these guys from the same people who sent the others. That's the gut feeling I get."

Paola touched his hand. "What is your plan?"

Carver picked up the binoculars and scanned the terrain. It was hard to see through the trees. The angle wasn't as steep on this approach. He could probably parallel the driveway going to the house. If there were only three guards, they wouldn't see him coming. One of them was inside the house right now.

The mayor might also call in more men. Someone at the police department had told the mayor that Carver was looking for Holly. That someone was Maberly. When Holly showed up on his doorstep, the mayor probably thought Carver was right behind her. That was what had triggered his suspicions in the first place. That was why he might want reinforcements from whoever supplied him the freelancers.

"I shouldn't have sent her." He'd known the mayor might have his suspicions, but he hadn't expected him to act so overtly. Especially not against a cop.

"I can't believe he took a police officer hostage." Paola clasped her hands tightly. "People like this don't follow the rules."

"That's what I was trained for," Carver said. "I don't follow the rules either."

BUCK SHOVED HOLLY on the floor next to the other women.

Maberly had told him Carver was looking for her. That he was going to meet her. Then she showed up on his doorstep to talk about the dead men found in the boiler tank. He'd immediately put two and two together. She was actively working with Carver. They knew he was connected somehow.

But how?

He turned to Reggie. "Who's the best interrogator? You, Jack, or Alex?"

Reggie answered without hesitation. "Alex."

"Get him. I need some answers."

Reggie double-timed it outside. Returned a moment later with Alex. He was short and wiry. He had that lean kind of muscle everyone underestimated until it knocked them on their asses. He was also ruthless and efficient.

Alex looked over Holly. "What you need, boss?"

"I want to ask her some questions. I want her to answer them quickly and truthfully."

He looked her up and down. "I'll need to test her limits. Find her tolerances."

"Why are you doing this, Buck?" Holly tried to stand, but Reggie shoved her back down. "Who are these girls?"

"Don't play dumb, Holly." Buck stared right into her soul. "You're working for Carver. I want to find out what he knows."

"I just came up here to—"

Alex twisted her pinky finger. She screamed in pain. He eased off. Watched her carefully. Buck didn't know what he was looking for, but he let the man do his job.

Jensen walked into the den eating a bagel. He grinned at Holly. "I told you police work was no good for somebody as pretty as you."

"Fuck you, Jensen."

"I'd love to." He looked at his dad. "Can I?"

Buck nodded. "When we're finished getting answers."

Alex pinched the space between Holly's thumb and index finger. She cried out. Tried to wrest her hand free. He pinched tighter. Released the hand and watched her again. Then he took her arm and twisted it behind her back. Holly gasped. Tried to stand to relieve the pressure. Reggie pushed her back down.

Alex pulled a little harder. Holly screamed. "Answer the mayor's questions and I'll give you some relief."

"Carver doesn't know anything! He said he wanted to know if we found out who killed Settler and those two men. I swear it!"

"That's not true." Buck knelt in front of her. "Because Carver is the one who killed them."

She gasped. Her eyes flared. "What?"

Buck laughed. "Ease up, Alex."

He released her arm. "Might have to go with pliers and fingernails, boss."

Holly rubbed her arm. Stared at Buck in disbelief. "How in the hell could Carver kill three men while he was in jail?"

Buck kept laughing. The look on her face was priceless. "Because those morons were supposed to kill him. Make it look like a hanging. He killed them and covered it up. I had to admit when I found out about it, I thought it was genius. That boy is good at his job."

Her gaze went distant. "That asshole. Why wouldn't he tell me? I can't believe it!" She pounded her fists on the floor. "I hate liars!"

"He's been lying to you all this time, Holly." Buck put a sympathetic hand on her shoulder. "You owe him nothing. Now, tell me, why did he send you here?"

"He thinks you killed Rhodes. He wants to know why."

"That boy is in over his head if he thinks he's coming for me." Buck sobered. "Reggie, call your boss. Tell him we can end this today. I just need more men."

"Yes, sir." He stepped out of the room.

Holly looked confused. "More men? Who are you working for?"

"No one, dear." Buck traced a hand down her face. She slapped it away. He nodded at Alex. The other man twisted her arm behind her back again. "Tell me everything Carver knows."

"What he knows?" Holly winced in pain. "How should I know? He's been lying to me all this time! He asked me to come up here and tell you about the three dead men to see what your reaction was. I was just bait!"

"I'm afraid so." He unbuttoned her shirt. She tried to struggle, but Alex ratcheted up the pain. He caressed her bra. "I've been wanting to do this for a while."

Tears trickled down Holly's cheeks. "You sick bastard."

"Alex, take her to the basement bed. Tie her up nice and tight."

"You got it, boss."

Reggie stepped back into the room. "I couldn't reach them, so I left a message."

"It's fine, just—" The front door creaked open, and all hell broke loose.

CHAPTER 32

Carver watched the house with the binoculars.

The short guard went inside. The third guy stood on the south side looking into the big window. Watching whatever was going on in there.

He rotated out of the SUV. Went to the back and opened the hatch.

Paola scrambled out after him. "What are you doing, Carver?"

"I'm going in."

"Now?"

"Now." He slung on his belt. Loaded magazines into the ammo pouches. Slid Ruben's knife into the thigh sheath. Slung a Kalashnikov over his back, strap across his chest. Holstered the Glocks.

The switchback road cut through open pasture until it reached the house. There was no good way to drive across the road and up to the house without being seen. The forest on the right side of the road was dense enough to hide him, but too thick to run through. He'd have to run alongside it and hope everyone was too busy looking at the house to notice him.

Carver handed the binoculars to Paola. "If it goes bad, take the money and run."

She nodded. "I will."

"You have documents?"

"I have a green card and passport, but they took them from me. I don't know where they put them."

"There's a guy named Jason Wilson in Benton, Arkansas. He used to be a CIA lawyer but now he's doing whatever that free lawyer stuff is." Carver tried to remember an address but couldn't. "Go find him and he'll get you new documents. Oh, and take care of those other women if you want to."

Paola took his hands. "I'd prefer you stay alive, okay? Don't die."

"I'll try." He slid his hands out of hers and jogged into the forest. The bushes were thick, but he pushed through. He wanted to get up the slope a little way before running out in the open. Further into the trees, the bushes thinned out. The ground was covered in leaves and pine straw. There wasn't enough sunlight for the bushes to grow thick.

Maybe the forest wasn't too thick to run through after all.

He hustled up the slope. His boots slipped in the pine straw from time to time, but his progress was steady. It was a long, hard quarter mile to cover. He hadn't stayed in top shape over the past few years. The humid air felt thick in his lungs. It felt hotter than the beach somehow. But he didn't stop. Kept breathing. Kept moving.

The slope turned to a rocky ridge where it met the plateau. It was too steep to climb. He paralleled it toward the driveway. Stepped out of the forest and into the pasture. The ridge was lower here. It had been blasted away for the driveway to pass through. He reached the driveway. Readied the AK-47. Crept forward until the house was visible.

The third guard wasn't in sight. The first guard stepped out of the house. Put a phone to his ear. Talked for a few seconds and went back inside.

A picture window faced the driveway. If he continued this way, someone might see him. Or they might be preoccupied with whatever was going on inside that they might not notice. He could see silhouettes moving inside, but he couldn't see faces.

Carver dropped to his stomach. Low-crawled the final few feet. Turned back toward the forest and kept crawling. He heard footsteps coming around the house. Carver rolled into the bushes. Waited. The third guard entered his view. The guy looked preoccupied. Like he wanted to be inside with the others instead of out here.

He was just a hired hand. Not much different than a maid or a gardener. Except he was armed. He knew the mayor was using sex slaves. He was okay with it. If he was just a guy who didn't know anything, that was one thing. But this was something else. This guy was complicit.

The guard stopped. Listened. Frowned. He readied his rifle and walked toward the ridge. Carver didn't know what he'd heard. Birds were singing. Bugs were chirping. But he hadn't heard twigs snapping or anything rustling in the leaves.

Carver watched the guard go past him. The man looked out over the ridge. Carver rolled onto the grass. Drew his knife. Eased up behind the man. The guard relaxed. Turned around. Ruben's knife went into his throat. Carver gripped the man's trigger finger to keep it from clenching.

The guard's eyes were wide with shock. He gurgled. Tried to fight off Carver. But he ran out of blood and strength.

Carver checked the man's rifle. It was a classic Colt M4A1 carbine with an aimpoint on the top. It was a good reliable weapon. He cleared the chamber and ejected a 5.56 round. He picked it up and looked it over. It was a tungsten-carbide core armor-piercing round. Standard range combat. He popped the magazine and slid the cartridge into the top.

It would be hard to use inside a house. Carver preferred pistols for close quarter combat. He frisked the body. Took the sidearm and a knife. Some ammo. A pair of flashbang grenades. Military grade, not civilian.

He rolled the body over the ridge. Put the loot to the side of the house. Then he considered his next step. A flashbang might do the trick, but if there were a lot of people in proximity, it might do more harm than good. And if all the targets weren't in one place, it would just announce his presence.

Carver dropped them into one of his pouches. They were already so heavy with ammo that he hoped it didn't hinder him if he had to duck or roll. He dumped the .762 magazines on the ground. Dropped the Kalashnikov and switched to the Colt. The two extra magazines would hopefully be enough. Four 9mm magazines were clipped to the side of the belt so they didn't affect his mobility.

He went to the front door. Crouched. Eased it open. It creaked. There was a foyer. The guy who'd been on the phone was there. He spun toward Carver. Carver fired the Glock three times. Two in the chest. One in the head.

But the guy changed his spin to a dive at the last minute. Two rounds hit his ribs. The other round missed completely. The man shouted in pain. He should have been lethally injured, but he wasn't. The bulky tactical gear wasn't just for show. He had on body armor.

The mayor flashed past the foyer. Ran out of sight. Jensen ran after him.

Carver switched to the M4A1. He swiftly rounded the corner. The first guy was still rolling into his back. Rifle coming to bear. The Colt boomed. A hardened round went through the guy. Ricocheted off the hard floor beneath. Blasted through the wall above the fireplace and kept going somewhere outside.

Keeping an eye on the aimpoint, Carver spun. Visually cleared the room. The second guard wasn't in sight.

The den was big and walled off from the foyer. A doublewide entrance led to the kitchen. An open space beyond had a stairwell to the second story. Two women were huddled in the corner of the den, shaking and sobbing. No sign of Holly.

Buck, Jensen, and the other guard were missing. They probably had Holly. Probably upstairs. In seconds, they'd all be armed and sheltered in a room. The situation would be next to impossible unless he was okay with losing Holly.

He ran upstairs. Cleared the hallway in both directions. There were two bedrooms on the left. One on the right. Without a team watching his six, this was going to be hairy. He guessed they'd gone to the single bedroom on the right. It was probably the master suite.

Carver kept his eye on the aimpoint. Treaded carefully toward the door. He waited outside. Listened. It was quiet. Too quiet. He cleared the left, then the right. The room was dark. There was a bed, a dresser, a closet, a bathroom. All places for a shooter to hide. He crouched and listened. Still nothing.

He picked up a pair of pants discarded on the floor and tossed them at the bathroom. Still silence. No movement. No one was in here, or they were unarmed and hiding. He reached back and flicked on the lights. The bedroom was empty. He cleared the bathroom and the closet.

Carver went to the two bedrooms on the other end of the hall. Cleared them and their bathrooms. Even if he suspected no one was up here, it was better to be safe than sorry. But now he was ten minutes behind. They were somewhere else, ready and waiting.

He went back downstairs. Checked the kitchen. The door was closed. He checked the other rooms. Found a door and carpeted stairs leading down to a basement. It was walled in so they couldn't see him coming and he couldn't see them until he reached the bottom. The wall was probably just wood and drywall. Bullets would punch through it like paper.

Carver returned to the den. He frisked the dead guard. This guy had the same weapons and ammo. He wore a thin armored vest beneath his shirt. It would stop nine-millimeter, but definitely not the hardened 5.56 ammo in the Colt.

He moved the body and looked at the floor underneath. The bullet had gone into the carpet and hit a slab. The basement was encased in concrete. Normally there would be wood subflooring under the carpet. Not in this rich man's house. The basement was hardened. There might even be a saferoom.

The dead guy might be useful. First, Carver needed to test something. He went to the basement entry. Fired a round into the wall. The bullet pierced the drywall. Bounced off concrete beneath it.

Someone shouted in alarm. Gunfire erupted. Bullets whined off the concrete.

"Stop firing, you idiot!" Buck shouted.

Carver knelt at the top of the stairs. "Armored piercing rounds sound cool, don't they? Not so cool when you're surrounded by concrete."

"We have Holly, Carver." Buck sounded confident. "Surrender and she can go free."

"Answer some questions and I'll consider it."

"No. Surrender now or she dies."

"And then what?"

Buck hesitated. "What do you mean?"

"What happens after you kill her?"

"We storm up there and kill you!" Jensen shouted. "There's three of us against one of you, asshole."

Carver aimed the rifle at the corner of the wall at the bottom of the stairwell. "I don't think your bodyguard would agree with that strategy."

"He's right," someone said with a light Hispanic accent. "But we hold the winning hand."

Carver fired. The bullet pinged off the wall. Zinged diagonally into the room below. There were three shouts of surprise, all males. If Holly was down there, she was gagged.

"You're insane!" Jensen screamed. "That nearly took off my head!"

"Shut up, you idiot!" Buck shouted.

Someone murmured in hushed tones. Probably the guard. Probably telling Buck that Holly was useless as a hostage. Carver didn't want her dead, but he wasn't negotiating for her release either. He figured Holly was laid out flat somewhere. Bound and gagged. That gave her a good chance to avoid being hit by bullets.

While they were talking, Carver went back to the dead guard. He recovered two flashbangs from him. Stripped off his holster and belt, then hoisted him. He lugged him to the stairwell. The vest would probably fit Carver, but there was no sense messing with it considering the armor-piercing ammo.

He imagined the layout of the basement. Judging from the sound of their voices, they were positioned to fire on anyone coming downstairs. The staircase was against the back wall of the house. If the space was as large as the house, there would be concrete support beams. Maybe even walls.

All they had to do was fire into the stairwell if they saw him. The ricocheting bullets would do the rest. The other problem was the noise. Firing a gun in that concrete tomb was deafening. In the field they wore headsets that mitigated loud noises while allowing communications. Carver's ears were already ringing from firing twice into the stairwell.

The biggest issue was keeping the mayor alive. Carver wanted answers. He needed the man to live, but that would be difficult. There weren't many options, so he went with the plan he'd concocted just a moment ago.

The dead guard was five feet, seven inches. He was slim, maybe a hundred and ninety pounds. Not too heavy, but still dead weight. Carver wrapped an arm under the dead guy's armpits and over his chest. He walked him down the stairs. The carpeting on the stairs muffled the noise.

At the bottom was a small five by five landing and a double-sized entryway to the basement. Not a lot of space for maneuvering and certainly not for avoiding ricocheting bullets. This would have to be swift and immaculate. The surviving guard would be the first to catch on. Jensen would probably fire until he emptied his magazine. The mayor was a wildcard.

Unless they had on ear protection, they'd be just as deafened as Carver when Jensen opened fire. Jensen wouldn't hear them shouting right away. He'd empty his magazine. Buck might do the same. The guard would be the problem. He'd spot what was coming and react properly.

Carver readied himself at the bottom. He heard Jensen arguing. Heard the guard answering. They were distracted. He gripped the dead guy by the top of his vest with both hands. Angled himself. Put a boot on the guy's back and gave the body a vicious shove.

He grabbed the flashbangs the instant the body went sailing into the basement. Looped a finger through both pins and pulled them. Gunfire erupted. The body danced in a hail of bullets. Carver reached around the corner and threw both flashbangs. Booms echoed. He crouched and poked his head around the corner.

The basement was wide open. No concrete pillars. It was covered in thick red carpet. There were ropes, chains, contraptions. A big bed at the far corner with a struggling figure on it. A red leather couch was positioned about twenty feet from Carver. It had probably been dragged into place for cover. There wasn't anything else down here that could hope to block bullets.

Jensen was shouting. Crawling on the floor blindly. The flashbangs must have hit him directly. The guard was prone on the floor. Squinting and aiming. He'd probably averted his eyes at the last minute. Carver put the red dot in the aimpoint on the guy's head and fired. It grazed the side of his face. He adjusted quickly and fired again. Blood and brains misted.

The guard went down.

Carver rushed the couch. The carpet behind it was black. A flashbang had landed perfectly behind it. The other one had bounced off the couch. Mayor Buck Morgan lay prone right next to the black mark. A piece of metal jutted from his temple.

He wouldn't be answering any questions.

CHAPTER 33

The mayor was dead.

"Damn it." Carver booted Jensen in the side. Rolled him over. The kid's face was covered in blood. His and his father's rifles were on the floor. Carver checked Buck's pulse to be sure. He was dead.

Maybe the kid could answer his questions. He grabbed Jensen by the shirt and yanked him to his feet. Jensen flailed his fists. Carver batted them aside. Gripped him by the throat and squeezed. "Calm down or I'll put you down."

Jensen whimpered. Went limp. "Don't kill me."

"I won't. But you need to answer some questions." Carver shoved him toward the bed. "First, let's get Officer Holly off that bed."

Jensen shuffled over to the bed. There were leather straps with metal buckles holding Holly down. Her shirt was ripped open, but she looked okay otherwise. Jensen unbuckled the strap on her right foot, then her right wrist. Carver watched him walk to the other side and unbuckle them. Holly slid off the bed. Kneed Jensen in the crotch.

He screamed and went down. Rolled on the floor. Whimpered.

Holly stared at Carver with a mix of fear and gratitude. She pointed to a mark on the wall over the bed. "Your bullet did that."

"Sorry."

"You didn't care if I lived or died, did you?"

"I cared, but I had to take a chance. I didn't know the layout."

"You barged down here blind."

"Yeah, but I made them blind first." Carver dragged Jensen to his feet. "Holly, grab the rifles and ammunition."

Holly glowered at Jensen. "You brought me to your sex dungeon, you sick son of a bitch? Were you and your dad going to take turns with me?"

"No!"

She tried to kick him again, but Carver blocked her. "I need him. Please get the weapons and ammo and meet me upstairs."

Holly worked her jaw back and forth. "Fine."

Carver pushed Jensen ahead of him. The kid was holding his crotch and limping. "Don't get any ideas, okay?"

Jensen glanced back at him. "I won't."

They walked past his dad's body. Past the dead guard. Turned the corner and went upstairs. The kid didn't cry. He hardly reacted. He was definitely a psychopath. Just like Carver.

Paola was upstairs with the two women. Carver looked outside and saw the SUV parked in the driveway. "Why did you come up here?"

"I thought you might need help."

"I thought you agreed to run if things went bad."

"Things went good, though. You're still breathing." Paola gave glasses of water to the women and sat them on the couch. "I thought I'd get the women out." Her nose wrinkled. "It stinks in here."

"Gunfire, flashbangs, and the loose bowels of dead men." Carver shoved Jensen onto a padded chair. "Okay, Jensen. Tell me why your father had Rhodes killed."

"He didn't. I promise he didn't. It was some other people who did it."

"Who?"

"I don't know. He just said they were important people. Well connected. I don't know how long he knew them or how they met."

"When was the first time he mentioned them?"

Jensen frowned. "Maybe a year ago. Right around the time he hired Chief Rhodes."

"Why did he hire her?"

"I don't know. He did a background check and didn't like what he found. He said it looked strange, like maybe some of it was faked. He asked around for people to look into it and I think that's when he found these new people. Then he hired her."

Carver thought it over. It didn't make sense. "He didn't want a competent chief, did he?"

"No. That was why I was surprised he hired her. But the old chief made it known he wanted her to replace him." Jensen shook his head. "Not that he had any power to make a decision like that." He glanced at Paola. "Why are you here?"

Paola smiled sweetly. "My new friend killed Jasper and all his Brazilian friends at the paint factory."

Jensen paled. "All of them?"

Her smile grew even sweeter. "All of them."

He gulped. "How—"

"Who killed Charlotte Cunningham and Renee Smith?"

Jensen blinked. "Who?"

"Two women that Rhodes associated with."

"I don't know. I never paid attention to any of that."

Holly came upstairs, arms full of rifles and ammo. She dumped the loot on the floor. Took out a cell phone. "This was Buck's."

Carver took it and activated the screen. It was secured with a four-digit PIN. "What's the code to open this, Jensen?"

"I don't know."

"What's your dad's birthday?"

Jensen spat out the numbers. Carver tried the birth year then the day and month. No go.

"Where's your cell phone?"

Jensen pulled it from his back pocket. He unlocked it without being asked. "There's nothing on it. Dad said to never text anything explicit."

Carver read the texts to Jasper. They were vague. Simple things like, *Need a date for tomorrow.* There was probably plenty of useful information. Locational data and other things that a good crime scene investigator could use. But nothing that was useful for Carver. It wasn't like this kid was going to have a jury trial anyway.

"Did your dad go to meet these people?"

"He went to Atlanta sometimes. I think they're headquartered there. Or maybe that's just where they met. I don't know."

"The one guy went outside to make a phone call. Was he calling those people?"

"Yes. Dad wanted more men to come."

"Are they coming?"

"Reggie said it went to voice mail."

Carver had to assume they'd get the message. And more men would come for him. This was nowhere close to being over.

Holly sat next to the two women on the couch. She stared with dead eyes at Jensen. "You did rape Melissa in high school, didn't you?"

He gulped. "She was into it. Then she changed her mind. It wasn't rape."

"She said no?"

Jensen stiffened. "It wasn't rape."

Holly laughed like she'd heard a bad joke. "You've been raping sex slaves, but you can't admit that you didn't do the same to Melissa?"

"None of that was rape. These women made their choices."

"How long have you and your daddy been doing this, Jensen?"

"Not long."

She walked over to him. Poked a finger in his chest. "I asked you how long." She pulled a knife. It had probably belonged to the guard downstairs. "Tell me."

"The first time was in high school, okay?" Jensen shrank into the chair. "We'd go to strip clubs or brothels in Atlanta. He paid for it."

"That's different. That's consensual. When did Jasper start getting sex slaves?"

"A few years ago. Right after the Brazilians took over. He tried to use them like a peace offering to dad. But that didn't clean the bad blood."

"Thank you for the truth." Holly looked at Carver. "What now?"

"I think before much longer we'll have a small army rolling in on us. I don't know anything about these people. Their capabilities, nothing. But they'll be capable. Dangerous." He looked around. "Where did Paola go?"

Paola walked into the room. "I found his office. Maybe there's something in there."

"I looked through his office before," Jensen said. "He was careful. He didn't even keep anything on his laptop."

Carver hauled Jensen out of the chair and pushed him after Paola. They went into an office near the back of the house. It looked down on Morganville. The entire valley spread out below them.

"Dad used to come here and stare out the window," Jensen said. "He'd curse Jasper up one way and down the other."

"Because he ruined the town." Holly shivered. "I thought it was a great place to grow up, but it was always rotten to the core."

Carver looked around the office. There were some hunting trophies on the wall. Sports trophies in two large glass cases. A liquor cabinet stocked to the brim. A desk and a laptop on it.

Jensen pointed at it., "I can unlock it, but there's nothing on it."

"Do it," Carver said.

He unlocked it. Paola sat down and started looking through it. Holly went to the liquor cabinet. She grabbed a bottle of aged whiskey. Poured a glass full.

Jensen glowered but covered it up when she looked at him.

Paola shook her head. "His history is full of news and porn sites. And he visited a church website a lot."

"Church is important to him." Jensen flinched like he suddenly remembered his dad was dead. But he didn't cry.

"Oh, is he a God-fearing man, Jensen?" Holly got in his face. "Did he think Jesus would forgive him for his sins?"

Carver walked around the desk and looked at the history. Nothing looked important. Paola clicked on one of the church links. It was a page with pictures from church events. One of them caught his eye. "Click that one."

She did. Rhodes's smiling face appeared in the middle of a group of women. They were all smiling. A table full of cakes was in front of them. A placard said, *Best Dessert Contest.* It was beyond strange seeing Rhodes grinning like that. Seeing her happy. It hit him like a bullet to body armor. Almost knocked him on his ass.

"Carver, you look pale." Paola touched his hand. "Is it because of Rhodes?"

He nodded. "Yeah. She was alive. Happy. I don't understand why they killed her."

Holly joined them, drink in hand. "That's Renee and Charlotte on either side of her."

Carver had hardly noticed the other women in the picture. He focused on the pair next to Rhodes. He looked harder. They were familiar. Their faces were clean. Happy. But he'd seen them before. It hit him in the gut when he realized where.

"Carver, what is it?" Holly watched him. "You look like you saw a ghost."

"Because ghosts are scary?" Paola smiled. "I like that English saying."

"Shit." Carver grabbed the laptop. Walked to Jensen and turned the screen toward him. "You don't know these women?"

Jensen shrank back. He looked. Nodded. "Yeah, they moved to town a few years ago. First new people we've had in ages. They bought one of the foreclosed properties from the bank."

"Know anything else about them?"

He shook his head. "No, I never talked to them."

Holly took a long drink from her glass.

Jensen glowered again. "That's thirty-year Glenfiddich you're drinking. Have some respect for it."

"I'm sorry." Holly tossed the rest of it back. "It's expensive?"

"Fifteen hundred a bottle, so yes."

Holly took the bottle from the shelf. It was cylindrical. Had a decorative metal lid. A deer logo on the front. "So, in addition to raping sex slaves, you're also a whiskey aficionado?"

"It's not rape—"

Holly smashed the bottle into the side of his head. It clanked hard but didn't break. Jensen went down like a sack of bricks. She took out the knife. Slashed open his jeans. Yanked and tugged and ripped them off while screaming like a madwoman.

"You're a little emotional, Holly." Carver reached toward her, but she pointed the knife at him. "Shut up!"

Paola put a hand on Carver's shoulder. "Let her do what she needs to do."

He held up his hands in surrender and backed off.

Holly tore down Jensen's pants. He groaned. His eyelids fluttered open. She grabbed his privates and put the knife right under them where they attached to the body.

Jensen shivered.

Holly pressed the knife to his skin. Blood trickled down his thighs. "I wouldn't move too much if I were you."

He whimpered. "Stop, Holly. Stop, please. I'll give you a million dollars. I'll give you anything you want."

"I just want one simple thing from you, Jensen. I want a confession. Tell me that you raped Melissa."

"I raped her, okay? I raped her and all the other women. Just please stop."

"You liked it, didn't you? Tell me how much you liked it."

"I loved it, okay?" Jensen started crying. "Please don't hurt me."

Holly smiled. "Thank you, Jensen. That's all I wanted to know." She yanked his privates out and slashed upward. The knife was razor sharp and took everything off in one smooth motion.

Jensen screamed. Grabbed his crotch. Holly staggered to her feet, Jensen's genitals clutched in one hand. She threw them on his face. Dropped the knife. Doubled over and vomited on him. She heaved and heaved until her stomach was empty.

Carver looked at Paola. "I don't think this is healthy."

Paola was looking away. "I think you're right."

Holly ran out of the office, staggering against the walls.

Carver picked up the discarded knife. He looked down at Jensen. He might survive. He probably deserved to. Carver wadded up the torn jeans. He pulled Jensen's hands away and pressed the cloth down over the bleeding. "Keep pressure on it."

"She cut it off!" He wailed. "It's gone!"

Carver looked at the discarded parts. "Keep pressure on the wound, okay? If you survive this, I suggest you go somewhere far away. Maybe become a monk. Try to atone for your sins, or something." He shrugged. "If I ever find you again, you're a dead man, got it?"

"Y-y-yes," Jensen sobbed.

Carver dumped the rest of the whiskey on the vomit to dilute it. Hopefully to destroy it as evidence. Then he left Jensen. Rejoined the others downstairs. Holly was covered in blood and dry heaving in the den. The other two women seemed to be coming out of their drugged stupor.

"We need to leave," Carver said. "The cavalry might be coming."

And hopefully with it, the people who'd started this sordid mess.

Paola guided the women into the SUV.

Holly leaned her head on her cruiser. She was crying. "I don't know what I'm doing. I don't know why I did that."

Carver put a hand on her back. "They almost raped you. They were bad people. You don't need to feel guilty."

She turned and looked up at him. "You killed Settler and those other men. You lied to me about that!"

"I didn't lie. I just didn't tell you." Carver shrugged. "I didn't think you'd understand."

"Thanks to the mayor, I understand perfectly. They came for you. You did what you had to do."

"Yeah."

"And then you locked yourself back up? Who does that?" Holly pushed him in the chest. "You went right back to playing the prisoner with the perfect alibi. I'll bet you were laughing at us the entire time."

"We need to go." He opened her car door. "We need to go now."

She pointed finger in his face. "This isn't over. We're going to talk about this."

"If it makes you feel better, sure." Carver gently guided her into the driver seat. "We're going to Jasper's mansion. Meet us there."

"First I'm going home to shower."

"Just be careful. Maberly told the mayor I was looking for you. That's why they took you."

"I know." She revved the car engine. Made a U-turn around the SUV and roared down the road back to the highway.

Carver climbed into the SUV. Turned it around.

"You knew the women in the picture with Rhodes," Paola said. "Who are they?"

He guided the car down the long driveway. "I think they're the reason this all started. I'm not sure why just yet, but now I see another connection."

"What connection?"

"I'll tell you later. I need to think about it some more. I want Holly there too. I don't want to repeat myself."

"Just tell me!" Paola gripped his arm. "Repeating yourself isn't that hard."

"Give me some time to think it over, okay?"

She slapped his arm. "Stupid."

Maybe he was being stupid. But these women were a pivotal part of his past. They'd changed everything. Destroyed his career. And now they were trying to get him killed.

CHAPTER 34

T ony rolled his neck and groaned.

The long meeting with the senators and House members was finally over. Dorsey had dragged him into a closed-door meeting to give final reassurances. Yes, their men were highly trained. Yes, they'd all come from American military branches. Yes, they were absolutely loyal.

But now they were getting paid right. Getting treated like humans instead of trained animals. They weren't political pawns. They could handle affairs both foreign and domestic. The US military couldn't do that. The National Guard was fine and dandy, but they didn't have the training.

Their private elite forces were superior in every way. Their training was honed and enhanced once they joined. They were small and efficient. Their proactive missions avoided large-scale conflicts and saved billions of dollars and hundreds of thousands of lives.

Aside from the usual holdouts, both sides of the aisle had been convinced. It was going to be a landslide victory. The first round of votes would give them authority to act domestically. To enhance efforts by the DEA, the FBI, and other local law enforcement. Once they dazzled them with their proficiency, the foreign clause would go into effect.

Then they would finally be positioned perfectly. Hundreds of millions of dollars in funding would increase to billions. They would supplant covert ops around the world. They would still interface with the CIA but wouldn't be beholden to their politics. The top military chiefs were eager to finally slip the leash of civilian oversight.

They'd be a special private military company.

Dorsey grinned madly when they left the Capitol Building. He and Tony climbed into the stretched Bentley and toasted their success.

"We made it." Dorsey tossed back a finger of whiskey. "Just tell me your boys have finally solved the Carver problem."

"I hope so." Tony turned on his phone. It had been off all day and stuck in a secure locker. Congressional leaders didn't allow cell phones in secret meetings like that. They couldn't risk their dirty dealings going public with a cell phone video or recorded audio.

It finally came on. There were a dozen missed texts and several phone calls. He worked through the texts first. They were from the operations center. Just standard notifications about personnel and training exercises. He didn't like people in the field texting him directly. Everything had to go through the operations center where they filtered the noise.

But there was a phone call from one of his guys. Reggie Winfield. One of Mayor Morgan's bodyguards. He was part of a package deal they'd worked out in exchange for the mayor's help in what would soon be their first major domestic victory.

Tony didn't know why Reggie would call him directly. He listened to the voicemail while Dorsey droned on about his victory. As if he'd been the entire reason things were going so smoothly. Tony had been the one to talk the most. To convince the others. His specialty was psyops. Of course, he'd convinced them. Dorsey's specialty was being rich. End of story.

Reggie's message crackled on his phone. "Sir, sorry to call you directly, but the mayor asked you to send more men. He says there's a local cop working with Carver, and he thinks he's coming for him. I don't know if he's right, but I'm just passing this along." The message ended.

Tony mulled it over. Which local cop would be working with Carver? The man was a murder suspect. He switched to his encrypted messaging app and texted Ritter. *Is Carver working with one of your people?*

Ritter answered fast. He knew the consequences if he didn't. *I saw him talking to our clerk, Maberly on several occasions. He talked to Detective Davis as well. He was trying to find out who killed Chief Rhodes.*

Tony pondered that. Then he texted Maberly. *Is Carver working with one of your people?*

Maberly took a little longer to answer. *He keeps coming by and asking for Holly Robinson. I told him she was on duty, and he went looking for her.*

Are you the one who told the mayor about that?

There was a full minute pause. Maberly apparently thought he was in trouble. He finally answered. *Yes. The mayor told me to keep an eye on Carver.*

So did I.

I texted you before I texted the mayor, I promise!

Tony skimmed down the unseen texts on his encrypted messaging app. He found Maberly's. The fat man was telling the truth. *Where are Holly and Carver now?*

I haven't seen them. Holly went to handle a rabid raccoon incident. Carver asked for her and I gave him the address. I'll call her on the radio and find out where she is.

Do it and get back to me right away.

Dorsey was watching him carefully. "What's wrong?"

"Carver again, damn it." Tony texted his cleanup crew. Demanded a status update. How had they not tracked him down yet? *Clean the damned laundry today!*

BLOOD TRICKLED DOWN the drain at Carver's feet.

He leaned against the tile wall and let the hot shower rinse the filth from his skin. Jasper's mansion was clean, but obviously hadn't been used much. The accumulated dust told him the cleaning crew didn't come often. Hopefully they wouldn't come this week. If they did, they'd have a surprise waiting.

The shower was a large, tiled space. Two generous showerheads rained down from above. There were water jets on the sides. A bamboo bench in the middle. It was the nicest shower Carver had ever experienced.

Paola stepped into the bathroom. Closed the door. Carver looked over at her. "What do you need?"

She slipped out of her clothes. Opened the glass door. Stepped inside. She unhooked the loofa from the wall and stood under the other showerhead. Let the hot water run through her long, black hair.

Carver grabbed a bar of soap and lathered. Rinsed. Took a dab of shampoo and lathered his hair.

Paola wrapped her arms around his chest from behind. Pressed herself to him. "Is something wrong with me?"

He looked over his shoulder. "No. I'd say everything is pretty perfect about you." She was tall. Curvy. Full lips. Eyes like black pearls. It felt like he was really noticing her for the first time.

"You're very different from most men. You didn't try to touch me when I got in the shower."

"You don't like being touched." He shrugged. "It's fine."

"It's okay if you touch me. I trust you now."

Carver put his hand over hers. He turned, kissed her. She smiled. Kissed him back.

"It's been a long time, Carver."

"For me too." He smoothed back her hair. Ran a thumb over her lips. "You're beautiful."

"I'm alive again. Thanks to you."

Carver didn't have a response to that. He hadn't gone there to save her. Everything he'd done had been out of self-interest.

She smiled. "Don't worry. I know it wasn't for me."

He couldn't respond to that either. So, he just kissed her again and enjoyed the best shower of his life.

CARVER WAS DRESSED in fresh clothes by the time Holly arrived.

Her hair was still wet. She was wearing jeans and a t-shirt. Black hiking boots. She looked over the women lounging in the den and cooking in the kitchen. "Carver, what have you gotten yourself into?"

Paola sat on a chair across the room. Her hair was also still wet. "I'm ready to hear the full story, Carver. What shook you about Renee and Charlotte?"

He motioned them to follow. Went into a study and closed the door behind them. There was a big mahogany desk in front of a window. Bookshelves running all the way to the ceiling. An empty liquor cabinet. Carver imagined old Nathan Whittaker sitting behind the desk, a vintage phone in hand. Making calls. Sealing deals. Creating a legacy for generations to come.

Now this place was a ghost house. Haunted by the bad decisions of Jasper. It smelled of aged wood. Cleaning oil. It was an old house. It had probably been built not long after a Morgan founded the town.

Carver dusted off a wooden chair and sat down. He didn't know how to talk about the day his career ended. The day everything went south for him. The plea deal had placed everything under seal. Non-disclosure agreements had been signed under threat of jail time.

"Spit it out, damn it." Holly slumped on a leather sofa. "I cut a man's junk off today. If I can do that then you can talk about the past."

Paola laughed. "Have you ever cut off a man's penis, Carver?"

"I've done worse." He leaned forward on his knees. "We'd been on deployment in Crimea, Ukraine. Pinpoint strikes. Assassinations of pro-Russian separatists. We were trying to tilt events in favor of Ukraine. Then our team separated to complete final tasks. I went with Rhodes to identify separatist leaders. New targets for another mission, probably."

Carver remembered those days clearly. She was all business on missions. But solo, she was a different person. She wasn't the hard-ass tactical leader. She was smart, funny. A force to be reckoned with. He'd liked her.

She'd admitted to him that she'd thought he was just a trained animal. A killer without a conscience. They were drinking at a bar. A night of free time before rejoining the others and leaving the country. But she'd seen something in him. Something human. But also, something feral. He'd told her about his childhood. About hard lessons learned.

Rhodes had understood. She'd seen the real Carver. Not just the guy who followed orders blindly. Who showed no emotion no matter what.

"Carver?" Paola snapped her fingers.

He continued. "We finished the side mission. I took an early train back to the capital. Rhodes was coming later after meeting with a local loyalist. I got off the train and took a dark ride onto the military base."

"What's a dark ride?" Holly asked.

"It's a specially designated vehicle for carrying top secret operatives onto foreign bases. It can't be searched. It's protected by diplomatic immunity."

Holly whistled. "Never heard of it. You must have worked for a real dirty special force."

"The dirtiest." Carver nodded. "The truck pulled onto the back of the cargo plane that was our ride back to the states. It unloaded supplies and four coffins. Americans who'd died and were catching a ride back with us."

"Americans in Ukraine?"

Paola propped her elbow on the sofa armrest. "Were they members of your team?"

"No. We didn't lose anyone on that mission." Carver frowned. "The other members of the squad were back already. Menendez, Rocker, Jackson, Angel, Fry, Jericho, and so forth."

"How many members did your team have?"

"It depended on the mission. Our core crew was Rhodes, Menendez, Rocker, Angel, Fry, and me. Rhodes was the commander. Menendez and Rocker were advanced scouts, demolitions, snatch and recovery, and so forth. They were our advance team. Rocker, Angel, and Fry were support, snipers, and fire. I was infil, exfil, CQC termination—"

Holly stopped him. "CQC?"

"Close quarters combat."

"So, you weren't the guy to snipe people from a mile away."

"I was a sharpshooter, but Fry was the best. Nobody could outshoot that guy long distance."

Paola clapped her hands to get their attention. "Okay, so that was your team. What happened?"

"Everyone was back but Rhodes. She showed up an hour later in another dark ride. Hers was a sedan, not a truck. It dropped her off in the cargo bay then left."

"How big was this plane?" Holly asked.

"It was a C-17 Globemaster. Big enough to haul a hundred troops or even tanks." Carver remembered feeling like an ant inside the belly of those things. "You could play basketball in the cargo hold."

"Did you?" Paola asked.

"Yes." Rocker had once pulled a knife on him during a game. Accused Carver of cheating. Being tall wasn't cheating. He got back to the story. "We arrived on US soil. Military police locked down the plane. Wouldn't let us off. They came inside with a warrant to search."

Holly looked surprised. "They can do that to a covert ops team?"

"They're not supposed to, but they had evidence of a crime and a warrant. Rhodes let them search the plane." Carver clenched a fist. "They went right to the coffins. Sprang them open. There were women inside the coffins. They were hooked up to oxygen tanks and sedated. One of them was dead. Her oxygen ran out and she suffocated. The other three were alive."

"What the hell?" Holly leaned forward. "Someone smuggled women on the plane?"

"We were escorted to separate holding cells while the MPs worked it out. The women were given medical attention. When they came to, they fingered me as the one who kidnapped them and put them in coffins. I was accused of human trafficking."

"That's ironic," Holly said. "I hardly know you and would never suspect you of that in a million years."

Paola's eyes flashed. "Carver isn't that kind of man."

Holly raised an eyebrow. Looked from her to Carver. "No, he isn't."

Carver kept talking. "Menendez, Rocker, Angel, all the others said the coffins had been in the truck that brought me in. The driver said he never looked in the cargo space. He just met me at the designated truck. Drove me onto base." Carver shook his head.

"What happened to you after this? Did you get court martialed?"

Carver shook his head. "They couldn't seal the proceedings. Too much dirty laundry to hide. They also couldn't prove I was the one who loaded the truck. The entire unit was under suspicion. Our earlier missions were scrutinized. There were ten instances of coffins being loaded on our planes. They suspected we'd all been involved. Apparently, our unit wasn't the only one accused of this. Several other black ops teams were accused of smuggling money, sex slaves, and other contraband into the US."

"This makes no sense." Holly shook her head. "A single rotten apple is one thing, but several of them in the same basket goes against the odds."

"Our squad was disbanded. Discharged without benefits. I signed a deal to take responsibility for everything, so they'd get their benefits back. It didn't matter. Everyone blamed me. Hated me. Rhodes told me she never wanted to see my face again." Carver bit his lower lip. "I went off the radar. Lived my own life."

"Back up," Holly said. "How do Charlotte and Renee fit into this?"

"It's obvious." Paola rapped her fingers on the armrest. "They were in those coffins."

Holly gasped. "They were the women being trafficked? It's no wonder they were so quiet and secretive."

"It's why they're receiving money from a blind trust. One that's probably controlled by the DoD." Carver strained to piece together what had happened. "The last time I saw Rhodes, she said she couldn't believe I would do it. That I didn't fit the personality profile of someone who would break everyone's trust. She couldn't understand how she'd been so wrong about me."

"But you obviously aren't that kind of person." Holly raked her fingernails across the leather couch. "It was a lie, right? Or did you really do it?"

"I had nothing to do with it." Carver imagined Rhodes after all of this. Imagined her pacing back and forth, furious about being disgraced. She was relentless when it came to finding the truth. "I think Rhodes never gave up. I think she tried to find the women, but the DoD put them in witness protection. Somehow, she tracked them down. Found two of them in this town. But she was smart. She wouldn't just barge in and start questioning them."

"Wouldn't they have recognized her?" Holly said.

"The women barely saw the others. They mainly saw me. Fingered me as the one who kidnapped them." Carver felt his hackles rise at the memory. Then he thought about Rhodes. About how she operated. He laughed.

Paola frowned. "What's so funny?"

"Rhodes." He laughed again. "I know why she became the police chief. I know why she did it all."

CHAPTER 35

R hodes was relentless. Determined. Unstoppable.

And Carver knew how and why she'd done everything.

Holly waved him on. "Tell us!"

Carver continued. "She located the women somehow. Came to town. Realized she couldn't just interrogate them. So, she infiltrated the town. Set up a fake past. Got hired as police chief. Became best friends with Renee and Charlotte." His smile faded. "Someone found out. Someone didn't want her finding the truth."

"They killed her, Charlotte, and Renee, and set you up as the fall guy."

"That's why she contacted me!" Carver slapped his knee. "She must have found the truth. Realized she was right about me all along. Wanted me to come help her."

"Finally, the answer." Paola smiled softly. "Now you know the why. But you need the who."

"I think the who will be coming to town shortly." Carver sighed. "If only Rhodes had left something for me to find. Names, a file, anything."

"Rhodes was brilliant," Holly said. "I guarantee you she left something for you in case anything happened to her. She probably put it where no one would think to look."

A thought hit Carver. He took out Renee's phone. Went to the encrypted app. Showed it to the others. "Like in an encrypted app on Renee's and Charlotte's phones?"

"Wouldn't that be the first place they look?" Paola said. "They killed them."

"Why would they? These women obviously helped point the finger at Carver." Holly pounded a fist on the couch. "They were working for the people behind it. They were killed so they wouldn't spill the secret."

"But their fingerprints don't open—" Carver stopped midsentence. He stood. "Let's go."

"Where?" Holly asked.

"To hopefully find the answer." Carver left the study. Went outside and climbed into the SUV. Paola took shotgun. Holly slid into the back. He gunned it down the long drive. Steered onto the road and headed toward the county lockup.

Holly buckled in. "Where are we going?"

Carver didn't want to say anything. He was probably wrong. Rhodes was the smart one, not him. If she'd left him anything, the puzzle might be too hard for him to solve. But there was something in that message she sent him. Something that made him think he was right.

The answer is at the tip of my finger.

He went past the prison. Veered into the medical examiner's office. Walked inside. "Holly, get us access to Rhodes's body."

She went to the secretary. Flashed her badge. "We need to see Rhodes."

The secretary buzzed them back. They went to the room with the freezer doors. Carver opened the one Rhodes had been in last time. She was still there. He took out Renee's phone. Opened the encrypted app. Put her finger on the print reader. Nothing happened.

"I need water." He found a large beaker. "Hot water."

Holly took it and turned on the sink. The water started steaming after a few seconds. She filled the beaker. Carver soaked Rhodes's right hand in the water for a minute. Then he pulled it out. Tried her thumb. Her index finger. Her other fingers. Didn't work. He soaked her left hand. The left index finger worked.

The app opened.

Inside was a DoD classified witsec file. It had the real names of the three women. Their aliases. The third woman had died in a car accident shortly after assuming her new life. The other women moved to a small town in Georgia. A place with a low population. A place no one would think to look.

Rhodes had catalogued her progress. Someone at the DoD owed her. She'd waited until the heat died down on the case. Waited a full year. Contacted her source and got the file on the women. She'd gone to the town. Watched them for weeks. Saw how furtive and secretive they were. These women were living under threat of death if they ever told the truth. Rhodes realized she'd need a strategy to get the truth from them.

So, she infiltrated the town. Created a fake job history using her contact at the DoD. Gotten appointed as chief of police. She'd just been aiming to become a regular officer, but the outgoing chief had been so impressed with her fake resume that he chose her as his successor.

She'd become friends with the women. Started to elicit tiny bits of truth out of them. But it was slow going. They didn't trust anyone. It took her a year to gain their trust. At long last, the women relieved the burden of their guilt. Told Rhodes everything.

They told their new trusted friend how they'd really come to the US. How an anonymous man approached them in the Ukraine. Told them he'd take care of their families in Russian-controlled Crimea. That he would pay them well just to do this one thing for him. Four women accepted the proposal. He showed them a picture. Told them this was the man to frame.

That man was Carver.

But they didn't know who the anonymous man was. He was Ukrainian. Probably hired to contact them. They didn't know who was behind the setup or why Carver was chosen as the target.

Carver was guilty of a lot of things, but now Rhodes knew this wasn't one of them.

Carver read the files from beginning to end. The files on Charlotte's phone were the same. He tossed the thermos with her rotting finger into the garbage. He didn't need it anymore. The file didn't tell him enough. It didn't give him the who or the why.

He knew why Rhodes had done what she'd done. He knew why she and the women were dead. But he didn't know the who or the why behind the original scheme. What was their motive? Why had they gone through so much trouble?

Holly asked the same questions aloud. "This is a lot of effort. Whoever did this had very high-level clearance. They had access to black ops teams. And I guarantee they had a lot of money riding on this."

Carver nodded. "You're right. It has to be someone high up in the chain of command. Someone with access to the black-ops teams. But there are only a handful of SOCs."

Holly tapped a finger on her chin. "What are their names?"

"I don't know. Rhodes's immediate superior was SOC Holt."

"SOC?" Holly frowned. "Carver, start spelling out these military acronyms, please."

"Special operations commander. They didn't use standard ranks in our section."

Paola wrinkled her nose. "No generals, majors, captains?"

Carver shook his head. "It was an inter-branch task force. Best of the best from the other special forces. Although I gotta say I met more SEALS there than green berets. Several Marine sharpshooters as well."

"You don't know Holt's commanding officer?" Holly asked.

Carver shook his head. "I don't even think Rhodes knew. And there's no way for me to find out."

Holly rapped her fingers on a stainless-steel table. "Someone powerful has a financial interest in getting rid of special forces teams, especially this special branch you were in. Someone high enough in the military ranks is responsible. But there's got to be a private corporate interest involved, because that's where the money is."

"Follow the money." Paola said it as if it was that easy.

"Plenty of money at the paint factory." Holly blew out a breath. "But that was a false lead."

"They wanted me dead for different reasons." Carver looked around the morgue. He assumed this place would be full of bodies from the paint factory soon. The mayor would be here. His bodyguards. Maybe whoever started this mess.

But hopefully not Carver.

The next few hours would be crucial. If that phone call went through for reinforcements, then his survival would be severely tested. But it was necessary. If he wanted the root of the problem, he had to pull up some weeds.

Carver headed for the exit. The women followed. He went outside. Climbed into the SUV. Turned on the air conditioner and stared out the windshield for a moment. It was obvious what he needed to do. Pulling it off would be hard, but it was doable.

He wheeled the car out of the parking lot and headed back to the mansion.

"What now?" Holly asked.

"Get some rest." He checked the time. "We'll meet up in the morning."

Paola stared at him. "Where are you going?"

"To my motel." Carver hooked a turn onto a county road. "You all should stay at the mansion."

Holly snorted. "I have a house, thank you."

"I don't think you're safe there right now. Stay at the mansion."

She looked out the side window. "You might be right. I need to get some things from my house though."

Carver dropped them in front of the mansion. Holly got out. Paola stayed in her seat.

"Why aren't you staying here, Carver?"

"I need to do some things on my own."

She watched him for a long moment. Reached over and squeezed his hand. "I hope you survive those things."

He put his hand over hers. Squeezed it back. "Thanks, Paola."

Paola looked like she wanted to say more. A whole lot more. But she nodded and got out of the car. "You know what you're doing. You will survive." She closed the door and walked away without looking back.

Carver watched her until she entered the mansion. Holly climbed in her cruiser and peeled out. Headed back toward town. Carver gave her a minute to get well ahead of him, then he headed for town.

He went straight to downtown. Parked on the street. Walked around. Went into the sandwich shop and ordered a donut even though he wasn't hungry. When he came out, he saw the guy from before. The guy with the monocular. He didn't have the monocular now. This time he was sitting on a bench reading his phone in ninety-degree heat.

Carver pretended not to notice. He walked into the hotel. Went to the clerk. "Lots of tourists today?"

"Not as many as usual. It's so damned hot I think they're waiting on cooler weather."

"Fat chance of that," Carver said.

The clerk laughed. "Yeah. It's July. It ain't getting cooler anytime soon."

"Yeah. Have a good one." Carver left. Walked to the SUV and climbed in. He put on the AC and waited a moment. Pulled onto the road and headed toward the motel. It was remote. Then again, everything was remote in these parts. This one was farther from town than the one he'd stayed in before.

He paused until the count of three at the stop signs. Kept going. He had a tail. They were far back. There weren't many places to turn out here. Not a lot of traffic either. They were smart. Playing it safe. That was ok by him. He was going to make it easy on them.

Carver parked in front of the motel right outside the end unit. Like most motels, it was L-shaped. The office was the bottom of the L. The rooms were along the top. It was on a road between two mountains, surrounded by forest. Just like everything else around here.

Most of the cash and weapons he'd taken were at the mansion. But he had the Colt rifle and six mags of ammo from the mayor's people. He had two flashbangs and the Glocks.

It wasn't much, but it might be enough. He carried the duffel bags inside before his tail was in visual range.

He turned on the TV. Switched to the news and turned the volume to a low drone. Then he went to the bathroom. The window was on the back wall. It was just large enough to squeeze out of. That was another reason he'd chosen this motel over the other ones. He slid it open. Slipped the duffel bags outside. Climbed out and closed the window behind him.

Carver walked into the forest behind the motel. Walked up the slope of the mountain a little way then found a place with a clear view. He took the binoculars from the bag. Looked back down the road. Saw the tail coming into view. It was the same Jeep Gladiator he'd seen the other day. The man with the monocular was driving. Another guy was with him. The sunlight on the windshield made it hard to see his face.

The passenger pointed to the SUV. The Jeep parked out of sight on the side of the motel behind the office. A moment later they came around the backside of the motel. They walked past the other units. Stopped outside the window of his unit and listened. Spoke to each other. Nodded. This was the place.

Carver recognized the other guy. He'd been with the second group of tourists that had drawn his suspicions. There had been five of them. That was a lot of men. He wondered how they'd do it. How they'd kill him. The standard method was easy enough. Storm in and shoot.

They went back around the corner. The Jeep pulled out a moment later. Both guys were in it. Headed back to town. It was almost nine and the sun was trying to end the long day. Come nightfall, this motel was going to get a lot more activity than usual.

Carver left one duffel bag in the bushes, took the other with him. He went down the slope to the window. Walked around the side and went to the office. There weren't any other cars in the parking lot. Yesterday there had been two. Maybe more would come today. That would be bad.

He went inside. Rang the bell. The clerk, an old guy with no hope in his eyes came out.

"Yeah?"

"Anyone else got a room here tonight, or is it just me?"

"Just you so far." He slumped. "Damned Morganville Hotel gets all the business."

"How much for all the rooms and for you to take the night off?"

The clerk frowned. "I live here. Why?"

"I want to have a party. It'll be loud."

"You wreck that room, you're gonna pay for it."

Carver pulled ten stacks of twenties out of the duffel bag. Each stack was about a thousand dollars. "How's ten thousand dollars?"

The man's eyes went wide. "Shit, you can buy the whole damned place for fifty."

Carver laid out fifty grand. "I don't want to buy it, but hopefully this will cover any damages."

"Hell, yeah it will." Drool dribbled down his chin. "I ain't never seen this much money in my life. I ain't gonna ask where you got it, either."

"And forget you ever met me, okay?"

"Already forgotten."

"That's for the best." Carver glanced around the office. "When you clear out, turn the lights off."

He nodded. "Mister, I'll be out of here in thirty minutes."

Carver checked the time. "That works." He went to the SUV. Started it up and took it to a diner down the road. He had a hamburger, fries, and extra coffee. He was going to need to stay awake tonight. After filling his belly, he returned to the motel. He looked at the side of the motel the Jeep had parked at earlier. It hadn't returned. He parked and went inside the room. Turned off the TV. Took the pillows from the first bed and fashioned a sleeping form underneath the covers of the bed furthest from the door. He turned out the lights. It would look convincing enough.

He went outside and walked across the road. Hiked up the slope and into the woods. Found a vantage point and went prone. It was a good spot. It was getting dark, so he hustled across the road and up the slope behind the motel. Grabbed the other duffel bag and hoofed it to his new spot.

Carver settled into place. He pulled out the camouflage paint and covered his face. Put on a new pair of the thin, leather gloves. He cleared and checked the Colt rifle he'd fired earlier. Cleared and checked another one. Loaded them both. Gave the Glocks the same treatment.

The clerk left the motel. Got in an old eighties model car and squealed out. Carver waited until he was out of sight before he moved onto his next phase of readiness. He was about to make some noise and didn't want anyone around to hear it.

When the car disappeared over a hill, Carver adjusted the aimpoint for the first Colt. Imagined a target on a tree and fired. It hit dead center. He aimed down the iron sights and tried them. They were accurate. He tested the other rifle. The aimpoint and iron sights were on target.

Then he practiced his route, clearing twigs and leaves. Made himself a short dirt path. Hacked any bushes that might get in his way. Absolute silence was going to be key. Once he had all his ducks in a row, he settled in.

Waited for the men who would come to kill him.

CHAPTER 36

They came at midnight.

It demonstrated a lack of patience on their part. Or maybe just an abundance of confidence. It was dark, there were five of them, and only one of him. Even if he wasn't asleep, they'd have him dead to rights. That was the problem with motels. There was just a door standing between the occupant and whatever was on the other side. No safety at all.

A few hard kicks and these doors would punch inward. The wood and safety latch gave a false sense of security. Most of the time it wasn't a big deal. If you stayed at enough motels like this one, you'd eventually have a problem. But most problems weren't lethal.

A crazy guy might beat on the door. A drunk might think it was his room. Most robbers wouldn't bother breaking and entering. The people who rented motel rooms weren't the kind with much money.

But tonight, death was coming for Carver in the form of five men. They came in two cars, the Jeep, and a black crew cab pickup truck. They parked on bottom of the L, the side of the motel office. Slid out and gathered in proper team formation.

These guys were fully outfitted. Black fatigues with standard military issue body armor on the outside. Black helmets with night vision goggles attached. M4 carbines with optics and suppressors. It was maximum overkill for a single supposedly sleeping target. Carver was surprised these boys didn't have the Sig Saur XM5s that were all the rage now.

The M4s showed they had some common sense. But not enough.

All they needed were handguns. Not this crazy show of force. Maybe they planned to take Carver alive so they could stage his death somewhere else. That seemed even more likely than filling a motel room full of bullet holes.

The squad leader rounded the corner. Checked the motel office. Cleared it and gave a hand signal. Three men prowled along the wall behind him. The fifth man walked around the back corner to cover the window. They weren't taking any chances.

Carver's position was right on point. He was about four hundred feet from the parked Jeep. His position gave him line of sight to the side and the front of the motel. He started making his way down the slope. Following the dirt trail he'd cleared. Making almost no sound.

One of the men pointed to the streetlamps. The squad leader waved a hand over his neck. He wanted the lamps out. That would give them a tactical advantage with the night vision goggles. But it was a dumb move.

They already had a tactical advantage. Knocking out the streetlamps might alert the occupant. Maybe the target wasn't asleep. Maybe they were tossing and turning in bed and saw the streetlamps suddenly blip off. Then they'd be alert. They'd go to the window and look outside. Maybe catch a glimpse of the soldiers.

Carver made sure the other soldiers were out of sight, then glided across the road. He put his back to the side of the motel and slid between the front bumper of the wall and the Jeep. At the back corner he looked around. The back lights of the motel were dim, but he saw the fifth soldier kneeling not far from his room window.

He set down the rifle. Drew the knife. Walked slowly across the hard packed dirt and grass. The guy had all his attention on the window. Tunnel vision. It shouldn't cost him in a situation like this. But tonight, it was going to. Carver got right behind him. The man was practicing trigger discipline and the safety to his rifle was on. He was a freelancer just doing a job. Making some money. Maybe feeding his family. Maybe feeding his vices.

Everyone had a job, some more dangerous than others. Under normal circumstances, this wasn't a capital offense. But this guy was at the very least aiding in a kidnapping. At the worst, abetting a murder. It was a dangerous line of work. Especially dangerous, considering the target.

Carver slapped a hand over the guy's mouth and slashed his throat in one fluid motion. The man struggled hard. Flailed and thrashed. The desperate exertion made his heart beat harder. Emptied the arteries faster. He went into the great unknown shortly after that.

The body slumped. Carver laid it out. Took the rifle. He cleared the chamber and checked the round. It was standard 5.56, not armor piercing. They didn't want to enter an enclosed space, open fire, and kill each other with bullets ricocheting off the cinderblock walls. He unlocked the magazine, slid the round back in, then clicked it in place and pulled the charging handle to load the chamber.

Carver took the helmet. Adjusted the straps and put it on. He tested the NV goggles. They were high quality. Probably as good as the ones he'd used in the field. He took the dead man's headset and put it on. Radio silence. They were just using hand signals. That was smart.

The streetlamps flicked off along with the lights along the back of the motel. Carver retraced his route to the side of the motel. He put on the goggles and watched the four men slinking down the walkway to his door.

The squad leader went to the opposite side of the door. Readied his rifle. Another man took the opposite side. One man readied a kinetic battering ram. Carver had seen them before. They used blank forty-five caliber ammunition to propel a flat piece of metal into the door. One shot was normally enough to break it in.

These kids had all the new toys.

The only guy facing Carver was the squad leader. Carver had parked the SUV so it blocked a clear line of sight from anyone outside his motel room door. He crab-walked into the parking lot until the SUV blocked him from vision.

He needed to be behind the SUV the instant they breached the door, so he quick-stepped it until he was behind the vehicle. There was a click. Another click. The door broke open. Three men burst inside. The fourth guy covered the doorway.

Carver pulled the pins on two flashbangs. He lobbed them inside the room. Closed his eyes and looked away. There were two blasts followed by cries of pain. That much light in the NV goggles seared their retinas medium rare.

He looked through his NV goggles. Aimed. Put two bullets in the neck of the guy at the door. Aimed inside. Fired four quick rounds into the legs of the soldiers inside. They went down howling.

Carver popped the closest two guys in the face. Shattered their goggles. They went down. The squad leader was still alive. Rolling, aiming his rifle. Still blind.

Carver shifted position. Put his back to the brick wall outside the door. "Drop it or you're dead. I just want to talk."

"Fuck you."

"Who do you work for?"

"Come inside and ask me nicely."

"If I have to come in there for answers, you won't like it." Carver heard the guy crawling. Groaning. "Who do you work for?"

"The Salvation Army."

Carver sighed. "You can survive tonight. Go home. Rethink your life choices. Or you can die because someone gave you money."

"I almost died because the government gave me money. This is no different."

"Loyalty to a country is different than loyalty to a criminal organization."

"My work is legit." He groaned. "I'm taking down terrorists like you."

"Who said I was a terrorist?" Carver took the helmet off the guy who'd been guarding the door.

"Don't even try that with me."

Carver put the helmet on the tip of his rifle. Held it out like it was peeking around the door. A volley of bullets smacked it off the rifle. "Blind loyalty is stupid. You don't even know what you're fighting for or why you're dying. But if this is the hill you want to die on, be my guest."

The man inside grunted. Metal clanged on the sidewalk. Carver dove behind the SUV. A flashbang popped. Bits of shrapnel struck the side of the car. The manufacturer of the flashbangs needed to work on their design. They weren't supposed to be that dangerous.

Carver went prone behind the SUV. He couldn't see the inside of the room from here. He slid sideways. Two bodies lay on the floor in front of the beds. The squad leader wasn't visible but the tip of his rifle poked out from behind the second bed. He'd taken cover. Was probably calling for reinforcements.

These mercs were a different breed if they were this loyal. Maybe it was just this guy. Maybe he was related to whoever was behind this. Maybe he was the top dog himself. That was highly doubtful. He might be a squad leader, but he was still just a grunt.

The sidewalk curb was maybe two inches high. From the prone position that put the rifle about even with the underside of the beds. The covers didn't let him see beneath the beds, but he could estimate where the target was from the location of the rifle's barrel. He imagined the guy flat on his stomach. Legs bleeding. In pain. He couldn't kneel. He could only lay flat. The best firing position would be on the side so he could angle the rifle around the bed.

"Last chance," Carver said. "You got a wife and kids? Anyone at all who cares if you live or die?"

"Come get me," the other guy shouted back. "Face me like a man."

"You mean like you were going to do? Five versus one? That's manly all right." Carver watched the barrel of the rifle. It was inching forward. The guy wanted to take another shot. "Last few seconds of your life. This is it. The big black ocean is about to swallow you. You sure that's what you want?"

"You'll have to come in here to get me." The squad leader barked a laugh. "Good luck with that."

Carver fired. The rifle coughed. The bullet punched through the bottoms of the two comforters. Smacked into something solid. The man shouted.

"I don't know where that hit, but I know it hurt. I'm going to fire again and again until you answer me, or you die, okay?"

"Fuck you!" The squad leader's barrel moved. He was squirming into a firing position.

Carver fired twice more. The man shouted in pain. Cursed. The rifle barrel twitched and went still. Carver pushed to his feet. Rushed inside. Put a foot on the rifle barrel. But this guy wasn't going to move it anymore. He was dead.

"Stupid." Carver blew out a breath. "So damned stupid."

He dragged the bodies into the parking lot. Walked around the back of the building and hefted the last guy. Dropped him next to the others. He frisked them. No wallets, no IDs, no phones. Just radio comms. He stripped off their body armor, helmets, and NV goggles, even the ones that were broken.

He found the keys to the Jeep and the pickup. He drove the Jeep around. There were duffel bags in the back with more ammo, flashbangs, and body armor. He shoved what he could of his loot into the bag until it was bulging. Then he dumped the bodies in the bed of the Jeep.

Carver went to the pickup truck. Found another duffel bag of equipment inside. No cell phones, wallets, nothing. Not even a car registration. These guys were thorough on covering their tracks. Then he went into his motel room and turned on the lights. They didn't work.

He went to the motel office. The door had been knocked open by the battering ram. The main circuit breaker was off in the back room. Carver turned it back on. The streetlights flickered to life. He went to his room and surveyed the damage. There was blood on the thin carpet. Blood on the bedsheets. A few bullet holes here and there.

The question was, how clean did the scene need to be? The clerk knew what Carver looked like even if he swore he'd forget ever meeting him. Even so, he didn't want the man to come back to a slaughterhouse. He took out his phone. Called Holly.

"Carver?" She sounded wide awake.

"Need your help."

"What happened?"

He told her what happened. Gave her the motel name. "I need a cleanup on aisle six."

"That's not funny."

"Making jokes isn't my strong suit."

"I know." Holly sighed. "We'll be right there."

"We?"

"Paola and me." She ended the call.

They showed up in a black Whittaker van. Paola, Holly, and four women piled out. Buckets, mops, vacuum, steam cleaner. The whole works.

"Where'd you get all that?"

"From the cleaner's supply closet at the mansion." Holly looked at the bodies piled in the back of the Jeep. "What are we going to do with them?"

Carver shrugged. "Dig a big hole?"

"I thought you didn't make jokes."

"I'm not joking."

She shook her head. "Best we can do is temporarily hide them." She snapped her fingers. "There's the old Granby mine out on Route Twenty-Four. We could drive the vehicles inside and leave them."

"Let's do it." He watched as the women went to work. They were all wearing thick yellow cleaning gloves.

Paola put a hand on Carver's arm. "I'm glad you're okay."

"Thanks. Holly and I need your help hiding the bodies."

"I would be happy to help you hide the bodies."

Holly sighed. "True friendship right there."

Paola smiled. "Yes, I think so." She told the other women what they were going to do. Then she and Holly put on cleaning gloves to avoid leaving fingerprints.

Carver climbed in the SUV. It had a couple of bullet holes in the side and the engine rattled when it started. The engine must have taken damage. But it was drivable. Paola drove the Jeep with the bodies in the back. Holly drove the pickup truck and led the way. They traveled a few miles. Turned off the road and into the bushes.

Just past the bushes was an overgrown gravel road. It went up and around a mountain. The road was in bad shape. Washed out in parts. One curve had a steep drop off into the trees. It reminded Carver of a mountain pass he'd traveled in India a long time ago.

They eventually ended up at a quarry in the middle of the forest. Holly drove carefully, skirting the lip of a big black hole. They followed a rusty fence and arrived at a large wooden double-door.

It was made of tarred timbers, thick and resilient. There was a heavy padlock and a chain securing the two doors together. There was a rusty old sign from the state park service. It warned people not to go inside.

Holly produced a keychain and unlocked it.

"How do you have the key?" Carver asked.

"The state doesn't have rangers out here, so they gave us keys in case of emergency. There's enough slack in the chain that people can get through. Every once in a while, we have to come rescue some idiot who went inside."

"They can get in but not out?" Paola asked.

"They go too far inside, and someone gets trapped or stuck." Holly shook her head. "People are stupid." She tugged open the doors, one at a time. The opening was large enough for dump trucks to enter.

"I'm putting the SUV inside," Carver said. "Keep the pickup truck out here."

"But it belonged to these people," Holly said.

"So did the SUV." He drove it in. The headlights illuminated the bedrock tunnel. The engine was smoking. A bullet must have hit an oil line. He went in about a hundred yards and parked. Paola parked the Jeep behind him.

They'd been wearing gloves, but he spritzed the interior of the SUV with the cleaner and did the same the outside. He didn't bother doing the same with the Jeep and took the cleaner back outside. He and Holly closed the doors. Carver pulled all the slack out of the chain, straining his muscles so they were tight as possible. Holly put the padlock on.

"I don't think tourists will be squeezing through that," Holly said.

Paola laughed. "If they do, they're in for a horrible surprise."

"That's not funny." Holly laughed too. "Why am I laughing? This is horrible."

Carver grinned. "Gallows humor is the only way to keep your head straight."

"Gallows?" Paola looked confused.

"It's where they hung people," he said. "People who deal with death use dark humor to keep from going crazy."

Tears trickled down Paola's cheeks even as she laughed. "Yes, it's the only thing keeping me from screaming right now."

"Me too!" Holly wiped tears off her cheeks.

Carver didn't feel one way or the other about the events of the night. Some people had to be put down. That was just a fact of life. But he was frustrated. He still didn't know who was behind this or why.

But if the mayor's bodyguard had put out an SOS, then he was probably going to find out soon.

CHAPTER 37

Tony was grinning ear to ear.

"They were headed to his motel." He checked the time. Three-thirty in the morning. "They told me they were going in at three A.M. so they should have him by now."

Dorsey nodded eagerly. "Finally." He tossed back a glass of expensive whiskey. "This has been a clusterfuck from the word go."

"Carver always was hard to kill. I thought he'd be sloppy after three years. I was wrong."

"We can't afford to be wrong." Dorsey poured himself another three fingers. "We need to carry out Operation Paint Factory two days after congressional approval. I want to prove our worth so fast it makes their head spin."

"We should give it another few weeks," Tony said. "They might think we've been holding back from them if we hit a target so fast."

Dorsey groaned. "I hate all this waiting! I've been working on this for years. Years!"

"I know, I know." Tony held out his hands. "But slow down. We don't want to blow the gig right after we get it."

Dorsey yawned. "I'm going to get some shuteye. Wake me up when they arrive with Carver. I want to kick that son of a bitch around just for all the trouble he's caused."

"You got it." Tony looked at the time. The team was on radio silence. Protocol forbade taking any personally identifiable items with them or a cell phone. It was too easy to track things like that. They'd secure Carver and return to their makeshift HQ then make contact. Then they'd pack up and leave. Carver was going to be here soon, and he couldn't wait to see the look on that bastard's face when he saw Tony.

THE BLOOD AND GORE was completely gone.

A blacklight would reveal the traces, but there probably wouldn't be an investigation. The bullet casings were in a trash bag along with all the other debris. The steam cleaner had worked wonders on the carpet. If anything, it looked too clean. There were still bullet holes in the wall. Carver figured the motel owner could patch those up himself.

The women piled into the back of the van. Paola climbed into the driver's seat. Holly and Carver stayed in the pickup. He figured he'd stay at the mansion tonight. Plan his next moves whenever he woke up.

He started to pull out when Paola honked the horn. He stopped. She got out and ran to his window. Carver rolled it down. "What's wrong?"

"These men, they were posing at tourists in town for days, right?"

He nodded.

"Carver, they must have a hotel room in town. There must be something in their room that can tell us who they are."

"Holy shit, Paola." Holly looked astonished. "Why didn't I think of that?"

Carver had thought about that already. "They wouldn't stay in a hotel room, especially not one like the Morganville Hotel since it requires an ID. They probably set up in an abandoned house nearby or somewhere that couldn't be traced."

"Oh." Paola frowned. "So, no hotel room?"

"If they were halfway smart, they picked an abandoned property. If they were working with the mayor, then he probably set them up somewhere off the record."

"Okay, so we have to find this place," Holly said.

"It'll be off the records." Carver shook his head. "Untraceable."

"Let's say they got an abandoned house somewhere. Probably near downtown. They still need utilities, don't they? Five men aren't going to live in a place without being able to flush a toilet or plug in their laptops."

"You're right, but what good does that do us?" Carver said.

Holly grinned. "The electric company."

Paola frowned. "Huh?"

Carver wasn't convinced. "Don't you need a warrant?"

"Not in these parts. Everyone knows everyone here." She bit her lower lip. "I know who to call. I'll tell them it's a police emergency."

Carver checked the time. "At this hour?"

She nodded. "They'll answer."

"They must really like you," Paola said.

Holly made the call. "Hey, Andy, so sorry to call at this hour, but I have an emergency request and you're the only person who can help me." She nodded. "Aw, you're the best." Nodded again. "I need to know if any houses near downtown Morganville activated their power over the last week." She paused. "Thanks, sweetie!"

She ended the call. "He's remoting into the database. He'll text me in a few minutes."

"Let's get the women back to the house," Carver told Paola.

She nodded. "Okay. But don't go anywhere without me."

They got on the road and headed toward the mansion. Holly's guy texted her an address by the time they were pulling into the driveway. "It's the old Cooper house. One street over from the town center. The mayor requested electricity for it a few days ago."

"Good work."

She beamed. "I hope this pans out."

"Me too."

Paola parked the van. The women climbed out wearily and carried the cleaning supplies inside. They were too tired to ask questions. Maybe at this point they didn't want to know what happened.

Paola hopped in the back of the crew cab. "Did you discover anything?"

Carver was already headed back to town. "Yep."

She clapped her hands. "I hope this is it."

"Has to be." Holly grabbed hold of the door handle as the truck veered around a curve. "Why else would the mayor ask for electricity at an abandoned house?"

They arrived at a gray brick house with boarded up windows. No light leaking beneath the plywood. No exterior lights on. Carver viewed it with the NV goggles. "Let me have a look. Wait here."

He walked the perimeter. Examined the front door. Looked it over for any traps. Then he tested the doorknob. It was locked. He looked under the concrete planters on the porch. Checked on top of the door and window frames. He found a fake rock at the bottom of the stairs. The bottom swiveled open and a key fell out.

Carver unlocked the door. Turned on the lights. The foyer was a small room. Next to it was the den. There was a long foldout table with two laptops on it. Power cables draped along the surface. A small black safe with a digital keypad on the end. He turned on the lights in the rest of the house.

There were twin sized mattresses on the floors in the bedrooms. Duffel bags with civilian clothes. Separate bags with spare fatigues and body armor. These men didn't travel light. There was a long travel case with a Barret fifty caliber inside. It was a beautiful specimen with a high-power scope and bipod. The kill squad must have thought they could take Carver alive. Make his death look accidental instead of sniping him from a distance. There was antipersonnel ammo and antimaterial ammo in the case as well.

Carver went outside and waved the women in. They were already waiting outside the truck and hurried inside. They tried the laptops, but they were locked down with en-

cryption software. Three wrong tries and the laptops bricked themselves. The hard drives
could be removed, but the data would have to be decrypted.

The safe was strong and heavy. It wasn't one of the cheap personal safes. This was designed
to hold cell phones and other personal items. It would take a hydraulic press or explosives
to break it open. Even that would be futile since a thermite charge would destroy the
contents of the safe the moment it was breached.

"Damn it!" Holly stared at the laptops. "Nothing."

Paola echoed her. "Nothing."

Carver dumped out the duffel bags. Nothing but clothes.

Holly hefted the safe. "We can take the safe. Maybe someone can open it."

He shook his head. "If it's forced open, the contents are fried with a thermite charge."

Paola was frisking the black fatigues. She pulled a slip of paper from one of the pockets.
Unfolded it. "It's a delivery receipt to Breakstone. What's Breakstone?"

Carver googled it on Renee's phone. Found a website. The image of a young man in
military fatigues standing in front of a group of soldiers. No, not soldiers. Freelancers.
Mercenaries. This was where Ruben and Jimmy had come from. The proof was in the
picture. They were standing in formation clear as day.

He didn't see the five men he'd just killed in the picture. Nor did he see the three who'd
been guarding the mayor. But he did see another familiar face. One that made him zoom
in to be sure he was seeing right.

"Menendez?"

Paola looked closer. "You recognize someone?"

Carver pointed out the three. "Ruben, Jimmy, and Menendez." He saw a fourth. "And
that's Rocker."

"Ruben and Jimmy are the two who tried to kill you," Holly said. "Who are the last two?"

"Guys from my squad. They were the advanced team. Scouting, demolitions, snatch and grabs." Their presence was hard to chalk up to coincidence. But it had to be. Lots of former military types went into private security. Firms like Breakstone were a dime a dozen. But they paid better than the military and treated you better too.

Carver flipped through more of the website. They had packages. Bodyguards, drivers, even tactical units for foreign visits. The whole menu. No prices listed, of course. Probably plenty of off-menu items as well. Kill squads like the one that came for him. Wannabe kill squads like Ruben and Jimmy.

Carver tried to fit the pieces together. Rhodes, Breakstone, Menendez, Rocker. There was no bad blood between the three of them. Everyone loved Rhodes. The same couldn't be said for Carver. He was the one sent to get his hands the dirtiest. The shit jobs nobody wanted on their conscience.

Breakstone was behind the fake human trafficking charges. They'd paid the women to finger Carver. But Carver hadn't been the only one to catch blame. The entire squad had been disbanded. And their squad wasn't the only one affected. Other special squads had been disbanded on various criminal charges.

The pieces were jumbled. But they started to sort into piles. Started to form the bigger picture. The clouds thinned out. The stars became visible again. Carver wasn't lost at sea. Wasn't relying on dead reckoning to find his path. Now he saw it clearer than ever. It was right there in the Breakstone mission statement.

The future of the military is private. Lower costs. Less red tape. No politics.

Dorsey was behind the women who'd fingered Carver for human trafficking. He was the reason the squad had been disbanded. Discharged. And he was soaking up the casualties of his campaign. Recruiting the best of the best into his private military company.

Carver felt a little left out. Why hadn't he received an invite? It looked like they'd snapped up Menendez and Rocker. Probably hired others from his squad. He wondered if they'd tried to recruit Rhodes. They would have to be stupid if they didn't at least try.

Rhodes might have been so focused on the truth about the trafficked women that she opted out. Or Dorsey thought she was too dangerous to bring onboard. She might discover the truth and that would be the end of that.

Because Rhodes's biggest character strength was also her greatest weakness. She believed in justice. In truth. It made her a thorn in the side of her commander. But it also made her invaluable.

Dorsey would have found that out from her records. It would have been a red flag for an operation like his.

"Carver, you've been staring at the screen without blinking." Holly snapped her fingers. "What did you find?"

"Dorsey is the person behind all of this. He has to be. Right along with other higher-ups in the company." Carver continued flicking through the website. He couldn't find a page dedicated to the company leadership. "I need to have a conversation with him."

"How do you plan to do that?" Paola looked confused. "He owns a private military company. There's no way to get close to him."

"She's right, Carver." Holly bit her lower lip. "Maybe it's time to let the law do its job. The more vigilante justice you dish out, the harder it'll be for you to avoid prison time even if we cover for you."

Carver thought it over long and hard. Shook his head. "Holly, I need you to get something for me. Then we're going to have a talk with Dorsey."

"Carver, please don't do this. Let me make some phone calls."

Paola shushed her. "You can't be serious, Holly. Not after everything these people have done. Dorsey has a crazy amount of money and influence if he was able to fake a human trafficking crime to take down a black ops squad. Normal justice doesn't work for people like that. They'll win and you'll die."

"Paola's right, Holly." Carver reached over and squeezed her hand. "If you can just do a couple of things for me, I can handle the rest."

Holly looked at his hand. At his eyes. She shook her head. "I'll do what you want, but you're not doing this alone."

He smiled. "Thanks."

"You can thank me if we survive this." Holly sighed. "What do you want?"

He told her. She grinned. "I like where this is going."

Paola grinned. "Me too."

Carver gathered the duffel bags and the equipment left by the kill squad. He examined the safe and looked up the model on Renee's phone. It was an expensive personal safe. Designed to destroy the contents if force was used to open it.

It also detected if it was being moved via GPS and an accelerometer. If it was moved, it would beep until it was returned to its starting location. If it wasn't returned within thirty seconds, it would destroy the contents. The cell phones were as good as lost.

Carver took body armor and two pairs of fatigues that fit him. He took the case with the Barrett in it as well. They were still wearing gloves, so they hadn't left any prints behind. Holly turned off the lights and they closed the house.

Then they drove back to Jasper's mansion to catch some shuteye. They'd need all their wits about them in the morning.

CHAPTER 38

Tony wasn't grinning anymore.

He was angry. Frantic. He'd expected a message on his cell phone this morning. But the kill squad hadn't reported in. He'd called them. Texted them. Tried the mayor's bodyguards. No one was answering. It was like they'd all gone radio silent.

A half-empty bottle of bourbon sat on the table in front of him. He'd resisted as long as he could but the stress was killing him. He took a shot and considered his options. There weren't many.

He contacted Maberly. Asked him to go check on the house where the cleanup crew was staying. Maberly checked. The house was locked up. He broke in and found nobody there.

Tony almost smashed his cell phone. He sent another text. Told Maberly to check the motel where Carver was staying. Maberly went. Contacted him thirty minutes later. The motel was completely empty. Not even the clerk was there. The door on the end unit was broken so he'd gone in there.

What did you find? Tony asked, unable to keep from being impatient.

Maberly answered a moment later. *It's empty. Clean. Smells like bleach and chemicals.*

Tony couldn't understand. Had the crew been forced to shoot Carver? Had they moved the body and cleaned up the scene? He sent another message back to Maberly. *Keep looking until you find something to report!*

Something wasn't right. If Carver was dead, the crew still should have reported in. He couldn't avoid this any longer. Couldn't keep putting off the inevitable. It was nearly nine in the morning. This needed to be finished today.

Tony called Dorsey. Told him everything he knew.

"How are these idiots so bad at their jobs?" Dorsey growled and something shattered. "Get Sam. We're going."

This time, Tony didn't argue. He messaged Sam. Told him to gear up and ready for deployment. He finished off another shot of bourbon. Went to the bathroom and stared at his bloodshot eyes. He was going to gut Carver personally.

Sam and Dorsey were waiting on him by the time he pulled into the rear parking lot. Sam looked tired but happy. He'd been the reason the Senate had cleared that final vote. Sometimes talk wasn't enough. Sometimes you had to play hardball.

"Hey, brother." Tony gripped the other man's hand. Pulled him in for a hug.

"Good to see you, brother." Sam slapped him on the back. His nostrils flared. "You been drinking?"

Tony shrugged. "I needed it."

Sam nodded. "I don't blame you, given the circumstances. Just be careful. Don't forget what made you stop in the first place."

"Hey, brother." Dorsey went for a handshake and a hug too. "Good to have you."

Sam faked a grin. Gave him a half-hearted clap on the shoulder. "Yeah, boss. Good to see you."

Tony almost rolled his eyes. "Did the Senator's daughter make it home okay?"

Sam laughed. "Yeah. A little worse for the wear, but she's back."

"Just like Ukraine, right?"

"I might have had a little too much fun with this one." Sam's grin faded. "So, what's the emergency?"

Tony told him.

"Fucking Carver." Sam spat. "Why don't we bring Leon along?"

Tony shook his head. "He's on mission. Plus, I don't think we could count on him for this."

Sam spat again. "Fucking Carver."

Tony nodded. "Fucking Carver. Hop in. Let's finish this."

Sam whooped and patted the vehicle. "Damn, this thing's a monster!"

Tony climbed into the driver seat. Dorsey got in the passenger seat. Sam rode in back. This SUV was one of their new urban combat vehicles. Bulletproof glass and armor. Extra shielding around the engine. It could withstand gunfire from AK-47s at close range. The tires were armored with a solid core composite in case a bullet penetrated them.

These vehicles were supposed to get their first real-world test during Operation Paint Factory, but Tony wasn't taking any more chances with Carver. This needed to be finished today.

Dorsey removed his body armor and helmet and tossed them in the back seat next to Sam. He buckled his seatbelt. "Roll out."

Tony gunned it to the security gate. It slid aside and he pulled onto the road. Navigated to the interstate and hauled ass toward Morganville. He pulled off the interstate and onto the highway leading into town about an hour later.

"I want to kill Carver myself." Dorsey was polishing his handgun. Examining the short scope on the top. Testing the laser sight. "I've been dying to try this out on a moving target."

Tony glanced at Sam. "You ready for this?"

"Yeah." Sam had that dead look in his eyes. The look that said he'd seen and done it all. Doing it here was no different than anywhere else.

"Maybe we can torture him," Dorsey said. "This asshole has caused all kinds of problems."

"I can get behind that." Tony brought the SUV to a cruise at eighty-five miles per hour.

"Pull his fingernails out. His teeth. Chop off his balls and make him eat them. "Dorsey glared at the racing scenery. "I just don't get how one guy is such a pain in my ass."

Tony saw something ahead. Something in the road. It was small but stuck out. He slowed. Stared at it. Was that what he thought it was?

Dorsey saw it too. "Is that a toy gun?"

It was a gun all right. The same gun Tony had used to kill Rhodes with. Her hot pink gun. He laughed. "Okay, asshole. Give it your best shot. Let's see where you are."

"Carver did that?" Dorsey had his pistol out. "What's happening?"

"He thinks he's springing a clever trap." Tony stopped the car. "He doesn't know what he's up against." He slapped the steering wheel. "I hope he comes out and empties a clip into this beast."

There was a distant crack. A clank. The vehicle rocked on its springs.

Tony blinked. "What the hell?"

Another crack. Another clank. The SUV shuddered. The engine clattered. Rattled and died.

"What the hell?" Dorsey looked up the hill toward the mayor's house. "What's going on?"

"Carver has a fifty cal. That's the only way he could have done this." Tony looked for a glint of sunlight off the lens of a scope but didn't see anything. "We need to get out of the vehicle on my side. He's up there on the hill shooting down at us."

"Go!" Dorsey shouted. "I'm right in the line of fire!"

Another bullet smacked into the side window. The thick glass puckered inward.

Dorsey screamed. "Go, go go!"

Tony slid out. Ducked behind the SUV. Dorsey slid over the driver seat and down to the ground. Sam was already out. Already scanning the hillside with a monocular through the windows on the SUV. Tony was starting to wish he'd brought another team with them.

"Shit." Dorsey was pale. "Guess a fifty cal can punch through the armor."

"I don't see anyone on the hill," Sam said. "If they fire again, I can pinpoint it."

"They're not on the hill," someone said from behind them.

They spun around.

A big man stood there with a rifle trained on them. He scowled at Tony. "Well, shit."

CARVER TRAINED THE rifle on the three men.

He recognized Dorsey from the website. Recognized his former squad mate Tony Menendez. Recognized Sam Rocker as well. All the pieces fit so neatly together in an instant. It was enough to make his head spin.

"Well, shit."

"There are three of us, Carver." Menendez grinned. "All armed."

"And?" Carver shrugged. "You think I'm alone?"

Tony's grin faded. "So, that's how you evaded us so long. That cop is helping you."

"Something like that." Carver kept the rifle steady. "Drop all your weapons."

Rocker's hand flicked upward. Gunfire cracked. Struck him in the armor and knocked him sideways. A pistol dropped from his hand.

Carver hadn't fired. The gunfire had come from Holly's position.

Menendez scowled. He dropped his handgun. His rifle was in the back of the SUV.

Dorsey dropped his fancy pistol on the grass. Held up his hands. "Now what, asshole? Do you know who I am? What I'm capable of doing?"

"At this point, I'm well aware of your capabilities," Carver said. "What I want to know is who pulled the trigger the first time?"

"What trigger?" Dorsey said.

"The one on the gun that killed Rhodes." Carver stared at Menendez. "Don't tell me it was Jimmy or Ruben. I'm guessing you didn't allow Dorsey to come here. That means you or Rocker did it."

"Who the hell do you think did it?" Menendez said, almost proudly. "I hated that bitch."

"Why?" Carver couldn't figure it. "I thought everyone loved Rhodes."

"I couldn't stand that self-righteous bitch." Rocker spat on the ground. "I'd have done it if Tony didn't. Anything to shut her up."

"We could have been making serious bank on our missions, Carver. We had free license to take anything home from our missions." Menendez scowled. "Rhodes wouldn't let that happen. Then I met Dorsey, and we found a better way to do it."

"Taking over military ops with a PMC sounds like a way to make millions," Carver said.

"Billions!" Dorsey spread his hands imploringly. "And you can have a cut. Whatever you want, just tell me."

"Not interested." Carver looked at Tony. "Only one thing I'm interested in right now."

Paola walked out of the woods. Picked up the hot pink handgun and brought it to him.

Menendez frowned. "You're that girl from the paint factory. What the hell are you doing here?"

"All the cartel members are dead," Paola said. "I had to find a new job."

"What?" Dorsey went pale. "How?"

"That's not important right now." Holly emerged from the forest to Carver's right. She held her rifle at the ready. "I'm guessing your goons killed Renee and Charlotte. Probably raped them first too."

Dorsey held up his hands. "Just read us our rights and get me my lawyer. I'm going to have all of you in jail by the time this day is over."

Menendez narrowed his eyes. "This is the United States, Carver. We're protected by due process here. Do anything stupid and you'll never see the light of day again."

"That's a chance I'm willing to take." Carver walked up to Tony. Pressed the hot pink Sig Sauer to his forehead. "I would tell you to say hello to Rhodes for me, but I don't think you're going to the same place."

Rocker lunged. Carver fired. Tony's head whipped back, and his brains painted the side of the SUV. Carver rammed his knee into Rocker's gut. The other man drove his fist into Carver's ribs. Carver grunted. Drove his knee into Rocker's gut again. Pushed him back.

Dorsey went for his handgun.

Shots rang out. Bullets bounced off the armored SUV. Carver felt a hot sting on his arm and his back. He dove to the ground. Found the pink handgun. Rolled onto his back and fired. The first shots caught Rocker in the groin. The man went down. Carver put a bullet in his head.

He turned to Dorsey. The man was bleeding from multiple wounds to the chest. Gasping for air. "Help me. Please."

Carver frisked the man. Took his cell phone. It required a PIN. He held the phone in front of Dorsey. "Tell me the PIN and we'll get you to a hospital."

Dorsey shivered. Rattled off seven numbers.

Carver unlocked the phone. Opened the encrypted messaging app. The messages from the last twenty-four hours were there. A long list of orders telling Tony and Rocker to kill Carver. Their affirmative responses. It was just what he needed.

"Help," Dorsey gasped. "Help."

"I called an ambulance." Holly knelt next to him. "You're going to be okay."

"Liar," Paola said.

Holly nodded. "Yeah, sorry, I lied, Dorsey. You're a dead man."

"No." He struggled weakly. The blood loss was too much already. "You promised."

Carver looked him in the eyes until he went still. Then he turned to Holly. "It's all up to you to sell this. Think you can do it?"

She nodded.

Ritter walked around the SUV. The Barrett fifty caliber was strapped to his shoulder. "My goodness, this thing packs a punch."

"You're going to back up Holly's version of events. Maybe help her come up with something." Carver took the Barrett. He gave the PIN for Dorsey's phone to Ritter and Holly. "Take photos, screenshots, whatever. The messages in the encrypted app vanish after twenty-four hours. They're going to be vital evidence."

Ritter looked at the bodies. "These are the people who kidnapped me? Who threatened my wife and daughter?"

Carver nodded. "That was one of their specialties."

Ritter kicked Tony in the head one good time. "Rot in hell." He brushed off his hands. "Okay, Holly, let's figure this out."

Carver wiped down Rhodes's handgun. He was wearing gloves but wanted the weapon clean. Then he pressed it into Tony Menendez's hand. Used the dead man's finger to fire a shot into the forest. Holly put the gun into an evidence bag.

Carver plucked hairs from the three dead men. Used medicine droppers to suck up blood from each of the men. Holly put those into another bag.

"Drop the hair and blood around the carpet and bedroom," Carver said. "Don't put it all one place. It'll look staged."

"Framing the guys who tried to frame you." She grinned. "If this isn't karma, I don't know what is."

"It's not framing if they did the crime," Ritter said. "We're just making things right."

Carver and Paola hoofed it back to the pickup truck. They dumped the weapons inside. He hated to lose the Barrett, but it needed to be placed at the paint factory. That would tie the deaths of these three men to the drug cartel. He wanted the feds to have an easy time of it. Tie things up nice and tight with a bow on top.

He headed down the highway. Skirted town with a side street and headed for Jasper's mansion. It was time for the women to be free. For some of the truth to come out. This was going to be tricky, but there was no way around it.

"Carver, you're bleeding." Paola touched his arm.

"I know. Two of Holly's bullets grazed me when they bounced off the SUV." He steered around a curve. "The body armor protected me from the worst of it."

They reached the mansion. He gathered the women. Told them the time was coming for the truth to come out and that they'd have a vital role. He ended with the most important part. "You need to forget me and Paola. We were never here. This was a war between a cartel and a private military company, okay?"

There were nods all around.

"You were never here," one of them said. "But thank you."

Others echoed her words.

"You're welcome." Carver told them the other good news. "We took a lot of money from the cartel. The police are going to seize it. They're going to give you a lot of that money tax free to make up for what you went through."

"It doesn't make up for the horrors," Paola said. "But it's something."

There were a lot of tears. A lot of crying women. Hugs.

Carver backed up before they hugged him. Then he turned and made a retreat for the bathroom. He was in desperate need of a shower.

Paola followed him. "What now?"

"Now I vanish. I'm finished here."

"I'm coming with you."

"You won't like being around me for long. Holly and Ritter will find your documents at the paint factory. You'll be free to go where you want. Do what you want."

"This is what I want." Paola touched his arm. "At least for now."

Carver nodded. "Okay."

CARVER WAS DEAD tired.

He was sitting on the beach watching the sun set after a long day of learning how to wind surf. It was a lot harder than it looked.

Paola was in a lounge chair next to him watching something on her phone. "It's happening."

"Is it?" He scooted his chair closer. Watched the video. A news anchor was talking about the major news out of Morganville, Georgia. How a war between a cartel and a private military company had claimed nearly twenty lives. How a major conspiracy had possibly been uncovered. The FBI was investigating Breakstone for reasons unknown.

It showed a group of FBI and military investigators in Morganville. None of them would comment.

"No mention of Dorsey's cell phone." Carver watched a reporter speculate. Watched them interview Holly and then Ritter, the officers who'd stumbled upon the remains of a battle where the cartel had killed Dorsey and two associates. There was a video of the female sex slaves the officers had rescued. Another video of piles of cash and cocaine, all seized by the Morganville police.

The new Morganville police chief, Chief Ritter, was awarding seized funds to the sex-trafficking victims and making sure they were taken care of. As the highest-ranking official, he was effectively the acting mayor as well.

Even more evidence had linked Mayor Buck Morgan to the sex-trafficking ring. The cartel had killed him, his son, and his contingent of bodyguards. No one knew what had started the war, but some suspected it had to do with the mayor wanting more money from the cartel.

Carver grunted. "I guess Junior didn't survive having his manhood sliced off."

Paola switched it off. "It's an open and shut case."

"It should be." Carver closed his eyes and listened to the waves lapping the shore. "But the government is good at covering things up."

"You think they'll succeed, even with all the evidence?"

"Best not to think about it." Carver sipped his beer. "Just enjoy life."

Paola touched his hand. "You're not so bad to be with, Amos Carver."

"It's only been three weeks."

"A nice three weeks." She squeezed his hand. "Especially watching you do something you're not good at."

He cracked his eyes opened and looked at her. "You mean wind surfing?"

She laughed. "Yes."

Carver smiled at her. "For what it's worth, I like having you around."

"I know."

For the first time in a while, Carver felt human again. He felt a sense of completeness. It wasn't perfect, but it was good enough for him. He hoped wherever Rhodes was, she could rest in peace.

Justice was hers.

Books by John Corwin-

Books by John Corwin
Join the Overworld Conclave for all the news, memes and tentacles you could ever desire!
https://www.facebook.com/groups/overworldconclave
Or get your tentacles via email: www.johncorwin.net
Fan page: https://www.facebook.com/johncorwinauthor

AMOS CARVER THRILLERS

Dead Before Dawn

Dead List

Dead and Buried

Dead Man Walking

CHRONICLES OF CAIN

To Kill a Unicorn

Enter Oblivion

Throne of Lies

At The Forest of Madness

The Dead Never Die

Shadow of Cthulhu

Cabal of Chaos

Monster Squad

Gates of Yog-Sothoth

Shadow Over Tokyo

Conrad Edison and the Infernal Design
Conrad Edison and the First Power

STAND ALONE NOVELS
Mars Rising
No Darker Fate
The Next Thing I Knew
Outsourced
Seventh

About the Author

John Corwin is the bestselling author of the Overworld Chronicles and Chronicles of Cain. He enjoys long walks on the beach and is a firm believer in puppies and kittens.

After years of getting into trouble thanks to his overactive imagination, John abandoned his male modeling career to write books.

He resides in Atlanta.

https://www.facebook.com/groups/overworldconclave

Join the Overworld Conclave for all the news, memes and tentacles you could ever desire!

https://www.facebook.com/groups/overworldconclave

Or get your tentacles via email: www.johncorwin.net

Fan page: https://www.facebook.com/johncorwinauthor

Made in the USA
Columbia, SC
06 April 2024

5cb10165-e988-4838-9316-cc69a37fbb87R01